RAVENOUS

SWARM
BOOK 1

JT SLOANE

MIKE KRAUS

MUONIC
P R E S S

RAVENOUS
Swarm
Book 1

By
JT Sloane
Mike Kraus

© 2022 Muonic Press Inc
www.muonic.com

www.MikeKrausBooks.com
hello@mikeKrausBooks.com
www.facebook.com/MikeKrausBooks

CONTENTS

WANT MORE AWESOME BOOKS?

Find more fantastic tales right here, at books.to/readmorepa.

***

If you're new to reading Mike Kraus, consider visiting his website and signing up for his free newsletter. You'll receive several free books and a sample of his audiobooks, too, just for signing up, you can unsubscribe at any time and you will receive absolutely *no* spam.

***

Thank you for checking out Swarm! This series was written as a collaboration between Mike Kraus and several individual authors listed below, the collection of which appears on the cover as J.T. Sloane, and is the result of many months of hard work. We hope you enjoy it!

Aidan Pilkington-Burrows
J. Mannix
E. L. McCabe
Michael Raymond
S. E. Gilchrist
B.K. Boes
Liam Pickford
Jack Caspian
Kate Pickford

***

Special Thanks

Special thanks to my awesome beta team, without whom this book wouldn't be nearly as great.
Thank you!

READ THE NEXT BOOK IN THE SERIES

Swarm Book 2
Available Here
books.to/QJnWP

SPECIAL THANKS

Special thanks to my awesome beta team, without whom this book wouldn't be nearly as great.

Thank you!

PROLOGUE

ALEX STEELE, ILLINOIS.

Sometimes you're the windshield, sometimes you're the bug but for several thrashing, spitting moments, Alex Steele was both; the massive flying cockroach or stinkbug or *something*, jammed in his windpipe, making him cough and gag and thump himself on the sternum.

He threw himself up against the door of the Old Country Feed Store, sending his fellow shoppers running for the exits, but the bug didn't budge. He shoved his fingers into his mouth and wrestled with the slimy critter. He couldn't get ahold of the invader. It was too far down his gullet.

His neighbor, Ned Wilding, smacked him on the back once, twice, three times, but his assailant had other plans.

Jonny Pepper wheeled himself close to the action, jabbering to the 911 operator. "The man's fixing to die, right here, in my store!"

Alex stopped dead still and tried to breathe through his nose. No go. He might as well have been gargling acid and chewing tacks. The bug had plans to end him. That wasn't going to happen. He wheezed and gurgled and choked and, finally, hacked hard enough to dislodge the twitching lump of ack.

He staggered through the doors to the gate in the parking lot—hands around his throat, tears and snot and spit streaming down his face—and sucked down the sweet, fresh country air. He stumbled, sweating and swearing, to the water pump and jacked the handle then rinsed and spat several times before returning to the scene of the crime.

A crowd had gathered, friends and neighbors all ogling the winged invader, speculating about whether it was a crop-destroying locust, like the ones over the state line out by Battle Ground.

"Stripped the soy crop down to the ground and finished off cousin Dale's prize pig." Harry Fabish was a gossip and a fearmonger and Alex didn't believe a word that came out of the man's mouth. There were no *locusts* in Illinois or Indiana, or any other place west of the Mississippi.

"Let's not get ahead of ourselves." Alex wanted order and calm, not panic and pandemonium. Even in a town as small and close-knit as Watseka, five-thousand residents and dropping, a malicious rumor like that could have folks boarding up their businesses and packing the kids off to their grandparents for the summer. Their little town couldn't take that kind of economic hit; it was already struggling. Alex didn't want their way of life—measured, kindly, driven by the seasons—to be upended by some dunder-headed gabbing from a spineless twit like Harry. "It was just one, lonesome critter, fool enough to slap into my ugly mug."

Jonny poked the outsized bug with his cane and brought the end up to inspect the viscous gloop that had oozed from the critter. "Pests. Gross. Kill them all. Sevin's in aisle four, get yourself a gallon or two." He wiped his cane down with a tissue, grinding it into the floor to get the residue off.

Alex bent low to see what it was that had caused such a ruckus. His assailant twitched. It was deformed and broken from its time inside his mouth, but still whole enough to be identifiable. It had the waxy carapace of a carrion beetle but with an oversized abdomen and freakishly large wings. He smashed the thing with his heel, sending insect guts for several inches in each direction.

"Hurts like the dickens." A blister, smaller than a nickel but bigger than a dime, sat squarely in the middle of Jonny's palm. He poked the taut, round bump and hissed.

Alex spotted Jane on the other side of the crowd, elbowing her way toward them. He pushed his way through the nattering neighbors, smiling and shaking his head, waving her away. She hated bugs, as in borderline phobia. She'd have a cow if she knew that *thing* had been inside him. Best just pack up and go home to the kids.

"Going to need someone to lance this for me. Now!" Jonny held up his palm for inspection. The boil had doubled. The crowd dissipated as fast as it had gathered, leaving Alex and Jane with the old curmudgeon. "You going to leave an old cripple, too?"

"Of course not, Jonny." Everyone said their other half was one in a million, but Alex knew that his wife—her skin glowing with all those pregnancy hormones and her smile just as sweet as ever—was a bonefide saint. There wasn't a broken wing or crushed paw or grumbling, wheelchair-bound neighbor that she'd ever turned her back on.

"Do me a favor, dollface, and roll me to my kitchen." Jonny had a small house attached to the back of his shop. Jane pushed him past the chicken coop, the goat run, and the barn—letting him rattle on about how well his girls were laying and why goat's milk was the panacea for all ills, "Especially your pregnant-gastro problems!"—and finally made it into his kitchen.

Alex dug under the kitchen sink and found the first aid box while Jane boiled some water, chatting about the kids and their projects, keeping Jonny's complaints at bay. "Samantha's smart as a button. Keeps her teachers on their toes. Her science project was on the e-coli inhibiting factors of spices in hamburger meat." She sorted the supplies into a neat row. Disinfectant. Needle. Swab. Band Aid. "Did you know that oregano does more to stem the growth of harmful bacteria than garlic? You do now!" She paused to let Jonny raise an objection, as they both knew he would, and then went on to outline Sam's entire dissertation, which had not only won her a gold medal at the state fair, but also jammed their freezer full of hamburger patties for three months straight.

"Let's have a look." Jane took Jonny's hand gently in hers.

Jonny stretched out his fingers for inspection. The boil had spread, turning his palm into a mountain range. "It's throbbing to beat the band."

Jane swiped the bug bite with an alcohol-free wipe, took the needle to the stove and held it over the flame until it glowed orange, then dipped it in the peroxide and—holding the old man's hand until the shakes subsided—pricked the center of the carbuncle. Nothing happened. She dabbed the site with some antibiotic cream then wrapped it. "Keep it clean and dry, Jonny. Samantha would have plenty to say about the number of germs in your average pot scrubber and the resultant infection rates!"

Even Jonny Pepper—who rarely smiled, let alone laughed— relaxed into Jane's gentle banter about her kids. His assessment boiled down to: Samantha was a pistol, Eli was a sweetheart, adding, "May they stay that way, whatever life brings."

"Amen to that." Jane packed away the supplies, washed her hands, but gave the rag that hung by the sink a wide berth. She winked at Alex as she brushed past him. That tiny gesture—even after all the years they'd been married—made his guts flip and his pulse race. She was one in a million and he was proud to call her his wife.

Jonny pointed his cane at the cupboard over the sink. "Want to join me in a glass of rye?"

Alex found the bottle and a single shot glass. "The kids are waiting on us. Family dinner tonight. Hey! You should come. There's always plenty."

"I've got a stew on the stove! Beef and barley. Your favorite." Jane rested a hand on Jonny's shoulder.

"Next time, doll." He poured himself a triple and raised it for a toast. "Here's to good friends and better neighbors. Especially ones with a good supply of oregano!"

They left him, sipping his rye, with promises to return in the morning but Jane insisted they clean the bug goo from the shop floor before they left. Alex wasn't having her do that, not in her condition.

He gloved up and wiped down, then grabbed the store keys to lock up for Jonny.

"Alex?" Jane's voice wobbled, her pitch too high. "What's that?"

A black smudge hovered over the top of the cherry trees, shifting on the wind. It was too dense to be a flock of starlings and, in any case, they didn't shimmer like— "A swarm! It's a swarm!" He shoved Jane out of the shop doors. "Get back to the house. Now. Get Jonny out of that kitchen."

The couple pounded through the parking lot, Alex checking and checking and checking over his shoulder. The swarm pulsed and rose, clearing the distance between them like it was nothing.

"Doors and windows." Alex raced through Jonny's house, rattling windows and inspecting vents. "We want this place sealed while they pass over."

"Get back here! What's happening? Hey! Talk to me!" Jonny peppered Alex with questions, but there was no time for answers. Alex had to make them safe. "Take him to the bathroom, Jane. Hurricane prep. Stay there. Don't come out until I give the all-clear."

Jane grabbed Jonny's wheelchair and charged out of the kitchen.

"His livestock!" The feedstore owner kept goats and chickens. He'd even kept the horse who crushed his seventh vertebrae, consigning him to a chair. Alex was a farmer, deep in his soul. He couldn't leave those animals out in the swarm.

He opened the back door on his worst nightmare. He flailed, smacking away squadron after squadron of hissing, clacking dive bombers, tucking his chin into his chest. The bugs were on his back, his legs, in his ears. He shook himself like a dog and grabbed a tree net off the back of a chair. He slung it over his head and stuffed it into his waistband. His thick, stupid, worthless thumbs had swollen to twice their normal size and it took him a whole minute to get the wretched thing tucked all the way around—only to discover he'd locked himself inside the net with three waxy-backed villains. He rammed himself into the wall mashing them against his shirt.

The bugs swarmed over the stove. Alex threw himself at the pan of boiling water, hollering obscenities and set part of his net on fire. He did what he was trained to do: stop, drop, and roll. The fire was out, but the bugs swarmed in through the gaps, nipping and biting and stinging and setting his skin on fire. Fire. That's what he needed. A flame thrower.

He blinked and spat, stretching the tattered remains of the net over his nose and mouth, making a rough mask. Peroxide! That was flammable. He turned and ran slamming into the nightmare wall of aerial attackers. They weren't a curtain or a flock and "swarm" didn't capture the magnitude of the invasion. They were everywhere. On everything. In everything. Overhead, underfoot, on every side, the bugs were thick as molasses and twice as dark. They'd turned day to night, pleasure to pain, heaven to hell.

He knew the way to Jonny's barn without the need of working eyes or fully-operational legs, which was just as well because someone had poured glue into his veins and made him a jellied man, better able to crawl through the onslaught than walk.

Josie the mare was on her side, her beautiful huge eye crawling with bugs, her side heaving and jerking.

The bucket at the side of her stall was loaded with Epsom salts, but that wasn't what he needed. It was the ichthammol. Derived from Sulphur, the medicine was viscous but water soluble, and most importantly, flammable. He shucked his useless, tattered tree net and felt his way through the mash of eyes and wings and stingers and jaws, all of them pressing against him and blocking everything from sight. This was a touch-mission. Good job everything was in its place. Being in a wheelchair meant Jonny kept his supplies on the lower shelves and in strict order. The ichthammol was right where it was supposed to be, next to the gauze and the clean rags.

Alex squeezed the tube of goo into the bucket, digging his face into his shirt to keep the bugs from scraping their way up his nostrils. Squirt bottle. Where was the squirt bottle? He dumped out the water and filled the bottle with his makeshift concoction, then dug the lighter out of his pocket, sprayed the air, and lit the jet of fluid. His screams met the screech of popping bugs as he annihilated two, three, four hundred. Behind them were two, three, four thousand more.

He pumped the feeble handle of the spray bottle and misted a boatload of beetles then torched their sorry hides. Not enough. The swarm kept coming. It dwarfed the barn, the pasture, the feed store. Everything his neighbor had worked so hard to create—the house, the livestock, the fruit trees, his entire life—was being eaten alive by a mighty pestilence of onyx insects.

Alex's nose split open, blood spraying over the fallen battalions, but he wasn't done with those suckers. No way, no how. He dragged himself through their carcasses to the bucket and fished around for a rag then palmed his way around the stable until he found the rake.

He brought the wooden shaft down on his knee, but his sausage fingers and boiled-ham hands didn't have the strength to snap it. He ripped the top off his squirt bottle and drenched the rag with ichthammol, wrapped it around the rake head, lit it, and swiped at the air sending bugs hissing and popping and screeching into the hay.

He pushed himself up the wall. His legs barely kept him upright but he still managed to swing that flame through the endless onslaught of crisped wings and singed mandibles.

The straw by the door caught on fire, lighting the squirming, flailing mass of insects. They blanketed the floor, the walls, the ceiling, the windows, and the exits. Hell had belched the Devil's own bugs into the land he loved and buried it alive.

The tsunami of killer bugs roared toward him, hissing, buzzing, and finally drowning him in acid but he kept spraying and praying as he dropped to his knees. Spraying and praying. "Not Jane, Lord," he begged. "Not the kids."

His head rested on Josie's side. Alex Steele had seven seconds of relief before the mare's belly split open and the swarm engulfed him.

His cell phone buzzed in his pocket. Text message. From Jane. *Love you, Alex. Best husband in the World.*

CHAPTER ONE

DR. DIANA STEWART. ILLINOIS.

Wrinkling her nose at the ungodly stench that rose from the field before her, Dr. Diana Stewart suppressed the urge to swear, which was hard for a Briton with a built-in taste for more colorful language. "Well, that certainly isn't just Feedit."

It was a beautiful day in Illinois. There was a pleasant breeze and the never-ending sky stretched, cloudless and blue, over the plains. But in the green expanse in front of her, the wheat was far larger than in any of the studies, and she had a strong suspicion it was related to the stink. "What did you do to our fertilizer, Jonah?"

The farmer pushed his hat back on his head awkwardly. "Fish meal."

She shook her head in dismay.

Jonah hurried to explain. "Arron Mackee said he'd had big results with this stuff." He looked down at the boy who crouched at his feet, all tousled curls and mischief, drawing lines in the dirt with a stick.

"He said it won't affect your study, and I... I need a good harvest this year."

Diana sighed. The man had lost his wife and was trying to manage the farm while looking after Jesse, his son. And a grieving six-year-old had to be exhausting, particularly when you're grieving yourself. "Jonah—you should have talked to us. This makes the study completely useless. We can't tell what growth is due to Feedit and what isn't."

He glanced at her. "They'll still pay me, won't they?"

"How can they?" She felt for the phone in the pockets of her trench coat; it was there. "I'll do what I can but there's a strong possibility they'll have to burn the crop, which means you won't get the money."

Jonah's breath hissed out between his teeth, and he strode into the crops and tore a stalk of wheat from its roots, twisting it between his fingers like a noose.

She turned away to mask the anger on her face. *So that's why Dan sent me here - to do his dirty work again.* The little boy was playing with a bug, guiding it around with a stick. Another bug fell off a tree, and rolled to its feet.

"What have you got there, Jesse?"

"Cicadas. They came out of these holes in the ground, see?" He waved at the dirt under the tree which was pocked with holes.

Diana looked closer. Great streams of the creatures were clambering up the tree. Hundreds clung onto the leaves, many wriggling out of splits in the top of their carapaces. The empty cases littered the ground below in a thickening carpet and the pale soft imagoes waved stubby appendages in the breeze as they expanded out into something more like wings.

Jesse followed her gaze. "They're waiting for their wings to dry so they can fly away."

"They are." Diana paused. Something about them wasn't right, though. Not just one of them. They were all slightly off. "Jonah, is this a cicada year?"

"No, that's a couple of years off yet. Why?"

A blackbird flew down to feast on the grubs, and a second

joined it.

"They're—" A gunshot went off on the other side of the valley, and the background murmur of faraway wings suddenly became louder. There was a rising buzz from over the hill, a chitinous scritching that made the hairs stand up on the back of her neck. "They're swarming! It's going to be painfully loud if they stop here, Jonah. We should get inside. Come on, Jesse. Leave those be."

"Go on, boy!" Jonah rumbled. "I'm right behind you." He slapped at a cicada that had settled on his shirt.

Diana hurried Jesse away. Clouds of insects unsettled her, and these were big ones. The thought of them crawling all over her made her shudder. Besides, if they were cicadas they weren't like any she'd seen before.

The razzing sound of the cicadas skittered along her nerves, cold as fear. She lengthened her stride until Jesse was running to keep up, ducking as the cicadas tumbled through the air around them.

Jonah was still wading through the wheat when the first insects zipped past like rattling bullets. Then the swarm enveloped him. He screamed.

"Dad!" Jesse stopped in his tracks, dropping Diana's hand.

Jonah staggered forward out of the swarm for a moment, his face a mass of blisters and weals, and coughed a great spray of scarlet over the green stems. "Go! Doc, please!" His hoarse wheezing turned to horrible choking noises and, clutching at his throat, he collapsed amongst the wheat.

Diana's heart missed a beat. She swept Jesse into her arms and sprinted for both their lives.

"Dad!" Jesse's voice was high and shrill.

Insects buzzed past as she stumbled along the path; her heart beat so hard she thought her lungs might explode. *No chance of reaching the house. The truck, maybe.*

Shifting the shrieking child to her hip, she fumbled in her pocket. The cicadas were everywhere, swarming more intensely with every pounding heartbeat. The keycard stuck in her pocket, snagged on a thread. Their buzzsaw scream was deafening, hurting her ears; she couldn't think straight.

Wrenching the keycard free as she rounded the corner, she unlocked the truck. Cicadas were settling, the ground thick with a crawling carpet of bodies.

"In the truck!" She yanked the door open, shoved the boy inside and leapt in after him, slamming the door behind her. Jesse scrambled to the far side of the truck, setting his back to the other door, his eyes wide with fear.

Diana's heart was thumping madly. *Quick! Shut the windows!* She twisted around to check no cicadas had gotten in. All clear. She forced herself to slow her breathing, trying to get control of the painful pounding in her chest.

Just as she felt her pulse slowing, an impact thwacked on the window beside Jesse's head. She jumped as he recoiled. The fat black body of the cicada slid down the glass, twitching feebly, leaving a loathsome trail of yellowish fluid in its wake. But as it dropped out of sight, another hit the windshield; then increasing numbers of them, coming in great waves of dull impacts, one after another, relentless.

"They're coming to get us!" Jesse shrieked, his eyes glassy with terror.

"They can't get us in here," she quavered, but he was too far gone to listen, and cowered in the footwell.

She stabbed at the truck's start button. The engine roared into life, but the windshield was smeared and she couldn't see properly. The wipers kicked in, but they only smeared the stains into a sickening mess of yellow fluid and twitching shadows, where split and dying cicadas struggled weakly in the vile ooze.

Away! Quick! Her breath was coming in short gasps. Visualizing the yard as best she could, she reversed the truck out. Which way was the road? She eased the vehicle forward blindly. *Please be here...Please be here...* There was a harsh jolt.

We need to get away! NOW! She backed up again, but the shock had flustered her and she had lost her sense of direction. There was another crunch. Her nails dug into the steering wheel. She had a sudden urge to smash her way out of there; but if she broke the windows or bent the bodywork of the truck enough, the cicadas would get in.

They would have to stay put till the swarm passed.

"No, no, NO!" She slammed her hands on the steering wheel. In the footwell, Jesse cried out. He was beyond terrified, and she had left him to it. Who did that to a child? She needed to calm him down. Gripping the steering wheel tightly, she took a breath, and got herself under control. "Jesse. It's okay. They can't get us here." *I hope that's true.* "Jesse?" Her shoulders were so tense it was almost painful. Turning off the engine, she moved onto the bench seat of the truck, and pulled the boy up into her arms.

What about Jonah? Her stomach dropped. She'd been about to abandon him, even though she had no proof that he was dead. A sob slipped out, but she bit the inside of her lip; the pain centered her. *Get a grip, you fool! There's no time for this. You need to get this situation under control before anyone else dies!*

"I'm sorry, Jesse. It's okay. We're safe, we are. We just... We can't drive away yet. But we will soon." The swarm was getting louder and she had to raise her voice to be heard.

She hid his head in her shoulder so he wouldn't see the insects crashing barely inches away from him, in the sticky gunk on the other side of the glass. He clung to her, his cries fading to hysterical sobs while around them the truck rocked and rattled with impact after nerve-wrecking impact, and the swarm's shriek drowned out all other sounds.

Eventually the battering faded and the noise of the swarm eased, and with them, Jesse's sobs. When Diana could hear the words she was murmuring to Jesse, she sat back and took a few deep breaths. *I have to call this in. The police need to know about it, maybe the ambulance service too. But just contact with the cicadas and Jonah was... They won't have the PPE to cope with it, not on-hand.* She was too shaken to work it out. Dan would know how to handle it.

"Jesse, I need to make a phone-call." Her voice wobbled; she cleared her throat. "Can you sit quietly so I can tell them where we are?"

The boy nodded, his face wet with tears. He slumped back against the seat as she dialed.

The phone rang for what seemed like forever before it was picked up. "Hello?"

"Dan, it's me."

"Diana?"

"I went to Jonah's. Saw the crop."

"And?"

"I think he's..." She caught herself, looking at Jesse. *I think he's dead.* "Cicadas came, lots. When we were in the field. I'm in the truck. You can hear them on the windows."

"Cicadas?" He was as baffled as she was; what were cicadas doing, swarming a farm in Illinois? They weren't due for a couple of years. And, in any case, cicadas weren't... she balked at the memory of Jonah spewing blood... they weren't lethal. "Diana? You there?"

"Yes, dammit!" It was almost a shout. She brought herself under control again. "Yes, Cicadas, Dan, years early and not like any I ever saw before. It's bad. We need an ambulance. I don't know, maybe the fire service. We should probably let the police know."

"Whoa, Diana, I'm in an open office. Give me a moment." The sound of a door, steps echoing in the stairwell, voices and then another door closing. "Okay. I'm in Victor's office and we're both listening. What's going on?"

She reported what she'd seen, trying to phrase it so as not to alarm Jesse any more than she had to. "I need to get the son to safety. Then I'll come back for samples. Will you send the clean-up team? I'll brief the police and hand this over to them—"

"You'll do no such thing," Dan interrupted.

It took Diana a full two seconds to accept that she'd heard that right. "I beg your pardon?"

"You signed a Non-Disclosure Agreement. You will not bring this company or its products into disrepute. It's all set out very clearly."

"But... But..." Cold horror trickled down Diana's back. "People will die. We can't just walk away without warning anyone. The swarm is moving on. There are dozens of farms around here!"

The friendliness faded from Dan's voice. "You can and you will. That's a direct order, Diana. There is nothing for us to report here. It's nothing to do with Feedit. A man had an allergic reaction to some cicadas. That's all there is to it, and that's what the police will find. I'll make sure of it."

Diana knew she should be angry—no, bloody furious—but she had no fury left. She stared at the windshield. In the mirror, her eyes were dark and wide against the pallor of her skin. Another insect hit the glass, another shadow twitching next to a hundred others in the thick, viscous fluid that coated the truck. It made her want to retch.

"Diana, I get it. You saw a man die. You're in shock," Dan had his fake-sympathetic voice on again. "However under the terms of your NDA you can't mention Matreus Inc., or Feedit to anyone outside the studies. You know the consequences as well as we do. We don't want to have to go the legal route."

"It won't come to that," Victor interrupted him. "Di is too valuable a member of staff. Di, leave it with us and we'll take everything in hand and get it all sorted out. Are you all right, though? Are you hurt?"

"No." She leaned her head back on the chair. Victor would make things right. He'd get Dan in line and make sure it was dealt with properly. "No, not hurt, just shaken."

"That's something at least. Where are you now?"

Diana rallied her thoughts. "Illinois. Farm 124 in Study B, near Danforth."

"Good." Victor replied, and now his voice was all Caring Boss again. "Hand the kid over to the family, find a hotel, and stay put. Dan will fly over tomorrow and debrief you. And then you should take time off and recover, okay? But in the meantime, remember; you didn't see anything, and you aren't involved. Got it?"

A triple whammy of insects hit the truck and Diana started so badly she nearly dropped the phone. It was all too much to handle. She sagged back in her seat. "Yes, Victor."

"Good. We appreciate your loyalty." The phone went dead.

Diana stared out of the windshield bleakly. The bumps and bangs had nearly stopped. It was all wrong. She couldn't leave Jonah there lying in the field. Whoever his family were, they deserve to know the truth of his death. If the swarm landed somewhere else, people would get hurt, even killed! They couldn't ask her to keep silent about the attack—it made no sense! But they'd given her a direct order. And there was the NDA. She couldn't lose her job, her livelihood, her everything. She had no choice, she had to remain silent even though it made her sick to her stomach.

She turned on the engine again and squirted some windshield fluid onto the glass and this time the windshield washers began to clear the sticky mess into neat, if gross, arcs. As soon as she could see, she backed the truck slowly toward the lane, crunching through the fallen cicadas.

Jesse hoisted himself out of the wheel well and onto his seat. "Where are we going? Where's my Dad?"

Diana stopped the truck and racked her brains for ways to explain, but there was no set of words that would do. Jesse was six, but even he would see that it was wrong.

She tried to get her head around the fact that she'd tacitly agreed to keep her trap shut, to persuade herself that it was a necessary evil, but the more she did, the more the ice clumped in her stomach. Her limbs ached with exhaustion. Despite her best efforts, it was a step beyond what she could tolerate. *If I do what they want, it will be sheer cowardice. People will die because of me. Again.*

"No," she whispered. "Not happening."

Jesse's voice scaled higher. "Dad? We're going to get him, right?"

She leaned her elbows on the wheel and dropped her head into her hands. *I can't do it. I... I can't.* Which left only one course of action. *I must be mad.* She rubbed her eyes briefly. "I'm going to take the truck closer to where we were. It may be that we can see him from there."

She pulled in at the edge of the field and clambered into the back, crouching to unpack her PPE in the limited space. Jumpsuit, face-mask, gloves: she lay them out and started to wriggle into the jump-suit. "Jesse, I'm going to need you to stay here, okay? I have no protective gear for you. You sit tight here."

Jesse just looked at her, his eyes wide and scared.

She pulled on a set of gloves, careful not to rip them, and made sure her mask was on properly. Then she grabbed some containers and paused to listen. Outside everything was quiet. The buzz of the swarm was gone. "I won't go far, I promise." She slid out of the door and closed it behind her.

Looking back at Jesse's white face pressed against the window, Diana was seized with dread. Birds were everywhere, gorging on the cicadas still on the ground. She trudged past them to where Jonah lay, and the hairs on the back of her neck rose at the sight of him.

His arms and neck were two or three times their normal size, the skin raised in great blisters which had all merged to make one horrendous fluid-filled distortion. His face was virtually unrecognizable.

"Jonah?" she whispered. "Jonah? Oh hell." She pressed a gloved finger to his neck. He was not breathing and he had no pulse. "I'm so sorry. I'll look after Jesse as best I can till we find the rest of your family, I promise."

Her chest was so tight she could hardly breathe, but she jolted herself into action. *Back to work, quick, or I'll freeze.* She took samples of everything; bugs, the discarded grub cases, swabs from Jonah's face, and the fluid from his blisters. She couldn't let Jonah's death go uninvestigated, whatever Victor said, but he couldn't know she was, in essence, opening an investigation. There was one person who might help her.

Hurrying back to the truck, she stripped off her protective clothing and carefully bagged it up. "I'm so sorry, Jesse—"

He wasn't listening. "One got in..." He was staring at a smeared mess on the dash.

Fear prickled her skin. She grabbed her coat and tucked it over the air inlets in case any others were in there. "Are you okay?"

"It buzzed at me and I squashed it."

Diana grabbed his hand to look at the red welt, puffy and swollen already. Her heart thudded so that she could hardly breathe. *Oh no. I killed him, just like Charlie. I killed him.* She revved the truck till it screamed, stabbing her GPS as they veered onto the main road. "TomTom, find me the nearest Emergency Room."

"Methodist General Emergency Room is 235 miles." The soft voice of the GPS purred.

"Hospital," she yelled. "Find me a hospital."

Beside her, Jesse wheezed and slid off his seat.

CHAPTER TWO

ANAYELI ALFARO. OUTSIDE WOOLDAND, CALIFORNIA.

The line of flames darted and flickered in the corner of Anayeli Alfaro's eye despite her best effort to keep her gaze trained on Josh Bertoli, the only farmer willing to talk to her about the controversial "controlled burn." What a joke. No farmer burned their fields in California anymore. Too dangerous with the drought. Which was exactly why she had gotten up at dawn to stand on a low rise overlooking actively burning farmland. She was pursuing what she hoped would be her first front-page, above-the-fold story. The story that would free her from the detestable weekend crime desk.

"This is on the record, so let me get this right." She used her best journalist voice as she secured her face mask and pulled her reporter's notebook from her back pocket. "Every member farm of the Frontier Farmers' Co-op is burning their entire crop today, the last day before the fire season officially begins, on orders from the co-op?"

"Orders from Matreus. The seed company." Josh's voice was slightly muffled from the bandana he wore against the smoke. She strained to hear him, trying not to be distracted as the flame licked toward the row of farmworkers stretched across the field, all dressed in hats, long-sleeve work shirts, jeans, battered boots. Protection from the sun, not the fire, for which they were armed with nothing but shovels. Her papa was one of those men, had worked for Bertoli Farms for more than twenty years, while Josh's dad was the one taking over the reins from his father.

"Are controlled burns usually this fast-moving?" Worry prickled at Anayeli as the flames crept forward, eating up grass that was lush and full, two feet tall and maybe two weeks away from its first cutting. She searched for her papa and found him at dead center, obvious in his signature yellow and blue Sacramento River Cats Dorados cap, the one she'd given him.

Josh shrugged and pulled at his bandana. "It's been dry." He let out a burst of ragged coughing as smoke wafted past them. His dog, an Australian shepherd, sidled up next to him and whined.

Anayeli blinked, her eyes stinging as she trained them on the crackling blaze. She was glad there was a water truck idling at the ready at the base of the hill if the fire needed to be doused quickly. And at least she had an N95 mask, and she'd made sure Papa did too. They were basically required for half the year in California, ever since the drought had made tinder out of every stick and blade of grass that wasn't irrigated, sent wildfires raging through the forests, and left farmers up and down the Central and Sacramento Valleys desperate to grow anything that didn't require copious amounts of water the way almonds and rice did.

"What crop are you burning?" Anayeli pressed. She only knew the little Papa had told her: "They're burning the loco grass." *Loco grass.* There had to be something bad about whatever it was. Because even though it wasn't technically fire season yet, and Josh had the required

19

burn permit, it didn't make sense that farmers up and down the northern part of the state would risk burning their hay crop and losing so much potential income unless something was really wrong. Papa had told her about a few *campesinos*—friends of his—who had suffered terrible allergy attacks after seeding the hay in the spring. "Asthma so bad they had to go to emergency." But no way a few asthmatic immigrants would have convinced Josh Bertoli to incinerate his entire crop.

"Teff." Josh wiped at his eyes.

She had just scribbled that four letter word on her notepad, when a yell went up from below. Her breath caught as the flames found the dense grass growing toward the center of the field and shot higher, sending a plume of dark smoke billowing into the morning air. Both she and Josh took a step back as the flames swelled, gobbling up the buffer between it and the *campesinos*, forcing the men back.

But one man below retreated too slowly. Anayeli's stomach lurched as he spun into a screaming panic, arms flailing as flames crawled up his pant leg. The nearest *campesinos* cried out to him as they shoveled dirt faster, lobbing it at the man or at the fire—they were the same thing—but the flames kept advancing. Someone charged the burning man and tossed water from their canteen at the base of the flame, to no effect.

She was not going to watch a man die. She refused. "Drop and roll!" The words tore from her throat, even as Josh let out a stream of curses. She shouted again—maybe someone would hear, would tell the burning man what to do—and as she did, a figure in a bright Dorados cap—Papa!—dashed down the line, toward the man on fire.

Papa tackled the man, pushing him backward away from the burning field and forcing him down to the ground, rolling him over and over until, after an eternity of seconds, the man's pant leg was smothered. The two men lay there, and she couldn't breathe—not until Papa leapt up. Safe. Unscathed. And angry, from the looks of it. He gestured wildly at the blaze, bolting back to take his place on the fire line as the burned man curled into the fetal position.

"This isn't safe!" Her voice was diamond hard with fury. It wasn't right that a man lay injured and her papa was risking his life below while she stood with Josh trying to get her story. More people were going to get hurt and she knew most of the men on that field. She'd grown up going to their daughters' *quinceañeras*.

It was Josh's dog who responded, letting out a sharp bark that sounded like agreement to her, while his owner kept his mouth shut, wiping at his eyes again. You're right, she silently agreed with the dog, it's not safe. Not okay, either.

The *campesinos* were dark shapes moving through the billowing smoke, while the heat blasted upwards, making Anayeli's skin taut and painful. Her heart sped, a slight wheeze tightening her lungs as she saw that many of the men below were bent double, coughing, even as they shoveled desperately. One man slumped, clutching at his throat, and another dragged him back to where the burned man lay, motionless.

It was when a third man sank to his knees and had to be carried to the base of the hill that the water truck finally rumbled to life, lumbering over the uneven ground toward the fire line. Relief flooded her as the truck let out a huge fan of spray, dousing the men and the flames. An ominous hissing rose from the field—steam mixed with an ugly, thick smoke. The fire died down for a second—but then the blaze shot upward in a furiously crackling firework of sparks. Fierce tongues of flame surged into the sky, as the wall of seething orange bore down on the men, burning hotter and brighter than it had before the water truck had made its pass.

She startled as Josh's dog let out another sharp bark—not at her, at Josh, as he dissolved into a violent coughing fit. *The asthma.* It wasn't tears he'd been wiping away from his eyes. The backs of his hands were smeared with something. Soot, her brain tried to tell her. Ash. But it wasn't. In the horrible orange flickering glare of the fire, it could only be one thing. Blood. More oozed from his eyes—eyes that were so bloodshot the whites had gone completely red—and trailed down his cheeks.

She tried to make her mouth form words, but before she could, from down on the field came a sound unlike any she'd ever heard before, a roaring from the fire itself as it sucked in oxygen and created its own scorching wind.

The dog barked again, and then again and again, as if it could ward off the monstrous blaze that towered over the *campesinos*, their shovels pitifully useless.

Anayeli stumbled backward, away from the searing heat and smoke. A blizzard of ash swirled around her, obscuring her vision. She couldn't find Papa, his hat. At the same time, Josh bent in half, still coughing, and frantically clutching at his bandana.

"No! Leave that on!" But Josh either didn't hear her or couldn't respond, not with all the hacking he was doing. His dog pawed at his leg, still barking, and when Josh straightened, Anayeli was stunned into motionless horror. His mouth was frothing with pink bubbles, and when he coughed, it was blood that came up. Bright red blood, staining his lips, his teeth.

"*Ay, Dios!*" The words came on a gasp as the roar of the fire turned to screams of a pitch Anayeli had never heard before—screams so wrenching—

Her every muscle was at sudden attention. Ready. But she wasn't running. Not when Papa was still below, fighting the blaze.

She whirled from Josh back toward the field, and before she'd even processed what she saw, she was screaming in wordless terror and anguish and helplessness. The flames twisted and spun forward—a firenado, that was the only way to describe it. It overwhelmed the men below, devouring even those who turned and ran from it. She wanted to clap her hands over her ears to drown out the sound of the men's screams. Instead, some desperate voice in the back of her mind told her that maybe the workers were okay, maybe the fire would burn past them so quickly they would be mostly unharmed. *Lies.*

There were several *campesinos* on the ground, rolling out the flames, she thought at first—but no—they were writhing in agony. Her soul cried out for her to bolt down the hill, toward those men, to help them, to do something—but the fire had already surrounded and raged past the still-spraying water truck to the base of the hill she stood on, as if the truck had poured gasoline on it instead of water.

She blinked to clear her eyes of the acrid smoke so she could search for Papa, and in that tiny fraction of time the fire exploded, fanning out across all the adjacent fields. It overtook the dead almond orchard off to one side, climbing the brittle trees, the flames like nasty clawed fingers scraping at the sky. It leapt up the power poles, lighting the wires up like garish swooping garlands. And then, worse, so very much worse, she saw a figure, running out of the flames, clothes afire, letting out a horrible, desperate wail—a Dorados hat—Papa!

"Run!" she shrieked, to Papa, to herself, to Josh, she didn't know, because she could never get to Papa in time, could never get away from the flames in time either. The fire was coming straight up the hill, gorging itself on everything in its path. And then Papa went down. Not rolling. Not even writhing. Just dropped. Motionless. Even as the flames raged. Her sweet, laughing Papa, the man who had called her only yesterday saying, "Maybe I got that big story you always say you need before you settle down..."

Her eyes stung and her nose burned, with smoke and tears. There was a keening coming from somewhere. From her. From down below. Everywhere. But at the same time, a strange clarity flashed through her. It was too late. There was nothing she could do for Papa. Nothing at all to do, except live. *Vive*, Papa's voice commanded in her head. *Escribe*. Write.

"Run!" But it didn't matter how loud she screamed. Josh was rooted, his eyes wide and streaming blood, his mouth agape.

Her notebook flew as she grabbed Josh's arm and yanked him around, in the direction of her car. Even if he was the worst kind of jerk she wasn't leaving him behind—he was going to live with the consequences of whatever hell he'd had a hand in creating down on that hay field. He was going to answer not just her questions, but for what he'd done.

Except Josh didn't move. He was paralyzed, and in the orange flickering light of the fire, she saw he was bleeding from his nose too. His dog barked and nipped at him but he just stood, watching the sky go night-dark with smoke, the sun a red-orange orb. She yanked at Josh again and he stumbled forward, the word *run* blaring in her head like a siren. *Corré!*

She was strong, but with her short legs, she'd never been fast. With Josh staggering behind her, coughing an awful, wet, wracking cough, even with his dog nipping at him—herding him—they were never going to outrun the flames. The heat blared across her back and she knew without looking that it was getting closer. She cursed herself for parking so far away. Papa—her eyes streamed at the thought of him—had said the Co-op had hired their own fire crews to supervise, but those crews were nowhere to be seen. If she made it back to her car—no, *when*—she would call 911.

But the instant she caught sight of her little red hatchback, Josh collapsed, his head bouncing as he hit the ground, blood snaking from his ears.

"No! Get up!" Her voice was ragged and more tears—oh she hoped they were tears— welled, barely tracking down her cheeks before they evaporated in the heat. Josh didn't move.

Or rather, he did—*No. Please no.* He was convulsing, his back arched as he writhed, struggling against some unseen enemy, a desperate rattling sound coming from him, loud enough she could hear it over the howling, snapping fire. She'd been mad at Josh before, she was still furious that he'd had the irresponsible audacity to set such idiotic fires, stealing her precious Papa's life and all those other men's too. But Josh's dog was frenzied, pulling at his sleeve, licking at him, barking, pulling again. The fire was coming for her now, crackling and hissing and she was coughing too. Whatever advantage they had would be gone in seconds. She would never get Josh to her car, even if she could somehow get him up, but she didn't want to leave him. She grabbed for his arm, the one the dog didn't have, to try anyway, when Josh went slack, the fight gone out of him, just as it had gone out of Papa.

She threw a glance over her shoulder. The fire had crested the low rise and raced toward them, fueled by the smallest of weeds. There was no time to check Josh's pulse and see if he was truly gone, not when the soles of his boots were already warping from the scorching heat.

It wasn't even a thought. She snatched the dog's collar and bolted, scurrying bent sideways to lug the dog in the direction of her car, parked too far away. The dog resisted, dragging back toward Josh, but then another wave of heat crashed over them and the dog suddenly

24

bounded ahead of her, hauling her faster than she thought she could go as she kept ahold of the collar. The fire roared louder, belching so much smoke it was like running through thick black fog. She couldn't see her car. Without letting go of the dog she tore at her pocket, then the other, cursing herself for forgetting which one, for picking her tightest jeans to wear as she struggled to get the keys out. But then she had them. She hit all the buttons—the alarm went off, the lights flashed through the dense, enveloping haze. She lurched for the car door handle, screaming as the handle melted her palm. She flung the door open, half dragging the dog in after her, and slammed the door shut. But as she jammed the keys into the ignition the flames lit her car in hellish brightness and the engine stuttered to life. The bitter tang of singed hair hit her nostrils. The dog was smoldering.

CHAPTER THREE

SAM LEARY. BERKELEY, CALIFORNIA.

Sam straightened in his chair, his spine rigid. He jammed his phone against his ear as his friend, Dr. Diana Stewart, whispered on the other end.

"It was a swarm of Biblical proportions." She was never like this. She was the unflappable type. It was one of the reasons they'd clicked. "They came out of nowhere and took Jonah down like he was a marshmallow man."

Sheesh, was she crying on the other end of the phone? "Are you hurt?"

"I'm fine. No, really, I am." All evidence to the contrary. "They intubated Jesse after he coded." She blew her nose. "It was..."

Sam had no clue who Jonah, the Marshmallow Man, or Jesse 'who'd been intubated,' were, but he wasn't supposed to interrupt a friend when they were crying. That was their "private time" and his job was to "wait." Diana had taught him that back at college when he was struggling to connect with the other—baffling—humans. Diana spoke their language, whereas he never had. Sam Leary, genius? Yes. Social animal? Most definitely not.

"I'm bringing them to you. California's safe, right? No cicadas? Invading, I mean."

Sam spun his fidget spinner, letting the spin calm him. "Nothing invading." There were fires somewhere—north? South? He hadn't been paying attention—but there were always fires in Cali and, in any case, they weren't close to the campus. Much more exciting was the fact that Diana had samples! Insect parts! His specialty. He grinned, glad that she'd sought him out. He might not understand why someone wept uncontrollably, but he was the top man at the University of California, Berkeley when it came to bugs and nymphs and life cycles that were out of whack. He'd even been awarded the Physiology, Biochemistry, and Toxicology Award from the Pacific Branch, Entomological Society of America (PBESA) and was the youngest recipient in history at the age of nineteen. She was right to bring the bugs to him. Though, practically speaking, it was a long drive. He was about to suggest she FedEx them rather than driving from Danforth to Berkeley when she dropped her voice so low he had to cover his eyes and concentrate even harder to pick up what she was saying.

"You tell no one that I am involved. Are we clear? Not a single being. Not even Henry."

Sam stole a look at his dog, curled in the soft, round bed below the steel desk. He told Henry all his secrets and Diana knew it. That was code for, 'This is serious, Sam.'

"Your secret's safe with me."

"I'll be there as soon as I can." She hung up without saying goodbye which was weird because she usually said a hundred goodbyes. She'd explained that it was because she'd grown up in England and that's what they did over there, though it always struck him as a terrible waste of time to say goodbye more than once.

He slid the phone into his pocket and frowned. He didn't remember reading any articles involving swarming cicadas in large numbers. There'd been a blurb in American Entomologist in the August issue, 2018 about the insects, but nothing like Diana described.

He rolled his chair back and forth. The rhythmic grinding was soothing and helped him switch from "people mode" to "science interface." He pushed away from the lecture desk and rolled over to his computer in the corner of the lab. A crinkling caused him to glance down. The bold lettering on the envelope suggested official business, and it bore the university post-room's stamp. A colleague next door received one just like it, and now they no longer worked at the college. He wanted to open it, to prove it wasn't a letter of dismissal, but now wasn't the time. He had a scientific conundrum: what were cicadas doing in Illinois? How had they killed a man? And what could he do to prevent that from happening again? He set the letter on the desk and logged into the computer.

There was a thump, then another; two lazy tail wags from his shaggy-haired dog. Then Henry huffed in true Henry fashion.

"That's all very well for you to say, but it doesn't make any sense. No swarms are being reported, and the cicada population isn't supposed to show for another year or so. They sound like Tibicen Bermudiana Verrill, but they're on the wrong continent and have been extinct for years."

Henry let him know what he thought of that theory by getting up, circling twice, and tucking his head under his front paws.

"I agree," Sam muttered. "Extinct means extinct. It doesn't mean killer bugs."

He tapped cicada variation into the search bar at American Entomologist and scrolled. Genes and morphology. Biomimetic wing structures. Psychoactive mushroom alkaloids. "Ah, there it is." Prof. Keiko Sato of Tokyo University had submitted a paper in 2018, just as he'd remembered. He scanned it but was bitterly disappointed. Her report was on the use of cicada sloughs in creating high-performance electrodes for use in supercapacitors. He'd been hoping for an anomalous swarm report.

Henry grunted and shifted, signaling the end of that particular venture. Henry always knew best.

Sam opened a new window and navigated to his favorite low-brow forum. Scientific Puzzlers was where you went for hot-off-the-press science gossip, rather than learned opinions. It was populated with geeks and nerds, just like him, but geeks and nerds with wit and humor and, best of all, off-the-wall answers.

"Cicada swarm," he wrote. "Anyone caught the buzz?" He hit return, smiling at his own pun. It didn't take much to make his online friends smile with an emoji in return. Another reason to enjoy their remote company.

He grabbed a piece of printer paper and a pencil and started sketching. Images were the keys to the brain's deepest structures. If he drew for long enough he'd find the answers he was looking for. He glanced over to the ninety gallon aquarium at the far end of the lab where the caterpillars he raised were currently waiting to start their transformation. If only Diana had asked him about Megalopyge Opercularis he wouldn't have had to start from scratch. His pencil glided over the paper. The wings were always the most rewarding. Diaphanous as silk, yet strong enough to carry a cicada over eighty miles of terrain each day. What a marvel.

Henry growled as the door slammed open to reveal the hulking form of Frank Dorset, the University's forensic entomologist. Sam returned to his drawing hoping Frank would get the message to leave, but pretending to ignore the brute hadn't stopped him before.

Frank clomped over to Sam's desk. It was his usual practice to play with everything that wasn't tied down, no matter how fragile or valuable it was. Sam slid the letter under his drawing to keep Frank from noticing the official stamp but was too late. Frank grabbed the letter, ripped open the envelope which Sam had deliberately stashed for later, and clucked his tongue. He leaned over Sam's shoulder to wave the document in his face. "It's a shame you won't be able to present next month."

So it was a letter of dismissal. That meant his research would be shelved once he was gone. Sam ignored his buffoon of a colleague and continued sketching his cicada, with its bug eyes and fat body. "I'm busy."

Frank stuffed the letter into his front pocket and headed to the fish tank sitting on the adjacent counter. Moments later the sharp tap of metal on glass rang through the lab. "You've got a couple of runners."

Sam dropped his pad and pencil, rushed to the back counter, and pushed past Frank who was holding a pair of forceps. "What do you mean?" He prowled around the tank, examining every corner for his specimens. They should be in there. He counted them just after putting out fresh leaves on Monday. Rising to his full five feet, six inches, he tiptoed to reach the top of the tank and lifted the lid. He swallowed. They weren't there. Not one. The lack of hairy brown caterpillars crawling over the fake terrain meant they were loose somewhere in the building.

He dropped the lid. Things didn't add up. There were no openings for them to escape, and he hadn't pulled any out of the tank for venom extraction in a couple of weeks. He checked the calendar pinned to the wall beside the tank, four days left to cross off. It wasn't time for them yet. He grimaced. That meant he had four days to find them, or all that time raising them was for nothing.

Sam whirled, jabbing a finger at his colleague. "What did you do with my Flannel moths?"

"What did I do?" He leered and jeered, his lip curling. "Come now, Samuel, this isn't fair. How can you blame me? I haven't visited you in weeks." *Liar.*

Sam hated when Frank mocked him. "They could be key to understanding evolutionary changes in insect populations!" He unbuttoned his collar to let some of the steam out, even though he knew the heat sensation was psycho-somatic. "If you didn't take them, then who did?"

"I can't tell you what I don't know, Samuel." Frank worked open the forceps, tried to pick up a pencil that lay on the counter, and put them back on the tray over the top of the other tools. "Unless you have something to trade."

Sam returned the forceps to their proper place and strode over to the opposite wall, his back turned to his antagonist, jaw clenched. Nothing had changed. Frank was just an older, fatter, more powerful version of the bullies in the schoolyard. After a year of being tortured, every deed the human-slug committed rose to the surface of his consciousness. His forehead and cheeks flushed, and his speeding heart thumped in his neck, pulsing out of control. Every square inch of his skin itched. He slammed his fist on the counter, rattling his microscope.

Frank continued, "Too bad you can't trust the people you work with. I bet it was Paula. Your ladybugs would look fantastic in her insect collection."

"They're not ladyb..." Sam whipped around to face his opponent.

Frank's grin said he knew that they weren't ladybugs and that he'd already won this round, smug reptilian slime bag that he was.

Henry curled his lip to expose his fangs. Hackles up, he moved, stiff-legged, toward Frank, a low growl rumbling from deep inside his chest.

"Woah... Hey... Play nice..." Frank backed away, ducking behind the lecture desk.

"It's all right, Henry. Settle down. Good boy." Nothing would have pleased Sam more than for Henry to sink his jaws into Frank's loathsome neck, but he didn't want his dog to catch anything from the slug man.

Sam weighed his options. Frank's greed was easier to deal with than Paula's advances. She draped herself on him whenever she came to his lab. She didn't seem to understand that not talking, not making eye contact, and never going for coffee, no matter how many times she asked, meant he wasn't interested. Frank, on the other hand, was up-front about what he wanted and Sam was generally in a position to hand over the goods. "What's your price?"

Frank beamed. "Now that's what I'm talking about. Cooperation." Whispering as if they were conspirators plotting something illegal, he cocked an eyebrow. "I want to know when the mayflies are going to hatch this season."

Sam tilted his head, confused. Frank was an entomologist. He could find that data in his sleep. The point, then, was to exercise power, making him run a rudimentary search, just because *Frank said so.* Sam rolled his eyes and sat down at his computer. "Bring my caterpillars back now and the information you requested will be waiting for you."

It took a couple of minutes to find the latest files, and he scribbled down notes as to where the most mayflies were going to be, making sure to mark down the times they were hatching.

The swish of the doors heralded Frank's return. He carried a jar with holes poked into the lid. Five brown caterpillars inched their way over each other in the crowded space. Where's my info?"

Sam ripped the page out of the notebook and held it out. "What do you want this information for?"

"Fly-fishing. The trout are going to be epic, and I just happen to have my gear here in case mayflies hatch this weekend." He folded the paper and hid it in his back pocket. "Now, about these caterpillars?"

"What about my caterpillars?"

Frank dug in his front pocket and fished out the crumpled letter from the head of the faculty. "Don't you get it, brainiac? They want you gone. I'm taking your slot."

Sam dropped his head to his chest, letting his hair fall over his eyes. Three colleagues had been cut loose in as many months. Now it was his turn. He hadn't made tenure and they were going to let him go.

"Don't go crying on me, flyboy. The Dean asked me personally."

"This isn't your field, Frank." He wanted to fight back, talk to the Dean, make the presentation himself. He'd worked day and night to collect the data. He deserved to be the one to step onto the stage and tell the world what he'd discovered. He might stammer and sweat, but the work spoke for itself.

Frank rolled the jar of caterpillars in his clammy hands, leaving ugly smears all over the glass. "What makes them so special?"

Sam glared at the guy who was muscling him out of a job he loved. Frank was no brainiac, but knew how to 'people' which was the only reason he hadn't been booted to the curb by the faculty.

"Earth to Sam. I'm waiting."

"The toxins from the caterpillar can cause rashes, vomiting, and swollen glands. In one case, a young boy almost had his system completely shut down from being stung."

Frank recoiled from the jar as if he'd already been skewered. The container thunked on the counter, tipped over, and rolled into the tank.

"If they'd attacked you'd know it. The pain is a seven on the Richter scale." It was a joke, but Frank didn't do nerd jokes, which made it all the more pleasurable. Frank was out the door and down the corridor, probably with some plan to suck up to the powers that be, to further cement his position.

Sam picked up his beautiful moths-to-be, unscrewed the lid, and lay them gently in the bottom of their tank. What he hadn't told Frank was that the more extreme responses were an anomaly, and few had been recorded in an official capacity.

The computer speakers let out a baleful ding and Sam took a seat. Scientific Puzzlers had belched up a response. Two new messages populated the otherwise dull forum.

Sam slid his chair back and let Henry rest his head on his knee; it calmed both of them. "There's new information from the boys in the INHS Medical Entomology Department. They usually cover ticks and mosquitoes, but considering the data, it doesn't sound like anything we've seen previously."

Sam approached his fish tank, leaned his elbows against the cool epoxy resin, and cupped his chin with his hands. His creepy-crawly friends inched toward the leaves, and made holes in the foliage as they fed. He was so absorbed in the live Discovery TV show he almost missed another ding from the speakers. He returned to the computer, scanning the feeds. Huh. Nothing new here, just the same event rehashed by someone else who wants their fifteen minutes. What a waste of time. The monitor went blank as he powered off the flat screen.

"What do you say we head to the park for a game of catch before dinner?" Henry jumped out from under his desk at the word 'park,' wagging his tail.

They were halfway out of the door when the computer started to bling, several times in rapid succession. Pressing the power button on the monitor, he logged back in. The science forum had exploded. Comments and bits of information filled the page faster than he managed to take it in.

Forsythe, Illinois. 300-acre farm. Stripped to the dirt.

Oreana, northeast of Decatur, seven-car pileup. Bugs reported on the highway.

Warrensburg, Ill. Woman and child killed. EMTs injured. Police have cordoned off the scene.

DO NOT APPROACH. BUGS LETHAL. REPEAT TOXIC TO THE TOUCH.

The reports came in so thick and fast that Sam couldn't keep up. He punched in Diana's number, but it went directly to voicemail. He had to warn her.

There was more than one swarm.

CHAPTER FOUR

DR. DIANA STEWART. DANFORTH/WATSEKA, ILLINOIS.

The nurse stuck his head around the door of Jesse's room and beckoned her out into the corridor. "Good news, Doc—Jesse is going to be all right."

"He is?" She leaned against the wall, limp with relief.

The nurse smiled. "He'll be kept under sedation for a while. Why don't you go get a few hours' sleep? Visiting hours are at six."

Returning to her truck, Diana leaned her head on the steering wheel. She was so tired. Probably shouldn't be driving. Maybe just sit in the truck and wind down for a bit.

She turned on the radio, which cut in with the news broadcast. "-we appear to have lost the feed from our correspondent. We'll come back and talk to her about the wildfires out West shortly. In the meantime, there have been calls from Forsythe, Illinois where a swarm of what look like cicadas have swept through the streets causing injury and mayhem. Onlookers, speaking to us from inside the buildings, have said that people are collapsing on the streets, and police and rescue workers have also fallen prey to the swarm. Firemen are now moving in, wearing full protective gear to try to reach the wounded."

Crap.

The presenter went on, "Reports are also coming in of injuries caused by cicadas in the area around Gilman and Danforth. Michael, is this the same swarm?"

"We can't be certain of course, but, a hundred miles is more than we would expect cicadas to cover in a day"

"So what you're saying is there must be a second swarm..."

Diana turned the radio off.

"A second one?" She couldn't breathe. "It's not just one mutation. It's more than that. We're going to need data. I need to go back to the farm." She started the engine, and googled the address of the Sheriff's office. It was time to break her NDA, and the Sheriff was the first place to start.

It took a while to drill down through the layers of emergency services, to get to the right local agency, but once she finally reached the local Sheriff, a man called Ben Ford, he sent people to remove Jonah's body and tape the area off, the second she finished her report. By the time she arrived back at the farm, all was still.

Pulling into the very same spot she had parked in before, Diana readied her cooler box, plugging it in to the charging socket in the trunk to prepare for the samples, and put on her protective gear.

The police car drew up beside her. The Sheriff was a tall, well-built man, and the protective suit he was wearing was tight across his shoulders. "Man, you wear this stuff all the time?" He pulled on the goggles with some difficulty. A tuft of curly black hair stuck up at an odd angle. "Drives me nuts." He looked around the farmyard. A pathway had been made through the cicada sloughs. "So, walk me through it."

"Literally." That won her a slight smile. She hefted her bag and the cooler over her shoulder. "This way." The strap of the cooler slid off her shoulder and she grabbed it.

"May I?" He held a gloved hand out.

"Thank you." As she handed it across, something buzzed past her head. She nearly dropped the cooler, and swatted frantically, her heart a-stutter: but it was only a bee.

"You're jumpy." Ben had caught the cooler, fortunately.

"You ever seen a man whose face is one big blister? That's why I'm jumpy." She shuddered. "Make sure they don't touch you, okay? Jesse's hand is a mess." There were dead and squashed cicadas everywhere along with a few crawling feebly on the ground. Focusing firmly on the task at hand, she scanned the place for samples and packed them into the cooler.

Finally, and with reluctance, she placed two or three of the live ones in a box with a small foliage-bearing twig. "These are the culprits, and they're not like normal cicadas."

"They aren't? They look more or less like cicadas to me." He bent to peer into the clear box.

She jerked it away from him. "Careful. The damage they caused Jonah was way beyond what it would have been with wasps or anything like that. Until we know what caused the injury, we have to assume the worst."

"Even in a box?" He raised an eyebrow.

"Jonah died fast." It wasn't the blistering that killed him, not on his face, anyhow. Was it huge levels of pain that caused a heart attack? Were there blisters in his throat and lungs? Was it some kind of lethal poison? She just didn't know. All she knew was that those cicadas were subtly different from normal cicadas and they killed.

"They're not supposed to eat foliage – cicadas don't eat at all as adults, but these clearly have." She frowned and pulled a magnifying glass out of her bag. There was a slit on the twig, and when she looked closely, more slices all over it.

A shiver ran up her back. "No."

"What is it?"

Diana hardly heard him. She went back to the tree. There were tiny cuts all over the bark. The twigs were starting to droop. And now she was looking for it, she saw that the remains of all the plants around were starting to droop too.

"These slits? Everywhere you see the plants drooping, that's because the cicadas have laid eggs."

Ben looked around and whistled. "That doesn't sound like good news."

"Each slit in the bark holds hundreds of eggs. And unless every tree and bush around is burned to the ground before the eggs can hatch, there'll be another swarm like the one that killed Jonah." For a moment the thought of it paralyzed her.

"Shoot. Okay. What do we do?" Ben paused as his phone rang. "Sorry, one moment. They don't ring this number unless it's important." He turned away and took the call.

Her scientific brain kicked in again. The eggs shouldn't hatch for weeks yet, and that meant that something could be done. Ben should be able to talk to the right people, and maybe a second wave could be avoided, though it would devastate the area. Forsythe too, wherever that was.

He turned back. "Multiple pile up on the main street. I've got to go. Call me tomorrow and we can discuss this further." Without waiting for an answer he raced back to the car and accelerated away.

Heading back to Watseka, Diana was brought to a stop as she came to the outskirts to find two cars had clashed bumpers and a body lay unmoving on the road. No one else was around. She got out of the truck, listening carefully, but of course there was no sound of cicadas. Sheriff Ben was right—the farm had made her jumpy. She fished in her pocket for her gloves and turned the man over; prickles coursed all over her body. His face was blistered, and he lay limp and lifeless. She shied back and hurried over to the other car, but the door was open, and no one was in there. Small mercies, at least. The swarm must have passed this way before it went to Jonah's, but she couldn't quite make sense of their route.

She hurried back to the truck, trying not to listen to the voice of unease in her head, but she'd only cleared two blocks when her worst fears were realized. There was a massive pile up on the west side of Main Street. Half a dozen cars were clustered, bumpers locked, crumpled and battered with smashed headlights. A beautiful Camaro was half up on the pavement on its side, scraped and buckled beyond recognition.

Ben had pulled up by the crash, and there was an ambulance just drawing up. A man crouched on the sidewalk talking gently to his wife. She let out little cries with every breath and did not seem to know where she was. Her arm was a mass of blisters, and she stared glassy-eyed at a severed leg on the road nearby. There was a mess of gore around the limb which led to a skateboard on its side and past to the rest of the body crushed under the car's axle. One untouched hand projected, pale and perfect, from the dark, bloody space.

Tearing her gaze away, Diana drove on, easing the truck past the cars abandoned or crashed on the way, desperate to get to the hospital and Jesse. People sheltered in the little stores that lined the road, crowding the windows. An old man staggered into view, and collapsed in front of her. A blond youth in a retro Aerosmith T-shirt dashed out of the pharmacy, a dark-haired teenager with him, and grabbed the old man.

Diana pulled over as they took him to their car, but right as the blond teenager opened the car door, he cried out and jumped back, tucking his right hand under his armpit. The old man crumpled, and the dark-haired guy guided him into the back seat, then lifted his feet in. The blond teen stopped him before he reached for the door handle. "Don't touch it. It burns!"

Diana had not taken off her suit, but she pulled on a mask and doubled up on her gloves. She hurried over with a spare pair. "Here. Wear these." She bent to examine the door handle, which was misted over with a slight film, smeared over the sheen of the metal. "There's something on it, and that stuff is dangerous. You need to get that seen to." She opened the car doors and bent to examine the old man. He had no pulse. Perhaps a weak heart? "Get him to a hospital. Now."

The boys didn't need more prompting to get out of there. They were in that car and heading down the road before Diana'd had a chance to inspect the next victim.

A woman lay curled on the sidewalk. She was dead, her face so swollen that her nose was hardly visible amongst the fluid-filled mass that covered her skin. Worse, she was curled around her child, a tiny baby. It was still. She had wrapped it in her jacket, so its skin was free of blisters or red marks but it was dead.

Diana's eyes filled, but she dared not rub them. "You did your best, Momma. They didn't get your baby. You kept her as safe as you could." But it wasn't safe enough. Just like Jesse.

She shook her head angrily. "But how? Why? It doesn't look like the cicadas got to her at all. You did everything right!" It didn't bear thinking about, a mother accidentally smothering her child.

Two men, armed and masked, ran around the corner and shoved their way into the pharmacy. A shot rang out and suddenly the people in the pharmacy were fighting to get out into the street and away from this new threat. It was only a little mom and pop store, with a big glass frontage, The men went up and down the aisles of the tiny shop, tumbling pills and medicines into bags, and the pharmacist fled as they battered on the door of the storeroom where the prescription drugs were kept.

"Masks! Get the masks and gloves!" a male voice yelled. "You saw what this stuff did! Don't touch it!"

"There's hardly any," came the reply.

"What about her?"

Several people turned toward Diana. Cold fear stabbed through her as she ran for the truck and dived in, locking the doors behind her. They clustered around, more and more of them, banging on the windows and shouting, words tumbling over each other in a frenzy. A middle aged man, his face blotched and red (agitation? bugs? she didn't know) jammed himself against her window. "Tell us where the masks and gloves are and we'll let you go!"

She could taste the mob frenzy rising. Adrenaline kicked her into gear. She had to get out of there. She ripped off her gloves, careful not to touch the outsides, and started the truck. The sweaty-shouty guy tried to pull away, yelling and screaming as she revved the engine, but he was kept in place by the crush of people behind him.

"She's electrified the truck," he screamed. "She's one of them! She's part of it!"

Part of what, she had no idea, but the mob roared. Panic surged up in her body. She was trapped! There were people on either side but not in front of her.

She edged away slowly. The truck crawled forward so as not to hurt anyone, but more people were moving toward the front of the truck to head her off. "Get out of the way!" she growled, but they kept going. The banging and thumping sent her adrenaline into over-drive. "Stop it!" Nervous energy built up between her shoulders like lightning waiting to strike. "Get out of my way!" The scream burst out of her. She revved the engine again and steered to the right, pushing a few of them backward, but her sweaty palms made the steering wheel treacherous, and the mob just pushed in closer on the other side. "Move, now!"

Her hands were shaking. She was getting nowhere. The incessant thuds were like immense cicadas on the truck. She was trapped, and if they broke in she'd be done for. A smash right in her ear, and the driver's window cracked into a cobweb of fractures. The man outside raised the stone in his hand to strike again.

Diana found her angry center. She slammed down the gas pedal, the engine roared and the truck leapt away down the road, throwing her assailants to either side. She swerved around the corner, down the next street and the next, and nearly mowed down a woman who stepped out from the curb with a loaded shopping cart.

She stamped on the brakes. The truck screeched to a halt, sending the shopping cart careering sideways to overturn on the pavement. Bottles smashed and a thread of milk began to unwind across the road as Diana sat shaking, her skin prickling with the near-ness of the encounter.

"You idiot! You could have killed me! Watch where you're going!" The woman thumped the side of the truck then recoiled. "What the hell? It burns!!"

But the thump sent Diana accelerating away, past the others scat-tering across the town with their shopping carts, past the smashed window of the supermarket, and the two men having a fistfight over a sack of rice, and the spill of watermelons that looked horribly like severed heads, smashed all over the road.

Her breath was coming as fast and hard as if she had just taken part in a sprint, and she was starting to feel lightheaded: a panic attack coming on, dammit! She had to get herself under control, and fast. She slowed her breathing, and then the truck, trying to drive more sensibly, but it was a battle to keep herself calm enough to function.

The turnoff to the hospital was blocked full of cars and shouting people so she drove around the back and pulled into a lane marked 'deliveries only,' parking the truck by the recycling bins.

The porter at the back door took one look at her protective gear and opened the door for her without query. The antiseptic tang of hospital disinfectant always made her want to run away, but she hurried in.

It wasn't good. The whole of reception had been turned into a triage ward. People were streaming in with various levels of swelling and blistering. Gurneys lined all the walls, some people moaning in pain and convulsing. Others were ominously silent.

Nurses and doctors ran from one to the next. "Nurse, tell me about this one." The doctor didn't touch his patient. They were learning already.

"He's unconscious, the trachea is nearly closed, the convulsions are getting steadily worse." The nurse fought back the tears.

The doctor's face was stone-hard with grief. "Give him morphine for now. That's all we can do."

The nurse marked the order on her chart and the pair moved on.

Diana spotted the two teens she'd seen on the street. "Hey. How's your hand?"

The blond boy was wheezy. His hand was grossly swollen, one massive blister. "Hurts so much I can hardly breathe."

The dark-haired boy blinked as if trying to focus. "I can't believe it. The insects, what are they?"

She shook her head. "I've never seen anything like this before today."

Looking past her, he jumped out of his seat. "You little turd, you're not getting away." He stamped on a cicada, leaving a yellow mess on the hospital floor.

Diana felt the blood drain from her face. All that stood between the inside of the hospital and the cicadas was a couple of pairs of glass doors, and several smears on the floor suggested that more than one had gotten in. They weren't safe. She fought through the chaos to the entrance, pushed her way out and retched onto the grass.

"You okay?" A man came around the corner with a cigarette in one hand and a clear bag containing a bottle of water and a Tupperware container. It was Jesse's nurse. "Doc, is that you?"

She took the water. "Thank you."

"Your boy's fine, Doc. Safe in his room." He watched as she swigged the water. "You should go home. This isn't going to be a good place to be for long. All the ambulances are out. Some are not responding. The police are doing what they can, but there are only a handful of them and this is too much for five people. If you don't have to be here, you're safer elsewhere."

The coolness of the water had cleared Diana's mind enough to assess the situation. He was right on all counts but one. "This place isn't safe for Jesse either. I need to take him away, somewhere the swarms haven't reached."

The nurse stubbed out his cigarette. "You think the cicadas will come back?"

"I heard on the news there's another swarm an hour south from here. If they come this way, they could be here tomorrow."

The nurse leaned back on the wall. "Can you look after him?"

Diana bit her lip. "What does he need?"

"We don't know what caused this, so treat the symptoms. He has blisters and inflammation of the skin on his hand and around his eyes. He needs anti-inflammatories, antihistamines, saline eyebaths if you can..." He trailed off, looking at her.

"I can do that, meds and eye baths."

"When the swelling on his eyes goes, you're going to need to get them checked for damage. And it will be painful till then. He needs strong pain meds, but until you can get to a doctor you'll have to get what you can from the pharmacy."

"The pharmacy's been looted. There will be nothing left there. Can you help?"

"I could lose my job just for helping you this far. But…" The nurse wiped a hand across his face. "But if you were to pass back through here on your way back, you might find that someone had accidentally left a lunchbox here." He nodded at the Tupperware he held. "Litter should be cleared up."

"Thank you. Thank you so much."

The nurse shook his head. "Jesse needs to be somewhere quiet and restful, and we need the bed. They'll argue, but don't give up. It's for the best, even if it's not in the rules." He rolled his shoulders and walked a pace or two toward the door. Diana followed. "Where will you take him?"

She grimaced, ducking through the door as he held it open for her. "My father and his wife live in Davenport. They love kids. I'm sure they'll help him, even if we turn up unannounced."

The nurse left with a salute and a smile. Getting Jesse out of his hospital bed would normally have had the staff swarming her, demanding she sign a release to say that they were leaving against medical advice, but there was no one left to care about legal niceties. They were too busy trying to hold back the tide with the medical equivalent of a spoon.

She lowered Jesse into the back seat and tucked a blanket around his shoulders. He didn't stir. Whatever they'd given him had him out for the count.

With the Tupperware of meds in hand, Diana hit the road.

A couple of hours of quiet driving as the sun went down did much to calm her nerves, if only because there were no cicadas or crowds of people to be seen. She was exhausted, and despite her reservations, had to pull off the road.

She had intended to have a quick nap and move on, but when she woke up, the sun had cracked the horizon. It took her a moment to realize that she'd slept through the night. Jesse was still asleep or unconscious. It was 8 a.m., and she was stiff as a board, but on the plus side, her parents were early risers. She started up the truck and headed back onto the main road.

Despite those few hours of sleep, her exhaustion hadn't lifted and she was grateful when she reached her dad's house. She drew into the driveway, pausing to check that she had the right house number, then got out and went to check on Jesse. He was three quarters awake, very sleepy but blinking and straining to open his swollen eyelids.

She leant over him. "Hey, little guy. How are you?"

He didn't answer. She wasn't even sure that he could see her through the swelling and inflammation, but it was a balm to her heart to see him stir. *See? He's gonna be okay.*

She stroked the hair away from his face lightly, careful to keep away from the sore places. "Come on, Jesse. We can go and rest now. Father and Angelica will adore you, even if they don't like me very much." She eased him out of the truck and into her arms. He was heavy, but she propped him on her hip and rang the doorbell.

"Father—" But the man who opened the door was a stranger. "Oh no! I'm so sorry. I'm looking for the Stewart-Millers at 1154. Have I come to the wrong house?"

"The Stewart-Millers?"

She nodded. "My father and his wife."

The man cocked his head on one side as a lady came to peer over his shoulder. "Why, this house is theirs, ma'am. Or at least it was."

"It was?" The words didn't make sense. *Was?*

"We moved in in February. Your parents don't live here anymore."

CHAPTER FIVE

ANAYELI ALFARO. EAST SACRAMENTO, CALIFORNIA.

Anayeli burned. Every time she moved her melted, oozing hand, the fire raged all over again. Whenever she took a breath, her lungs screamed. And each time she glanced at the dog who was now curled up at her feet on an old towel, the fur on his entire left side singed almost to nothing, his skin angry pink and oozing in patches like hers, furious heat blazed through her, eating her up from the inside. But she was home. She was alive. And so was her family—most of it. She'd gotten them out in time. She looked at her little brother Ernesto, curled in the fetal position at the other end of the futon, snoring in the asthmatic way that had made Papa call him *el gatito*—kitten. Safe. Her family was safe. Except Papa.

She blinked hard, clearing the tears that welled. She'd been the only one to make it off Josh Bertoli's farm, and she wasn't going to waste the second chance she'd been given. She let out a shaky sigh that made the dog look up at her and turned back to the cool glow of her laptop, trying to block out the sobs coming from the other room—Mama, or her sisters, or all three of them. Her memory kept turning that ragged sound into Papa's screams—No. Not now. She had work to do.

But that was the problem. She couldn't do it in her tiny duplex. She was stuck. Ever since she'd cleared the worst of the blaze, her phone had been worthless. She'd never even been able to call 911 for the farmworkers. She had no idea if it was the cell towers that were down or her crappy phone crapping out, but as many times as she'd tried, she hadn't been able to get through to her editor Sid at the paper either. And since her phone was also her hotspot—her only Internet —its failure meant she had no information, no way to do any reporting, no story. Until she could reach someone at Frontier Farmers' Co-op or Matreus, the story she'd spent the last hour writing was what Sid would call tortilla thin. Papa wanted her to write this story. He'd given it to her, and then he'd died for it. She had to write it and she had to do it right. The newsroom would be fully operational, of that she was certain.

Down the hall, the bedroom door opened. The sobbing blared loud for a moment, then was muffled again as the door snicked shut. Footsteps padded closer and Anayeli cursed herself. She should have left for the newsroom when she'd had the chance to go without having to explain herself. She clicked 'save' one more time, then closed her laptop—not fast enough.

"Still with that story? While your sisters and I go hungry?" Mama's voice was like an electrical current, snapping wildly, the wedding photo she'd snatched from the hallway of the family house clutched to her chest. "When your whole family is falling apart and needs you?"

At the other end of the futon, Ernesto groaned, stretching his legs out to push against her thighs. He scrubbed his face with his palms, cleared his throat the way he did when an acute asthma attack was brewing, and sat up, mumbling, "What's going on?"

Anayeli opened her mouth to answer, but Mama went right past her, straight into the kitchen. "I cannot stand another minute. If we do not feed that sister of yours, I don't know what I will—"

Of course Carlota would be hangry on top of everything else.

There was the quiet sucking sound of the refrigerator door releasing its seal, and its pale light washed into the dim living room. Anayeli pushed herself to standing, and the dog at her feet stood too, toenails clicking after her into the kitchen doorway.

Mama stared into the mostly empty open fridge, her back ramrod straight.

"You have no food." Mama's voice was the flat, quiet voice Anayeli hated most, the one that made her think of that song lyric: calm like a bomb. Even the dog knew it. He sat on Anayeli's foot and whimpered as Mama very carefully set down the wedding photo on the counter and then rounded on Anayeli.

"Why would you bring us here? To this empty, lifeless house of yours. How are we supposed to feed ourselves, let alone that beast?" She shot a glare at the dog, then flicked on the kitchen light like she wanted to murder it and slammed open the cupboards that were also mostly bare, leaving the doors gaping wide. There were Anayeli's two bowls, her mismatched plates, the jars she used as glasses. In the next cupboard, there were a few cans of beans. A box of Cheerios that had long since gone stale. A pile of granola bars. A box of instant Mexican rice. An unopened jar of spaghetti sauce next to an open box of noodles, not even enough left for one person, which is why they were still there. "What have you even been thinking? I left a kitchen full of food for *this*? How did you expect to feed us?"

Somehow Anayeli didn't think *takeout* was the right answer. She didn't know what was.

"We have to go back home. *Ahorita*. Your papa will come, and it will all be fin—"

"Mama, I told you—" It had been horrible enough to get the words out the first time. She couldn't believe she had to repeat them. "The fire—I saw Papa—" She swallowed the hard, painful thing in her throat and forced the words out. "Papa isn't coming home. He's not going to be there. Not ever." She swiped at her tears. She could not give in to them. Not until the story of how Papa had—not until she'd filed her story.

Mama looked at her, shaking her head faster and faster. "No. We have to go home. We have to wait for him there. We have to all be together." Anayeli had thought the denial would get better, the longer Mama sat with the news, the farther they got from the house. But it was getting worse.

"It's not safe there!" Anayeli's voice was loud. Too loud. She tried again. "We're better off here, farther from the fires." She had no idea how many farmers had decided to torch their hay fields, or where those farmers' fields even were—another set of details she needed for her story and couldn't get until she got to the newsroom—but in all the recent years of fires, there had never been a big one in Sacramento. They'd always been in the foothills, in the forest, never in cities. "And we're closer to the big hospitals, in case Ernesto needs a breathing treatment, or...." She flashed her red, melted palm, forcing it open, cracking whatever thin scab had started to form.

"Ayyyyy," Mama cried, and burst into tears.

"And you think the smoke is bad here?" Anayeli pointed out the kitchen window at what looked like a heavily overcast sky, but was actually a smoke-filled one. Maybe it was too much, going too far, but she didn't want to have this conversation again. "You really want to drive back home and be breathing worse the whole way?" She lowered her voice, "And with Ernesto's asthma?"

"I hear you," Ernesto grumbled from the other room. They both ignored him.

Driving back to Woodland was the last thing she wanted Mama to do, not only because what should have been a thirty minute drive had taken them hours, but because if Mama insisted on going back, Anayeli would have to go too. The only way she'd gotten Mama to come to Sacramento in the first place was by agreeing they'd all drive together in the family minivan instead of taking both cars. If Mama and her siblings left, Anayeli would be stuck in yet another way because her car was back in the driveway in Woodland, its tires half melted. Without a car at her disposal, she couldn't get groceries—or takeout—or even *be* a reporter. Without a working phone, she also had no way to check the news to see which way the wind had blown the fire: North, away from Woodland, or worse, East toward Sacramento. On the drive, she'd learned the hard way that the radio in the family minivan had quit working ages ago.

A hand pressed against her elbow. It was her littlest sister, Luz, her face puffy and streaked with tears.

"Yeli?" Luz's voice was just above a whisper, her eyes darting to Mama sobbing and back to Anayeli. "Something for Lota?"

"Yogurt in the fridge. Granola bars up there." She pointed to the cabinet at the left of Mama, letting Luz decide which gauntlet she wanted to run.

Luz sidled past, skirted Mama, and opened the fridge, her presence instigating an uneasy truce. She picked the yogurt from amongst the collection of random condiments, half-used salsa, and old Styrofoam takeout containers, glancing at it suspiciously before letting out an under-the-breath *ewww*. With a too-loud thunk she dropped it into the garbage, giving an apologetic shrug in Anayeli's direction before hurrying past Mama to snatch up two granola bars.

"Food. We need food." Mama whisper-yelled, the restrained fury in her voice enough to stop Luz in her tracks, her lips pressed, her eyes pinned to Anayeli's—the sweet, always-agreeable, youngest sister, afraid she'd made things worse.

Anayeli jerked her head toward the bedroom and mouthed, "feed Carlota."

As soon as Luz was gone, Mama went on, her voice thunderous. "You think we can live off granola bars? You think your job is more important than this family? I'll tell you what—whatever information you have, it isn't so big it's going to make any kind of difference. No one is going to listen to you, and care what you think, not when there's fires like this. Do you see this smoke?" She stabbed a finger toward the window. "Everyone is going to be thinking about themselves and what they need. And you know what? They're right to look after their own family, because that is what matters most!" She flung her hands in a wide circle, as if encompassing everything inside the house. "Your family. Us. I don't understand why you can't put aside that *story*"—she spat the word, and stalked to where Anayeli's laptop peeked out from under the blanket Ernesto had tried to cover it with —oh, Anayeli loved that brother of hers—"when your family needs you!" Her words were coming fast now, another kind of fire, and as much as Anayeli knew they were fueled by grief, each accusation was a stab that found its mark.

"You don't understand—" It was stupid to try to defend herself. She knew it, but she couldn't stop herself. "I haven't slept, I haven't eaten, I haven't stopped moving since this morning, all so I could get to you and get you safe and tell this story—"

"We have no food, Anayeli!" Mama roared, suddenly a dragon, swooping to snatch Anayeli's laptop out from under the blanket. "There are fires—we don't know where! Everywhere, maybe! If we don't get to the store now, there will be nothing left, and all because you wanted to work on your little story."

"Papa wanted me to write it!" Anayeli screamed back, and in the split second that Mama looked as if she'd been slapped, Anayeli grabbed for her computer, yanking it from Mama's hands. The dog barked twice in warning, but what Anayeli heard was, *Vive. Escribe.* That was what Papa would have wanted. That was what she was trying to do. She would make sure that no one was ever endangered in the way those farmworkers, her Papa, had been. That would be the good to come out of the fire's devastation and her family's grief.

"This family is all I have. I will not lose any more of it!" Mama broke down into sobs, worse than the ragged ones from before. On the futon, Ernesto was squeezed as far into the corner as he could get, his knees tight against his chest, making himself as small as a thirteen year old boy could get. He didn't need to see this kind of argument. None of them did.

Anayeli pressed her good palm to her forehead. Her head ached— had not stopped pounding since she'd stood on the hill overlooking the burning teff field. Maybe it would never stop aching again. She filled her lungs, held her breath, then let it out slowly. Mama was right: they did need food. But also: Anayeli had an idea.

"Okay, Mama. Fine." She willed herself to be calm as she slipped

51

the laptop into her backpack. "You're right. I can't finish the story anyway. So fine. I'll get dressed and go to the store, bring back whatever you want. Okay? You make a list and I'll get ready."

Mama shook her head. "No."

"No? But you just said—"

"We all go. We stay together."

Not Mama's obsession with all sticking together again. Anayeli wanted to scream.

"It doesn't make sense for us to all go out in the smoke—" It was a weak argument, but for her idea to work, she needed to go alone. "We need to preserve our masks, in case it gets worse—"

The light in the kitchen flickered, the fluttering reminding her of a moth beating its wings, and then went out. A split second later, it came on again, then faded to half-strength, before bursting on again, far too bright. The bulbs above the sink popped and shattered, glass tinkling into the basin, scattering across the linoleum. At the same time, a sizzling sound and a little shriek came from the bedroom. Luz burst into the hall, followed by Carlota, her long hair mussed and crackling with static.

"Did you see that?" Carlota was apparently restored after the granola bar Luz had taken her. "I was trying to get my phone and something *blue* came out of the plug!"

Ernesto stood up, flipping on the living room light switch, the four bulbs in the ceiling fan light fixture making them all squint.

"New plan." Anayeli's voice was one she'd never used before, one that shut everyone up. Usually when she yelled, it just made her sisters yell right back. But this time they listened. She did not need anyone panicking and she needed to get moving, quickly. "Mama—I know you don't like it, but we can't all go to the store. If the power company is going to do a safety shut off, we need to be ready—more ready than we are." She had some bottles of water under the bathroom sink, but they were all old and filled with tap water. After there had been multiple days' long emergency Public Fire Safety Power shut offs, she'd been pretty good about having supplies on hand—water, baby wipes for fake showers, the granola bars Luz had found—

but she'd gotten lackadaisical in the last year. And she definitely had never been prepared for five people.

"You all are going to stay here." She held up a hand when Mama opened her mouth to protest. "It's not a suggestion. This is what's happening." Mama closed her mouth and Anayeli went on, wondering what had changed. The sense of emergency, she guessed. They'd felt almost safe for a few hours, here at her little duplex. They'd been able to sleep a little, and forget, maybe. "Luz—" her youngest sister's eyes snapped to hers. "You and Carlota are going to fill up every container you can find. Jars. Pots and pans. Bowls. The washing machine. And after everyone's taken a shower, fill up the bathtub, okay?" Luz nodded, then elbowed Carlota, who nodded too. "Ernesto—" she wracked her brain for what he could do. "You're going to sweep up the broken glass. Then get the baseball bat next to my bed and put it by the door and find my flashlight and see if it works or if it needs new batteries. I need to know before I leave. After that, dig up a lighter from my junk drawer and gather all the candles and put them on the kitchen table. There's some in my room, and some in the drawers in the kitchen. Got it?" He nodded. "After that, make sure everyone's phone is plugged in and charging." The phones would likely still be useless, but that wasn't a given and they could still be flashlights, and it was something for him to do. "Did you bring your inhaler?"

He patted first one jeans pocket, then the other, before pulling out the thing, showing it to her.

"Okay, good. When you're done with everything else, if the power's still on—"

His face creased with worry.

"—which I'm sure it will be, this is all just-in-case stuff... if the power's still on, you're going to put on your mask, and turn on the sprinkler out front. Okay? Don't stay out there in the smoke. Just put the sprinkler on, and leave it. I want the whole front yard watered really good so my grass doesn't die if the power's off for a few days." Her grass was the least of her worries, but he didn't need to know that. If the power was going in and out, it meant whatever was happening was unofficial—not an emergency power shut-off, but the result of the fires burning up something important. Which meant the fires were still spreading. Having the grass watered probably wouldn't save her house, but it was worth trying.

Everyone looked at her, waiting for her to say more. But what she had to say to Mama, she didn't want anyone else hearing. She clapped her hands, making the dog sitting at her feet drop flat on his belly. "Don't just stand there! Get going!"

She waited two heartbeats, for her siblings to get about their tasks, and then she turned back to Mama. "Write a list of food. Whatever you think we need. And then start packing, in case we have to evacuate. Clothes, towels—" She shook her head. "I don't know. Maybe just make sure everyone has a backpack with some supplies in it? The granola bars? And I've got a couple metal water bottles in the kitchen—make sure those get put in." She had no idea what they would want or need if they had to leave. It wasn't like she had very much, and the rest of the family had already left behind almost everything back in Woodland. She'd made them all pack a few changes of clothes before they'd left, but that was it.

But Mama patted her arm. "You forget. I left everything once before. In Mexico. I know what we need most."

Anayeli's one-handed shower took too long but it was hard to bathe quickly with her injured hand cradled against her chest—a feeble attempt to protect it from the burning water and stinging soap and still get it somewhat clean. By the time she'd changed into clean clothes, brushed her hair, slathered her palm with antibiotic ointment and put on a fresh mask from the stash she kept in her bathroom, a collection of candles was on the kitchen table, and the kitchen counter was cluttered with water containers.

"Someone should come with you, *mija*." Mama held out a page torn from one of the journalist notebooks stashed everywhere around the house, her writing scrawled down it. The grocery list. "It's not safe for you alone—"

"I won't be." Anayeli stroked the dog, who had been velcro'ed to her side, no matter where she'd gone. "Cricket's coming with me." She had no idea where the name had come from, but the dog looked up at her when she said it. Her editor Sid had a dog, and he was a sucker. He'd take Cricket on, once he heard the dog's story, and he would take better care of the dog than she could. Because that was where she was headed first—the newsroom. To use the landline to put in calls to Frontier Farmers' Co-op and Matreus, finish her story, file it in person, and foist a new dog on Sid. It wouldn't take her long, and once that was done, she'd get the food Mama wanted. There was a store right by the newsroom, and despite Mama's fears, there was no way its shelves would already be bare, not when the fires had been burning for just over twenty-four hours.

Anayeli checked to make sure the minivan keys and tube of antibiotic ointment were still in her pocket, then handed two packages of N95s—one opened, one still sealed—to Mama. While Mama bent to put the masks inside a reusable shopping bag near the door, right where Ernesto had leaned the baseball bat—good brother—Anayeli slipped her laptop bag over her shoulder and sidled outside, into the haze. Even though the sun was still up—a red-orange disc against a charcoal gray sky—it was barely light outside, the smoke as dense as fog, the lights of the neighboring houses dim and fuzzy. It had gotten worse, not better, since they'd arrived.

"I'll be back." She poked her head back in the door, keeping hold of the belt she'd used to fashion a makeshift leash for Cricket, even though she doubted she'd need it, and giving Mama a confident smile. "Lock the door and don't open the shades, and don't worry if it takes me awhile. It might be busy at the store." And then, because she'd never forgive herself if she didn't, she added, *"Te quiero mucho." I love you very much.*

CHAPTER SIX

SAM LEARY. BERKELEY UNIVERSITY, CALIFORNIA.

Sam's sneakers squeaked as he paced through the lab. "Something isn't right Henry. Diana always picks up when I call. Even if it's late." Henry snorted and placed his chin on his paws. "I know, she's in Illinois, which means general mountain time and that's two hours later than Pacific standard... but..." He glanced at his wristwatch. "Maybe she needed to charge her phone."

The monitor flashed, and he rushed to the computer, sliding his chair underneath him. Someone had left a message on *scienceforums.net*. Two clicks popped open the electronic envelope. "Guess what? Our friend Cockroach is back on the chats." Henry's ears perked up as Sam inched toward the screen.

Cockroach's text was succinct and to the point. "Forecast calls for hurricane-force winds and torrents of hail. Best to remove oneself from the equation before it hits landfall."

He shot over to the NOAA website. No storms off the Pacific coast. It was a coded message. Sam clicked the reply button and paused before typing. "Weather is fine here, how bloweth the wind in your climes?" He grinned. Cockroach loved puns, codes, and wordplay and delivered them with wit and intelligence. While some people (naming no names, Frank!) used language—especially metaphors and similes—to confound Sam's hyper-logical mind, Cockroach used them in a way that didn't feel spiky or mean.

Even the name, Cockroach, fit his mysterious chat partner. The dude never typed more than a couple sentences at a time, and there were pauses of at least thirty seconds before a response. If anyone else joined the chat, he frequently disappeared. Sam hoped no one else would show. Not this time. Not with a coded message in the mix.

Sam checked his watch, eight thirty. Maybe he should try to call Diana again.

Henry stretched, trotted over to Sam, nudged his hand and whimpered. When Sam didn't respond, Henry flopped under the desk and gnawed on a yellow-gray tennis ball.

"I'm sorry, Henry. Something came up." He grabbed the ball, propped the door open, and chucked it down the hall. Henry took off like a shot, barking with joy, claws scrabbling on the hard surfaces.

A ding resounded, and Sam twisted to view the message. The box of text stood out in bold red letters.

"Urgent: find a safe harbor somewhere else, say, Montana?"

Sam scratched his head. "Why are you telling me to go north, is that where you're going?"

Henry whined and dropped the ball at Sam's feet. Reaching down, he grabbed the slobbery ball and tossed it over one shoulder. The shaggy-haired dog took off again. Wiping his hand on his pant leg to remove the drool, he tapped his keyboard: "Clarification?"

Cockroach's message shot right back. "INHS states toxic."

Sam rolled his eyes, stretched his neck and popped his knuckles. "Alright Cockroach, apply that big brain of yours and tell me something new." He finger-pecked the keys.

"Data incomplete," came the answer. "First swarm was a radius of a quarter mile. Multiple broods appearing with a mile radius in an average six mile spread north to south. Evidence of rapid breeding. Oklahoma city is now a shelter-in-place disaster, as well as Jonesboro, Arkansas. Insects most likely affected by cooler climate, get high and cold."

Sam slid his chair back. Cockroach had written almost an entire paragraph. Things must be serious.

"Et tu blattodea?" And you Cockroach? What are you going to do?

The blinking cursor sat unmoving. Cockroach wasn't revealing his plans.

The ball bumped into Sam's foot, and he tossed it back down the hallway. He couldn't leave before Diana arrived, but there were cicadas to the east and fires to the north and Cockroach saying "move," which meant he needed to be ready for anything.

Sam walked out of the lab, pulling the door closed behind him. Henry brought him the ball and Sam tossed it down the hallway, jogging to keep up.

Climbing the stairs from the first floor basement to the atrium on the second floor, Sam stopped by the Tyrannosaurus Rex in the center of the lobby. The rotunda was the perfect place to house the fifteen-foot spectacle along with another predator, the pterodactyl, which hung at an angle to make it look like it was flying above the king of the lizards. Sam reached out to the fossil's leg and touched it lightly. For luck. While not the largest specimen on earth, it was still one of the coolest pieces to have at your work.

He craned his neck back to get a better view of the staged battle. The winged menace dove at the T-Rex with its pointed beak, and if allowed another three measly feet forward, would have pierced the king's back. Sam smirked. *As if it stood a chance.* A cold wet nose nudged the tennis ball in his hand. "All right, enough day dreaming. Let's go."

By the time he got home, Sam was sweating and his throat felt scratchy. There was a smoky haze all across campus. The air inside his house was better, though it was stale and hot. He'd forgotten to turn the air conditioner on before leaving that morning. "No point turning it on now, Henry. We're not going to be here long enough."

But he miscalculated. They were there, sorting, cleaning, and packing things away, for four very sweaty hours.

The exterior was finished, and every window in the house was covered with plywood to keep the insects out, if they came West. The smoke—and the fires—he couldn't do much about. Those were a California summer staple. They'd weathered worse. If they made it all the way to the campus, well there were people who'd come with their fire engines and hoses. Berkeley was far too well funded to burn to the ground!

He jogged back inside. Cracking open the closet door he checked the water heater knob, making sure it was turned all the way down. The fuse box lay open with only one more to switch off. He'd wait until he was ready to leave to hit that one.

He drew out a blanket from the linen closet and spread the microfiber cloth over the arm chair, smoothing out the wrinkles. Satisfied, he counted every piece of furniture in the living room, and pulled the corresponding number of coverings. Snapping the cloths open, he waved them high, one after the other, over each piece of furniture. They floated down, outlining a chair here and a couch there. Having finished covering the furniture, he moved to the walls, removing the pictures and paintings. He stacked them in a corner, their wooden frames butting against each other. When the walls were bare he draped the thickest blankets he owned over the art. The living room looked like a haunted house, empty and lifeless.

In the kitchen, Sam raked all of his food into an iron wagon, its tires squishing under the weight. He frowned at the unorganized mess, shifting a couple bags of dog kibble, one case of SpaghettiOs, baked beans, and chili. He lugged a black garbage bag on top of the cans; contents: one lone gallon of Sevin (main ingredient carbaryl, he'd checked), various bug sprays, zippo lighters, mouse traps, candles, plastic bags and duct tape. *Don't forget the lamp or Henry's treats or the N95 masks. Can't leave those behind.*

The secret compartment of his roll top desk hung wide open as he dropped two thumb drives into a manila envelope. Scrawling the words, "just in case," on a Post-It, he stuffed the square paper into the package with the vital info. He licked the glue and gagged. "I hope this is enough postage to get it to Cockroach, I can't lose these."

While he hadn't met Cockroach in person, and didn't know his true name, they'd swapped gifts for most major holidays for the last three years. He was the one person he trusted other than Diana to take care of the drives. "I'll put these in the drop box on our way to school." Henry woofed again, confirming Sam's suspicion that he was on the right track. People who didn't talk to their dogs were missing out. Henry gave the best advice ever. In dog. Which Sam spoke fluently.

He placed his coat on top of the mounded supplies and bungee strapped it to keep everything secure. He very deliberately didn't blink as he took a last walk through the house, creating a mental recording as he made sure everything was protected. "Stay safe house. I'll be back."

The air quality had gotten even worse while he'd been inside, but he didn't want to take the time to dig out a mask. It wasn't a long walk. He ignored the sideways glances that were cast at him as he hauled the wagon behind him with both hands. The trek on foot was wearing him out and he was in no mood to deal with neurotypicals that were looking to make fun of him. No matter how he'd tried to fit in as a kid, he'd never gotten the hang of the *code* everyone else used to communicate. Apparently, his 'say it like it is' and 'answer the question as asked' style of speech wasn't what humans were supposed to use. There was an undercurrent of understanding—transmitted with eye contact, hints, and innuendo—that most humans shared and he did not. It left him on the outside of most social and interpersonal events, but he'd long since given up caring. Let them stare. One day he'd do something that blew them all out of the water and then they'd regret mocking him. Maybe. Or maybe not. Whatever.

He approached the basement door to the university, squinting. Its newly whitewashed walls dazzled and shimmered in the afternoon heat, even with the gathering smoke. The wagon wheels thumped in rhythm over the cement pathway toward the lone metal door framed in brick. It was the only exterior door on the east side of the building and the perfect way to slip inside unnoticed. Stopping at the entrance he passed his faculty card over the reader, and red turned green as the lock clicked, permitting access into the first floor.

Henry ran ahead and Sam followed, huffing as he lugged the cart down the stairs and inside. He rounded the corner to find the mutt sniffing at the crack in the lab door. The dog growled and snorted as Sam opened it. "Frank, why are you here?"

Frank hunched over a console, the keyboard keys clacking their mechanical monotone music. He turned and raised his eyebrows. "What's with the wagon? You know it makes you look like a hobo." He laughed.

"What are you doing?"

Frank shrugged. "Trying to figure out your password so I can log in."

Sam dropped the handle onto the tile floor. "What?"

"I feel for you, bucko. Reduction in forces are being handed out left and right. But the data you've collected on the puss caterpillar is school property."

Sam lunged for the computer, but Frank's outstretched hand stopped him from reaching anything past his elbow. They tussled, like a couple of scabby-kneed schoolboys, but eventually Sam yanked the cable and the whole thing skidded off the desk. He tumbled back, crashing to the floor.

Frank glowered and stood up, towering above him like Goliath. "I want the file on Megalopyge opercularis."

Sam scooted on his behind, edging further away from the man who threatened to flatten him. "There are no files. I only told you that so you would give me back my insects."

His raging colleague stomped forward. Sam crab walked over to the wagon. He stretched out his arms over the stash of canned goods and essential supplies, but the wagon was too big to cover. Frank leaned against the center desk and focused on the wheeled treasure box. His muscles relaxed, the blood drained from his forehead, and he forced a smile. "What do you have in the wagon?"

Sam played goalie as Frank approached but was brushed aside as the offense undid one of the bungees. The coat slid off the top as he rummaged through the goods and picked up the bottle of Sevin. "Insecticide?"

Sam ignored Frank, instead choosing to haul his wagon to the corner closet. Opening the door wide enough to fit the wagon through he disappeared inside and started to unpack.

Frank leaned against the doorpost. "There's something you're not telling me."

Sam kept his back turned. Let's see, move the broom and dustpan, the canned food goes on the left, dog food to the right, extra propane canisters for the stove, check. Henry flitted around Sam's feet. The closet meant one thing to the dog: treats. Sam tossed him a Greenie.

Frank barged into the closet, eyeing the stacks of food and supplies and muscling his way up to Sam. If it hadn't been so ludicrous, it might have been threatening, but Frank had no power anymore. As soon as Diana arrived, he'd be leaving the university. With any luck, he'd never see Frank—or anyone like him—ever again. Sam clamped his lips tight, elbowed his sometime nemesis out of the way, and returned to organizing the closet. Maybe if he stopped answering, he'd go away.

"Come on, I've heard the rumor straight from you. Those bugs are dangerous and you're preparing for their arrival. At least tell me when they're going to get here."

The guy just wouldn't take the hint. Sam needed to find a creative way to get rid of the intruder. He pushed the cans further down the shelf to make room for the boxes. "You're a smart fella. Figure out which way the wind's blowing and you'll figure out what time they'll get here."

"What *time?* Soon then? They're coming soon?"

Good question. One he needed to ask Cockroach. Where the swarm went next really was going to depend on prevailing winds and if the fires spread. There was no telling where or when either would alight next. Fine if Frank believed they were in imminent danger. Let him sweat for once. Sam's job was to hunker down, assess the situation with Cockroach's help, and guide Diana to safety. He shrugged at Frank and kept on stacking.

"You're all set up here, Sammie boy. Let me stay. You can afford to feed one more person."

It was so rare for Sam to have the upper hand with Frank he decided to play along; let Frank think it was time to shelter in place. Looked at a certain way, hauling your food half way across campus and stacking it in your office might seem like you thought it was time to SIP, immediately, but Sam was nothing if not cautious and he was only doing what any smart scientist would do and preparing for all eventualities. In his heart of hearts, he didn't believe the cicadas would make it from Illinois to California against the Gulf Stream. That simply wasn't good science. But Sam was about to have the last laugh because Frank couldn't think his way out of a paper bag, let alone walk through the logical steps required to come up with a plan. Upshot: Frank was panicking. Score one for the good guys! "Your key card can access the faculty room. Stay there if you must, but you aren't staying here."

"Well, if that is the case, how about you spot me some supplies? I won't last long living off of staff room snacks."

Sam smirked at the thought of his portly 'friend,' wasting away until he was his size. "No. I only have enough for me and Henry. You can live off of water and chips for at least a month. But with your bulk, a fair bit longer I would say."

Frank stretched, expanding his body so he filled the doorway. "Low blow, bro."

Once again, Frank sounded like he'd never made it out of grade school. Why hadn't he grown out of that crap? Didn't really matter. Sam turned to face the man who'd made his academic life a living hell. "Or else what, Frank?"

Frank belted out an enraged roar and Henry stepped forward, hackles raised. Frank backed out of the enclosed space and came level with the fish tank as the dog showed his teeth. "Okay, nice Henry, no need to get tough, I'm leaving." Frank gave a sly grin and retrieved the jar of caterpillars from the tank, backed closer to the exit, and took aim.

"Henry, no, stay." Sam brought his hands down, but was too slow. The dog darted between his legs and toward the door.

Frank threw the jar at the floor in front of the dog, breaking it into a thousand shining shards as the tiny occupants landed on Henry's feet. He let out a yelp as Frank dashed out into the hallway. Seriously, grade school antics with aggravated assault. One day that asshole was going to get what was coming to him.

"Henry. Sit. Stay."

Sam pushed the dog back with his foot and hopped over the mess. He grabbed a magazine from his desk and used it to herd the creatures together and swept them up, making sure to not touch them. Depositing them back in the tank, he grabbed scissors and tweezers, and rushed to Henry's side.

Henry limped, favoring his left front foot. Sam combed through his grey and white hair. The stiff brown barb from the caterpillar stuck out like a wire. He extracted it, placed it in a test tube, and returned to the injured paw. Giving him a small dose of Diphenhydramine from the container on his computer desk, he cut away the hair surrounding the sting, washed it, and rubbed calamine on it. "The next time you see that ogre, you have my permission to attack."

Sam got Henry settled in his basket and used the broom from the closet to sweep the shards of glass into a pile. One clean swish and the entire mess was dropped into the trash can. Putting his tools away he made for the hallway closet. "Be a good boy, I'll be right back." He tossed the ball into the bed as a distraction.

He dashed across the hall, swiped his key card over the lock, and pushed the door inward. Inside the storage room, Sam shifted microscopes and test tubes until he reached the back corner. Removing the lid on one of the crates, he bumped the container next to it, holding small vials of nitroglycerin. Sam flinched. Even with the liquid suspended in a frozen state, nitroglycerin wasn't something he wanted to disturb. When he wasn't consumed in a ball of fire, he whispered a silent prayer of thanks and fished out his silver laptop from the crate. As he pressed the power button, a reassuring whir from the fan confirmed its operability. He closed the clam shell and tucked it under one arm.

Poking his head out of the storage room, he surveyed the hall before slipping from the storage room back into his own lab, flipping the deadbolt latch. His shaggy companion was nowhere in sight.

"Henry?" Sam hurried into the middle of the lab and put his laptop on the lecture desk. No animal. A slight crunching snuck out from the closet. Four steps and he was in the doorway. Henry's head was buried in a family sized sack of kibble, bits spilling about as he tried to gobble down as much as he could.

He hauled on the dog's collar, dragging him away from the food. "I see the sting from the caterpillar didn't affect you much." Sam scooped handfuls off the floor and dropped them back into the bag, using his body as a shield to keep the dog from eating more. With the mess cleaned he rolled the top shut, raised up on the tips of his shoes, and set the bag on the highest shelf.

Henry sat, looking up with puppy dog eyes.

"Don't look at me like that, you've already eaten more than you should have. You'll be lucky if you don't get sick." The dog whimpered, eyeing the blue bag as access to the closet was denied.

Sam pulled out his phone and flipped it open. Still no message or call from Diana.

Please hurry Diana. I don't know how long I'll last.

CHAPTER SEVEN

RON FROBISHER. GALEN CASTLE. HAMPSHIRE, ENGLAND.

Everything about Galen Castle reeked of old money: wood paneling, crystal chandeliers, a sweeping staircase, not to mention Wilbur, the butler, who both served and judged in a single unsmiling smile. You couldn't get more English than Wilbur and it showed in his squared away shoulders, handlebar mustache, and plummy vowels.

Ron threw his hat at the butler. Not because he wanted someone to hold his hat, but because he knew it irked the old man to have a low-rent American treat him like a coat stand and annoying people was one of the great pleasures of Ron's life. He cruised down the hushed corridors toward his employer's office. Couple of taps on the door and the familiar, rasping voice invited him in.

"You are late." The Right Honorable Ann Pilkington didn't like to be kept waiting and she let it be known in each well-enunciated word. Even if she was busy, you appeared on time or faced her wrath which was icy cold and measured in the zeros she took off your check. "Take a seat."

The seat she wanted Ron to take was an ancient chair, one leg deliberately shorter than the others. It sat at a ninety degree angle to her desk so you had to face away from her while you waited for her to lower her glasses, put down her pen, and deign to speak to you. But the money was good, so what did sitting on a wobbly chair matter? Ron took his place, hands held loosely in his lap, and stared at the carpet while she decided the fate of some shell company or other.

"I have a job for you." Ann screwed the lid back on her pen and placed it at a ninety degree angle to her blotter. "It's dirty, dangerous, and therefore lucrative."

Ron waited. Ann didn't like to be interrupted.

"You'll take it, I presume?"

"Sure thing. When?"

"Now." She pushed a box across the table. Unlike the rest of the room, the box was an understated wooden affair. No inscription, no engraving, no carving. Nothing. Also, not dirty. "Don't open it and don't let it out of your sight."

Interesting. Not the weirdest thing she'd ever asked him to do, but interesting. He turned the box over in his hand.

"Careful," she barked.

"Plutonium?" He couldn't help himself. She wouldn't think he was funny, but he did and that was all that mattered.

"You open it and you forfeit your fee. You lose it, you forfeit. You fail to deliver it to the customer on time... you get the picture."

She wasn't done, so once again Ron didn't speak.

"The customer is in Lagos."

"Nigeria?"

"No, Lagos, Ohio." It wasn't like her to be sarcastic. The merch had her on edge—useful to know. She lowered her glasses and smoothed her hair, though not a strand was out of place. "Yes, of course Nigeria."

Small box. Fit in the palm of his hand. Not to be opened. And to be delivered in person. He would have guessed 'heirloom' but she'd said the job was dirty, so it couldn't be that.

"You will avoid airports."

Ron had no facial tics or tells, but if he'd been a less prudent or less well-trained man he'd have shown his surprise right then.

"You will travel steerage and you will deliver the merchandise two weeks from tomorrow." The fact that she didn't elide her words made her sound angry all the time. Brits were like that, uptight and judgy, looking down their snouts at their poor Yankee cousins, while hiring them to do their 'unpleasant' work. Or at least that was how Ann was. If she'd been an American he'd have pegged her as a WASP. As it was, she was part of the landed gentry. The main difference between her and her fellow Lords and Ladies being, she was also rich as freaking Croesus. She tapped on her phone's little keypad. His phone vibrated in his pocket. "The address."

"Anything else?" She was holding out on him, more than usual.

"You will draw no attention to yourself. None of your theatrics this time." She was referring to his propensity to blow things up which wasn't fair. He'd never set a timer or laid down a trail of gunpowder for anyone who didn't have it coming. He might be an annoying asshole, but he had principles. "I have booked your passage on *The Fairwinds*. You are an entomologist studying the life cycle of the glowworm. Your name is Peter Columbus."

He couldn't figure out what the hell was going on. Things didn't add up. It was like being told two and two was equal to the square root of a banana. She didn't provide his cover. He did that. And who the hell would believe he was a bug scientist? Talk about drawing attention to yourself. An insurance salesman, surely? You wanted an identity that was as bland as semolina, so that the, 'What do you do?' question didn't lead to 'Oh, that's interesting, tell me more' but rather, 'Ah...' and a glassy stare.

"Glowworms are, as you know, bioluminescent."

Now it made sense. Addison, her husband, had succumbed to a rare form of cancer; ate him down to a nub in record time. She was looking at medical applications of light-'em-up proteins. Ron had read about them in a doctor's waiting room when he was undercover as a sales rep. "What's so special about this one?"

"This one what?" She wasn't good at lying and shouldn't try it. Her face was a contorted mess of eyebrows and fake smiles. Her irritation couldn't have been more obvious if she'd taken a full page ad out in the *Sunday Times*.

Ron tapped the box. "Why am I taking a glowworm to Nigeria?"

"That is not a glowworm."

Liar, liar pants on glowing fire.

"What's in that box is none of your business. I am simply telling you what your cover is going to be so when the rest of the merchandise is delivered, you'll be the right man for the job."

If it hadn't been for the obscene uptick in his bank balance every time he worked for the Right Honorable Ann, he'd have left his rickety chair and gone someplace less irritating. It wouldn't have killed her to lay the job out in plain English. But, no, she had to get cryptic about it. She wasn't a spymaster and this wasn't some James Bond nonsense he was undertaking for her. She was a business woman with an empire that spanned the globe and he was a fixer who was willing to take on wet work when it was called for. Still, there was the money. It kept him sitting, silent, waiting.

"The cargo will be live."

It was hard not to sit forward in his chair.

"You will live alongside the crates. Make sure they're safe. You will be armed, naturally."

Armed? To protect glowworms? Yeah, something wasn't right.

His phone buzzed in his pocket. A deposit. His hands itched with the effort of not reaching in and checking it. Ann wouldn't approve of anyone staring at their screen during face to face time. She was as old school as her surroundings.

"Please, look." She waved him on with an imperious gesture several hundred years in the making.

It was his turn to fake his emotions. He'd never seen so many zeros. And he'd been late to their meeting, but she hadn't punished him. Or if she had, he couldn't feel the sting. "Thank you."

"The second installment will be delivered when the job is complete."

Second installment?

She screwed the lid off her pen and returned to her documents. He was dismissed.

"Double it."

Ann was a thin-lipped woman, so it was hard for her mouth to get smaller, but she managed it. "Greed doesn't sit well on you, Ronald."

No one called him Ronald. Not even his mother. But no matter how irritated Ann was, he had the upper hand. She'd signaled her desperation with every word she hadn't said.

"Steerage doesn't sit well either. Double." It was a massive gamble, but one that would tell him what he needed to know about the next two weeks of his life. She'd said "dangerous and dirty" but nothing about the mandate she'd laid out for him fit that bill. If she doubled his fee it meant there were competitors in the arena. Armed men. On his tail. Wanting what he had.

"Fine."

A jolt of adrenalin ran through his huge frame. He was not given to getting overexcited, but she'd just made him a very rich man. He could retire to a small island and live on coconuts and beer if he wanted to. He didn't, but it was good to have options. There was the matter of other people gunning for what he had, but he'd been in deeper than that a dozen times or more and lived to tell the tale. He wasn't worried about the competition.

She turned her back as she dialed whoever took care of her banking matters, muttering figures in German. Offshore accounts, then. Switzerland most likely. God bless the Swiss and their impartial banks. They made for the kind of transactions that kept men like Ronald Frobisher in business. No tax, no trail, no muss, no fuss. Just the way he liked it.

"I don't need to tell you how important this mission is, Ronald." She didn't, but she was going to. "Hundreds of people die of preventable diseases every day." So he was right. It was about the hubby and his cancer. "Our ability to catch mesothelioma early is the difference between life and death." He knew this tone. She was about to lecture him. It would be dictionary dry and devoid of real data. He zoned out while she pontificated on the medical and industrial applications of luciferase, "the enzyme involved in the production of the glow in glowworms." *Bad choice there, scientists; you could have come up with a less ominous-sounding name than LUCIFER-ase.* Her pacing picked up. Not like her. Again with the hair smoothing and face crunching. What the hell wasn't she telling him. "...so you see, I needed the top operative to hand deliver the vial."

Wait, what? He'd spaced out precisely when he shouldn't have. A vial? The box took on a dark blue hue; thunderclouds gathered over Ann's desk; men in white coats with stethoscopes stalked the perimeter of the room. "There will be paperwork. Customs and Excises."

"You're not going through Customs."

Cool. Right. Well, that explained the price tag. He was a smuggler now, as well as a courier and a killer. But he still had no idea what he was transporting into the African continent.

"Captain Alva is a trusted operator who knows how to navigate the port authorities."

It wasn't often that Ron questioned the motives of his employers. They paid, he delivered. It was as simple as that. But if glowworms weren't native to Nigeria, wasn't that going to bring down a whole heap of problems on the flora and fauna, the giraffes and the rhinos? The zeros on his phone—morphing into zeros in his bank account— laughed in digital at his momentary pang of conscience. "Excellent. And he thinks I'm a specialist? A biologist?"

Ann smirked. It didn't suit her. "Captain Alva knows better than to ask foolish questions."

A rap on the nose and three demerits for Team Ronald. He didn't care. The money covered a whole host of insults. She could metaphorically pee on his loafers and he'd be chill with it.

"Anything else?" Ann hit the buzzer on her desk. Time for her afternoon tea, no doubt. For the second time in fifteen minutes, he'd been sent on his way.

Too bad his rear end was still parked in the chair. He had questions, she had answers. "The box. Is it toxic?"

"The box? No."

His turn to smirk. She was being cute with her answers. "What's inside the box is toxic, though, right?"

"Highly. A single drop can kill a colony."

Colony. There was a word he hadn't counted on hearing. Did glowworms live in colonies? He had some reading to do. "And we don't want to kill this colony?"

Ann rounded the desk in record time and planted herself at his feet. "Mr. Frobisher. I pay you to do as you're told. If I wanted to answer your questions, I'd be related or married to you. As we are neither, I would request that you remove yourself from my office and thence my home. You have your instructions. If you're having second thoughts..." She took the box from his hand and waited.

She was slight and fair; generally considered attractive in a well-heeled, over-powdered kind of way. She stood close enough that he could identify her perfume. L'air du Temps: carnations and bergamot with a musky undercurrent. She even smelled of money. In another life he might have hit on her simply to see what she'd do, but there was no point souring their relationship for a little romp in the hay or a slap in the face.

Ron towered over her when he stood but she didn't back away. He took the box, gave her a curt nod, and let himself out of the study.

Wilbur was standing to attention outside Ann's door, Ron's hat on a silver platter. The metaphor wasn't wasted. 'Get this right,' the hat said, 'or your head will take my place.' Ron fished a fifty pound note out of his wallet, folded it and tucked it into Wilbur's top pocket. That would irritate the hell out of him.

Wilbur shoved the note back at Ron. "One does not tip in a residential setting, sir."

They'd had this conversation many times before. Ron did what he could to switch it up and get a rise out of the dear old butler, but the wizened old man stuck to his script.

"Re-gift it." Ron didn't take the money back. "See if one of the chimneysweeps want it."

Wilbur matched Ron stride for stride, even though his knees clicked when he hit more than three miles an hour. "There are no sweeps, Mr. Frobisher, as well you know. Chimney cleaning is automated these days."

Ron didn't know, but neither did he care. His mind was already in the lab with his favorite technician, Amy Halder. He might not be able to open the box, but he sure as hell planned to scan it. "The scullery maids, then. Surely they need a bit of extra, what do you people call it, dosh."

"Goodbye, Mr. Frobisher. A pleasure as always." Wilbur was an even bigger liar than his boss, but his job demanded he say these things, so Ron didn't hold it against him. Had to be a sucky job, always bowing and scraping, no matter how big an a-hole the guest was. Ron had a second flash of conscience. Man, two in one day. That was a record.

His beat up Chevy Impala was parked right where he left it but someone had washed his windows and buffed his hubcaps. More fool them. They'd be muddied in minutes. He shot Amy a text, littered with emojis, the way she liked it. Digital hearts and flowers and the occasional GIF kept her on his side. *Any chance you can squeeze me in? Heart, heart, kissy face, heart.*

For you, lover boy, I can squeeze anything in. She was a mother of five and frumpy as hell, but she flirted like she was twenty and a hottie. He had to hand it to her, she got her fun where she could.

Be there in an hour. Heart heart heart heart. Was that too many? It was one thing to fake-flirt, it was quite another to lead someone on. He was no predator. An asshole, a liar, a thief and a smuggler, yes, but not someone who'd pretend to be interested in a woman when he wasn't.

The drive across town was a breeze. That's why he planned his meetings with Ann in the early afternoon; he missed rush hour on both sides that way. St. Jerome's Hospital was bustling. Sick people being ferried in and out by the people who fretted over them. He didn't know what that was like, being 'cared for' by someone else. He'd never married, never stayed with anyone longer than it took for his ardor to cool, never put down roots. It wouldn't have made sense in his line of work. What would he tell a wife? "Sorry, honey, I'm heading off to Nigeria for a week. I might be hunted by trained assassins. Love you." Yeah, no. There wasn't a woman on Earth who'd put up with that.

He stopped by the kiosk by the front doors.

"The usual, Mr. F?" The clerk dashed over to the wall of sweets and grabbed a box of fancy, high-end Belgian chocolates. No one else bought them. Who'd shell out forty smackers for a snack? Ron Frobisher, that's who. They stocked them just for him. "Flowers, too?"

The roses were tatty and browning around the edges. Tracy tutted and carried them behind the counter. "If I'd knowed you was coming, Mr. F., I'd've got something in fresh."

"Not to worry." He peeled a hundred pound note off his roll.

Tracy flushed to her roots. "I can't take that, Mr. F. It's too much."

He'd just been given over a million pounds to deliver some bugs to Lagos. What kind of cheapskate was he, giving her such a lousy tip? He separated another picture of Her Majesty from his wallet and left it on the counter. "Take the kids to Nando's. They love the piri-piri chicken, right?" Personally he wouldn't have been seen dead in a restaurant that took superb dishes from around the world and Angli-cized them to make them tame enough for the English palate, but he knew Tracy's kids rarely got to eat out, so it would be a thrill for them.

He didn't wait to hear the end of Tracy's thank yous. She meant well, but it was embarrassing that so little could make a grown woman tear up that way. Four right turns down four identical corri-dors took him to the Imaging Suite. Amy, her uniform as crisp as ever and her lipstick freshly reapplied, held the door for him. "You took your time."

"For you, madam."

She took the chocolates with the obligatory 'you shouldn't have' but her smile said she was tickled pink that he remembered to bring her something every time he needed her services. "What are we investigating this time?"

"No clue."

"Ooooh, we like the mystery ones." She stashed her chocolates under the counter, took his mystery box, and placed it inside the MRI. "Start as we mean to go on, by playing it safe."

The machine chugged and whirred and an image populated the screen inside the tech's hutch. Not a vial. Not even a bottle. Ann Pilkington was the Lyingest Liar in all of Liardom. She was sending him to Nigeria with a beetle.

CHAPTER EIGHT

DR. DIANA STEWART. DAVENPORT/LINCOLN, NEBRASKA.

Diana couldn't get her head around what she was hearing, even though she'd been told the same things three or four times over. She grabbed at Jesse who was slipping off her hip again. "My father moved away?"

The man shrugged and glanced sideways at his wife, the two of them hovering in the doorway like a couple of garden gnomes.

It made sense that her stepmother wouldn't have forwarded their new address, and her father would have put it off until the obligatory Christmas card but the fact that neither of them had given her a second thought stung. If she hadn't been so exhausted, she'd have lost her temper, but instead she blinked away tears.

The woman pushed past her husband and held the door open. "Come inside before you drop that child. You look... well, come in anyway."

She didn't need to say it, Diana knew she looked a wreck. She'd been in and out of PPE for the past day. Her hair hadn't seen a brush in over 24 hours and the bags under her eyes were a dark shade of blue-gray. She laid Jesse, still sleeping, on the sofa in the neat little lounge. "Thank you so much. I'm Diana Stewart, by the way and this is Jesse." She held out her hand, but her hosts didn't return the gesture.

"I'm Emily Hart, and that's my husband Thomas. He's a grouch, but a good man." Emily hurried into the kitchen leaving Diana and Mr. Grouch to ignore each other in the living room. After an eternity, Emily hustled back with a pitcher of her homemade lemonade and four glasses and proceeded to play hostess.

"Hmm, delicious." Diana lied—the stuff was awful, twenty parts sugar to two parts lemon—but what else was she supposed to do when they'd been kind enough to let her rest and organize her thoughts?

Emily leaned over Jesse, inspecting his wounds. "What happened to his face?"

"A swarm of cicadas descended on Watseka and he had some sort of allergic reaction."

Emily nodded primly. Thomas picked up a newspaper and disappeared with a grunt. "Cicadas, my ass."

Diana got enough of that nonsense at work, thank you. Time to change the subject. She nodded at the family photographs on the dresser. "Your children?"

"We see them when we can." Emily got up and passed the photo to Diana.

"Lovely." She stood and looked along the rest of the shelf. "Oh, I had that exact same T-shirt when I was a child. It was one of my favorites!"

Emily took the photo from her and set it down, flicking dust off the second. "Happier days. That was my youngest, Rebecca. She died not long after this in an accident, but she was a happy child."

Diana turned away. "My younger brother died when he was five. It's very hard when they are so young. I'm sorry."

"Thank you."

Jesse groaned and writhed, reaching for his face. Diana held his hands away from his eyes, but he whined and twisted under her grip.

Emily raced out of the room and banged around overhead returning with a pair of pink, knitted mittens on a long string; the kind that used to hang from your coat sleeves in the winter. She pushed past Diana and sat herself beside Jesse, crooning and oohing at him. "Such a good little boy. Let's put one handie in here. There we go. It'll feel better soon." She paused, her voice dropping to a whisper. "What do you have him on?"

"Morphine?" Diana flinched. "Was that wrong?"

Emily shook her head. "What time?"

For a blinding second Diana couldn't remember when the child had been dosed. "At the hospital. So, about 4 p.m. yesterday."

"How much did you give him?"

Diana drew a total blank. It was on the bottle the nurse had left her in the Tupperware container. She'd given him a quarter of an adult's dose. "Not much... Like..."

Emily shot her the kind of look reserved for someone who'd tracked manure into the house. She held her hand to Jesse's forehead. "We need to get that temperature down if he's going to pull through."

Diana's stomach dropped through the floor. Pull through? He was that bad? She'd taken him out of the hospital when he was still critical and in need of expert care.

"Get me some ice chips." Emily was in full Momma Bear mode and Diana ran to the kitchen. It was weird to see her parents' kitchen full of strangers' belongings and it took her a couple of seconds to find what she needed. She grabbed a rolling pin and bashed ice from the freezer, bringing it to Jesse's new nurse in a dishtowel.

Emily dripped water into Jesse's mouth, but he squirmed away, moaning. His eyes were glued shut, his forehead covered in sweat, and the welts on his neck had spread up toward his ears. "Tom, I need my First Aid kit."

Mr. Hart huffed, slamming his paper on the side table and

stomping upstairs. You'd have thought he'd been asked to perform surgery or do something onerous, not traipse upstairs and get his wife some supplies.

"Is it that bad?" Diana hung back, worried that her presence was only making things worse. "Do we need a doctor?"

Mr. Hart stalked across the living room and dumped the First Aid Kit on the table, hitting the jug of lemonade and sending a pile of books cascading onto Jesse's arm.

The child screamed and thrashed, bucking up against Emily.

"In the back of the kit." She held Jesse down and pushed the red box toward Diana with her foot. "Brown bottle, clearly marked. Rebecca's name, child's dose."

Diana dug through the first aid supplies and found the decades-old prescription of Dilaudid and thrust it at Emily.

"Two drops. No more." Emily was fully occupied with Jesse and Mr. Hart had removed himself to the far side of the room.

Diana drew the liquid into the pipette and timed herself to drop the meds into Jesse's mouth while his head was turned. He hollered and fought for six minutes and forty-two seconds before finally subsiding into a rhythmic sob that snagged at Diana's brain and lodged itself deep. When the crying stopped, Mr. Hart returned to his seat and hid behind his paper again. "I don't think we should let them move on tonight."

Emily nodded slowly.

Diana couldn't hold back the tears. People were kind when the chips were down. "Thank you," she mumbled.

"I'll make up the beds and, once we're sure he's settled, you can carry him up." Emily left Jesse in her care, which seemed like a poor choice, but her husband was solidly absent even though he was in the room. Nursing was women's work, he'd made that very clear.

They sat in uncomfortable silence for what seemed like forever while Emily was fussing with the guest room. No doubt sorting towels and getting little guest soaps from her stash of never-used-Christmas-gifts. She seemed like that type: kind and fastidious, but not given to frivolous nonsense like hand-sized soap.

Jesse was, thankfully, in a drug-induced stupor so Diana checked her phone for his father's data. There had to be a grandparent or an aunt or someone who could take him. She went to her notes on her 'Feedit' farmers. There was no other family listed on Jonah's contact notes, and she wasn't familiar with the name listed as his emergency contact: Sarah Heller. She jotted the name and number down in her diary, but she couldn't make a call with Mr. Hart sitting in the room and she couldn't leave Jesse alone. She didn't recognize the area code but was relieved there was somebody Jesse could go to.

There was a tap on the window. "Oh no." A cicada was on its back on the windowsill. Another one hit. There was a vast cloud of them sweeping in along the road. She could hear the swarm through the double-glazing.

She leapt out of her chair and checked the windows and the vents. All were closed.

Mr. Hart lowered his paper. "What are you doing?"

She turned to Jesse. He was still asleep. She pulled the crocheted blanket off the back of the couch and lowered it over his face and hands just in case a cicada got in before she got back from her inspection. All doors and windows throughout the house had to be sealed.

"They're here!" she gasped. "The cicadas. They stung Jesse, and all those people at Watseka."

"Cicadas don't sting humans—" he started, but she wasn't listening.

She checked the kitchen windows and the back door for cracks or openings—they looked okay—and ran through to the bottom of the stairs. "Emily? Emily, are you there?"

Emily hovered at the top of the stairs.

"Don't listen to her, Em. She's lost her mind. She's talking nonsense." Mr. Hart was right behind her, lecturing his wife on how safe the situation was.

Diana broke in. "The cicadas are here. And they are not normal ones. They're vicious, poisonous, attacking."

Emily frowned. "Cicadas won't harm you, dear. They're just a little noisy—"

"Please!" Diana tried to keep her voice level. "You saw what they did to Jesse. We need to cover the vents and anywhere they might get in."

The old lady threw her an irritated nod but came downstairs, leading her into the kitchen. She opened a cupboard and passed Diana some tape and Saran wrap. "Don't you think you're over-reacting?"

The swarm hissed and buzzed, louder and closer; the hits on the windows coming in clusters. Diana pulled at the end of the Saran wrap, tearing it in her haste. She suppressed the urge to swear.

"What's this nonsense?" Thomas demanded, coming in to find her taping Saran Wrap over the air conditioner.

"I need Jesse to be safe, and these things are dangerous." Diana felt like a fool, but she couldn't risk it.

"That tape will mark the wall." He grabbed her wrist.

She wrested herself away and pressed Saran Wrap all over the window then taped around it. "This must seem so rude, but it's for your safety as well as his. I promise."

"You come into my house, act crazy about a bunch of cicadas and wreck my paintwork? Who the heck do you think you are, lady? This is not your parents' house now, you know!" He was red-faced, and a vein in his temple throbbed. For a moment she was afraid he'd throw them out.

"Thomas!" Emily snapped.

Diana clambered down from the stool. "Mr. Hart, please. I know what I'm dealing with here. This is what hurt Jesse... in a matter of seconds. I have no problem with you thinking that I'm overreacting or crazy or whatever. Maybe he had an allergic reaction, and maybe so did all those people in Watseka. But what if it's not just him? I will pay to fix the walls so you can't see the tape was ever there. I just need Jesse and the rest of us to be safe now."

He rolled his eyes at Emily and shook his head. "If the swarm will make the child ill, then you must stay until it passes. But once it does, you leave."

"That's all I ask. Thank you."

"Stay in the living room with the kid. I don't want to see you." He

81

stalked across the kitchen and into the hallway to his study, slamming the door behind him.

Diana, already keyed up, jumped at the sound. The cicadas' screeches played on her every nerve and made it hard to think.

Emily pursed her lips sourly. "When he gets his hackles up, there's not much to be done."

"We're absolutely ready to leave as soon as they've passed. We never meant to inconvenience you. We're very grateful for your hospitality." Diana took the Saran Wrap, tape, and scissors as she spoke and went back through the living room to cover the front door.

Jesse had clawed his way out from under the blanket. "They're here, aren't they? I can hear them!"

"It's okay, Jesse. I'm here." Diana knelt by the couch, one arm around the back of his head, the other close to his mittened hand.

"Doctor Stewart?" He inched to the edge of the couch and pressed himself against her, clinging tightly to her with his good hand. The noise outside screeched louder, and she was not surprised to feel him shaking.

A door opened in the kitchen and the murmur of conversation started; then Emily's voice became louder and shriller. Diana hoped she hadn't caused trouble between the Harts. They had been kind, and though Thomas was unwilling, he'd gone along with her plan.

"Thomas! You heard what the lady said!" Emily yelled. "Don't you dare! Just wait. Thomas! I'm telling you—!"

A door banged, and a second clatter followed from the screen door. "No!" Diana disentangled herself from Jesse and ran to the window. "Oh don't, please! Get back in! Please!"

Thomas had pulled on a long coat and a hat and was walking down to the garden shed. The cicadas tumbled and buzzed around him, several landing on the back of his coat.

"Thomas!" Emily dashed into the front room, leaning on the windowsill to watch.

He coughed as he reached the shed and opened the door. As he touched the handle, he shied away as if burned; the door swung back and slammed into a tree. With a great angry roar, a thick cloud of cicadas erupted from the tree, flying away in all directions, and he was lost in the whirring of wings.

"Doctor Stewart?" Jesse whispered.

"It's okay, Jesse, they're all outside. They aren't going to get in here." Diana soothed.

When the cloud cleared, Thomas lay on the ground, red to the top of his bald head. His hat had fallen off as he jerked and convulsed. He clawed at his throat, and went still.

"Thomas! Thomas!" Emily shrieked. "We have to help him!"

"We can't!" Diana told her. "Not while the swarm is out there. My protective gear is in the car. There's nothing we can do."

"There must be something!" Emily turned to her. "You're a doctor —do something!"

Diana paced away from the window in frustration.

"Don't go! Don't leave me!" Jesse wailed, reaching out blindly toward her.

"I'm here, Jesse, it's okay." Diana went back to the sofa and held his hand. "Emily, do you have a mask and snorkel or a scuba tank? Even a motorcycle helmet might do. We can probably make some kind of covering for your body. Unless you can get out there and back without being touched, you'll die too."

"I am not letting my husband die out there because I haven't got the right coat!" Emily spat. "Are you going to help me?"

Jesse clung onto her arm. "Stay here. Please. Don't leave me. I'm scared."

Diana looked helplessly at Emily, wracking her brains desperately for a way to help. "Wait. Saran Wrap. It might help protect you against touching anything toxic. We can wrap your hands and neck with it – maybe parts of your face."

Emily slapped her, hard. "He's out there dying, and you're fiddling about with Saran Wrap. You won't help a dying man. I'm not surprised your parents didn't tell you when they moved. If my daughter was such a selfish brat I'd lose touch with her too." Emily paused in the doorway. "When I get Thomas back in here, I expect you to be gone. Swarm or no swarm, I don't want you under my roof." She stormed out, leaving Diana clutching Jesse, one hand raised to her stinging cheek as the cicadas thwacked against the window in their thousands.

The back door slammed. The screen door screeched. Barely two steps from the house, Emily Hart cried out. She tried to run, lost her footing and dropped to the ground, her choked screams lost in the ever-present shriek of the cicadas.

CHAPTER NINE

ANAYELI ALFARO. NEAR THE STATE CAPITOL BUILDING. SACRAMENTO, CALIFORNIA.

A light, powdery ash had covered the world. Anayeli cleared her scratchy throat and peered through the thick smoke, her vision obscured by bits swirling like snowflakes. She eased the family minivan into the newsroom parking lot, startled as a car loomed out of the murk. "That's not a parking spot," she muttered, but she wasn't really sure. She couldn't see the lines that marked the asphalt.

She navigated around the cars that emerged out of the smoke, their edges ominously softened by soot as she trawled through the lot, trying to remember the last time she'd seen it so full—Election Night, probably. But the paper ran a skeleton crew on weekends and nights when she usually worked so she had no idea what *normal* looked like. "Guess everyone got here before us, Cricket." The dog sat on the passenger seat, alert instead of cowering the way he had on the drive away from Bertoli Farm. Using the wrist of her burned hand to steer, she reached over with her good hand and stroked his head—

one part of him that was mercifully un-singed—but he barely noticed. He stared out the windshield, trembling. From the pain of his burns, maybe. "But it's a big story. Lots of angles to cover. Lots of reporters on it, I guess." She had to get in there, hop on the phone, crank out the last few lines of her story, and get it fired off to Sid. Nobody was going to scoop her. She owed as much to Papa.

Every thought of Papa brought a fresh wash of tears, her vision going wavery. But crying in the parking lot wasn't going to help anyone. She pressed her enflamed palm against the steering wheel, sending a different sort of pain shooting through her. She jerked the car around and swung into a gap she hoped was actually a parking spot.

"C'mon, Cricket!" She used a too-bright voice as she hauled her satchel from behind the seat and slipped out of the van. "Let's go meet Sid! He's going to love you!" The dog cocked his head at her chirrupy tone like he knew better than to trust it, but then he scrambled across the cab and shot past her, the belt-leash dragging behind him.

She manually locked the minivan door, turned to go and shrieked. Someone was in the car she'd parked next to—a woman, her mouth open in a scream that matched her own. Except the woman's scream was silent, her eyes glassy, her stare so dull it was clear she was dead— and had been for hours. Dried blood trailed in coagulated rivulets all down the woman's front, and there were smears of blood on the window. With a terrible sinking feeling that started in her belly and radiated everywhere, rooting her, Anayeli swept her eyes over the cars she'd driven past. So many of them pointed toward the exits, canted at strange angles, too close together. They hadn't parked, they'd crashed, trying to get out. In the windows of a few of the nearest ones, she could make out the shapes of people, sitting motionless in the driver's seats. At her feet, Cricket whimpered and backed away.

"Yeah, let's get out of here." She took up Cricket's leash and broke into a run, refusing to look anywhere except the low-slung, non-descript stucco building at the center of the office park instead. "Inside will be better."

Inside was almost normal, except there was nothing and no one to see, which was weird. When she worked on weekends, there was always at least one reporter rushing out the door, off to some story, notepad in hand, or else rushing back in, hurrying to meet a deadline. But she was the only one in the lobby. Even the security guard who usually sat near the door was gone. Cricket pulled at the leash, dragging her a step closer to the guard's usual station. There was a strange pattern on the industrial-linoleum tile floor—a smattering of random rust-brown spatters making a halo around the stool where the guard usually sat—blood. She retched, the horrible acid taste stinging as Josh Bertoli's frothing mouth appeared in her mind's eye. *Focus Anayeli. Escribe.* She had to get out of here—up to the newsroom. That's probably where everyone was, eyes glued to the TV.

She dashed to the elevators, but as she reached to push the call button, Cricket sat at her feet and whined. Her hand hovered. The power could go out at any time, leaving her stranded in the last possible place she'd ever want to be. The doors could open and reveal something worse—an elevator that wasn't empty and instead held more people like the woman out in the car. That was more like something out of a horror flick, not real life, but the image had lodged itself in her brain and she couldn't shake it. Nope—the stairs it was. They were faster anyway. "Good call, Cricket." She had to smile at the sweep of the dog's tail across the floor—just one wag and then they were moving, Cricket trotting at her side as she ran down the corridor. She needed to get to the newsroom where she could actually do some good.

She ran down the corridor, past the long line of windows that looked down into the lower floor where the printing press kept up a steady hum. Except it wasn't. "What the hell?" She'd never seen the press not running. Near one of the machines—she was embarrassed that she'd never learned what any of them were called—a man was slumped, his body wracked with coughs. She knocked on the glass, and when his eyes met hers, she pointed to her mask, then dug a spare out of her bag and held it up for him. He made a face and shook his head, then coughed again, bright red splotches blooming at his feet.

"Machismo moron," she muttered and took off running again.

If the press wasn't running, there was always the online version of the paper. Her story could be posted within the hour if Sid liked what he saw.

It was a relief when she threw open the door to the newsroom. Inside, a sea of twisting screen saver images danced across the multiple computer screens. The corner of each desk sported either an abandoned to-go coffee cup or mug or water bottle pushed precariously near the edge, and every other flat space was strewn with reporter's notepads, scraps of paper, stacks of old print editions of the newspaper or books, a scattered spray of pens.

On the wall-mounted TV, the national news blared, a perfectly coiffed newscaster nodding seriously at the correspondent. The only thing missing was *people*. Sid was nowhere to be seen. Even when all the other reporters were out on stories, Sid was a permanent fixture, perched at the largest desk in the corner nearest the police scanner, refusing to use his own editorial office. "I like the buzz of the newsroom," he'd told her once, when he was in a friendly mood. "Gives me a little contact high, like being on a deadline with a Pulitzer-worthy story." She'd worked with him for another full year before she'd been inside his office and seen the framed front-page story that had actually won him a Pulitzer.

"He's probably in his office, don't you think, Cricket? On a big news day like today? I bet he's editing and posting stories like a madman."

She dropped Cricket's leash, so he could wander for crumbs, and dove for the nearest desk. She ignored the incessant static of the police scanner—more activity than usual—and vaguely heard the national newscaster say "dry weather conditions and a spate of seemingly disconnected fires leave authorities and firefighters scrambling as flames threaten the entire Sacramento Valley and surrounding foothills..." Good. They hadn't figured out the agricultural burn angle yet—it was still hers, thanks to Papa.

She typed *Matreus Headquarters Seed Division* into a browser with her good hand, clicking on "Who We Are," scrolling to find the names of the highest ranking research staff, and then typing Dan

Jensen into the Lexus Nexus database. "Yesss!" she whisper-exclaimed when she hit the button for speakerphone and the landline's dial-tone droned, painfully loud. At this hour, she usually wouldn't expect anyone to answer, but they were in the midst of a crisis. It had to be all hands on deck at Matreus. She punched in Jensen's direct line, then scribbled it onto a notepad, in case the Internet went down.

According to their website, Matreus was based out of Chicago, Illinois. Also good. They'd be well out of the range of the fires, though there was no way they could be caught unawares after this long. She jiggled her knee as the phone rang and rang. Don't go to voicemail, don't go to voicemail, she prayed as her mouth went dry and her heart rate skittered. She wanted to talk to the man who was responsible for her papa's death.

"Hello?" a wary sounding voice crackled into the newsroom, startling her enough that she bounced her foot into Cricket's face, unaware he'd curled up right under the desk.

"Hi Dan, this is Anayeli Alfaro of the Sacramento Bee. I'd like to ask you about the controlled burns you ordered out in California. What caused those fires to burn so rapidly and cause the deaths of multiple farmworkers?" She said it fast, no gaps, the words all blended together so Dan Jensen didn't have a chance to say no or deflect.

The line went dead.

She swore. She let loose every curse she could think of, even as she went back to the website and scrolled for a different name. Taylor Muckenfuss, Junior Research Agronomist. From his picture he looked young and eager and so open-faced he might spill something he shouldn't. And he was lowly enough that maybe he'd be one of the last to know a reporter had made the connection between the fires and Matreus, but not so junior that he wouldn't know anything at all. She punched in his number and added it to the notepad with Dan's.

The voice that answered this time was just what she'd hoped—not wary and closed like someone who expected to be called by reporters. Before she even asked her question, he interrupted her intro.

"Are you calling about the infestation?"

"The Teff infestation? Yes. I'd like to ask you about the controlled burns Matreus ordered out in California."

There was the tiniest pause and she cursed herself for allowing him to get her distracted and off-track. She thought he too was going to hang up, that she'd taken too long to make her calls and the company had officially gagged all their employees, but then Taylor said, "Ummmm. No comment?"

But where there was uncertainty there was opportunity. "I'm sure you want to do the right thing here, Taylor, for yourself and for the company and for the families of the farmworkers who have died and I wonder if, as an agronomist, you might know what it is that made the company decide to burn all those Teff fields?"

"Look." Taylor's voice hardened in a way that made a certain swear word repeat in Anayeli's head. "I'm not authorized... I mean, I have nothing—No comment. On teff or cicadas or anything."

There was always that moment where normal-person-Anayeli would back off and apologize and end the call. But Reporter-Anayeli pressed. She worked her source the way she'd been taught. "I understand, Taylor. You've got to protect yourself and your job. But men have lost not just their livelihoods, but their lives"—her voice wavered but she forced her voice through the sob that was threatening to close her throat— "and their families want to know why. Everyone in the state of California wants to know how something like this could happen, how a few fires—how many farms was it? 53?"—she picked a weirdly specific number so high he'd be eager to deny it—"could get so out of control."

His voice, when it came, was lower, an almost-whisper. "It wasn't 53. But that's off the record!"

"Oh. That's not how 'off the record' works." It was a gamble telling him, but if she quoted him and he found out, he would never answer her questions again. Instead, she could develop him as a source, make him believe he could trust her. She was going to lose him if she didn't explain fast. "I won't quote that, but you should know, next time you talk to a reporter, you have to say 'off the record' *first*, before you say anything at all. Otherwise they can use it."

Taylor swore under his breath.

"So it wasn't 53 farms. How many was it?" She wrote 53 on her notepad and circled it.

"Off the record?"

"Of course. Or you can be an anonymous source. Either way I'll keep your name out—"

"Off the record," he repeated, more firmly this time.

"Okay." It wasn't what she wanted, but it was better than nothing. In the pause, the police scanner crackled to life, a series of calls coming in, one on top of the other. But she had to get this story. She'd worry about the police scanner after.

"I don't know where you got the number 53," Taylor said. "That's not accurate. And they've got some specialist—from the Australia branch—who's heading up the response—"

"Do you have the name of the specialist? And why an international response to a series of regional fires? Isn't that strang—"

"I gotta go," Taylor said, and the line went dead.

She fired up her laptop, opened the story she'd already written, and updated it with the official "No comment" responses from Matreus Head Agronomist, Dan Jensen, adding the information about Matreus's international reach. She looked up Frontier Farmers Co-op, based in Capay, not far from Josh Bertoli's farm, and tried calling them, but every number she tried was disconnected—the lines burned up, most likely.

The whole time, the police scanner crackled with a steady stream of the mostly unfamiliar codes—10-80, 11-59. Taken all together, the codes she did recognize—10-91D—dead animal, 10-67—call for help, 10-54, 10-54, 10-54—possible dead body—were the kind that would normally have sent her flying off to cover an accident or crime. She uploaded her story into the inter-office system, then opened up her email and typed in Sid's name. Even though he was just down the corridor, it was the polite way to let him know her story was ready for his editorial eye instead of barging into his office. If he was in his office his door was closed, and that meant you didn't go in. The end. It was an unspoken rule and if it would help get her off the crime beat and onto better assignments, then Anayeli was all about the rules.

Señor Ed Sid,

The fire story is ready for you. It's slugged FarmFire. Think it's a big one. Could develop more—follow up?

-A

She hit send—and nothing happened. She hit send again. Still nothing. "Dammit!" In the span it took her to write three tiny sentences, the internet had gone down.

On the scanner, in a tone she'd never heard before—not the usual low, fast-speak mutter cops liked to use, but something frantic, higher-pitched—came the code, "52F, Jackson Highway and Hedge! Big! Moving fast!" Jackson Highway and Hedge was South Sacramento. Not all that far. And she didn't need the code sheet to know that 52F meant fire.

She snapped her laptop shut, shoved it in her bag and bolted, Cricket glued to her side. She had to get her story to Sid, and she had to get it to him now, because if that fire was what she thought it was—

She'd done a story out on Hedge Avenue a couple years back—a fluff piece on a local farmer who ran a pumpkin patch. A hay farmer. She'd done the whole tour on a hay wagon pulled by a tractor. She'd seen the huge hay barns stacked high, and he'd even told her how the whole thing had gone up in flames when a batch of hay had been baled too wet and had spontaneously combusted. If it was burning now... if that farmer had been growing Teff, too... It was obviously a possible link to her story. "We should investigate, Cricket." The dog looked up at her. "You wanna drive out there with me and see? It's not far."

But just the thought of getting that close to a fire again, the idea of setting foot on another farm had her stopped dead in the hall, her stomach twisting. She didn't want to see anything like what she'd witnessed on the Bertoli farm, ever again. She pushed the panicked men tearing ahead of the gobbling flames, Josh's frothing-mouthed flailing last moments from her mind.

Cricket sighed and put his head back down. "Yeah, me neither. Besides, Mama's probably worried. We've been gone way too long already, and we still have to hit the grocery store, get us some triple antibiotic ointment."

Cricket eyed her with his head cocked to one side.

"We'll file the story first. I bet Sid will have an opinion." She'd ask Sid, see if he wanted her to go investigate out on Hedge. And if she could leave Cricket with him, that would make things easier, be one fewer worry.

She rounded the corner that led to the editorial offices and both she and Cricket skidded to a stop.

"No. Please no."

She was on her knees in an instant, kneeling beside Sid's rounded form. She couldn't count how many times he'd patted his belly and said, "You don't get a gut like this without having some fun, at least!" Then he'd elbow her. "You ought to try eating some time, kiddo. I'm gonna bring you a slice of my famous lemon tart tomorrow." Whatever he was famous for cooking changed every time he said it, but he'd always made good on his promise. And he was a good cook.

She already knew, the moment she saw his hands flung outstretched, something clutched in one of them, that she was too late. She'd been too late before she'd ever even arrived at the newsroom. The blood on the floor around Frank's face was a dark congealed jelly. His neck when she tried to find his pulse was cold, his skin still, in the way that skin with blood flowing beneath it wasn't.

"No!" she wailed, and Cricket licked the side of her face until she quieted.

Anayeli carefully pried the object from Sid's hand, trying not to let herself notice how cold and stiff his fingers were, telling herself she couldn't hurt him now.

It was a picture of his dog. Roxy. "My best girl," Sid had always said about the dog. "Queen of my heart."

She'd wasted all this time on her story—her small, insignificant, tortilla thin, "no comment" story—and the whole time Sid had been dead. The security guard was dead, and by now the man draped over the printing press was probably dead too. She gasped a sob, and Cricket licked her again, whimpering this time. Her Papa was dead and instead of protecting his family like he would have wanted, she had focused on her stupid little story. She had put her career over her family, just like Mama always accused her of, and now her family was even more at risk. There was a new fire raging—not in Woodland, or Capay or Davis, but in South Sacramento. Ten miles away. Maybe fifteen. Mama had been right and Anayeli had been so terribly wrong.

Cricket barked, and Anayeli staggered to her feet. She ran back to the newsroom, yanked the police scanner's cord from the socket and felt the tiniest zing of hope when the emergency battery-operated mode kicked in. At least she'd have some way of knowing what was going on, once she was home. She slung her satchel to her back, tucked the scanner under her arm and ran to the break room next, grabbing a trash bag out from under the sink. She filled it with anything that looked half edible. Plastic cup-lets of creamer from the counter. An open bag of coffee. The herbal teas she was pretty sure were the same ones from her first day on the job.

In a cupboard she found a cluster of shrimp flavored ramen, a box with three energy bars. They all went in the bag too. The fridge was a wasteland not all too different from her own, except with more moldy food. In the freezer though, were a few microwavable meals— beef stroganoff, chicken tetrazzini— "Ew, weird stuff office workers like," Carlota would say, but it was better than the nothing she had. Mama would be furious if this was all she came home with.

She thought about ransacking her colleague's desks for the secret stashes of candy they all had, but in her moment of hesitation, Cricket barked.

"You're right, not enough time." She ruffled the dog's ears, and then they were moving again.

She was just about to the stairwell when she remembered the supply closet Sid had called the Closet of Obsolescence. "All kinds of goodies in there that no one knows how to use anymore," he'd said. She dashed back, half surprised when the knob turned easily. She yanked the door open.

Inside was a jumble of boxy black things with large buttons and tangles of cords. "What the hell is this stuff, Cricket? Do you know?" It wasn't just that she didn't know what most of it was but even if any of it still worked, she had no idea how to use the stuff. She pawed through it anyway, and found a box full of walky-talkies and something that looked like the two-way *el radio* her *tío* had showed her once. Maybe Ernesto could get it working, so at least they'd have another source of news besides the scanner. She jammed it into her satchel, dumped the walky-talkies into the food bag, and then she and Cricket raced for the stairs.

She had no idea if anything she'd found would make any difference, but she'd already wasted too much time. She had to get to her family.

CHAPTER TEN

SAM LEARY. BERKELEY, CALIFORNIA.

Sam sat on the end of the cot and rotated his head. When the popping stopped he bent his neck forward, put his hands on the back of his skull, and pushed forward with a light pressure. Muscles twinged as they stretched, and he rubbed his neck in a soothing downward motion. Henry stretched too, splaying his front legs as he yawned.

"Quit complaining. Your bed is probably better than mine. Maybe we should switch tonight?"

Henry snorted.

"You're right. I wouldn't fit." Stretching his back, Sam rolled off the cot and zipped up the sleeping bag. He glanced at his watch. "Ugh, I should have been up an hour ago." Bringing his shoulders back until his shoulder blades touched, a massive pop escaped from his chest, and he relaxed. He checked the door to the lab, twisting the deadbolt into the open position and then back to closed. It was his practice to check the locks at home every morning just to make sure that someone hadn't unlocked them in the night. You could never be too careful, even more important when Frank was gunning for him, for no apparent reason. Sam slumped in his chair. Frank wouldn't harass him for 'no reason' which meant there was something he hadn't understood about their interactions. He raked through his memories, checking everything Frank had said to him in the last week, ranking them in order of importance, but all he could come up with was 'the university wants my research, but not me." *Why? When I'm clearly the best man for the job. What does Frank bring to the table that I don't?*

Henry scratched at the closet door.

"Yes, I'm coming." He grabbed the dog bowl and kibble from the top shelf, pouring a fair amount into the dish. Henry sat, gave a paw, and waited—as ordered—before finally chowing down.

Sam snatched a granola bar and eased into his ergonomically unsound chair. The University funds didn't stretch to 'things that are good for your joints.' Still, worse things could happen. He didn't live in his mom's basement like Cockroach.

"Talk of the devil." The mail button popped, dinged, and a single message appeared.

"Springfield, Missouri and Topeka, Kansas have fallen victim of The Winter's Tale, Antigonus sighted."

If there was one thing you could count on when you talked to Cockroach it was that his references would be literary, possibly Classical, and New York Times Crossword worthy. Luckily Sam was cut from the same cloth so he understood the reference. Perdita, the heroine of the story, had been left alone in the Deserts of Bohemia to live or die, but during those sixteen years she'd grown and matured under the shepherd's care. Sixteen years. That must be a reference to the cicadas' cycle. Antigonus, the one who abandoned Perdita to her fate, was chased off and eaten by a bear, and the crew he sailed with was destroyed by a storm. Translation: lots of death and destruction for Missouri and Kansas. Of course, in a genuine emergency, he'd have to talk to Cockroach about getting right to the point, rather than talking in code. It could save lives.

Sam opened the minimized internet browser. "That's great, Cockroach, I'm sure Diana won't give up the child even if she faces a swarm of cicadas. I'll pass on the message."

The science forum continued to update.

Matt from Indiana wrote: "Got a glimpse of the insects as they passed by the shop window, they look smaller than the average cicada."

Lightning Rod from Wisconsin: "Yeah I saw, and they're tough too, one smacked into the windshield and was still moving when I used the windshield wipers on the little bugger."

Moonshine from Kentucky: "Is it just me or do their wings look like they have an edge on them? Of course, I'm not getting out to take a closer look, what with everyone running for their lives. My property is littered with dead people because of these things."

Sam turned away. *You can't save the dead, so don't even think about them.* His phone beeped, and he flipped it open. The battery was full. He unplugged the device from the wall charger and checked the message. It was Diana. "Got your voicemail. Am good. Jesse is with me at my parents' house."

Why was she at her parents' house? She needed to get those samples to his lab while they were fresh. Stopping to visit with family wasn't an option. Sam slid his chair along the wall, bumping into the vinyl base molding. He came to rest under a cork board with supports that held a map of the United States. All occurrences of the swarms that had been reported in the forum were marked with red ball-headed map pins. He pulled a couple more from the edge of the cork and sunk them into the new locations, running his index finger over the road Diana would need to drive to reach Lincoln.

"She's not far enough away from the swarms."

Henry pawed at his bowl, tipping the plastic over onto the curved side. Sam glanced at the rolling container. Time for water. As soon as the rubber grip on the bottom of the bowl touched the floor the dog lapped the water down in under a minute, drops splashing on the tile. With a satisfied lick of his chops, he sat and waited.

"All right, let's walk you before you have an accident."

Sam waited outside the first floor exit, eyeing the smoky sky and every pedestrian that passed by as he used his peripheries to track his dog. Satisfied that Henry finished the job he set out to do, Sam jogged over to bag the waste, and tossed it into the garbage on their way back to the lab. He glanced at the time. *Three minutes. Way to go.* With the terrible air quality, he didn't want to stay outside any longer than he had to.

Safe inside the lab, he double checked the deadbolt and turned to Henry. "What do you want to do now?"

He grinned as the furry hound wobbled over to the bed, grabbed the knotted rope that lay over its edge, and dragged the toy over to Sam, dropping it at his feet.

Grabbing the closest end of the rope, Sam wrapped it once around his wrist and clamped his other hand down on the knot. Henry lunged, grabbed his end, and the tug of war commenced. Using what little weight Sam had, he levered himself backward so that the dog had to jump and shake to pull him forward. Henry jerked several times, offsetting his balance. As he stepped forward to catch himself the mutt jagged to the left, and Sam jerked to the right, and he let go of the rope.

His shoulder throbbed and ached. Probing the joint, he rotated his right arm in slow circles. His left fingers connected with a spot on the back of his shoulder and he stopped. The area was warm. He winced, and dropped his shoulder. Bruised again. "You need to take it easy on your old man." The dog wove around Sam's legs with the rope still dangling from his mouth. With a hand cupping his shoulder, he stepped over the moving obstacle. "No more today."

Henry nudged up against his leg, staying put until Sam bent down, using his left hand to rub the mutt's belly and pat his side. "It's okay Henry, you don't know your own strength." Sam wrapped a long sleeve tee shirt around his neck, tied the arms in a knot, and tucked his arm through the loop.

Henry trotted to his bed and flopped down. His tongue lolled about as he rolled onto his back.

Sam plugged his laptop in and waited for it to boot. The non-networked machine was the only computer on campus to hold his findings on the puss caterpillar's venom. Once he was positive his hypothesis was correct, he would share it with the others but until then it would remain a secret. The desktop finished loading with a bright colored monarch butterfly and two folders next to a garbage can with crumpled paper in it.

He scrolled through the hard drive until reaching his private files, located under the hidden folder labeled 'Dr. Hyde,' and opened the incomplete digital image containing the puss caterpillars' molecular structure. There were many tests that had to be run before he had a complete model. He zoomed in on the amino acids that had been identified then slid over to his desktop computer.

The molecular and cell biology division of the school should be done with the chromatography of his venom and posted their findings by now. The files he wanted were underneath Dr. Albright's shared folder and he highlighted all the scans from all the venoms of the past year and pressed enter. As the documents populated Sam's desktop, Henry snorted and began to snore, his nose twitching as his legs folded in. Sam ignored the noise and dove into reading, scanning the molecular structures on the desktop, comparing them to the ones on his laptop. When a structure didn't match up or come close, he closed the document. One by one, the windows disappeared until two remained.

Sam grabbed a sheet of paper and began sketching the two models, deft strokes outlining the molecules in vibrant color, as his phone rang. Diana. He stopped and pressed answer. "Hi. How are you?"

"I'm still at the Hart's—my parents' house." She sounded about the same as the last time she'd called. Her voice was still higher than usual. "I had to pull Jesse from the hospital early." Had she just sobbed? She wasn't going to start crying again, was she?

Her voice went soft. "The cicadas, if you can call them that, hit the town. It was horrible. I tried to help people, but they attacked me, and tried to steal my gear. It was madness. And then the Hart's— I tried, but..."

"You're still safe?"

She coughed, and her voice grew clear and strong. "I plugged up all the vents and windows to keep them out. I think we're better off someplace less populated."

"When can I expect you?"

"I don't know. It's going to take a while, so make yourself comfortable. Jesse's—not good. And—I'm sorry, I have to go."

"Hold on. One more minute." Sam ran his finger along Diana's path on the map. Highway eighty was the most obvious route. "My contact on the science forum, Cockroach, says the further Southwest you go, the worse the swarms will become. I would suggest heading Northwest. That should keep you safe. The insects can fly at most twenty miles before needing to rest and they can't swim, so stay near bodies of water if you can. The others are saying the cicadas are smaller with a harder exoskeleton, and possible sharp edges to the wings. This sound like what you saw?"

"Yes, that sums it up."

There was silence on the other end of the phone. Sam didn't have anything to say, so he didn't say it.

"Yeah. Right, well, bye, Sam. You and Henry be safe."

She said goodbye; that was a good sign. Sam glanced at the sleeping mutt. He wasn't going to wake him. He'd wait until later to pass on her message.

He finished off his sketches and slid over to the laptop, increasing the brightness until the glare was too much to handle. He narrowed his eyes and hung the first drawing over the screen. The two molecules overlapped each other and he shifted the drawing until the structures lined up. No, too many deviations. "If I can find a similar venom, we can research modifications that were done to it. Then I can take those solutions and apply them to what I've been studying." Sam realized he was talking to himself and clamped his jaw shut.

He replaced the molecule with the next sketch. Angling the paper like he did with the last drawing, he folded the corner over the top of the monitor so he didn't have to hold it.

Crap. Some of the proteins don't match, but this looks very similar to batrachotoxin. I wonder if the lab boys realize this. I think it's time for another chat with Cockroach. Sam powered off the laptop and wrapped it in a trash bag. Stashing the computer inside one of the dog food bags, he placed it behind some canned goods, making sure it was hidden.

Returning to his desktop, he opened a new chat window in the forum.

SAM: Hey, Cockroach! You online?

The minute hand ticked down two minutes, and a new post appeared.

COCKROACH: Yup.

Sam tapped the keyboard.

SAM: Locomotion has not commenced. Developments necessitate a holding pattern.

COCKROACH: Listen to me; move.

"Yeah," Sam muttered. "I hear you. But in the real world, we have to adapt, Cockroach."

Sam pasted the molecule into the chat and waited the thirty second period. Another visitor entered the chat.

EARWIG: Greetings, Sam. I'm Earwig. Have you read about the strange cicadas appearing?

Sam groaned. *Please, Cockroach. Don't leave yet. We've still got a ton to talk about.*

SAM: Hello, Earwig. Yes, I'm keeping up on the insects plaguing certain towns. Why?

EARWIG: Will they find their way to the west coast?

Earwig with the million dollar question.

Sam didn't need that kind of speculation on the ether. People panicking was never good for business. Not even academia.

SAM: I don't think so. Observers say they travel about twenty miles or less, and their natural adult life cycle is about a month. The swarms are more than two thousand miles from California. If you're on the West Coast you should be safe.

EARWIG: Good.

Earwig's cursor blinked for a few seconds.

EARWIG: What's that picture you put up a moment ago?

Cockroach chimed in with a new post.

COCKROACH: Batrachotoxin. It's a potent neurotoxin

produced by a tree frog in Central and South America. It binds to and irreversibly opens the sodium channels of nerve cells and prevents them from closing, resulting in paralysis.

Earwig shot right back,

EARWIG: So why are we discussing frogs when the chatter is about cicadas?

Cockroach ignored Earwig and went right to the meat of the matter.

COCKROACH: Looked at the model you sent and compared it to last month's pic. There are startling similarities. I imagine the toxin would be similar in its actions but not its lethality. What's it from?

Sam didn't want to lay it all out in front of the new scientist, but Cockroach wasn't always available and his mind was easily the best when it came to solving puzzles, so he was just going to have to chance it.

SAM: Megalopyge opercularis.

Cockroach added a wide eyed emoji, then a grimace.

COCKROACH: If someone got it into their head to modify it...

Sam nodded at his screen.

SAM: Add subunit of protein to one of the bottom strands. The new molecule would counteract inflammation in the muscles.

That was the hope anyway. If all the research he'd done resulted with zilch, that was thousands of hours and taxpayers' dollars down the drain.

COCKROACH: Yes, but put the protein in the wrong spot, and you just created a chimera.

Cockroach never missed a beat. He got it. They were looking at a dangerous molecule.

EARWIG: What's a chimera?

Earwig, on the other hand, wasn't even close to understanding what they were talking about. Just as well. This wasn't a conversation you had with civilians.

COCKROACH: Greek mythology – a mix of lion and goat with a snake's tail. Deadly.

Cockroach couldn't help himself. He always had to show off with his knowledge of the Classics. Sam opened a PM window.

SAM: Dial it down in front of the stranger.

EARWIG: So you're saying this moth creates a deadly toxin, like those things swarming cities?

Earwig wasn't as stupid as he made himself out to be.

"COCKROACH!!!!" Sam pounded the keyboard, willing his friend to shut the chat down. Too late. Cockroach was already spinning a scenario for all to see.

COCKROACH: No, not even close. You would need to modify some of the amino acid chains in the makeup of the molecule, so they would react in different ways, increasing the potency of the original molecule, or changing it all together, thus making it deadly.

EARWIG: How much would something like this be worth with the proper documentation?

Earwig was on it like white on rice. Something wasn't sitting right; alarm bells were going off in the back of his mind, though he wasn't sure why. Sam bashed his fingers across the keyboard, ignoring the pain in his shoulder.

SAM: ABORT, ROACH. GET OUT. STOP TALKING. OUT. NOW.

Cockroach left the chat. Sam jumped at a tap on the lab door and spun in his chair as the Dean entered. He walked over to the cot and pushed his toecap against one leg. He crossed to the fish tank and stooped until he was eye level with the caterpillars. "They're fantastic specimens." He straightened and placed his hands behind his back. "I hate to give you more bad news, but your dog can't stay here with you in the lab. We've received numerous complaints from the faculty."

"But sir, Henry doesn't cause trouble. Most of the staff love him. Who's complaining?"

Dean Collins shook his head. "I can't give out that information. Confidential reporting."

"This is all Frank's doing, isn't it?"

The Dean lowered his eyes and crossed his arms. "Rules are rules. When I come back on Monday, the bed and Henry better be gone."

It was bad enough that Frank was taking his position at the end of the month, he had the gall to get Henry kicked out as well. If Diana didn't arrive before the weekend was over, he was going to have to figure out how to sneak back in.

Dean Collins took his leave, the swing of the door allowing a gust of cold air to swirl in. The chill froze Sam.

Rules are rules.

CHAPTER ELEVEN

DR. DIANA STEWART. DAVENPORT/LINCOLN, NEBRASKA.

By the time the swarm passed, it was nearly midday, and the Harts were well and truly lost. Jesse had fallen asleep again, so Diana crept into the kitchen and fashioned a make-shift protective suit from trash bags and Saran Wrap. Pulling on rubber gloves, she grabbed two bedsheets from the dryer and went outside.

The garden was thick with cicadas, which had settled over the bodies of the Harts. Thomas was unrecognizable, his face a vast mess of blisters and, where they'd burst, great raw areas of oozing flesh with a thick yellow crust. Emily's face and eyes were in a similar state; her scarf had come loose and a dried dribble of blood tracked down her chin.

There was nothing to be done. Diana covered them with the bedsheets and went back in, washed thoroughly, and woke Jesse for some toast, prior to leaving. She flicked the TV on, which was awash with images of stores being looted, flames, and destruction. "Oh goodness. I don't think we can rely on the supermarkets." She checked through the cupboards, one at a time.

"What are you doing?" Jesse asked from his seat at the kitchen table.

"We need supplies, Jesse. The shops are all being broken into by people who are panicking, and I think it would be a bad idea to try to get anything there."

"So, where will we get food?"

"I don't think that Emily and Thomas would mind if we helped ourselves." She sorted cans from the cupboard, placing them on the counter. "I'm going to see if there's anything we can use."

Jesse chewed his toast and swallowed before answering. "Isn't that stealing?"

"Normally, we wouldn't be doing this, true. But right now, things are very far from normal."

"Because of the bugs?" He set down the glass and felt for the toast in front of him. He opened his mouth and winced. That would be the blisters. She had no idea how to treat those.

"Uh-huh. The bugs are a problem." Understatement of the century. It was her English roots. She still fell back to talking like her mother when she was stressed. "Jesse... We need to talk about your family." She didn't know how to start.

"They're all dead, aren't they?" the boy asked in a small voice.

"No. Not all of them. I mean, what about your grandparents? Where are they?"

Jesse pushed his plate away with his good hand. "Grammy and Gramps died before I was born. Daddy said they would have liked me. Nana lived a long way away. We went to see her one time, but she didn't know who anyone was. Momma said that there was something in her mind that made her think we were strangers. We stayed with Aunt Sarah. She was nice."

"Sarah Heller? Is she your auntie?" Diana's heart leapt. If the contact on Jonah's emergency list was this Aunt, then even if it took months, she'd get Jesse back to his family. "What else can you tell me about her?"

Jesse pressed his lips together "She let me look at her false teeth in a glass of water one time. That was gross. She didn't have any real teeth. Her gums were all bald and pink."

Great. Ancient Auntie. Still, that was better than having no one. She didn't press the matter. He ate his toast and she ransacked the kitchen cupboards, filling bags and boxes with everything that didn't need an oven or—if the worst came to the worst—a flame.

By the time they were ready to go, Jesse's meds had kicked in and he was sleepy. She reclined the car seat as far as it would go and lifted him in, fastening the seatbelt over Emily's blankets. He winced and groaned, his hands batting her away from his face. His eyes were slightly less swollen than they had been, but he was still in a lot of pain.

Diana took one last look at the house. She'd expected to feel sad but, in fact, it was a relief to drive away. It wasn't as if she had any good memories there; Angelica had seen to that.

And now her father and his wife had dropped out of touch. The one time when her area of expertise might have actually come in useful and she couldn't warn or help them! She shook her head, not sure whether she was more irritated or frustrated.

But there was no time to waste thinking about her stepmother's latest ploy to separate her from her father. So long as her father hadn't changed his email address as well as his phone numbers, she'd still be able to find him.

That would have to wait. Her top priority had to be to get the cicada samples from Jonah's farm to Sam before they degraded. As far as she knew, that swarm marked the first sighting of the cicadas. Sam wanted her to head North, but that would take more time and she couldn't risk the samples getting too old to be usable. Besides, she knew how to deal with cicadas now. Suit up, stay in the truck, block the vents, keep moving. So long as the wildfires didn't get in the way, she'd just have to deal with it and push on. A little voice whispered that this logic didn't fly, but she ignored it. Getting the cicadas to the lab was just too important.

She followed the signs out of Davenport West, looking for some-where to gas up her truck. The city was only slightly less chaotic than Watseka, but it was going that way, fast. Someone smashed the front of the grocery store as she passed, and the glass fractured. Cars were mounted on the pavement, clusters of people helping others collapsed on the ground. A young woman in motorbike leathers and a helmet lay on the sidewalk, screaming, her leg crunched at an unnat-ural angle, while the remains of her motorbike burned fierce and strong, just yards down the road. A solitary ambulance went screaming past. The veneer of civilization was so thin. A week ago she wouldn't have believed they'd descend into chaos within days of a natural disaster, but here they were, ransacking and looting like it was the height of some global catastrophe.

The main street was solid with traffic, so she weaved through a network of smaller side streets, but that choice turned into a night-mare drive. She drove slowly, avoiding the blistered people staggering about, falling down, convulsing on the side of the road. There were too many, and she couldn't save them all. She couldn't even save the Gnome People who'd moved into her folks' house; how was she equipped to save strangers on the street? She wasn't. Best to keep driving.

They passed a park with a small playground, complete with a swing, a slide, and a climbing frame. She tried to look away, but too late. The stark figure of the child, dead at the top of the rope net, hanging from his perch, and the adult who had managed to climb two thirds of the way before succumbing, were etched into her mind.

"Where are we going?" Jesse murmured, making her jump.

Diana thanked her lucky stars that the seat was reclined so he couldn't see the playground, even with his limited vision. She mustered a smile. "We're still trying to get out of town. We'll find somewhere though." *Somewhere? Vague enough, Diana? Somewhere to what? Lie low? Get better?* The less she promised, the better.

Gradually, the car wrecks and writhing bodies gave way to old fashioned empty streets and then, thank heavens, signposts for the highway. They needed gas. Soon. The needle was inching toward E. But there was no going backward. Only forward. There'd be a gas station just outside of town. There always was. Right? And it was a lot harder to loot gas than groceries... she hoped.

The sign for gas was hidden by leafy branches. If she hadn't been driving so slowly, she would have missed it. She followed the narrow lane from the highway and pulled into a deserted courtyard. She left Jesse sleeping in the car, put on her gloves, and braved the tiny convenience-store, bathroom, coffee-shop complex that squatted next to the gas pumps.

Inside the complex were a couple of tables and some chairs set up outside the coffee shop. A heavily pregnant woman sat at one of the tables, her two children hovering behind her like hummingbirds. Could be the owners, could be other travelers. Probably best to check. "Is it open?"

"The cicadas have already been through here. Fiona was dead before the ambulance turned up. But the pumps are on, and you probably need the gas more than the company does." The woman had a pretty face, but it was unnaturally pale and her eyes were swollen. She held out her hand. "I'm Jane. Jane Steele. You're not from around these parts, are you?"

Diana took the woman's shaky hand. "Diana Stewart. Just passing through."

"We turned off the hot food shelves so they don't catch fire or anything. The food will go bad in another hour or two." The older of the children, a girl with hazel eyes and brown hair spoke up. "If you haven't eaten, you might as well."

"Thank you."

"I'm Samantha. And this is Eli." The girl held out her hand, but the boy hid and wouldn't shake, no matter how his mother fussed and tutted.

"Nice to meet you. Well, not the circumstances but..."

Samantha didn't react.

Even though she'd lived most of her life in the States, speaking American was hard. The rules of polite conversation were different. Back when Diana was a kid and they'd visited her aunts and uncles in England, the grownups would fill conversational gaps with chat about the weather or the awful new-fangled coffee shop that didn't even *have* tea on the menu or the price of petrol. There wouldn't be any awkward silences; just meaningless banter.

Not so here. The kids were mute, as was their mother. "Well..." Diana pointed at the glass doors. "Best go and..."

Jane hauled herself out of her chair and slunk to the cash register. "Eighty bucks on pump two?"

Diana thanked her and went to fill the truck.

A couple of minutes later, Eli scurried to her side, carrying a couple of plastic gas cans. "Mom says you might want these with a thirsty truck like that."

"That's so kind. Tell your mummy she's an angel." Diana took the cans. "Where's your car?"

"About 3 miles down the trail. It went off the road and broke the axle. This is as far as we could get, but there's nobody here."

Once she'd tanked up, Diana ambled back inside. "Jane, why don't you come with me? There's plenty of room in the truck and I wouldn't feel right leaving you stranded."

"You would do that for us?" Jane wiped her eyes. "Thank you. Thank you so much. I'm out of ideas." Diana handed her a Kleenex and Jane smiled wearily. "If you could help us get somewhere, we can rent a car, that would be such a help."

"Where are you heading?" Diana did not like the idea of leaving the family to fend for themselves in the chaos.

"West. I have family in California. There's nothing left for me here, and I'm seven months along. It just feels like time to go home." A tear rolled down her face, and she dashed it away.

"The cicadas?"

Jane looked away again.

"I'm so sorry. Jesse lost his father to them as well. Listen, I'm heading that way. I'm going to drop Jesse off when we find his people, but I can take you as far as I'm going. We can split ways whenever it suits."

Jane opened her satchel and dropped her wallet and keys in it. "We would so appreciate it. I'm shellshocked. The children need me to make decisions, and I just can't."

"We can trade. You can help me with Jesse." Diana ventured.

"He's been through a lot. It would be better for him if there was someone who knew what they were doing. He's lost his father, and the only relation I know of is an elderly aunt. I'm hoping she has other family that will help her with him, but it's the only lead I have."

Jane burst into tears, holding nothing back. Samantha took charge while her mother was sobbing. "We'll head back to our car. Collect our stuff. We'll be as fast as we can. C'mon, Eli." Samantha set off, throwing over her shoulder, "And no, we won't stop for anyone or talk to strangers."

And then the children were gone, leaving the women outside a store that hadn't been plundered.

There were photographs pinned to the corkboard behind the cash register; lots: A lady working in a soup kitchen, beaming at the disheveled man holding a tray out for his food. A newspaper article about the little octopus toys and sewed material squares she had made for the premature babies unit at the local hospital. Flowers for a wedding. A thank you card.

"Fiona would want us to take what we needed." Jane blew her nose and helped herself to a basket before inspecting the food aisle.

"We'll take this as a gift, and do what we can to pass that help on to someone else in her honor, eh?" Diana went right for the medical supplies.

Jane straightened a postcard, which had fallen over. "She'd like that."

"Me too," Diana murmured. In an odd way, it made it feel less like stealing.

Jane's children were slow in returning from their car and while they waited, Diana called the Sheriff's Office again. There was no answer. Even the answering machine had been turned off. She let it ring for a few moments. Just as she was about to give up, someone picked up. "Yes?"

"Hello, Sheriff Ford?"

"He's out."

"My name is Doctor Diana Stewart. I left a message yesterday about Jonah Sanders and his son Jesse. I need to know who Jesse's next of kin might be?"

"I heard the message." In the distance, there were shouts and the sound of breaking glass. "You need to talk to a social worker. The whole town is on fire."

"It's – what?" Diana strained to hear over the gunfire.

A shot rang out in the background. "Call the social worker, lady." The call ended in a click.

Diana Googled a number for the local child welfare services, and left a message. She didn't expect to hear back.

Jane was still packing and repacking the back of the vehicle. She had a 'system' she said. "What we need most will be at the front and what we won't need until later will be toward the back." She heaved a Coleman Stove and some propane canisters over the mountain of candy and chips and stashed them under a blanket.

Diana wasn't much of a packer, so she left Jane to her busy work and logged onto her remote working portal. She opened her file on the company's fertilizer, Feedit.

When she'd initially called Dan, she'd thought the cicada attack on Jonah's farm was a one off—nothing to do with Feedit, but the strength of her boss' reaction had made her wonder. And though she couldn't immediately find the relevant documents, she was pretty sure that the other instances she'd heard of —Forsyth, Oklahoma City, Jonesborough Arkansas—had been close to test sites, too.

She flicked through a few documents but couldn't concentrate. There was a lot to think about, and she wouldn't really get around to it until after Jesse was with his family. Her phone beeped again—a notification that she had almost used up her data allowance so she dug out a thumb drive and saved the most pertinent docs: Test sites and contacts; chemical analysis of sustained effects on the local environment; a file detailing tests in ...Australia? It must be misnamed. The study hadn't even started at that date. She made sure that she had her own latest data to hand along with the newer sets of data Dan had taken on his own visits.

A dialogue box popped up. "Access Denied. You do not have read-write permissions on this file."

Diana sighed. "Of course I do, you stupid machine! This is where

I put the updates for Victor and Dan." She got rid of the dialogue box and clicked on the file: access denied, again and again.

"Fine!" She flicked into the main folder and back. "What the...?" Her own folder showed about half the files that should have been there. She opened another file and tried to save it to her portable hard drive.

File path no longer valid. This file has been moved or deleted.

Her phone buzzed suddenly, making her jump. "Hello?"

"Diana, are you in the hard drive?"

Diana sighed. "Yes, Dan. I'm—"

He cut her off. "Bit last-minute. We had a cyber attack, so we're moving everything onto a more secure file server."

That didn't make sense. Any time they did server maintenance there were about a hundred and fifty emails about it; it was impossible to miss. "What do you want me to do in the meantime?"

"Hah." His little half-cough made her go cold. It was one of his tells. He was about to lie. "Don't do anything for now. Well, maybe finish up the notes you're making and put everything you have together on your laptop. That way when we move across to the new system you can fill in everything all at once. Yeah, that's the best thing. Don't access the system for the moment, we can't chance your computer getting infected if there's any of the virus they haven't cleaned up yet."

She stared at the screen, hitting refresh every few seconds. The files went missing one by one: her life's work disappearing before her eyes. It made no sense at all, unless someone inside the company was deleting her files. That had to be Dan, right? But why?

Dan's voice was smooth as cream. "I'm meeting a couple of senators in Lincoln, Nebraska. I should be free by four. Can you get there in time? We need to talk about how to handle the current incident."

"Lincoln?" It was on the way to Sam in Berkeley, so there shouldn't be a problem but maybe she could buy herself a few moments to get the files saved. "Hang on, let me just check how to get there from here." She navigated to the main directory and tried to drag and drop her own directory onto the portable hard drive. She couldn't let years of her research evaporate while she watched. It brought up errors, so in a fit of fury, she dragged the whole project across. If they'd moved her documents to some other place in the file, she intended to be able to access it. "Ah, Lincoln. Yes, I should be able to do that."

"I'm so honored you think you can spare the time." If she hadn't been so angry his sarcasm would have made her feel an inch high, but not today. He went on, "We need to sort out this mess of yours."

Her mess, was it? Her temper flared but fury aside, it was a bad situation. She was used to disrespect, but if he was talking openly about it being a mess of her making Dan wasn't going to help her sort anything out, he was going to make her the scapegoat.

Given the deaths and damage the insects had caused, that would most likely involve prosecution and jail time. She needed that data, to prove it wasn't her work! She said the first thing that occurred to her to keep him on the call. "I might still have Jesse with me if I haven't managed to contact his relatives."

The download was progressing painfully slowly. At the end, it brought up a dialogue box: *The following files could not be saved.* She copied the list of file names and pasted it into an email to herself.

"Jesse?" He'd forgotten who that was, for goodness' sake.

"Jesse is Jonah's son, Dan!" Anger showed in her voice, so she took a moment to get it under control and think about what to do next. Her data should help counteract any accusations he might level at her, but she wasn't sure how much she'd managed to save. Her only hope was to go to the meeting, see if she could make them believe she was on their side—or at least was playing along—and try to get access to her files again. Maybe to all the files. She ejected the hard drive and dropped it in one of the inner pockets of her backpack. At least she had some of her work saved. But she would need more. "He's six and he just watched his father die because of the cicadas—"

"Who are you, Mother Teresa?" Dan did not bother to try to hide his disdain. "Not your problem. Check your hormones at the door and do your job."

Hormones? She was mortified but he did not pause.

"I'll expect you at four. Meet me out front of the Capitol building, and don't be late."

CHAPTER TWELVE

ANAYELI ALFARO. EAST SACRAMENTO, CALIFORNIA.

"I do not have time for this!" Since Anayeli had whipped out of her parking spot at the newsroom she'd wasted too much of everything—time, gas, patience—driving around near the newsroom, hitting every single shopping center she could think of. At each one, cars spilled out into the street, jamming up traffic, which was already moving slow thanks to the terrible visibility. At the first strip mall, she'd figured the next one would be less packed. But it was the same at each place she'd tried. She gripped the steering wheel tighter and leaned forward, as she crept through traffic past yet another gas station mini-mart, this one just as crowded as the last. She let out a frustrated growl that made Cricket's ears pull back with worry.

"It's okay, buddy. It's just that everyone and their dog is getting gas, I guess." Cricket cocked his head at her and she ruffled his ears. "Not that you're my dog...Just 'til we find you someone better." Someone better was supposed to be Sid. She pushed away the memory of him lying in the corridor.

From somewhere behind her seat, where she'd crammed her satchel and the bag of supplies she'd raided from the newsroom, the scanner crackled with constant reminders that the fire was coming. From the updated locations the emergency responders sometimes called in, it was moving fast—faster than the fire crews. She'd already seen what that looked like, and she never wanted to experience it again.

"So *estúpida*!" She slapped her good palm against the steering wheel, as if that would help, scaring Cricket. "Mama was right. We should have gone for supplies first."

Since leaving the newsroom, the sky had gotten darker and more ominous, turning a strange yellow-gray color. It was getting harder to see through the dense haze and the falling ash, and her lungs hurt, despite the mask. If she didn't manage to get the stuff on Mama's list, her family wouldn't have enough supplies to shelter in place. Mama was going to be furious at her. Carlota would be hangry and horrible. And she would've let the whole family down. Again. She hadn't saved Papa. She hadn't told his story. And she hadn't done the most basic thing of all, the one thing Mama had asked her to do: get food. Worse, if she showed up with less than a quarter tank of gas, they'd barely have enough fuel to get out of town. If the fire couldn't be stopped before it got out of the farmland surrounding Sacramento and into the more densely populated city proper, they'd be in trouble. If her family was going to have to flee the fires again, they sure as hell weren't fast enough to do it on foot—no one was. She'd learned that much on Josh Bertoli's farm.

"We're not going home empty-handed or with less than half a tank of gas, not if I have any say in the matter, Cricket." She yanked the van into a U-turn at the next intersection. "We'll just have to wait in that ridiculous line."

But as she put her blinker on and edged over the yellow line, the car in the next lane blasted its horn. She sped up, angling into the other lane, but the driver honked again and shot forward, making it impossible for her to merge. She jammed on the brakes, flinging her arm out to stop Cricket from flying off the seat, and the driver behind her—from a car she hadn't even seen through the smoke, because they must have their headlights off—laid on the horn, making her jump, before veering around her on the left and cutting back in front of her, zipping across all the lanes of traffic and into the gas station line Anayeli was forced to blow right past.

She hurled every insult she could think of for both of those jerks and then repeated a few more of her favorites.

"We'll find a store closer to home, Cricket. That'll be better anyway." She headed up the overpass that crossed the American River. She had almost crested the top when the engine misfired and the van gave a little lurch. A golden yellow light came on above the speedometer, one she'd never seen before, but she kept driving.

She'd stopped going to church regularly ages ago, but she'd never really stopped praying. She prayed until she finally turned onto the major thoroughfare that split her neighborhood from the nicer ones. The traffic was heavy—worse than rush hour—but she was close enough now that she could spend an hour walking home if she had to.

"C'mon..." Anayeli urged the van, as if it were one of her *tío's* horses—they'd never once quit on her. Could go all day, her *tío* always bragged. Cricket whimpered. The van gave another lurch, but then they were on the downhill. The temperature gauge suddenly surged upward, then dropped back to normal. "Don't do that. Overheating is not allowed!" She eased off the gas pedal and coasted, but the traffic was too slow-moving for her to fully take advantage of the momentum and the gauge shot into the red. She frantically ran through the options. Nothing was close—except The Corner Market.

It was only ever a last resort. Even the fact the gas was cheap didn't make up for the fact that half the pumps were perpetually out of order and the convenience store was creepy in the dingy way that made her think of kidnappers and peep holes in dirty bathrooms where both the toilet seat and the floor were wet, the door didn't lock properly, and there were no paper towels.

The engine misfired again, then chugged forward, only to sputter again and then quit, the entire dashboard lighting up. She tried the ignition. Nothing happened except an awful screeching noise. "This is *no bueno*, Cricket."

She did not want to go to The Corner Market, but the van was already slowing. There was nowhere else. She kept her eyes trained on the stoplight ahead, the green light the dimmest of glows through the smoke. If it turned red now, she'd never make it through the intersection and into The Corner Market parking lot. Even if it stayed green she wasn't sure she would make it.

"C'mon, c'mon!" No way could she push the van all by herself if it stopped moving. Her foot hovered over the brake as the van inched closer and closer to the intersection, and the green light got more and more stale. Just before she hit the crosswalk, the light turned yellow, but she was going for it, if creeping at a snail's pace counted as going for it. Never mind she could barely see the cross-traffic, which meant if she got stuck in the intersection, she had a good chance of getting hit.

The van kept rolling. Without power, the steering was stiff, but she cranked the wheel and angled the van toward the entrance, praying she had enough momentum to make it over the little lip of curb. At least there wasn't a car blocking the path. The van hit the lip and bounced, and for a millisecond it could have rolled either way—back into the street or forward into the lot. She leaned toward the dash, as if that would help.

"Yessss!" Probably no one in the history of The Corner Market had ever before cheered to find themselves in its lot and she almost laughed at the absurdity. The nearest pump was available—which probably meant it was broken—but at least she'd made it. She'd grab some of the items on Mama's list, find some batteries, and by the time she got back, the van would've cooled off and she'd gas up and go. That the van would fix itself was magical thinking, but she needed something to hold onto.

"You stay. Guard our stuff." Cricket gave her a baleful, ears-flattened look as she slid out of the van, surprised the pump she'd chosen didn't have an Out of Order sign on it. Maybe she'd gotten lucky. It was definitely a sign. She jammed her ATM card into the reader and waited for instructions to pop up on the screen.. Nothing happened. But the cars parked at the other working pumps all had gas nozzles inserted.

"Excuse me, sir?" The only person outside was a man in dark blue coveralls bent over a red plastic gas can. Everyone else must be inside, getting supplies. Like Mama had said people would be. The man didn't respond. "Sir? Is the card reader on your pump working?"

"You blind or something?" He gestured toward his gas can without even straightening up to look at her. That was when she noticed the spray of mallard duck stickers across his truck's back window. It was her neighbor, whom she'd spoken to all of once. Maybe he didn't recognize her. Or maybe some people had neighbors they could ask for help and some didn't. If he wouldn't answer a simple question she sure as hell wasn't going to ask if he could help with her van.

She pulled her card out and tried again, just in case. Still nothing. Of course. Irritated that everything was taking longer than it should, she yanked open the van door to grab her purse and Cricket came flying out, gluing himself to her side.

"Well, okay." She stroked the dog's head and earned one sweeping tail wag. "I guess you can come." A creepy gas station quickie-mart wasn't going to enforce strict rules about dogs. She checked the sky to the south—it was a charcoal wall of smoke so thick she could hardly see the buildings across the four-lane boulevard.

Her heart sank as soon as she stepped inside the convenience store. There was a line the length of one of the aisles—people must have walked from nearby because there weren't that many cars outside—but the shelves already had big, empty gaps. Maybe everyone had just bought up all the candy and chips. Or maybe Mama had been right again.

"Hey!" a male voice snapped.

She jerked her head up from digging in her purse for Mama's list. It was the store clerk, a rough looking older man with a full scraggly beard.

"You can't bring that dog in here." He jerked his thumb toward the sign on the door—*service dogs only*—as the masked customer he'd been helping hurried past her and pushed it open.

Cricket was trembling and pressed to her leg. She wasn't dragging him back out to the van when he'd been so desperate not to be left in it. "He's an agricultural pest detection dog." The lie came quick. A lady had brought a trained sniffer dog to her high school once, for career day.

"Yeah, and I'm the President of the United States." Over his mask, the clerk gave her a dead-eyed glare, but the next person in line was leaning over the counter to put an armload of stuff down and he went back to helping his customers without another word. She didn't wait for him to change his mind.

Everyone in line had their arms full of beverages and beer and chips and whatever else they could find and carry. She hurried to the canned aisle. The Corner Market was the kind of place that only stocked a couple cans of any given item, and everything was gone except two cans of stewed carrots. She grabbed them, passing up a lone box of Shake n Bake. She hit a gold mine at the end of the aisle: two cans of dog food that had been pushed into the back corner. Candy—candy could tide Carlota over, and make Luz and Ernesto happy—but the only things left in the candy aisle were Necco wafers and Lemonheads. All the chocolate was gone. In the chip aisle, Hot Cheetos were gone—everything anyone actually liked was gone. She zipped around the end of the aisle, on a hunt for batteries that she was increasingly certain wouldn't be there, and ran smack into a barrel chested man.

"Oh, I'm so sorry!" She stooped to pick up the corn nuts she'd knocked from his hands.

The neighbor. She didn't have the slightest idea what his name was. Right after she'd moved in, she'd gone over to introduce herself, figuring if they were going to share a duplex and a driveway they ought to be on a first name basis, but when she'd introduced herself and extended a hand, the man had just stared at her before saying, "This ain't Melrose Place. I stick to myself," before closing the door in her face. But he had a cute little daughter who sometimes smiled at her—she'd never been introduced to her either, but the girl was called Brooklyn or Brynleigh or some other weird trendy white-girl name.

She held out the corn nuts and her neighbor muttered something that might've been "no problem" or maybe "thank you ma'am" but probably wasn't. She didn't know because Cricket barked.

"Ay, Cricket! Shhhhh!" She wished she could shrink. From the counter the clerk said something in a tone she didn't like about dogs and their female owners.

Cricket whined and that was when a trickle of blood oozed from her neighbor's nose. The man grabbed for his pocket, pulled out a faded, much-washed bandana and wiped at it.

She should've walked past. She should've minded her own business. But the man's daughter's smiling face swam through her mind. Papa's Dorados cap. Josh Bertoli, yanking down his bandana mask. "You should get that checked out."

"I'm fine." The man's voice was even more brusque than she remembered it. He always seemed so gentle with his daughter.

"It's just—" There was no way to tell him everything she'd seen, the people she'd seen die. "The smoke. It's been causing—I've seen a lot of people with bloody noses today."

"What's it to you?" He tried to push past her. Cricket whined again.

"Do you at least have an N95 mask?" she asked, from behind her own.

"What? No." He shook his head like it was a ridiculous question. Or maybe she was a ridiculous person. "Lay off it, lady."

He didn't recognize her.

"Okay, but—"

He stomped over to the refrigerator case where the sports and coffee drinks were, completely avoiding her.

Well, she'd tried at least. Batteries. She needed batteries. She found them on the end of the farthest aisle. Or rather, she found watch batteries, because no one actually wore watches anymore, and nine-volt batteries like the ones that went in her smoke detector. All the useful batteries were already gone. Still, she pawed through what was there, in case someone had put the ones she wanted in the wrong place. Mama was never going to forgive her. She'd already taken so long and gotten almost nothing they needed and probably the van was dead and she had no way to drive home with what she had gathered.

She was upset and in just enough of a hurry that she did that thing that always happens when you're in too big a rush—she knocked into one of the pegs on the battery rack and it tipped, enough that every package it held fell, scattering across the floor.

"*Chispas!*" The clerk was already pissed at her—no way she could leave the mess.

She forced herself to slow down and be careful, setting down her canned goods before crouching and using both hands—ignoring the pain and the fact that she was getting gross gas station germs all over her burned palm—to sweep the batteries into a pile, Cricket sneaking in the quickest of licks at her jaw.

"Ew, gross. *No me gusta,*" she told him, but she couldn't help smiling a little. She'd let him lick her before, when she was upset, so there was no way he could know she wasn't into dog kisses. "Such a sweet boy."

One by one, she deliberately slipped each package back on its peg, then crouched down to make sure there weren't any left hidden under the shelves. She stifled a little triumphant yell when she found a lone 4-pack of D batteries under the shelf, alongside two more stray watch battery packages. She sat up and put the D batteries she wanted down on the bottom shelf next to her other supplies. The instant she released the 4-pack though, Cricket let out a low, rumbling growl and a hand snaked out past Anayeli, forcing her off balance, and grabbing the batteries.

She yelped as she toppled over. "Those are mine!"

"You put them down." Her neighbor didn't even offer a hand to help her back up.

"I put them with all the other stuff I'm buying!"

The whole store had gone quiet.

"What's going on back there?" The clerk had come out from behind the counter and was part way down the aisle toward them.

Anayeli stood, her hands shaking at her sides.

"She says these batteries are hers." Her neighbor's nose was still bleeding, worse now. A steady stream rather than a trickle.

"Did you punch him?" It was more accusation than question, the way the clerk said it, his eyes gone flinty.

She'd been accused of shoplifting before. She had gotten mostly used to being followed in stores, or else having salesclerks at fancy boutiques pretend they didn't see her and then act surprised when she actually bought something. But she had never been accused of punching someone.

"What? Why would I—?" But the look on the clerk's face said not only that he thought she would, he was sure she had. And her jerk of a neighbor was so busy shifting his stuff—her batteries—so that he could mop up his own blood, that he didn't say anything to disabuse the store clerk of that notion.

"Look. I don't know what your deal is. You bring that dog in here. You make a mess. Now you punch a guy. Either you get in line and you stay there and you don't touch anything or make any more trouble, or you get out." He hooked a thumb toward the door. "I don't need your business and I got other customers waiting. On you."

The two people left at the counter openly stared.

Her cheeks flared hot. She wanted more than anything to storm out of The Corner Market in outraged indignation. But she still needed gas. She needed something to take home to Mama. She needed those batteries. Her neighbor refused to even look at her, still dabbing at his nose. The only person she'd ever hated more was Josh Bertoli.

She got in line.

"No," the clerk said to her and then looked to her neighbor. "You got everything you wanted?

Her neighbor nodded, then coughed.

"You go ahead then." The clerk waved her neighbor forward. "You"—he pointed to Anayeli—"go last." As if she hadn't already figured out what he was doing.

When it was finally her turn to make her pathetic purchase, she wordlessly put her stewed carrots and dog food on the counter, then held out her ATM card.

"No plastic." The clerk didn't even try to hide his irritation.

"What?"

"Cash only." The clerk spoke slowly, as if she were mentally defi-cient, then poked at the sign taped flat on the counter.

"But—" She'd been so furious, so ashamed, she hadn't watched as the customers before her paid. Maybe he'd just decided to only accept cash from her.

"Computer system is down. Can't do nothing about it. Cash or get out." He muttered something else under his breath that she pretended not to hear.

She dug in her purse but she already knew it was hopeless. She never carried cash. She pulled out the folded leather coin purse Luz had made for her one Christmas and found three quarters, a dime and two pennies. She put them on the counter.

The clerk heaved an exaggerated sigh. "You want me to put the other stuff back." A statement that should have been a question.

She kept digging. In the cash section of her wallet she found a dollar bill, folded small. Out of spite, she didn't unfold it. Let the clerk do it.

At the bottom of her purse she found a grimy dime and two nick-els. She set them on top of the dollar bill. It was enough for the dog food at least. She pushed those two cans toward him. Mama wouldn't know what to make of stewed carrots anyway.

"I'll take these." She kept her voice light, like nothing had tran-spired to make her hate the man. "And I need gas. Pump three."

"Ain't enough for both."

"Here." She pushed her credit card across the counter. "Take down my credit card number. I'll use that for the gas. When your computer system is back up, you can run it."

"I don't know what it is with you people." The man sneered. "Do you not *comprende* English? *Dinero* only." He shook the dollar bill at her.

You people. She would not react. She would not lower herself to this man's level. She would never allow herself to be so undignified. She swallowed the insults she wanted to fling back at him. She couldn't risk making him any angrier. She couldn't leave with nothing at all.

"Fine. No dog food. Two dollars and seven cents of gas. Regular. Pump three."

At least it took only a minute to pump her gas. A minute of repeating over and over, you will not cry, you will not cry, you will not cry while Cricket licked her free hand, the injured one. When the pump clicked off, she hadn't even added one gallon to her tank. Enough for maybe fifteen more miles, *if* the van would start.

Safely inside the van, she mapped her options, figured out which big box store was closest, which one was on the way home—that decided, she couldn't stall any longer. She sent up a little prayer —"Please let this work. Please"— and turned the ignition. The engine roared to life. The warning lights stayed dark. The temperature needle sat right at normal. Fixed. For now. Cricket whined.

"Don't question it, Cricket. Let's just go."

She was just about to turn left out of the lot when it hit her. If the computer system was down at The Corner Market, it was probably down everywhere. Which meant she had no way to pay for anything.

A voice floated up in her memory. "Best thing in life is to have options. Keep everything in play until you can't." It had been Sid who'd told her that. But she was out of options. Just like Sid who was dead in a hallway at the newsroom, a picture of his dog Roxy on his chest. Stout Sid, who loved to eat, and loved cooking even more.

That was when it hit her. She did have one more option, if the van kept running long enough.

"We're going to Sid's house," she told Cricket, and she turned right, back toward Land Park, where Sid lived.

CHAPTER THIRTEEN

SAM LEARY. BERKELEY, CALIFORNIA.

The chemistry lab's lights flickered, a select few giving off a dim greenish glow. Sam despised having to traverse the labs of the molecular and cell biology center in Weill Hall, but he was in need of answers. In the gloom, he gripped the counter's edge and approached Doctor Albright who sat at the far counter, head bowed over a microscope, a pair of glasses sitting on top of her head.

"Ouch!" His knee met a metal stool. "Janine would it kill you to wear your glasses and turn on a full bank of lights?"

She waved the spectacles in question over her head. "You complain about lighting in here every time you visit. Just accept that things are the way they are."

Sam boosted the laptop under his arm, quirked a grin, and flopped onto the third stool away from her. It had always been this way between them. Sarcastic and full of drama. But for some reason, the relationship worked and found a way to stay balanced enough to function properly. Several capped vials of viscous fluid sat in a rack close to her microscope, and he picked up the closest one. Its contents oozed to the side as he tilted a tube into a beam of light.

"Whose blood are you working with today?" He replaced the vial.

Janine kept her focus on the microscope. "Sam, I swear, if you mess with my DNA samples I will smack you into next year."

"So possessive, no wonder the lab guys upstairs refer to you as a vampire."

Janine swung an arm at Sam, catching the edge of the rack with her fist. It toppled over, but Sam's reflexes were quicker and brought up his forearm against the counter to keep the vials from crashing onto the floor. They spilled out of the rack, bouncing off each other like bumper cars.

Please don't break! I can't afford to ruin someone's work.

Janine pulled away from the microscope as the labeled containers rolled in wide arcs. "My samples!"

She grabbed fistfuls of the vials. "Five, ten..." Fire blazed in her eyes and she bit her lip. Sam was grateful she didn't say whatever it was that was going through her mind. He didn't need that kind of rage directed at him. She placed the vials in the rack alphabetically as Sam stood by, stoic, ready to offer a hand only if asked.

She returned to the microscope, pausing for a brief moment. "Thanks for stopping them. You saved three months' worth of work, even if you were part of the problem."

"Anything I can do to help."

For reasons that were entirely mystifying, that statement upset the Queen of Darkness. She shot daggers at him. Sam hunched inwards to make himself a smaller target. His arm burned and throbbed from Henry's playtime and he hugged it to himself to try to stop the spread.

"What did you do to your shoulder?"

"Nothing."

Her eyes said she knew otherwise.

Henry yipped and planted his feet on the side of Janine's hip. He stuck his tongue out, licking the air as he wagged his tail. "Oh, you brought Henry. Who's a good boy, huh, have you been a good boy?" Janine pushed away from the counter and scratched the dog behind the ears. Bending down to nuzzle his wet nose, she smiled and tossed her hair over her shoulder. Still scratching him, she turned toward Sam. "What do you need?"

Sam made his way to the lighting panel and stopped. "I need to turn on the lights, so I can see."

Janine pulled the pair of dark glasses from her hair and slid the arms over her ears. "I hate these things, the plastic bridge always pinches my nose." Sam flicked the rest of the switches, and the room flooded with light. She flinched and let her hair fall over the edges of the glasses, blocking the light from the openings.

"I hear keratoconus can be quite painful. Sorry." One's cornea turning into a cone would have to be.

She rolled her hand. "Get on with it already, so I can go back to my dark room."

"Ah, yeah sure. I was discussing a possible anti-inflammatory with an... acquaintance, and they mentioned something about the venom I gave you to analyze having potential to be modified. I was curious if anyone down here had explored this?"

Janine rifled through a drawer and pulled out a form with her signature on the bottom. She pointed at two paragraphs. This was not the first time she'd waved an NDA in his face so he knew what was coming next. "Sam, you can't talk about the work we do here to outside parties. Nothing, not even research theories. How many times do you need to be told?"

"They aren't aware of anything, promise. I pass them ideas, and they come back with stuff I'm able to try."

Janine curled her lip. "Right, like your venom isn't tied up with a military contract."

"The agreement I signed allows for disclosure *if necessary*. This is my project, which makes me the 'sponsor,' and the university the 'independent contractor.'" If she was going to quote chapter and verse, he could do the same. "I'm doing the experiments, so I take on both roles, and have free rein with the material. All I have to do is put into writing what I intend to reveal."

Janine's matter of fact tone dripped with frustration. "The military contract supersedes yours. If the school ever found out, you would be so fired."

Sam's cheeks warmed. He rummaged through his pockets and gripped his sketch from earlier. Pulling the folded paper out of his pocket, he opened his laptop, and offered the two drawings to her. "Why is the military funding my research?"

Janine retrieved a folder from her desk. "Modification of the molecule to enhance its properties. In this case..." She fiddled with the manila file, before putting it back. "Since you can't seem to keep things to yourself I better not tell you anymore."

Sam's veins flowed with a spike of adrenaline, ants scurrying along his limbs as he paced back and forth. What wasn't she telling him?

Janine backed away, placing a table between them. "Sam, calm down. I'm doing this for you. If anyone finds out that you've been sharing bits of information, I don't want to even think about the consequences. What I said before includes what the military can do to you. Whether or not you knew about the other contract, they could call it treason. You understand that right?"

Sam jammed the paper back into his pocket, closed his laptop, and stashed it under his jacket. "Come on, Henry."

"Wait, why did you want to know?"

Sam flipped the lights off and kicked open the door, leaving Janine to wonder.

The sun was bright red behind a scrim of smoke, but its warmth was a welcome relief from the cold reception at the genetics lab. Even though the faint scent of smoke tainted the air, Sam allowed Henry to wander, sniffing bushes, and people, as they headed back to the Life Science Hall. A squirrel bolted out of a nearby bush and Henry gave chase. The squirrel zig-zagged until reaching a tree and disappeared into its branches. The dog hopped in place at its trunk, barking at nothing. "He doesn't want to play. Come." Henry obeyed and returned to Sam's side.

The cool air from the air conditioner—filtered and smoke-free — rushed over them as they passed through the side entrance of the Life Sciences building and a crash reverberated through the walls. Jogging the short distance, they skidded to a halt in front of the lab.

Frank was surrounded by the remains of several beakers. Cans of food and camping gear lay cluttered on the tile at the opening of the closet. He ripped open a drawer, about to dump the contents onto the floor, but turned as Henry scratched to be let in. "Where did you hide the laptop?"

"What laptop?" Sam gripped the laptop with his arm, gluing it to his side. Frank would never see the computer at his angle.

Frank took a step forward, and Sam took one back.

Sam balled his fist and readied himself for the fight even though it was a fight he'd never win.

Frank locked eyes with Sam but—totally not what Sam was expecting—backed down, taking a seat on the rolling chair. "Stalemate. Come in." He gave a short, seated bow.

"I think I'll keep the door between us as an equalizer. Thanks all the same."

"Suit yourself." He inched closer to the map and pulled a pin from Illinois.

"Stop, I need those to track the cicadas."

"Knew it. I knew you were holding out on me." Frank gripped another red ball. "You're more than welcome to come in and stop me Samuel. I have five more pins I can remove."

Sam glanced down at Henry, doing his best not to move the laptop that was precariously balanced under his arm. In the years he'd worked on his venom, he hadn't given much thought to who was going to use his research for what, but being fired, having Janine hold out on him, and Frank being even more of a butt than usual added up to: the Army wants this for *something*. He didn't know what, and he didn't have time to think it through, but he knew he didn't want Frank to get his mitts on his research. Sam turned away. "If you'd please put everything back where you found it when you're done, I'd appreciate it."

He took off down the hall as Frank barreled out of the room, ten feet behind. Henry shot past Sam, racing up the stairs, taking two at a time until they reached the main entrance. Students—some of them with masks pulled down around their necks—milled about in the main atrium watching the dog's antics as Sam maneuvered to the other side of the T-Rex skeleton, placing it between him and his foe.

Frank caught himself as he tripped to reach the main floor, heaving as he tried to stand up straight. Sweat stained his shirt around his underarms and neck. Planting himself on the opposite side of the dinosaur, he held his sides and coughed. "Didn't think I could move this fast, did you?"

Sam crouched, feinted right, dodged left through the double doors, and outside. He wove through students and professors alike, apologizing as he went. Henry made no such apology. He was having the time of his life. Sam reached the recreational sports facility, burst through a set of double doors, down the hall, and into the men's locker room. Falling to the floor on his injured shoulder—but keeping the laptop safe from harm—he clamped his eyes shut, sweat dripping from his forehead, his throat burning. He propped himself up on a bench with his good arm, and popped open an empty locker.

Henry sniffed at a pair of cleats and moved on to a shirt hanging over another locker door.

"Leave it." Sam stuffed the computer into the cavity, slammed the thin metal door shut, and wobbled outside. He didn't really want to go back out into the smoke, but he had to lead Frank away from where he'd hidden the laptop. He and Henry made their way out onto the baseball field.

Frank appeared moments later from the outfield, stomping over second base on his way to the diamond. He stalked Sam like a lion or at least a moderately out-of-shape cat. Weary, Sam leaned against the backstop. An ancient aluminum bat clattered to the ground.

"I knew you wouldn't stay inside the building. Not enough places to run or hide. Now, let's talk about that laptop." Frank floundered, almost falling—maybe the smoke was getting to him, too—and reached down to pick up a baseball that'd had a fight with a lawn mower and lost. He smirked and threw the discarded ball sideways. Henry ran after the white streak.

"What's it to you? You've never cared about bugs before."

"Because you're hiding research from the last eight months on its hard drive. Do you think the Dean wasn't aware of you withholding information, only giving out the pieces you needed help to decode? You can bet that was one of the reasons they decided to get rid of you."

Sam's shoulder throbbed twice as hard as it had back in the lab, and his chest ached from running and breathing the hazy air. As Frank came closer, Henry returned and dropped the ball between them, waiting for someone to get with the program and throw the ball. Frank kept a wary eye on the animal as he neared, grabbed the sorry excuse for a ball. He waved it in front of the dog, teasing him before tossing it farther than the last throw. As Frank came closer, Sam crouched, grabbed the broken aluminum bat with his left hand, and inched his way up the backstop.

Frank paused at home plate. "You can spare yourself a lot of pain."

Sam lifted the end of the makeshift weapon up and coughed again, his throat dry. "Won't do you any good. There isn't enough information to be worth anything."

Frank laughed. "Spare me the diversion. I know about the venom and how it can be weaponized. You and Cockroach told me. Dumbasses. Didn't even know it was me. Just blabbing to the internet people because you can."

Sam dropped the bat. Asshole Frank—Earwig— had pulled one over on him, pretending to be a member of the science forum. Maybe he had more than one brain cell after all. He'd need to be even more careful what he said around the buffoon. He crouched to pick up the bat. "So? It doesn't mean I stored it on that computer."

"Why protect something with no value?"

Good grief, the thug wasn't going to stop. For once in his life, the meathead had thought things through. Sam couldn't give in to him though. He'd need the information for when Diana arrived. Sam straightened, his chest and legs burning, as he braced his back against the hot metal. "Take a long walk off a short pier."

Frank balled up a fist and drew his arm backward. "Suit yourself. You can have the beating *and* give me the laptop."

One, two, three...

His attacker was two steps away. Sam readied the bat, the head still resting on the ground.

Now...

Frank leaned into his swing, and Sam brought the weapon up hard right between Frank's legs. He crumpled to the ground, and Sam brought the metal down on his knee. Another swing battered his ribs, but the bully caught hold of the end of the bat, wrenched the metal from Sam's grasp and jammed the end into his chest. He fell to the ground as Henry returned with the ball. The mutt's head swiveled from Sam to Frank.

Henry lunged, biting Frank on the calf as Sam pushed himself off the ground with the metal tube. He sunk another bite into Frank's arm and shook until the assailant dropped the bat. Sam rolled toward the weapon. Snatching the handle, he swooped himself upright and struck Frank between the shoulders, once again dropping him to the dirt. Sam stood there, wide eyed. He'd defeated Goliath. It shouldn't have been possible. But there he was, the victor. He needed to get out of there before the giant woke up. Sam hobbled as fast as he dared around the corner of the Haas Pavilion.

Finally surrounded by people, almost all of them masked, Sam bent over as a Frisbee flew past his head, its colors attracting Henry who ran after the new toy. Sam tried to call, but his throat wouldn't let him.

"Dude, you need a mask. Or else get out of the smoke. Maybe get some water at the fountain inside?" The student pointed at the building behind him.

Sam nodded.

Distracted by Henry, the owner of the Frisbee whistled. "Come here boy, bring the disk here." The dog trotted over and laid the toy before their feet. "Hey, mister. This your dog?" Sam nodded. "He's pretty sweet, knows how to fetch. All my dog will do is dig up my mom's flowers. He makes her so mad." The student patted the dog's head and picked up the disc. "Later, dude."

Sam took the kid's advice and headed inside to the water fountain where he drank for a full two minutes. He'd been ignoring the fires but that was a mistake. The smoke was inching their way. If the fires arrived, all hell would break loose. He needed to rethink his SIP plan.

Every step back to the lab was agony and when he pushed open the door, Shane from maintenance was already waiting to fix up his windows. He stretched his measuring tape across the plywood and ticked off several marks with his carpenter pencil. He grabbed one end of the four-by-eight sheet and waited. "You going to give me a hand?"

Sam grabbed the other end of the plywood with his good arm and helped inch it over to the sawhorses. As they tilted the sheet sideways, the wood slipped, and he dropped the end. The corner splintered into a jagged angle on the tile.

Shane jounced with the vibrations and dropped his end. "You all right?"

"I think so... I might have a splinter. Sorry, my right hand is the dominant one and much stronger."

Shane stretched and rubbed the small of his back. "It's a good thing the school requires us to wear these supports."

"Sorry. I didn't mean to drop it."

"It's all right Sam, nothing a chiropractor and a massage therapist can't take care of. Besides, I should've had someone with two good hands come and help me."

Sam ducked his head and backed away from the saw. *This is one more reason I don't work with others. Except Diana.*

He pulled out his phone—and it was the best thing that had happened all day. There was a message—Diana had checked in while he'd been busy with Frank.

"Hi Sam. Just wanted to let you know I'm still on the road. My boss insisted I meet him in Lincoln, Nebraska. I'm not sure what he wants to talk about, but I'm okay and that's where I'm headed."

Nebraska. He checked the map, hoping she'd be safe there.

A knock on the wall startled him. It was Shane. "You're all set here." No matter what the rest of the staff said about the efficiency of the maintenance department, they were wrong. Every window had been boarded up within the hour. Shane propped the hand truck by the door and surveyed his work. "You understand this isn't to code. If word of these boards gets to the administration, they'll demand they come down."

Sam nodded as Henry stopped and sniffed, moved down a few feet, and sniffed again.

"Perhaps you can put on the work forms that they are to keep pests out until new windows arrive." Looked at in a certain light, Frank was a 'pest' though no one on the faculty would likely back him on that assessment.

"I'm not sure what you've gotten yourself into, but I sure hope it's worth blockading yourself in here." Shane wheeled the hand truck out into the hallway. "Good luck."

What had he gotten himself into? Direct, ongoing hostilities with a boy-man who was a living nightmare. Frank would stop at nothing to get his hands on the laptop, he'd made that much clear.

Sam sprayed the door's hinges with water. In time they'd squeak and he needed that last-ditch level of warning. He tied the handles with a stretch of para cord then kicked the door as hard as he could. It didn't budge. Enclosed in his new bunker Sam sat on his cot and scratched Henry's head. "Let's hope that holds. I wouldn't put it past Frank to murder us in our sleep after today's fiasco."

CHAPTER FOURTEEN

RON FROBISHER. SOUTHAMPTON DOCKS, ENGLAND.

Ron Frobisher knew a thing or two about seaworthiness and rust buckets; enough to know that *The Fairwinds*, which bobbed and swayed in the harbor, was a primo example of a ship that should have been scrapped some time before the Norman Invasion. The hull had been treated to a lick of paint, but nothing could disguise the fact that she was on her last legs. Too bad he had to transport live cargo from Southampton to Nigeria with strict instructions not to allow anyone to inspect, open, or otherwise tamper with his crates.

He had three hours to kill before his cargo arrived and no one to kill it with. Being a port town, Southampton had its pleasure palaces and dens of iniquity, but he had questions about his mandate and the WIFI at the closest pub had answers.

The pub was humming, even though it was only half past twelve.

People weren't just there for a "spot of lunch" as they called it, they were downing pints like beer was going out of fashion. There were two gargantuan TVs hanging either end of the bar, a darts board, and a jukebox, all of them sporting clusters of drinkers. No one was going to pay a blind bit of attention to him. They were plenty busy playing darts or watching their beloved footie and the less-loved, but much talked about news.

Arsenal Football Club was up two-nil. The Stock Exchange had taken a tumble. There'd been another mass shooting at a school in Oklahoma. Lady Gaga's Foundation had shelled out a cool million to help survivors. California was on fire. Again. And in the *Things That Never Happen Here* section of the broadcast, there were cicadas on the rampage in Eastern Illinois.

He'd been so wrapped up in his own mission, he hadn't paid much attention to the reports that were flooding the newsrooms. America was falling apart, fast. Ron waited at the back of the bar, his eyes fixed on the TV. What was that old saying, "Where New York goes, there goes the world?" Well, the cicadas hadn't gotten that far east, but there was more than one swarm, the newscaster said, "and in a year we weren't expecting them to emerge." The map that filled the screen showed the swarms, rising and massing, spreading over more and more land. If Ron was good at anything, it was tracking patterns. The States was about to experience the mother of all societal collapses and he needed to be far, far from that noise if he was going to cash his checks. And he had every intention of doing just that; keep his head down, eyes on the mission, and transport his—ah, shoot, there might be a connection; that would suck—his *bug* to Africa.

The guy in front of him—tatts, shaved head, nose that had been broken more than once—ordered a pint of Telford Ale and a whiskey chaser and proceeded to drop the shot into the ale creating what they affectionately called "a boilermaker." Should've been The Troublemaker, but no one had consulted Ron. He took a step away from the drinker and backed into a gaggle of secretaries, apologized, and turned back to the bar in time to be served.

"What can I get you, my love?" Weird how English barmaids

called everyone 'love.' Ron had learned it meant exactly the same as her low-cut top and bleach-blonde hair: nothing. She was in the business of making people feel "comfortable" and "at home" and he was in the business of parting with as much money as the pub would take.

"Pint of your best bitter and two packets of prawn cocktail crisps." He hadn't taken to many English 'delicacies'—there wasn't much in the national cuisine to like—but their synthetic not-at-all-prawn-like potato chips hit some taste bud that had been cultivated during his youth: much salt, some oil, and no vegetables. He fished a twenty pound note out of his pocket and left the change on the bar. The British might not tip their staff, but that didn't mean he had to stoop to their barbaric ways.

Ron tucked his laptop under his arm. A pint of bitter in one hand and his chips in the other he slipped into the corner booth, kept his back to the wall and the door in his line of sight, and fired up his lappie. Countess Ann Pilkington had been in the news often enough that the web was littered with features and exposés. For anyone who cared about these things, Ann was a Capricorn who liked fine dining, cultured pearls, and terriers. That crock of nonsense had been cobbled together by her PR team. She loathed dogs, preferred highly polished gems, and subsisted on a strict diet of organic lettuce and imported prosciutto.

Ron zoomed through the carefully cultivated image Lady Pilkington's people had curated for her and dug into the company's profile. With any luck, some dumb plonker—the English had such colorful ways of insulting each other—would have gone to town describing this new and/or exciting venture, thereby showing their hand.

Pilkington Industries International, LP (PIIL) was a "highly diversified consumer goods company, with interests in..." He skipped over the corporate speak: leadership brands, net profits, global business units, and zoomed in on the "social welfare programs." Softer target, less scrutiny, the place where he was going to find Ann's Achilles. If there was funny money being shuffled from pillar to post or shady deals that involved a shipload of glowworms—if in fact that's what he was escorting overseas—it was going to be funneled through one of the do-gooder programs.

PIIL had partnered with *Habitation for Humans*, *The Children's Growth Fund*, and *Hunger Out*. He cross referenced 'Habitation' with 'glowworms' and 'Nigeria' but the search terms netted him over five million hits. He wasn't going to find what he was looking for in that informational haystack. The Growth Fund netted a similarly broad set of results. Substituting 'Lagos' for 'Nigeria' didn't help narrow his search. He took a slug of his beer. Ah, the English and their warm brew. He wasn't going to miss it.

The next hour was a slog, accompanied by both packets of crisps, as he scoured the web for clues as to what he had gotten himself mixed up in. The normal channels were useless, all fluff and no substance. If PIIL had moved into pharmaceuticals or medical imaging, it wasn't showing up in any of their front-facing material.

Ron did an inventory of the bar. It paid to track your surroundings. The three secretaries had moved to a table and were on their second bottle of bubbly, though the woman he'd almost barreled over had a small glass of orange juice rather than a flute of champagne. Baby shower maybe? Or promotion? The barmaid was idling by the hatch to the kitchen chatting to the cook. The lunch crowd had thinned out, but there were a couple of card carrying members of the 'flat cap and elbow patch' crowd propping up the bar. Ron had learned to read the English by their clothing. The army-green coats with leather elbows and epaulets were worn by the "country" set, which was code for "monied" people. There were four of them huddled around their table, so deep in conversation their glasses stood empty. Not something you often saw in a pub. The occasional word drifted his way. "Cicadas" got top billing, but the huddle also covered "infernos" "food shortages" "gas hikes" "riots" and "gun culture." They left no stone unturned as they touted the vast superiority of the "English way" over their "special cousins, over the sea." Ron didn't join in, of course. He was to remain invisible. But if he'd been a regular punter—a civilian, rather than a specialist for hire— he'd have challenged them to consider what they'd do if their world fell to pieces around their ears and their neighbors came looking for what wasn't theirs. With any luck they'd never know, but he was sure glad to be armed and ready to defend himself.

The guy with the sleeve tattoo had amassed a stunning array of empties and was arguing with the newscaster about the football results. Apart from the ravages of fire and bugs back in his homeland, it was an average afternoon in an English pub.

Satisfied that no one was watching him, Ron dug down into PILL's holdings. Parent company. Subsidiaries. Offshore... *That's more like it.* There was no way the Pilkingtons were going to pay English taxes. He peeled layer after layer of shell companies away from each other until he was left looking at a footnote of a footnote in an appendix of an offering brochure which mentioned "*Bio Better, LP.*"

"Gotcha." Bio business. Bugs were bio. He'd hit gold. He downed the end of his pint and ambled over to the bar. He needed some light lubrication for the next round of investigation. It was going to involve phone calls and emails and some fancy tapdancing as he winkled information out of people who weren't supposed to comment. Another half pint wouldn't hurt the operation.

"Same again, my lovely?" The barmaid was already pulling the pint so he didn't correct her. "What are you doing here, then? I can hear an accent. Business or pleasure?"

Ron didn't have an accent. He was the most middle-America, no-drawl, no-twang speaker he knew. She was the one with the accent. "Pleasure." Lying came easily, which was good in his line of work.

"Been to Winchester yet? The cathedral's lovely."

"Did the Cathedral, then took the wife to see Jane Austen's ancestral home." British people went soft in the head when Americans talked up their literary heritage. "She just loves that Regency drama."

The blonde slid his pint across the bar. "I tried watching that. Bit snooty if you ask me. Nothing ever happened. But if it keeps Her Indoors happy, let her ogle Mr. Darcy all she likes, eh?"

Her Indoors was slang for "wife." Ron had learned to navigate their impossible version of English during his many trips to their fair isle. "She said she could die happy once she'd walked the halls of Chawton House." He was enjoying the fabrication. He'd never been close to the East Hampshire village of Chawton, where Jane Austen's fans made their pilgrimage, but there wasn't an English landmark he hadn't studied for times just like this one when he needed to be anyone other than Ron Frobisher, Fixer to the Rich.

"She's lucky to have you." The barmaid held out his change. "My old man won't even watch EastEnders with me."

"Keep it." He turned as the barmaid tucked the bills into her bra.

"Mr. Jane Austen Man?" The barmaid lobbed a bag of crisps at him. "On the house. For being good to your lady."

She was too loud and drew too much attention, but Ron laughed it off as he collected the bag of chips from under his chair. "Thank you, kindly."

The bar went back to its convivial hum and Ron returned to his inquiries. *Bio Better* had produced a bona-fide Private Placement Memorandum, grade one, which the Securities and Exchange Commission required when you were fundraising. The Pilkington Corporation had gone to America with the begging bowl. Raising money to develop "an unlimited protein source, which can be harvested and housed in..." He snapped open his free bag of crisps. 'Protein source?' That wasn't what he'd been expecting. Ann had stressed that she was using the glowworms for medical research. Then again, his radar had told him she wasn't being entirely forth-coming. If her company had developed a new source of protein there was every reason to keep that under wraps. Competition was fierce in the food industry. She'd want to be first to market to be sure of satu-ration and market domination.

A couple of taps in his search bar led him to the conclusion that glowworms weren't edible. They had a toxin they used to dissolve their prey, which sounded like a solid no on the yummy front. Then again, he wasn't entirely convinced his cargo was made up of glow-worms. The MRI had shown a beetle with a fatter thorax than your average glowworm. There were a million reasons Ann would lie about what he was transporting, but none of them were making themselves known to him. He went back to the only lead he'd uncovered.

The appendix of the Private Placement Memorandum was unlike any legal document he'd perused. There were names, dates, even references to 'batch records.' He scrolled back to make sure this was one of Ann's companies. It didn't seem like the kind of information she'd want out there. There'd be a trail of lawyerly breadcrumbs. Lawyers were smart about burying their clients' data, but not so egoless they didn't put their stamp on their own work. Edgar Allen, Esq. was listed as the attorney of record. A quick hop to Allen's website showed the man boasting of his recent work for "a multinational, with household brand-name recognition." His headshot had been replaced with a picture of him shaking hands with none other than Jeremy Kobler, Attorney to Ann Pilkington.

"She should hire me to show her what idiots these guys are. If I can find this in less than two hours, anyone can." Well, not anyone, but for a firm that was hellbent on protecting its own intellectual property, that was some sloppy work by the attorneys.

He sipped his too-warm beer and went back to the Placement Memorandum. For an investment of a measly two-hundred million dollars, you too could be in on the ground floor of *Bio Better* and "help heal the planet." Cool. How?

Ron dialed Edgar Allen Esquire's office. "Mr. Allen, please?"

The receptionist did the usual gatekeeping. Mr. Allen wasn't available at present. Who was calling. Might she take a number?

"I'm calling on behalf of Oblen & Spritz." He waited for the customary snap to attention. No one who walked in their circles wouldn't know who Michael Oblen was. The investment guru's pockets were deep and his appetite for risk deeper. If Mr. Allen's secretary was properly briefed she'd put Ron through to her boss right away.

"One moment, Mr...?" She trailed off, but Ron didn't fill the gap.

The jukebox blasted the unmistakable intro to *Come on, Eileen,* and Ron hung up. He'd gotten the info he wanted. The fact that she'd been willing to put him through that fast meant Mr. Allen was still raising money for *Bio Better*. He pushed his beer away from his laptop. Where to look next? The batch records. They'd have step-by-step instructions for testing supplies, raw materials, samples, products and the corresponding tasks and activities. If he could look at that data he'd know what *Bio Better* was hawking. The fact that such documents were mentioned in an offering memorandum was remarkable. It'd be too much to ask to find them online.

Seven pages of searching later, and no batch documents to be found, he decided to take a shortcut. Mr. Allen's website listed no email addresses, but the Contact Us button led to a form. His laptop would bounce the message off a proxy server in Lithuania; he was untraceable. He filled out the form, requesting the *Bio Better* brochure and "all relevant documents" and signed himself 'J. P. Losta, Private Secretary to M. Oblen.' If they were even half-way decent at their jobs they'd send him what he asked for in double time.

Meanwhile, he needed to drum up another lead. He scoured the peculiar Memorandum, digging for data. The protein source kept nagging at his brain. It was such a long shot he almost didn't plug in the search terms, but until he heard back from Mr. Allen, Esq., he was swinging in the wind.

"Dang!" Turned out, insects weren't just edible, they were an ecological dream-come-true. They thrived on organic waste which, according to the study by the University of Copenhagen, meant farmers would be able to cut back on those crops used to feed cows and pigs and other methane-producing nightmares. The familiar excitement of finding the clue that unraveled the mystery built in his gut. This was what it was all about.

He'd known about the Romans and their honey-covered ants, but it turned out crickets, locust, worms, and cicadas all graced the menus in countries as far flung as the Netherlands and Ghana. There were chocolate covered ants (minty), silkworm soup (nutritious), and salt-boiled larvae (gross). He couldn't help it, all the data in the world didn't make crunching crickets sound appealing. Then again, he had just downed three packets of "prawn cocktail flavored" crisps. What were prawns if not the cockroaches of the sea?

"You sly dog, Ann." He had to hand it to her, she never rested on her laurels. If she was exporting beetles to Africa to cultivate as a new protein source, more power to her.

His email pinged. As predicted, Mr. Allen's assistant or associate had forwarded the brochure faster than you could say spit. The jukebox whirred and clicked as it selected another record but in that auditory gap Ron felt the room tilt and shift. Gone was the gentle rumble of Englishmen and women getting buzzed in the afternoon, replaced by unmistakable sounds of trouble: a low, pleading grumble and a high-pitched whine. Tatts-guy had moved on from slamming boilermakers and was hassling the secretaries who'd dropped into a defensive formation to keep him from their friend.

"I didn't mean anything by it." Given how much booze he'd put away it was a wonder Tatts could talk at all. If it hadn't been for the slight stagger and the arm on the bar to steady himself, Ron would have thought the man barely intoxicated. "Just asked her for a friendly little peck on the cheek."

"Back off, Bert." The blonde barmaid's smile had been replaced with a face of steel. "She's not interested."

Ron closed his laptop and shifted his half-finished beer out of the way. He kept his shoulders down, but his spine up, ready for whatever happened next. He didn't like to brawl in public, but he wasn't going to sit back while some lout harassed the women.

Bert lunged for the secretarial scrum. He never saw the handbag coming. It was just a couple of kilos shy of being a suitcase and the thwack it landed sent him reeling. "Son of a bitch." He came back at his assailant, blood streaming from his temple and both fists flying. The handbag was now a punching bag, but the woman wielding it was no match for the bruiser who was pummeling her.

Ron leapt between them, jabbing Bert's face with precision hits. One of the great things about thumping someone in the nose is the automatic reflex of the lacrimal glands. A punch to that lump of cartilage makes you cry and men like Bert would rather die than be caught crying in public.

Bert's blood leaked through his fingers and dripped onto his shirt. "Didn't mean nothing by it..." His whine was no less annoying than it had been the first time. Ron grabbed him by the scruff of his sweater and threw him out the front door, which gesture was greeted by a warm round of applause.

"Let me buy you a pint." The woman who'd been drinking orange juice already had her purse out. "As a thank you."

Ron waved her away, tucking his laptop under his arm. "No need." He elbowed the door open. "I'm late. Gotta go."

She followed him out of the pub and onto the street. "Thank you all the same, Mr...?"

There was no reason to withhold his name. He was never going to see her again. "Ron. Ron Frobisher."

"I'm in your debt, Mr. Frobisher. The world needs more good men like you."

It didn't, but she didn't need to know that. He grinned and trotted back to the harbor where the floating tomb loomed over the dock.

CHAPTER FIFTEEN

DR. DIANA STEWART. LINCOLN, NEBRASKA.

It felt like a betrayal, leaving Jesse with Jane, even for the half hour it would take for her meeting with Dan. She watched Samantha and Eli run ahead into the little diner across from the Capitol. "You have my cell number, right?" She had promised to stay with him, but Jane had two children of her own; it was only sensible to leave him with her.

Jane moved into the front seat to be next to Jesse. "He's okay, Diana. He'll just sleep for a while now. He won't wake up till well after you get back."

"But if he does, call me. The meeting can wait. And tell him—"

"He won't. Not so soon after his meds." Jane ushered her away. "Now go! You'll be late."

Diana went to the back of the truck and opened the trunk. She reached for her samples and stopped. Better to leave them here. If it looked like Dan would actually take them to Victor—someone she outright trusted—she could always come back. But she didn't trust Dan to do so and she didn't want to risk him taking them from her if

—she slammed the trunk shut—if Dan was more dangerous than the asshole she'd always thought he was.

The Capitol building was on the other side of the plaza, and she was there at 4 p.m. sharp. She spent ten minutes pacing back and forth by the entrance. Was meeting him a stupid idea? Maybe. But she needed Dan's laptop to get her research back. Otherwise, she and Sam would be starting from scratch on the cicadas—and she'd have nothing to defend herself with when Dan threw her to the wolves.

Her boss didn't turn up for another ten minutes, and then it was in the company of his bodyguard, Aaron.

"Diana." Dan drank the last of his coffee and lobbed the cup into the trashcan. "Walk with me. I'm sure you know Aaron—my driver's sick so he's doing chauffeur duty today."

She did and was not keen to know him any further. He had about as much compassion as a rattlesnake. "Aaron."

"Doctor Stewart." He always had a speculative glint in his eye, as if he was judging his opposition and finding them far outmatched. She suppressed a shudder.

Instead of going back into the Capitol, Dan led the way down the road and around the block. "We have use of the business suite in the hotel here. It has better facilities than that ramshackle old place we used to use for meetings."

Up on the third floor, Dan let them into the suite of offices and conference rooms with a keycard. The office doors were frosted glass, the lower half clear; surely this was public enough to be safe? Might have been if that's where they stopped, but the room marked 'Victor Matreus' was at the far end of the corridor, opposite the bathroom and next to an empty conference room. Shoot. No one was working at that end of the corridor. She was careful to leave the door ajar.

Dan leaned on the windowsill. "This must've been very traumatic." Fake smile, fake interest, the man didn't give a good goddam how she was, but she smiled and played along. "How are you holding up?"

She took a seat at the table. "I'm exhausted. I've been running ever since it happened. The town was in chaos. People are dead and injured. The police are overwhelmed, and the hospital—"

"Tell me about the cicadas." He wandered over to the doorway, glanced up and down the corridor, and then shut the door. Aaron took up his position in front of it.

Great. The small talk was over. "They erupted out of nowhere—must have been in the woods. The swarm was enormous. It covered all of Jonah's field. I don't know how far behind us it stretched. Jesse and I only just made it into the truck, and we were there for some time before they calmed down."

"And Jonah?"

"Jonah was in the field when they struck. The swarm enveloped him and he collapsed. By the time they'd passed, his face was massively blistered and he was dead."

Dan paced. "That sounds like an allergic reaction to me; nothing to do with Feedit."

"Jesse squashed a bug that got into the truck. He had a very similar reaction on his hands and face. He survived the encounter, but if there had been more than one cicada, I don't think he'd still be alive now."

Dan stopped by the door again. "Jesse and Jonah are related. If Jonah had a strong allergic reaction, it's very likely that his son would."

"But he wasn't the only victim, Dan. The swarm caused carnage in Watseka. There were dead and dying all over the place. Most were blistered—they can't all be allergic reactions. A woman died holding her baby." She couldn't get the rest of the story out. The woman had barely had a scratch on her. Certainly, none of the welts she'd seen on Jonah. Was there something else in play?

Dan's body stiffened. "You're barking up the wrong tree, Diana. You can't drag the company's name into the headlines. Besides, what would they be allergic to? People have been handling cicadas for years with no bad effects."

Diana stopped listening. What about the teen's burned hand in Watseka? There had been very few cicadas on the ground there. The difference was clear: the farm was a food source, but there was little enough for them to eat in Watseka so most of them had passed overhead without landing.

And there had been that smeared film on the car's door handle.

She hadn't seen insects landing on the cars, but there could have been something—poison?—falling out of the air. If the substance that caused the damage was both on the bodies of the cicadas and in the air, that would explain the strength of Jonah's reaction. If he'd inhaled the toxin as well as being covered in it when the cicadas touched his skin, he would have had a double dose. That would explain why he'd gone down so hard and fast. "There must be something about it that isn't directly transmissible via touch, some sort of airborne toxin. And it wouldn't be so bad if it were just a handful of insects, but when the swarm comes over and all of them release it in a cloud, it would be lethal. Of course!" Uh oh. She hadn't meant to say that out loud.

Dan's posture relaxed, as if she'd given him the answer he wanted. He went to the desk by the door.

"You were close to Dr. Greenbaum, weren't you?" Dan lifted his briefcase onto the desk and clicked the locks open.

Aaron shifted his weight forward as if ready for action.

"Ed Greenbaum?" Diana didn't like how casually he had thrown that out. Mentioning her previous boss was a hell of a non-sequitur, but Dan spoke as if it followed on. "Not until nearly the end. We played chess at lunch sometimes. He said it cleared his mind." They were both between her and the door now, and an electrical charge of nervousness gathered between them.

Dan passed a small black case to Aaron, who turned and opened it on the desk behind him. Out of sight, and it wasn't accidental.

"You played often?"

"In the last few weeks, yes. He had some problem he was trying to distract himself from..." *Oh... Oh crap.* She didn't like where this was going, not one bit. She clutched at her abdomen. "I'm sorry, can you excuse me for a moment?" She nodded at the bathroom door as she stood. "I'll be back shortly. Women's problems."

Dan fell back a pace, his face a mask of disgust. "TMI, Diana."

She hurried past Aaron into the executive bathroom across the corridor and shut the door, locking it behind her. Backing past the shower stall to the far wall, she frantically assembled the pieces of information she'd just uncovered. "Ed... What did you get us into?"

Her head pounded. The room was humid and over-warm, the window and mirror steamed up. She ran a paper towel under the faucet, nearly slipping on the wet floor by the shower, and passed it across her face. The shock of cold helped her think through her nervousness.

Ed Greenbaum had been working on the long-term use of Feedit. He discovered something and was worried about how Dan would react. He'd suffered a fatal heart attack shortly thereafter. Had Dan killed Ed over their Feedit problem? A thrill of fear ran down her spine.

Another piece of the puzzle fell into place: Aaron. Dan didn't need a bodyguard for a simple meeting, and they normally used local drivers who knew the roads. But Dan wasn't the sort to get his hands dirty. And from the quiet clink she'd heard, what Aaron had been manipulating so carefully was glass, maybe a vial of some kind.

"Time for me to have my very own heart attack, maybe?" Her whisper was lost in the sound of the water in the sink circling the drain. If she disappeared, Jesse would be all alone. She had to get out, and quickly. They'd be watching for her to come out of the bath-room, and even if she got out, the keycard door was noisy and opened so slowly that they'd catch her before she could get to the stairwell. There had to be another way. There had to.

She dropped the paper towel in the trash and eased the window open as quietly as she could. They were on the third floor, but the window led out onto the open top floor of the parking garage. She'd have to jump across a gap of a couple of feet to get to that roof then drop down six feet to the garage below. It could be done if you were desperate enough, and the door to the stairs was just across the expanse of cars but it was risky. If she broke her ankle she was done for.

She fumbled in the pockets of her combat trousers pulling out her Swiss Army knife, with its various screwdrivers; and something else. The cigarette lighter. An idea began to form as she quickly rummaged through the bathroom for anything she could use. Oppo-site the cramped shower cubicle wedged in behind the door there was a shelf of folded towels. Someone had left a can of deodorant and a baseball hat. It would have to suffice; there were no other options.

A bang on the door made her jump. Dan. "You're stalling. It won't help you. Come out!"

"I won't be long." Flicking the screwdriver out of the Swiss Army knife, she worked manically to unscrew the retaining bolts so that she could open the window, but the window was covered in condensation which made the knife difficult to grip.

"We don't have time for this, Diana." He was losing the fake casual tone.

She redoubled her efforts, but the knife slipped out of her hand and fell to the floor, clanking on the tiles.

"Aaron, get in there! She's up to something." The first thud hit the flimsy door just as Diana managed to crack the window open.

She shoved at the frame with all the strength of desperation, but the top was higher than she could reach. She dropped an industrial-sized toilet roll on the floor and used it as a step to hike herself up onto the sill. Sitting on the damp ledge, she could reach the loosened top part of the window. She gave it a vicious shove. Caught by the rising wind, the window and its frame came free and toppled outward, but the screw was caught in her sleeve. She was dragged half out of the window, and only just grabbed at the walls around her in time to avoid falling out after it. The frame jolted to a stop, swinging from the tough material and she could not get enough purchase on the slippery windowsill to pull herself back in.

Aaron slammed into the door again, and the wood around the lock cracked and splintered, but—thank goodness—didn't outright give way.

She slid another inch out over a two floor drop onto concrete, but her foot clanked on the towel rail on the wall by the window. Out of options, she hooked her feet into it and freed a hand to unbutton her coat. The buttons were stiff and under pressure from the weight of the window, but in a fit of terror she ripped them free and wriggled out of the coat. The window plummeted to the ground below and shattered with a crash, the coat fluttering down after it.

"She's getting away!" Dan yelled. "On my count!" With a shower of splinters, the lock broke. The door slammed open and they erupted into the bathroom. "Get out there and catch her!"

"Thought she was a friggin' scientist, not an acrobat." Aaron jumped down onto the parking garage, landing with a thud.

"I'll head her off at the ground floor!" There was a beep as Dan swiped his way out of the business suite, fading thuds as he sprinted along the corridor to the stairs. And then silence.

Heart beating hard, Diana peered out from behind the shower curtain. All clear. She pushed at the bathroom door currently masking the shower and stepped out. She yanked an armful of toilet paper free from the roll and heaped it on a towel in the shower. Dan could return at any moment, and it was hard not to freeze but she had to get back to Jesse.

She grabbed the discarded aerosol deodorant. Her hands were shaking so badly it took a couple of tries to spark up the lighter, but once lit, she brought the spray of deodorant across the flame. It flared into a plume of fire which she used to light the toilet paper. Then she aimed it under the smoke detector. Nothing happened for a moment and terror slid like ice down her back. What if it didn't work?

She grabbed the discarded baseball cap and ran into the office as the alarms went off. The siren blared so loudly it was physically painful in the echoing confines of the tiny space.

Dan had left his briefcase in the office, along with his laptop. She slammed it shut and dashed out to join the throng of people shuffling into the stairwell with the rest of the hotel guests. As she reached the first landing, she saw Dan on the flight below.

"This is her doing!" he screamed into his phone. "Get back here and find her!" He turned to run up and Diana hunched over, hoping the crowded stairs were busy enough that he wouldn't see her.

A little girl in front of Diana stumbled, and as Dan passed, Diana bent down, making a show of helping the child up. "Are you okay, sweetheart?"

The little girl, wide-eyed, clung to the mother who smiled briefly. "Thank you."

Dan continued to shove his way up the wide stairwell back to the office floor. Once he found his briefcase had gone, he'd be right back. She had to get away now. Reaching the next flight of stairs, she took her phone out and dialed.

"Hello? Diana? Did it go okay?" Jane asked. "What on earth is that noise?"

"Trouble. Get everyone in the truck, wait on the road with the engine going. I may not be alone." She kept an eye out for Dan.

"Are you okay?"

"Not if they catch me. There's Aaron! I'll be there in ten. Be ready!"

"But—!" Jane's objection was drowned in the blare of the fire alarm repeater on the landing, but Diana didn't have time to listen. She ended the call as she reached the ground floor and scanned for the way out.

Aaron was coming down from the third floor, his eyes fixed on Diana.

"Aaron, she's gone!" Dan came back into the stairwell from the office suite, his face grim.

"There!" Aaron pointed.

Dan swore, and forced a way through the crowd. Diana's heart battered at her ribs. She scanned the atrium, looking for the quickest way out. A shriek from above; a woman dangled from the handrail, those around her trying to pull her back up. Dan ignored them and shoved his way on.

There! The main exit was thronged but an employee was opening a fire door at the side. Diana sprinted out and toward the Capitol building, Dan's briefcase still in hand. She didn't know if they would dare grab her off the street in broad daylight, but with the fire engines just starting to arrive there was enough chaos that they might try. Her ears were still buzzing from the fire alarms in the stairwell and her side was clenched vice-tight in a stitch, but she didn't dare to slow. She staggered on, her breath catching in her throat.

"There! Hurry!" Aaron's voice was audible even through the mishmash of screams and sirens. He must be close behind.

She was nearly at her truck but there was no way she'd get away before they got there. Jane was standing, anxious, by the driver's side door. Diana swerved around the corner and, while out of sight of her pursuers, tossed the briefcase into a bush. She'd need it later, and if they caught her, she could maybe use it as a bargaining chip to buy herself some time. But she would not risk Jesse, or Jane and her kids, falling into the hands of these thugs. She had to get rid of them and circle back. She risked a panicked glance back; Aaron was closing on her.

Anxious that he would ignore the pregnant lady in the parking lot, she dodged through the stationary traffic, cutting past the Capitol again. Ahead of her, tourists wandered in a thick stream across the road from their coach toward the Capitol. One man paused to say something to those behind him, and in that instant, there was a gap.

Ducking through it, she sprinted to an alleyway on the other side of the square. Judging by the shouts and screams, Aaron had gotten tangled up in the tourists.

She fled down the alley, looking desperately for a place to hide while Aaron was out of sight. She was painfully short of breath, gasping in great sobs. There! Behind the dumpster, stink or no stink! But as she skidded to a stop on the greasy tarmac, her ankle turned on a greasy food wrapper and she fell. She slammed to the ground, hitting her head hard. Everything went white for a moment. She blinked, trying to gather her scattered wits.

After a long, suffocating moment, she managed to force a breath into her lungs, and then another. But when she rolled to get to her feet, Aaron was standing over her.

"Stay down." He reached into his pocket—for a moment she was afraid he was going for a knife – and pulled out his phone. "She's here, boss. Yeah, two streets over, alleyway along the side of the sports store." He ended the call. "You're going to regret that, lady."

Diana sat up, dazed, and put a hand to the side of her head. It stung and blood was trickling down her face. That bloody fire alarm had made her ears screech and buzz as if she had her own personal swarm of cicadas and the only thought she could keep hold of was that she was in deep trouble. She was too dizzy to get up and worse, she was hidden from the main street by the dumpsters. If things went bad, there'd be no witnesses unless someone came out of the emergency door of the sports store, and what were the odds of two fire alarms in ten minutes? She needed to think, and quickly, if she wanted to get out of there unhurt.

"There you are." Dan appeared at the end of the alleyway. "You think you're so clever, and yet here you are, rolling in the gutter. Finally found your rightful place, eh?" He'd never liked her, she knew that, but the sheer malice in his voice was terrifying.

Aaron pulled her to her feet, but her balance wasn't right, and she had to grab at the dumpster to stay upright.

"What did you do with my briefcase?" Dan nodded to Aaron who slapped her face, hard.

She staggered backward, falling against the wall with a jolt that made the buzzing in her ears even louder.

"What did you do with it, bitch? Victor isn't going to save you now. There are no special favors left, and you aren't the golden girl anymore. You're a sad ugly middle-aged spinster with no life and no family who is taking up a job that a real scientist could be doing. What did you do with the briefcase?"

Her brain was clearing now. "I dropped it. I couldn't keep hold of it in the crowd."

He strode forward, standing nose to nose with her. "That's inconvenient. More than inconvenient. Not least for you..." The softness of his voice was somehow more sinister than the yelling. "But who's going to notice another dead body in a dumpster?"

He lunged forward and shoved her to the ground. She rolled, trying to scramble away, but he pinned her down on her belly. His foot came down on the back of her neck.

She'd fallen in a pool of filth. She strained away from it but couldn't get her arms under her and had to twist her head to the side, trying to get it out of the water.

He laughed. "Oh, this is sweet. Let's make it last, eh?" He pressed down harder and harder, forcing her down an inch at a time.

Her head was half underwater, the puddle cold against her ear, then her cheek. She shut her eyes against the gritty filth, gasping as the water reached her chin. Her mouth was flooded by the harsh metallic taste. She coughed and spat, trying desperately to fight her way out of it, but she could not get any leverage to push herself up and he was pressing down more and more with each passing moment.

The liquid reached the edge of her nostrils and she flailed her legs, trying to throw him off-balance, but in vain. He was going to drown her and there was nothing she could do about it. She'd failed Jesse so badly. But as water stung her nasal passages and there was no more breath to be had, the pressure on her neck eased. She wriggled to one side, coughing and spluttering, tears running down her face as the stinking mud from the puddle ran from her hair and clothes.

Dan stood back. "I'll savor this moment for a long time, Diana, a long time. You were never better than me, whatever Victor told you. And now everyone can see just how pathetic you are." Dan gave her one last kick as she curled limply half-in and half-out of the water. "Aaron, perhaps you'd see to this for me? Don't want to ruin my shoes. They're my favorite pair."

Aaron took off his signet ring and dropped it in his pocket. "My pleasure, Boss. My pleasure."

CHAPTER SIXTEEN

**ANAYELI ALFARO. NEAR LAND PARK. SACRA-
MENTO, CALIFORNIA.**

It had taken Anayeli longer to get to Sid's house than she'd expected
—just like everything else had so far—but relief washed through her
as she pulled into the narrow driveway in front of his fully restored
1920s bungalow. It was the kind of house she'd always envied—with
hardwood floors and built-in cabinets and fancy glass doorknobs, the
exact opposite of her shoddily constructed, slap-dash duplex, where
every fixture was the cheapest possible version available. Even
though his house was modest, it said money. Just like every other
house on the street. The lawns were manicured and green, the trees
were tall and ancient, the cars in the driveways were Volvos and
Lexuses and occasionally BMWs. Her parents' van looked even more
out of place than her own little red hatchback had, the times she'd
come over to take care of Roxy when Frank was on a rare vacation
without the dog.

. . .

"You're going to love Roxy. She's a little black dog like you." Cricket wagged his tail like he understood, even as a pang bolted right through Anayeli's belly. Roxy. Crap. No way she could leave Sid's dog behind, knowing full well that Sid was never coming back. Two dogs. Mama was going to flip.

She knew better than to tell Cricket to stay in the van, so she wasn't surprised this time when he vaulted out practically right on top of her, but her laugh at his leap died in her throat. A woman stood in the doorway of the open garage across the narrow street, holding a banker's box of what looked like fancy china, one gold-rimmed platter sticking out. The house was one of the few on the street that actually had lights on. Probably most everyone else had already evacuated, even though, from what she'd heard on the scanner, there weren't any evacuation orders yet for this part of Sacramento. Rich people had whole-house generators. Rich people with places to go got out early. With all their valuables. Not like her family, who had left nearly everything behind in Madera.

Anayeli lifted her hand and waved to the woman. Like she would if she lived in the neighborhood. Like she belonged. The way she still did every time she saw her own jerk of a neighbor, who hadn't even recognized her at the Corner Market. The woman didn't wave back or offer any kind of acknowledgement or go back to loading boxes into the open hatchback of her Volvo SUV either. Anayeli was the one to turn away first. "We don't have time for staring contests, Cricket."

Roxy was already barking before Anayeli and Cricket even made it up the front steps, her sharp woofs muffled by the heavy, ornate front door. "Hey Roxy! We're here to see you!" She swallowed a lump at the thought of Sid, lying alone in the corridor outside his office. It was the least she could do to take care of Roxy, Queen of My Heart. But when Anayeli keyed in the code for Sid's front door—"Nellie Bly's birthday! Easy to remember!"—nothing happened. She punched it in again, just to be sure. Still nothing. Just a red X on the little screen. She didn't think these fancy door knobs ran on the internet, so it didn't make sense that the code wasn't working. She tried again. Still nothing. The door had to be malfunctioning, because Sid wasn't the kind of guy who went around updating his security codes and passwords on a regular basis. He was the guy who always complained every time the work email system made them choose a new password: "Don't know how they expect me to keep coming up with passwords I can remember." She toed up the doormat, stood on tiptoe to run her fingers along the door frame, picked up the potted hosta next to the door. No spare key.

"Dammit!" She'd have to go around back. Maybe there was a window left a crack open or maybe she could get in the back door. But when she turned to go around the side of the house, the China Box lady had moved off her own property and was standing out on the sidewalk.

"Do you have business here?" The woman's hands weren't on her hips, but they might as well have been.

Anayeli's mouth went dry even though she had every right to be there. Sid wouldn't have minded. Sid would've been glad someone was looking out for his dog. "My boss is working late at the paper. I'm here to take care of his dog. Roxy." If the woman really knew Sid, she'd know his dog's name.

"Ohhhhh. You're the dog walker." It took every ounce of willpower Anayeli had not to roll her eyes. Of course China Box lady could only conceive of someone who looked like her working in the service industry. But it wasn't worth contradicting the woman so she said nothing. The silence stretched a moment past uncomfortable. "What a very strange time to be taking a dog for a walk."

The woman wasn't wrong. Though the tall oak and sycamore trees in the neighborhood obscured it to some degree, nothing could hide that the air quality kept getting worse—people's lives, people's dreams, incinerated, turned to the fine particles the living were forced to breathe.

"And you don't seem to have the key," China Box lady took a step closer, down off the curb, as if she might cross the street to confront Anayeli. "What's your name?" What a stupid question. A real criminal would just lie.

"Sid asked me to come pick up Roxy and take her to his office. In case he has to evacuate." Anayeli lowered her good hand down, put a finger under Cricket's collar. She doubted the woman could hear it, but the dog was letting out a constant low rumbling growl.

The word evacuate did something to the woman's face and since Anayeli was already lying, she figured a little more embellishment wouldn't hurt. She needed this woman off her case so she could get on with what she'd come here to do—get food and supplies for her family—and get the hell home. She took a gamble. "Heard on the radio they're issuing new evacuation orders." It was true, so far as it went. On the scanner evacuations had been announced for areas surrounding Hedge Avenue. Well away from Land Park. And this was the nice part of town. No doubt fire crews would work harder to protect it than her run-down, low-rent neighborhood. Maybe she should have brought her family here.

"Oh!" The woman wavered on the curb for a moment, as if she couldn't decide whether to keep questioning Anayeli or to run back inside to pack another box of family heirlooms. "Well. In that case— What did you say your name was?"

She gave China Box Lady the equivalent of nothing. "Ana."

"Well, goodnight Ana. Stay safe." There was nothing in the woman's voice, no warmth, to indicate she actually cared one bit if Anayeli stayed safe.

As soon as the woman's back was turned, Anayeli was on the brick path around the side of the house. Sid's back door was one of those cute paned French doors she'd always half-wanted. Half, because all that glass wasn't safe. She grabbed one of the cushions off the Adirondack patio chair, held it to the door with her injured hand and slammed her good fist into it. It made a terrible thudding noise that brought Roxy skidding and barking from the front of the house, but the glass didn't break.

Anayeli looked around. Sid was entirely too tidy. There was nothing to hand— no gardening implements lying about, no decorative rocks—

She ran back to the brick walkway. On the edge a few of the bricks had buckled and were canted oddly. She pried one up, tearing her fingernails, then ran back to the door. She didn't want to just throw the brick through the window. And she definitely didn't want the sound of breaking glass to alert China Box Lady. She tried the cushion again, wishing she could tell Roxy to stand back, terrified the dog would get cut by the breaking glass. The dog kept barking.

This time, the glass buckled and bowed, but her hands were too small to get a solid grip. Even though it hurt her injured palm, she tried using both hands. She pounded the cushioned brick against the glass once more, and was rewarded when a crack shot across the pane nearest the door knob. After that, it was easy to bash out the glass, reach in, and turn the deadbolt. Exactly why she'd always been leery of French doors.

As soon as the door was open, Roxy was out on the patio, wriggling her entire body with exquisite happiness, her ears pulled back in what Sid called her "happy ears," bouncing around Anayeli as if they were long lost best friends. Only after she'd thoroughly greeted her, did Roxy turn to meet Cricket, and in an instant she'd play-bowed and took off in a full out sprinting circle, her rear low to the ground, while Cricket just barked and barked, as if trying to tell her there was serious business at hand. Which there was.

Anayeli pushed the door open, toeing aside the broken glass, the dogs crashing in after her. It was hard not to think of Sid, but she couldn't. It would only distract her from what she needed to do. The french door opened onto a breakfast nook, and from there it was a straight shot into the kitchen. She went to the pantry first, where Sid stored the dog food. She'd told China Box Lady that she was taking Roxy to Sid, so that was the ruse she was going to keep up. The bag of dog food was half full—enough for both dogs for at least a week—so she filled it the rest of the way with staples. Bags of rice. Dried beans. Split peas. Cans of diced tomatoes, beans, various soups. Stuff Mama had actually put on her list, right in Sid's kitchen. Stuff that would go to waste if she left it here. And a few things—chocolate chips, brownie mix, and powdered hot cocoa mix—that would make her siblings happy.

The whole time she packed, the dogs hovered near her, and by the time the bag was full, Anayeli staggered under its weight. She waddled to the front door and stood on tiptoe to peek out its window. "Okay *perritos*, let's see if the coast is clear." Across the way,

China Box Lady's garage door was closed. "Good. No mean lady in sight."

Anayeli didn't bother trying to keep the dogs in. Neither one was running away, and they lent credence to what she'd told the neighbor. "Stay close you two."

She made two more trips like that—taking out more food rolled up in one of Roxy's beds each time—and both times there was no sign of the woman across the street. For her third trip, she loaded up Roxy's large blue plastic dog crate with perishables from the fridge and freezer—eggs, milk, bacon, avocados! She never would have guessed a single man would have so much food on hand. Except it was Sid and he loved to cook. And feed people. Maybe he even had a life outside of work? She'd never asked. She kept loading the dog crate—frozen tilapia, bison burgers, frozen vegetables galore. "Mama is going to be so happy, *perritos*." She would forgive Anayeli for taking so long.

By the time she was done filling the dog crate, it was a struggle to get it off the ground. Not only was it heavy, but it was cumbersome, and she had to stretch her arms as far as possible to get a decent grip. The plastic dug into her burned palm. Any other time, the pain would have been unbearable. But instead of dropping the crate, she made a mental note to check the bathroom for first aid supplies—triple antibiotic ointment. And the garage! Maybe Sid had a gas can. She would load those last few items into the van and then she would go home. Her family would be well-stocked, the dogs would each have a comfy bed, and they would be safe.

Luckily, on her last trip she'd left the front door open a crack. She bumped it with the crate and it swung wide. The dogs ran out and Anayeli sidled through, the crate so big she couldn't see over it or around it. She banged it into the jamb, jolting the crate hard against her hand, making her cry out and nearly lose her grip. She tried again, easing sideways, and almost dropped the crate again when Cricket let out the sharp single bark she had learned was a warning.

The China Box Lady was back. She stood next to the van, her hands were on her hips, murder in her eyes. Roxy danced around the woman's feet and the lady didn't even take notice.

A stream of curses went through Anayeli's head. "Hi again." She kept her voice cheery and kept moving toward the van. She moved sideways so she could see the woman, the crate's grated gate pressed against Anayeli's chest. The sides were solid. As long as the woman didn't see the food inside, she could still play off that she was taking Roxy to Sid, the dog supplies necessary in case of evacuation.

But the side door to the van was open—not shut, the way she'd left it—and the dogs—such good dogs—had both already jumped inside. Cricket was growling and Roxy had her hackles up and both were giving China Box Lady a hard stare. The woman tapped her foot. She wore pointy-toed leather flats, a pristine cardigan, and pearls. For evacuating. Posh white lady clothes.

"I've called the police." The woman flung a hand toward the open van door. She had unrolled the dog beds, leaving the pilfered food exposed. "And I see now I was right to do so."

In the same instant Anayeli let out a bark of laugh, she understood the fancy clothes. No one would ever believe Anayeli over a woman dressed like that. But it wouldn't matter. "I think the cops are a little busy with more important things right now. I'm just helping out a friend, picking up his dog and supplies." If China Box Lady had looked murderous before, it was nothing compared to the fury that twisted her face as Anayeli stepped forward, fully intending to barge past and continue loading the crate into the van. She couldn't hold it much longer.

"Don't you lie to me, Ana. You're no friend of Sid's." The woman darted forward and grabbed at the crate, hooking her fingers into the slats for a tighter grip. When she yanked, hard, there was no hope. Anayeli's palm ripped open as the plastic scraped its whole length, all the food inside shifting to one side and tipping the crate precariously as she lost her hold. She stumbled headlong toward the woman, her fury a physical force that surged through her limbs as she shoved hard against the crate. It happened so fast. One second the woman was rushing Anayeli and the next the crate was ramming her square in the chest. The impact sent her flying backward, her slippery shoes unable to gain any purchase. The crate landed with a heavy smacking thud that jarred loose the gate, eggs and milk spilling out. The woman stumbled, arms pinwheeling as she struggled to keep her balance on the slight downhill slope of Sid's driveway.

Time slowed, every detail standing out in sharp relief. The cardigan's pearly buttons matching the pearl necklace. The tastefully small gold hoops catching the tiniest shimmer of light sneaking through the murk. The woman's mouth going wide—so many open mouths in one day—a rictus of surprise and anger still darkening her expression as she fell. And then the horrible moment of impact. The woman landed flat on her back with a huffing whoosh, the wind knocked out of her for sure, and a split second later her head hit the concrete. The sound was that of a bat hitting a *piñata* hard enough to break it wide. The result was the same—everything inside spilling out everywhere, splattering across the driveway.

She would have stood there in horror forever, until the cops actually showed up, except a terrible commotion across the street snagged her eye. A man bolted out the door of the house across the way, shouting. He was making animal sounds that shouldn't have carried any meaning at all, filled with pure emotion. Desperation and anguish and something else.

Finally what he was shouting as he ran took shape in her mind. "Betsy! Betsy! Oh my love! Oh Lord, please help her!"

He lifted whatever was in his hands, something long, brown and gunmetal gray. "What have you done?" He leveled it at Anayeli from across the street and kept coming. "What have you done?" The something else in his voice was rage.

In the van, Cricket was barking, barking, barking. There was no time to slam the sliding door shut. The dogs would just have to hang on. She yanked open the driver's side door and was in, the key already in the ignition, her hands shaking as she wrenched it, praying it would start again. The engine roared. The lights on the dash stayed dim. "Get out get out get out!"

She threw the van in reverse, not even bothering to look behind her. She didn't want to know where the man was. The van flew backward, bumping over the curb, the tires screeching as she whipped the car around and hit the accelerator too soon. Something darted in her peripheral vision, disappearing into her blind spot. She checked the rear view mirror and screamed. China Box Lady's husband stood in the center of the street, legs spread wide, shotgun leveled directly at her rearview mirror, grim determination etched on his face. She screamed again and jammed the gas pedal down to the floor. The van lurched and the golden dash light blinked on just as her eardrums throbbed with a resounding report and the back window of the van shattered.

CHAPTER SEVENTEEN

SAM LEARY. BERKELEY, CALIFORNIA.

Warm ick squished between Sam's bare toes. "Oh, man. Come on, Henry! You were outside for almost an hour. Did you really need to drop a bomb right in front of the closet door?"

Henry ducked his head closer to his curled body and woofed.

Sam balanced on one foot, hopped to the closet to grab the paper towels, and sat on the counter. He gagged as he wiped the brown ooze from his toes. *Just what I needed, the stench of animal waste to add to my own unwashed crevices.* Three quarters of the way through the roll, he removed the last of the mess, and held up the paper for Henry to view. "Next time warn me. This was our only roll."

The four legged bomber trotted to the door, whined, and scratched the wood locking them in. "All right, let me look." Sam forced himself to untie the door brace and pry the door open half an inch. It took almost five minutes of listening and spying to decide it was safe. "You win. We'll go out, but when I say we're done, you come with me. Understood?" Henry wagged his tail so hard his entire back wiggled.

Sam settled on the cot and slipped the dirtiest pair of socks he had on, trying to cover the smell. With his shoes tied, he dug a mask out of his bag of supplies, slipped the ball into his pocket, and cracked the door open once more. "I think the faculty have gone home. Let's go." The pair headed down the hall and burst into the hazy afternoon warmth. Shadows grew as the sun followed its allotted path through the sky.

With the encroaching smoke, he was surprised how many groups of students were still gathered on the lawn outside of the building, their tribes segregating in clumps. Didn't they get it? Half the country was being ciccadaed to death while the other half was fleeing the fires. The third half—hahahaha, Cockroach would love that—the third half was panicking and running around like headless chickens as the Bread Basket imploded, along with every other inch of farmland that fed the country. They were going to hell, express edition, but the students of Berkeley were enjoying the ride, with only "a little light smoke" to contend with. Yet. He knew—and they could have known, if they'd bothered to take an interest in the real world—that it was only a matter of time before the sky fell. Literally.

Henry—bless his furry little paws, he didn't and couldn't know what was headed their way—took an interest in an afternoon picnic, the girls all too willing to part with bites of food for his tricks. He ran in circles, rolled over, even tried to play dead in his attempt to please. Giggles erupted from the group as Henry wedged his way between two girls, grabbed a chicken tender, and bounced outside the reach of the diners. He stood on two legs and 'walked' before dropping the snack onto the grass and rolling it around. His excited dance thrilled the audience and they clapped as he chomped down the stolen food.

"I sure hope it's not fried."

The student Sam had met earlier in the day tossed his Frisbee to a friend on the other side of the yard while a couple of members of the fencing team practiced their thrusts and parries to their right. A cyclist passed on the sidewalk, catching Henry's attention.

"Henry get back here, this instant."

The dog chased the cyclist for half a block before stopping at a fire hydrant to mark his territory.

"Henry, no. You go to the bathroom on a tree or bush, not on concrete and metal." Three of the girls from the picnic glanced his way as he ushered the animal away from the red target. They were cute and bubbly, but Sam had no idea how to engage with them; conversations that weren't about work, or better yet science, always veered off in weird directions and he got lost. "Let's take a walk and stretch our legs," he said, to no one in particular. He didn't know if the smoke would be bad for Henry, but the dog had too much energy after being cooped up all day.

Sam took the lead, walking ahead of his companion. The dog meandered through the plants. More than once he emptied his bladder on the unsuspecting objects. Sam made sure that it wasn't on walking paths or something that could rust. Two loops along the main path and the mutt lagged, done marking the boundaries. He trotted at Sam's side, eager for the next adventure.

Sam pulled the ball from his pocket, picked a spot free from pedestrians, and chucked the chewed up toy into the field. Henry perked up and gave chase, pumping his legs so fast it looked as if he wasn't touching the ground. He tumbled about the prey as he bit and jumped, pretending the rubber sphere was alive.

Sam placed two fingers into his mouth, and let out a shrill whistle. The fur-laden missile streaked straight for him. "Man, one day you're not going to stop and you're going to end up trampling me." He picked up the slobbered mess and threw it as hard as he could. Then again. And again. Sam wore his arm out lobbing balls, but Henry was still raring to go. He couldn't help thinking about what life might be like in the coming months. Would they have 'play time' when the supply chain collapsed? Would people look down on him for feeding a dog? Was there any chance they could just be left alone to do their work without having to worry about the end of the world?

As the sun dipped behind the tips of the trees, a red Buick Riviera pulled into the parking lot. The roll-top roof closed and a lady got out of the car, placed her coffee mug on the soft top, and adjusted her skirt. She shut the door and used the mirror to check her lipstick before pulling an N95 mask out of her purse.

Oh man, it's Paula. A whole different kind of trouble. If she spotted him, he'd never get back to the lab. He dropped to one knee and patted Henry's side. "All right, we had our fun. Time to go." The fur ball plastered himself to his leg. One more scratch of the ears, and they jogged back to the Life Sciences building.

Secured in the makeshift bunker, Sam rummaged through the closet and Henry sat at the door, waiting.

"What's your choice of meal tonight, monsieur? Chicken or beef?" He held the bags of kibble at dog height, waiting until Henry scratched at the white cartoon chicken. Dipping the bowl into the bag, he presented the meal and returned to select his own dinner. "One, two, three." He counted from left to right. "Yes, SpaghettiOs." He opened the can with ceremonial zeal and poured the tomato-based slop into a wax lined paper bowl. "Three minutes. Better follow the instructions." The microwave beeped the same time the speakers did.

Removing his meal from the microwave, he scooted his chair over to the computer, spooning a meatball into his mouth on the way.

Another coded message from Cockroach, fantastic.

COCKROACH: The ghost of Salt Lake rises in vengeance.

Sam frowned. Salt Lake? Ghost?

Google displayed a hundred links, and he selected the first page. 'Jean Baptiste, known as the ghost of Salt Lake, was a gravedigger turned robber. He was caught with belongings of deceased people in his house, most of it clothing. The investigators found out he boiled the outfits to remove any disease and used them as draperies or furniture coverings. Jean was tried, convicted, and exiled to an island in the middle of Salt Lake where he vanished, never to be seen again. On foggy nights he appears as a luminous being, holding a bag of rotting clothes.'

SAM: Very fitting for the situation, Cockroach. Thanks for the educational moment.

He stuck a pin in Salt Lake City, Utah, and flipped open his phone. The speed dial rang forever until going to voice mail. "I don't know, Henry. Should I be worried?" Henry yipped. "Yeah, you're right. She returned my call last time, but my gut is saying something's different." He glanced over at the map. "Wait a minute, Utah is only two states away. The cicadas are traveling faster than they should.

A newcomer joined the chat and posted a news feed, its blue underlined text taking him to https://abcnews.go.com. A white circle swirled around the center of the screen as the video buffered. After several minutes, the live broadcast turned from a pixelated portrait to a square jawed gentleman in a suit, who straightened some papers on his desk.

"In breaking news this evening, the Woodland Fire, south of Sacramento, has consumed acres of land in California. Experts are battling the blaze, and residents of the Sacramento Valley have been put on high alert, with evacuation orders in place for some communities. In other news, swarms of insects have ravaged cities all across the Midwest. The first sighting was in Illinois, but in less than forty eight hours over sixty major cities in the Midwest have been overrun by these lethal swarms. Looting is rampant and the police are swamped with calls. Local fire and rescue have created safe zones for those affected by what they are referring to as 'a toxic residue.'"

The video switched to a field full of broken stalks. The camera panned across the devastated crops.

"The insects behave like locusts, stripping vegetation to its roots. Uneaten plants are poisonous and unsuitable for human consumption. People touched by the cicada-like insects are experiencing everything from rashes and swelling to death. Citizens are instructed to stay inside and check for openings the pests might crawl into. If you come in contact with these creatures, make your way to a safe zone or your nearest hospital."

The video cut back to the newscaster who touched his earpiece and went silent, his eyebrows scrunched together.

"Ladies and gentlemen, it appears there has been another sighting, Salt Lake City—"

The live feed went fuzzy and blacked out. Sam closed out the web page in favor of the science forum. The ones who lurked around there knew more than those bozos in the news rooms by a long shot.

He rattled the keyboard as he searched for the group tracking the phenomenon.

"Cockroach?"

He must've been offline but Matt chimed in on the boards.

MATT: Why d'you think the site cut out?

LIGHTNING ROD: Don't you dummies know anything? All broadcasts are over satellite feed. If those swarms knock the dishes over or gum up the receivers, they won't be able to transmit outgoing signals.

MATT: DAMMIT! Is that why my cell phone won't work? Those bugs jammed up the signals?

Sam shook his head. This was heading in the wrong direction. Just in time Moonshine entered the fray.

MOONSHINE: Thank the Lord Almighty those critters are gone, took me two whole hours to settle Eileen. Got a scratch from one of them, but figured if my time was up, I'm going out with my boots on. A quick heads up, if you get some of their oily residue on you, wash. The area still hurts like a mule kick, but the swelling isn't so bad. Regarding signals, only the regular radio and television stations are affected by satellite. Internet broadcast runs over cable, so unless those things chew through plastic and metal there is no reason for a web-based news source to go down.

Intrigued, Sam shot a PM to Moonshine.

SAM: How many touched you?

MOONSHINE: Only two. Swatted the first down, but the others landed on me before I could shut the windows. With the rash, I look like Quasimodo, but after the shower my back looks like I was pelted with a couple of high-speed racket balls.

Moonshine copied a link to a video conference in the main room and the two of them switched out of messenger and returned to the main room.

MOONSHINE: Looks like we have a young-un on the line. He says some 'weird' bugs have shown up. Better pull out all the stops and make this real easy for them to figure out or they might not last long.

Sam closed out the side chat and addressed Bugluvr, a young boy who was so close to his camera, he was almost fogging up the lens. "They're here. A whole lot of them."

"What do they look like?"

"Scary. They make this loud buzzing and are as big as my super ball. Here look." The video wobbled as the camera was lifted and turned to face the window. The air was thick with flying insects.

Sam hit his mic. "First off, if you can, try to point the camera where you are so we can see and help."

The video spun until it stopped in the living room. "What do I do?"

"The first thing to do is make sure your windows and doors are all closed and locked. Can you do that?"

Bugluvr padded away from the camera. Five minutes passed like an hour. The house sure had a lot of windows to be taking this much time. The boy reappeared. "Everything is locked up."

Matt butted into the conversation. "Where are your parents?"

Bugluvr fiddled with a pencil on the table. "At work. This is my mom's computer. I stayed home because I'm sick."

"Why are you out of bed?" Matt teased. "If you're well enough to get up, you're well enough to go to school, right?"

Bugluvr doodled on a pad, not looking at the camera. "Well, um, I got better real quick and decided to play a game. My mom always leaves this page open."

Sam loved his internet buddies, but they sure had a way of going off on a tangent. What did it matter why the kid was off school? Like anyone could concentrate in the middle of a bug attack! They had to be practical in order to keep the kid safe. "Alright Bugluvr, you need to put something over the vent in the kitchen."

"What's a vent?" Bugluvr put the pencil down.

"It's a large silver rectangle over the stove with a few buttons on the edge."

Bugluvr pattered away, and his voice came back faintly. "I can't reach it."

"Find a chair from the dining room."

Bugluvr came back into view. "I'm not allowed to stand on furniture."

Moonshine chimed in. "Trust us. In this case, your mom will thank you."

"Are you sure?"

Moonshine nodded. "We know for sure that your mom will not get mad at you. But if she does, just have her message us on here."

The camera panned until the view of a sparse kitchen came into focus and a screech echoed from the speakers. Sam covered his ears as the young boy pulled a solid oak chair with ornate carvings past the screen.

Moonshine continued giving instructions. "Push the chair in front of the stove, hop up, and put some tape over the silver filter underneath. Do you have any duct tape?"

"Yes, Poppa keeps the stuff in the hall closet. He says it can fix anything."

"Well, your poppa is correct because it's magic."

"Really? How does it work?" Bugluvr pulled the tape out, frowning and shaking his head.

"We don't know, but it holds things together, so they will never come apart." Moonshine got him back on topic. "What you should do is cover the entire opening."

Bugluvr stood on the chair and started unrolling the extra-large roll of duct tape. He placed it on the vent diagonally and then pulled out some more without cutting it.

Sam leaned in, focused on the right bottom corner of the screen. "Kid, get a shoe, now?"

Bugluvr paused. "Why?"

Sam yelled into his microphone. "Just do it will you?"

Bugluvr jumped from the chair and returned moments later.

"Okay, whatever you do, don't touch it, but use the shoe to smash the bug on the floor behind you."

The kid turned around and clambered up the chair in record time. He waved the shoe at the cicada as it crawled toward him. "Go away, just stop."

The insect, drawn by the motion, opened its wings and hovered for a second before flying into the face of the child. Sam covered his eyes. A loud pop and clang, vibrated through the video.

Bugluvr screamed in triumph at his first won battle. The cicada was splattered across the air vent in gooey green and black. "What do I need to do with the bug guts?"

Moonshine took the lead. "Leave it there and don't touch it. Use the tape to cover all the holes you see in the house and make sure to turn on all the water faucets. Can you do that for me?"

Sam opened another side chat.

SAM: Good thinking, Moonshine. Those cicadas might wander down the air vents into the apartment. What about the shower?"

MOONSHINE: Nice catch, let's wait till the kid's back.

The stillness of the video became unnerving. Bugluvr hadn't returned. With a hunched back, Sam hovered over the keyboard.

Bugluvr huffed into view. "Hey, It took a long time to tape up the house."

Sam relaxed. "Did you remember to run water in the sinks?"

The boy grinned and gave a thumbs up. "I did better than that, I closed the drains and filled them full of water. Then I taped up every hole I could find. It took four rolls. Those bugs won't get to me now. Want to see?"

Bugluvr roved the webcam around the living room, and Sam covered his mouth as a laugh nearly escaped. The scene was chaos. Duct tape ran from window to door, across the room and over the electrical outlets in one long strip. Light peeped through what little glass was free of the gray menace.

"Great job! I don't think anything is going to get in the house now. Do you have any snow gear?"

"Yeah, in the closet next to my board and boots. Poppa takes me to the mountain every year. We always drive."

"All right. Go put on the gloves and mask."

The little boy dashed off and returned wearing a brightly colored bobble hat with matching gloves and a red ski-mask .

"Good. Find a spot in the house that isn't near a window. Stay there until you can't hear the bugs anymore," Sam told him.

"What do I do after that?"

"Wait for your parents to get home, and tell your mom to check the chats. If anything happens that seems weird to you, come back and tell us. We'll try to help."

Bugluvr nodded, the ridiculous bobble flopping back and forward comically. "Okay, bye."

Sam addressed the group as Bugluvr dropped from the video. "Well, fellas. One good deed done; I hope the child survives."

Lightning Rod started pushing out facts as everyone left the video.

LIGHTNING ROD: Egypt has these suckers as well. Chap from Cairo said they ate all the crops in their path. Yesterday.

SAM: Not possible. Insects like this stick to one region. Even if a couple hitched a ride overseas, there is no accounting for a swarm of this magnitude.

Sam glanced at the map locations on the wall. This wasn't a swarm, it was an army. Diana wasn't going to get through in time.

LIGHTNING ROD: Well, they said not only did the cicadas eat the crops but killed a bunch of livestock. Lots of blood and deformed bodies to deal with.

Sam pulled out his phone. *I have to get in touch with her.* He signed off and redialed Diana. No response. Instead of hanging up, he decided to leave a message. "Di, it's Sam. Some news from online resources, if you come in contact with the cicadas, wash the affected area with soap and water to reduce the swelling. I'm telling you this now, because if my calculations are correct, you're heading straight for a major swarm in Utah, and it promises to be devastating. Find shelter at all costs."

CHAPTER EIGHTEEN

DR. DIANA STEWART. LINCOLN, NEBRASKA

Diana was shocked that Dan hadn't just put a bullet in her brain, but it seemed he enjoyed taunting and torturing her, because the cycle of dunking her head into the rancid water until she was almost out of it, and returning her to the land of the living, had gone on for longer than she thought was possible.

There was a rattle of doorhandles, and a teenager in a shop uniform slouched out the store's emergency exit and into the alleyway, vape in hand. He stopped in his tracks. "What the hell—?"

Dan snatched his foot back from kicking Diana and she rolled away, coughing and gasping. She scrambled to her feet, dripping with the stinking water from the puddle. Her ears were buzzing even louder now, though it had been some minutes since she'd escaped the painfully loud fire alarms. "Get the police," she gasped.

"Who are you people?" The young man stepped back, but Aaron grabbed him by the T-shirt.

"Don't hurt him! Stop! Please." She limped toward them, but something zipped past her head and dropped on the ground in front of her. "Cicadas!" She shied back from it, nearly going over on the ankle she had tripped on. "Get inside, quick!"

Aaron shoved the boy to the ground and let Dan inside. He smiled sweetly at her as she limped toward them. "Convenient." He slammed the door in her face.

More and more cicadas spread across the sky, the buzz rising to a whine. She helped the young man to his feet as more tumbled through the alleyway, raising her voice over the din. "Cover your nose and mouth. They're toxic."

He pulled the neck of his T-shirt over the lower half of his face, and she held a handkerchief against her own. Hopefully the first stray cicadas hadn't released too much toxin but with the numbers in the sky now, they had a problem. She had no jacket and didn't know if her blouse would block the toxin, and his arms were bare. If the cicadas landed on either of them, it wouldn't go well.

"We need to get into shelter. Quickly!" She coughed hard. "If the fire door is deadbolted—"

He grabbed a sliver of plastic wedged in the doorframe and jerked it. "I smoke here all the time, lady."

"Don't let any of them in!" She slammed the door and doubled over coughing. *Shoot.* The toxin had gotten her after all.

"Are you okay? Do you need a glass of water or something?" He sounded like he was speaking underwater.

She fought for breath as she coughed and coughed. Her throat stung like fire, and the skin on the side of her face burned. After a moment, it eased enough for her to catch her breath. "Ladies' room?"

The boy led her down the hall, pointing to the sign above a door. "There."

"And..." She coughed again. "To get in the shop?"

"Back that way and right."

She nodded. "Your skin stinging?"

"No, ma'am."

"Good. Stay inside till they're... gone. Dangerous." Hacking up half a lung, she staggered into the restroom. She inspected herself in the mirror. She was a sight. Wet and muddy, of course, but the side of her face was shredded.

She washed her hands thoroughly with soap, then wet a paper towel and did the same for her face. The area on the right side of her forehead and cheekbone was red-raw and bled copiously when she washed it. Thank goodness she'd managed to get inside before the main wave of the cicadas.

Her throat and chest stung, and her breath caught and bubbled with every inhalation and exhalation. She'd coughed up a load of water from the puddle already, but with the cicadas overhead, she had to assume she'd breathed in enough toxin to be dangerous. And her skin was bloody and raw as if it was starting to melt away like Jonah's.

Closing the lid of the toilet, she sat down with the wet tissue against her face as her knees went weak in reaction. The images of those terrible blistered faces from Watseka and Lincoln rose to mind, unbidden. Her hands shook. "Stop it! Jesse needs you!" She jolted herself out of it.

At least her face had stopped bleeding for the moment. But she was on the edge of another crippling coughing fit with every breath.

She slipped out of the bathroom. Somewhere, Aaron and Dan were lurking. She had to stay away from them. But this was her chance to get back to Jesse and Jane. All she needed was a little equipment. The corridor opened onto the shop floor, a brightly lit expanse of shelves, mannequins, and sporting equipment. Slipping behind a row of clothing, Diana took a moment to orient herself. She was at the edge of the clear area by the tills. She couldn't see Dan or Aaron. Nearby, a few customers gathered at the glass front of the store where the nightmare was unfolding.

The cicadas descended in a cloud, blanketing cars so that they crashed. An old man staggered away from the store, clutching at his face, mouth working under his fingers. Whatever he was saying was lost in the avalanche of screams and shouts. One man had gotten through the outer set of doors to the store but as she watched, he collapsed across the threshold. He lay there while the doors opened and closed, and opened and closed against his body. Cicadas crawled all over him and fell off, to bumble around on the welcome mat. A store guard turned off the doors, while another taped over the crack between the inner doors. They were distracted enough not to notice her behind them.

Diana slipped past and into the back of the store, looking for anything that might protect her long enough to get back to the car. In the far corner was the scuba-diving supplies. A mask and breathing equipment, just the thing. She pulled a capacious backpack off a shelf and hooked it over her shoulder.

Staying low, she made her way over to the display, pausing at the end of each aisle to check that Dan and Aaron were nowhere in sight. Her phone vibrated in her pocket. She leaned back against a display of coats to shield her from view and flicked it open. Thirteen messages. Not good.

The first was a reply to her message from Jane. "Will get the kids into the car and have it ready. Ten minutes should be plenty." But then, shortly after that, there were several panicked messages "I'm with Jesse but Samantha and Eli went to the store and now cicadas have come. I don't know what to do." Next message: "Jesse and I are in truck with vents taped up. I need to stay here till kids come back. Probably after cicadas have gone. Are you safe? Can you come back?" The phone beeped, then ran on to the next message. "Diana? Please answer. I'm frightened. I can't lose the kids as well as Alex. I couldn't bear it." And, finally, "Hello? Are you there?"

It wouldn't help Jesse if Jane panicked and left him alone. Diana answered via text, though this was hardly the time or the place

DIANA: Hi. Stay with Jesse. Will look for kids soon as I can. Which store?

She put her phone away and considered the coats on the display. Having lost her own, she should pick up another. But a movement above caught her eye.

Dan was up on the mezzanine, keeping an eye on the shop below. He was right at the back of the store, so as long as she crept along close to the displays, it was possible that he wouldn't see her. But she'd have to be careful, and the catch in her throat was building up to another cough.

"All quiet here, boss. She's probably still lying in the alleyway turning into something unrecognizable; just another tragic victim in a town full of victims."

She froze. From the sounds of it, Aaron was standing on the other side of the coats, barely three feet away from her.

"I'll check, sir."

She watched him in the aisle-end mirrors as he strode into another aisle. She let out her breath softly, trying not to react to the itch and sting of her throat, and managed—just—not to cough. Staying as low as she could, she headed back toward the diving aisles and the scuba gear.

It didn't take long to choose what she needed. She put five masks with snorkels and a small tank of oxygen with a full-face mask in a backpack. The next aisle across held camping equipment, including a gazebo that came with a large clear curtain of heavy plastic, to shield it from rain or wind. She added the plastic curtains to her haul.

Now all she had to do was get out of there. Was it foolish to attempt to pay? Almost certainly but even now, she couldn't bring herself to steal unnecessarily.

She edged forward to the front of the store. The customers were standing silently at the windows. A man held his wife, who was sobbing into his chest. Outside, a businesswoman had tried to get out of a crashed car and lay half in and half out of the door, her immaculately coiffed hair now crawling with insects. There was a Chevy rammed into the remains of a sportscar. One man had fallen forward onto his steering wheel, and the long blare of his horn overlaid the shriek of the cicadas. People of all ages had fallen where they stood; their bodies scattered the pavements like broken dolls, crawling with bugs.

The windows were smeared, not so thickly as the truck windows had been, and the battering of the cicadas here and there was still enough to eat away at the last part of Diana that was not utterly terrified.

She moved slowly toward the till. A hand grabbed her, and she froze.

"Diana? Is that you?" Samantha was pale, and Eli stuck close behind her, his eyes wide and scared. "What happened to your face? Did you fall?"

"What are you guys doing here?" Diana whispered, her finger to her lips to shush them. "Look, there's trouble. I don't want you involved. Text your mom."

"My phone's out of battery. I was afraid you wouldn't know where we were—"

Aaron rocketed out of the aisle and took Diana down in a rugby tackle.

Samantha screamed, and the other customers turned.

The impact winded Diana, and she started coughing, painfully hard.

The manager hurried over. "Sir, can I ask what—"

Dan approached. "It's all right, ladies and gentlemen. This lady is wanted by the police in connection with a robbery. We caught her red handed." He yanked at her backpack.

"And heading to the checkout with them?" It was the youth from the alleyway, who was at the till. "Not much of a thief."

"Leon, don't talk back to the policeman." The manager grabbed his arm, pulling him away.

"He isn't a policeman. Neither of them are," Diana choked out, between coughs.

"They don't look like police. We need to know what's going on here."

"No, Leon, we do not! Let the police get on with their business. We don't want any trouble. People lose their jobs that way." The manager pushed him back toward the till, hard.

Diana was still coughing so she couldn't breathe, and she couldn't double over to clear her lungs properly with Aaron pinning her down.

"Stop it, you're strangling her!" Eli screamed. "She'll die! Stop it! She isn't a thief! She was coming to take us home!"

Samantha put her arms around him.

"If you don't want that woman to suffocate, you need to give her room to breathe." An older woman in expensive-looking shoes walked toward them.

Dan nodded at Aaron, who shifted away from Diana, keeping hold of her ankles. Curling into a ball, Diana finally got control of the cough and lay limp, trying to catch her breath.

The lady went on, "Hush, child. We'll get this all sorted out, never you fear. I'm Mrs. Beaufort. Is this your mother?"

Eli sobbed. Samantha answered. "Please, she didn't steal anything. How could she? We're all still in here."

Mrs. Beaufort straightened. "You, let her up! Explain yourselves at once!"

"Aaron," Dan snarled.

He let Diana up. She scrambled to her feet and put her arms around the children, quietly slipping the shoulder strap of the bag onto Samantha's shoulder.

Dan turned to the older lady. "This lady is a criminal, ma'am. We're just taking her in for questioning."

"You aren't taking her anywhere till the bugs have gone so you might as well let her recover from your uncalled-for assault." She folded her arms. "Now, I'd like to see your identification, please."

Everything went still. Some of the customers were taking an interest now, turning from the horror outside to the drama unfolding behind them.

"I don't have to show you my ID, madam—" Dan started.

"You do, though. We did it in class. You have to show your ID and give them your name." Samantha's voice was trembling, but she said it anyway.

"He does indeed." Mrs. Beaufort glared at Dan, whose composure was starting to slip.

"His name is Daniel Jenson, and he works for Matreus Inc., as do I." Diana ushered the children behind her. "He and his associate were about to assault me when the cicadas came, as you can see."

Mrs. Beaufort's eyebrows hitched at the sight of her injured face.

"Shut up, bitch!" Dan lunged at Diana, but a burly man intervened.

"Leave the lady alone, sir." He stood between Diana and her assailants.

Dan paused. The man was built like a linebacker. "The woman is a compulsive liar."

"But you *were* kicking her on the ground in the alleyway. You had your boot on her back. The footprint is still there." The young man left the till and came forward.

"Don't get involved, Leon," the manager pleaded. "How could you possibly know that?"

Leon grimaced. "Sorry, boss. Nipped out back for a quick vape. They stopped when the door opened, but the lady was on the ground and asked me to call the police. From what this guy said, the other guy was about to do something bad to her."

"Madam, do you have some form of ID?" Mrs. Beaufort took Diana's work pass and scrutinized it closely. "We have shares in Matreus, I believe. Well, if Doctor Stewart here can prove she is who she says she is, but you refuse to show your ID, then we must believe her."

Dan lost his cool. Fury flared in his eyes. He drew his gun and let off two shots at the ceiling. A young woman screamed and customers dove for cover.

Mrs. Beaufort and the football player flinched but stood where they were. The football player tensed to attack, but Aaron had his gun out too. Someone was going to get killed.

"Dan, stop!" Diana's voice erupted into a cough. Both guns swung around at her, but it distracted the football player too. She straightened up and croaked, "Stop. If you shoot out the glass, the cicadas get in, and we all die." She panted a little. "There's no need. You have me, I'm not going anywhere."

"You'd better tell your new friends to stay out of it then!" Dan lunged across and screamed in her face, his spittle hot against her cheek. Even Aaron was watching him warily now.

"Will do. Just give me a moment, okay?" She turned to the kids. "Samantha, Eli, I need you to go with this lady here. If anything goes wrong, I need to know you're safe."

Samantha went white. "But—"

She pressed her phone into the girl's hands quickly before Dan dragged her away. "It's okay. Help will arrive sooner or later. The swarm won't last much longer." She unlocked the phone as she handed it over. "Mrs. Beaufort, please keep these two safe. And away from any unpleasantness."

Aaron muttered to Dan, "I thought you said the kid was injured? And there was no mention of a girl."

"You *do* know her!" Mrs. Beaufort accused.

Dan shoved Mrs. Beaufort to the floor then smacked Aaron in the face hard enough to make him stagger backward. "Shut up, you moron! Are you so freaking stupid that you don't know better than to..." His tirade went on and on, and Aaron glowered but said nothing.

Diana knelt by Mrs. Beaufort. "Are you okay, ma'am? Are you hurt?"

"Bruised more than anything, I think. That's a dangerous man." She was pale but undaunted.

The football player joined them, helping them up. "Mrs. Beaufort here is right. You're in danger if you go with him."

"We're all in danger, if I don't."

Dan grabbed her by the arm, "Aaron, restrain the customers and leave them by the windows. First sign of trouble, we start pushing people out of the door. Kids first." The customers flocked together uneasily.

Diana raised her hands in surrender. She had to get him away from the kids. She turned her back to the customers so Samantha and Eli could not tell what she was saying. "If you hit me in front of all these people, you're going to have trouble. I don't want the kids to be upset, and you don't want trouble, right? I'll back over here and you'll be well away from them, see?" She backed slowly around the corner, and he followed, keeping his gun pointed at her, as intent as a cat stalking a mouse.

She paused once out of sight of the tills. He slapped her, hard. Her ankle gave out from under her, and she fell into a display of cooking gear. As it tumbled down around her, she curled up, protecting her head with her arms from the sharp impacts of the camping stoves and cylinders that bombarded her.

Dan backed away, his gun still trained on her, to where he could see the others, and shouted around the edge of the aisle. "Aaron! Tie those people up and get over here, right now! We have work to do." Diana swallowed past the soreness of her throat. Right there and then, if he flipped he would kill every person there without hesitation. She had to come up with a plan.

The cascade of cans stopped and she looked up cautiously. Butane, a brand she recognized. They were popular because they were cheap. She'd avoided it because the cans were old-fashioned and unsafe but...

"It's not that hard. What are those band things right next to you? Tie them up with those!" Dan was still concentrating on Aaron.

She had to do something, fast. She yanked the rubber "Live Strong" wristband she was wearing off her wrist and reached in her pocket for her lighter. She clicked it on and pulled the wristband around it to keep the button depressed, the flame flickering. If these were newer gas cans with valves, it would do nothing and even if they were not, she had no idea how long it would take to warm them enough, but it was all she had and the only way she could stop them from hurting the children. Hiding the lighter with her body, she pulled herself upright, dropping it in amongst the cans just in time.

"Get over there! In that corner!" Dan aimed a kick at her. "On your knees. Hands behind your head."

Aaron appeared. "All done, boss."

Hauling herself upright again, she limped across to the corner Dan had indicated. She tucked herself right in against the wall, kneeling as instructed and raising her hands to her head awkwardly. It hurt. Felt like she'd torn a muscle in that last fall.

"Finally." Dan lowered his gun and tucked it into the holster as he came to stand over Diana. "So, to pick up where we left off—" He kicked her in the ribs and she crumpled to the floor, falling with her back to the wall and her hands still clutching her head. "Let's discuss these files you stole."

CHAPTER NINETEEN

ANAYELI ALFARO. EAST SACRAMENTO, CALIFORNIA.

Anayeli couldn't sleep. Every time she closed her eyes, the faces would swim out of the darkness—Papa in his Dorados cap, mouth open in a yell as the fire bore down on him; Josh Bertoli, mouth frothing with bloody foam; the woman in the car, mouth wide in a scream; Frank; China Box Lady—all of them dead. *Your fault* they whispered in her head, the chorus of dead.

So instead of sleeping like everyone else, Anayeli listened. Not to the dead, but to the scanner, to drown them out. The scanner was the only thing working. The radio she had taken from the Closet of Obsolescence wouldn't turn on and the walkie-talkies and her flashlight were useless without batteries, which she didn't have, thanks to her *pendejo* of a neighbor. All night she'd kept one tea light burning and had listened, the calls getting less and less frequent as the night wore on. Maybe there were fewer emergencies. Or maybe there was no one left to call for help. Whatever it meant, she couldn't relax, especially when the only thing to listen to was Ernesto's rumbling breath. He was congested, the precursor to an asthma attack, and she had no idea if he'd used his inhaler or not. If it wasn't working she didn't know what they'd do. She'd lost too many people already. She'd been so unprepared—for everything. That was never going to happen again.

She'd almost cried when her almost-gasless van had lurched into her driveway and she saw the windows lightless, too afraid of what she might find inside to even move. But someone had pulled apart the slats of the mini-blinds, letting out the dim flickers of candle-light, and then the door had flown open and her whole family—what was left of it—had rushed out, all of them talking all at once, none of them wearing the masks she'd left for them.

"Oh, *mi Corazón!*" Mama's hands had gone first to Anayeli's cheeks, then her shoulders and arms, patting her as if to make sure she was whole. "Oh, *mi Corazón!*"

"We were so scared, Yeli!" Luz took up Anayeli's hand, the non-injured one thankfully, and squeezed.

"What took you so long?" Carlota stood back from the fray, relieved enough now to be mad. Because she was hangry. Because Anayeli had been gone forever.

But then Ernesto had pointed to the shot-out window of the van and that had set Mama off again. "Ayyyyy! I knew you shouldn't have gone *solamente!*" The only good thing about all the commotion was Mama hardly noticed the extra dog and it wasn't until she was actu-ally cooking dinner and realized they didn't have cheese—that was back on Frank's driveway next to the other thing she was never going to tell anyone about—that she started complaining about the meager supplies Anayeli had brought home.

Her head had bobbed to her chest, the faces rising, when the scanner crackled to life, jerking her awake. "52F! Moving north, just crossed highway—" The call cut out. She pulled the scanner toward her, frantic to know which highway the fire had just crossed, and Cricket and Roxy both stirred on the bed they were sharing. The little screen on the scanner, the one that showed which channel it was on had gone dim. She twisted the volume and channel selector knobs, but nothing happened. The screen stayed dark. The scanner was dead. She flipped it over, opened up the battery compartment. D batteries. Of course. She turned the batteries, took them out, put them back in, hoping to spark a connection. Nothing.

She was staring at the dead batteries, silently fuming, when Cricket whined. He was up, eyes glued to the wall she shared with her neighbor. He whined again. On her bed, Roxy looked between Cricket and Anayeli, her ears sticking straight out with worry—Yoda ears. On the futon, Ernesto stirred.

"Shhhh, *perrito*." She strained to hear what might be bothering the dog, but there was nothing except the steady buzz of her neighbor's back-up generator. Of course he would be one of the people who had bought the small gas-powered ones after the Safety Power Shut-offs. He was ten out of ten that guy. A tool guy.

But Cricket was pacing, pacing, pacing along the wall, occasionally letting out a high-pitched whine. She went to him, took hold of his collar, but he whimpered and Ernesto stirred again, letting out a little cough. Cricket stopped at a spot in the middle of the wall, ears cocked, listening. Anayeli pressed her ear against the surface. The walls in this place were paper-thin. She was acutely aware, for instance, that her neighbor loved every movie with The Rock in it.

Then she heard it: a deep wheezing cough. Her neighbor's face floated up in her mind, the trail of blood trickling over his stubble. She'd tried to warn him. The sound continued, overlaid with a second high-pitched voice, but she couldn't make out any actual words. The wheezing got louder and more intense until there was a heavy thud that made the wall shake. A cry came through the wall—clear now: "Daddy!" There was an answering gurgling noise, more thuds—as if someone were running or kicking, and then—nothing. Still Cricket paced and whimpered.

Anayeli's ear was still pressed to the cold wall when the neighbor's front door slammed, rattling the front window. Footsteps pounded outside, closer, closer. And then someone battered on the apartment door.

Everything happened all at once. The dogs bolted for the door—

both of them in a barking frenzy. Ernesto surged upright. "Yeli! What is it?"

Screams came from the bedroom, where Mama and her sisters had been sleeping.

The fire is coming, she refused to let herself say, thinking of the half-heard scanner call. *Maybe it's already here!* "Grab your bags!" They'd spent the first part of the evening, while Mama was cooking, adding supplies to the bags Mama had packed while Anayeli had been gone. They were ready. They could leave in a heartbeat. Assuming the van would start.

She dashed for the front window. Outside was pitch black, not orange, a beam of light—a flashlight?—sweeping wildly from the direction of her front stoop. No fire, then. Ernesto was on his feet, his backpack already slung across one shoulder, fully dressed because she had insisted, grabbing for the second backpack on the floor next to the futon—hers.

The pounding continued. "Please! Help! My daddy!"

In the dark, Anayeli went for the door, fumbling for the baseball bat she'd had Ernesto stash next to it. "Who's there?" Through the peep hole she saw only black. It had to be the little girl next door—Bronwyn or Bethany, or—but if it wasn't, if it were a ruse—

"Ernesto! Your phone! The flashlight!" They'd long since given up on the phones being anything other than a light source. And she only had one solar charger—a remnant from the Power Shut-offs—so they'd been using them sparingly.

"Please!" It was more sob than words, the banging on the door more spaced out, more feeble than it had been.

"You stay," Anayeli told the dogs the instant the room flooded with cold, bright light from Ernesto's phone. Then she gripped the baseball bat with her burned hand. She would have screamed at the pain—sharp even with the padding of her makeshift bandage—but she had to be strong. Fierce. Just in case. She yanked open the door with her good hand. The moment the gap widened enough, Roxy shot out, but Cricket stayed put at Anayeli's side.

The girl's face was streaked with tears, and there were splatters of something dark—blood—across her pajamas. Roxy circled the little girl, her entire body wriggling in happiness, pausing her happy dance only to lick at the girl's hand, the one holding a flashlight—the beam of light Anayeli had seen. Dimly, she was aware of noise behind her—Mama and her sisters, a torrent of Spanish—but the girl pointed toward the other half of the duplex with the cell phone she held in her other hand, sobs wracking her small body. "Something's wrong—my daddy, he's bleeding! 911 won't answer!"

Anayeli leaned the bat against the wall next to the door, but someone behind her, Ernesto probably, took it before she'd let go. It made her feel better knowing he had her back. She wasn't convinced what she was about to do was safe, but she couldn't leave a little girl crying on her doorstep. No way she could shut the door in her face. Instead, she opened the door wider, stepping out just enough to put her bandaged hand on the girl's shoulder. "You're okay. We got you."

The door to the neighbor's duplex hung wide open, a shaft of light spilling onto its stoop, thanks to his generator. Nothing else moved, not on the driveway, not on the street, but the flashlight beam showed a swirl of ash, the air chokingly thick. Locked inside, she'd been able to almost forget about the smoke.

"But my daddy!" The girl sobbed, punctuating each word. "Please! He needs help!" More tears spilled down her cheeks. Regular tears. Not bloody. So that was something. "Do something!"

Anayeli hesitated, half of a mind to go back inside and shut the door. She didn't trust her neighbor. He hadn't wanted her help before. She didn't think he'd look kindly upon her invading his home. And he was the kind of guy who had a gun. He definitely wasn't the type who'd appreciate his daughter being in someone else's—a stranger's—house. And if what had happened to Josh Bertoli was happening to her jerk of a neighbor, there was nothing she could do. But—

"Go inside." It was easier than she'd expected to usher the girl forward and through the door, Roxy following at her heel. "You'll be safe."

"But my daddy—" Standing in the entryway, the little girl dissolved into heaving, choking sobs. Behind her, Mama was shaking her head and Carlota wore her grumpy face, but Luz reached out toward the girl, taking her hand.

"Everyone! Masks on—now!" She'd made them all sleep with masks around their necks. In case they got evacuated, there'd be no time to dig around in their packs for the extras that were stashed there. But the little girl didn't have one.

The exact moment Anayeli touched her mask, Cricket bolted past her and out the door, straight for the neighbor's place. That clinched it.

"I'm going to check on him. You all stay here. Ernesto, get her a mask." She met his eyes, and the instant he nodded, she snatched the phone/flashlight from his hand and ran.

Behind her, Luz asked, "Are you hungry?" having been well-trained by Carlota to think food made everything better. Her youngest siblings were the best. They would take care of the girl. Maybe even find out what her name was. And she would do the thing she wanted to do exactly zero percent: she would see to the girl's father.

The scene inside her jerk neighbor's place was not at all what she'd expected. Instead of a bachelor pad full of dark fake-leather couches, beer signs, and hunting trophies, the overhead light glowed down on a cozy living room. There were pillows and a throw blanket on the plush couch. Instead of some framed sports-jersey hanging on the wall, the guy had a gallery of framed artwork, all of it clearly his daughter's, featuring rainbows and unicorns, the name Bailey Rae scrawled across the blue sky. *Bailey Rae.* On a console beneath the huge flatscreen TV she would have expected, was a large frame that said "World's Best Daddy." Inside was a photo of the two of them, complete with matching clothes and golden light. There were several other frames, full of more candid shots—the man fishing with his little girl, a camping trip, Bailey Rae beaming down from atop a horse. A pretty woman with a baby in her arms. Everything Anayeli thought she knew about the man fragmented and rearranged itself. She'd been so wrong about him.

But he was nowhere to be seen, and neither was Cricket. She couldn't hear anything, because on the coffee table, a black box with knobs—very much like the useless wireless radio she'd taken from the newsroom—blared with some talk show, judging from the tone. Maybe she could change the channel, get some real news, once she was done helping—her train of thought came to a screeching halt. Beneath the gallery of Bailey Rae's artwork, the mirror image of where Cricket had been staring, was a smear of blood. Fresh enough it was still red.

"Hello?" She stepped further into the room, her heart kicking.

Someone on the radio started talking—too fast. "That's just it, Jim. It isn't a grass fire! It's exploded everywhere. The whole of Northern California's Sacramento Valley is on fire—not just the area near UC Davis, and now I'm hearing there's fires all the way up into Southern Oregon. Not to mention these cicada swarms we're hearing reports of, all over the Midwest. It can't be a coincidence—"

Cicada swarms? That didn't make any sense. Some lunatic conspiracy theorist, then. But something nagged at her memory. Taylor Muckenfuss at Matreus had said something about "the infestation." She thought he'd meant the *loco* Teff grass, but casting her mind back she realized he *had* said "cicadas" and she had brushed it off, listening for what she wanted to hear. But she couldn't worry about that. Not anymore.

"—no one can even get out of the North state! It's a death trap! Bumper-to-bumper traffic along the I-5 and East-80 corridors, but where can they go that's safe? Not East, that's for sure. Bet even the liberals are wishing the governor had spent money on freeways now, instead of that high-speed train to nowhere!"

"Is anyone here? Cricket!"

A single bark came from the kitchen. It was dark in there—only the one living room light was on. She crept forward, her fear of being attacked shifting into a new worry. She didn't know what she'd find in that kitchen, or what was worse—a dead body or a terribly sick man. Cricket whimpered again and not even a second later there was an explosion of coughing.

She shot through the doorway, into the kitchen, and there they were. Cricket sat alongside her neighbor, who was on the floor, slumped against the cabinets. Blood still trickled from his nose, like the last time she'd seen him, but the glare from her flashlight showed blood trickling down the side of his face, clotting in his stubble. He was bleeding from his ears, too. His hands, held in front of his mouth as he coughed, were covered with blood.

"Your daughter—" At the word, the man straightened, his eyes boring into hers, his cheeks puffing out as he tried to control his coughing. "She's safe. Next door. At my house. I don't know what—"

"Sorry. For bef—" He swallowed whatever he was going to say as he struggled against another bout of coughing.

She put the phone/flashlight down on the counter, aiming the light upward, illuminating the entire kitchen, and sank down beside him, next to Cricket.

"Before. The Corner Mar—" The man tried again, his voice a harsh rasp. She leaned forward to better hear, and he burst out coughing again. The blood and who knew what else sprayed across her face. She reeled backward on instinct, gagging even as her feet slipped in whatever was on the floor—more blood, more mucus— and fell hard on her backside. But the man was reaching for something on the counter—not her phone, something heavier, bigger —a gun!

"Don't!" She scrabbled backward, and Cricket barked, barked, barked, a different bark, one she somehow recognized as protective.

But it wasn't the barrel of the gun the man pointed at her—it was the butt. "Keep...daughter... safe. I can't—" He fell to coughing again. She didn't move. She didn't want his gun. She didn't want to get near him in case whatever was wrong with him was catching. But she already had his blood all across her face. So it was too late. And besides, if it was contagious, she was in trouble. She'd been right next to Josh when he'd died, and by the looks of it, this guy's symptoms were the same. She sat on her heels and waited for the fit to pass. There was no mask anywhere. Maybe it was too late for it to do him any good but she took hers off—it was spattered with his blood anyway. No way she was going to keep wearing it—and held it out to him.

"Take it." He thrust the gun toward her between coughs. All she had next door was the baseball bat. She grabbed hold of the pistol, but he didn't release it. "Keep her safe—" He wouldn't take his eyes off hers.

"I will. She's safe now. My whole family—" He let go of the gun. She still held out the mask. His mouth opened, closed, then opened again and she knelt forward, to be sure to hear, still holding out the mask. He didn't take it.

"More ammo. In the safe. 773—"

From the other room, the radio suddenly burst louder, startling her, snatching her attention away from her neighbor. "Farm fires across the Pacific Northwest, cicada swarms in the Midwest and Egypt of all places! And just in, there's news out of Australia of more fires popping—"

She missed whatever her neighbor had said, because her brain had snagged. *Cicada swarms. Australia.* It made no sense. It was all too disconnected.

The neighbor grabbed her hand, hard. "The code. 773—" He coughed again, but this time the coughs were somehow deeper, wracking his body more heavily. Cricket barked, then pulled on the man's shirt. Like he'd done when Josh Bertoli— before she could even think what to do, the man jerked into convulsions—his arms flinging wide, narrowly missing both her and the dog, his head drumming into the cabinets behind him over and over.

Her papa's smiling face swam before her eyes, then the little girl's tear-streaked one—She should have done more to save her papa. She would do anything to keep Bailey Rae from knowing that same pain —*Do something.*

She bolted for the couch, snatched up one of the plaid pillows. Still the radio blared a list of names she didn't recognize—towns in Australia, maybe. There was too much noise. Coughing and pounding and barking. She dashed back into the kitchen just as the man went the wrong kind of still. Her mask lay in a puddle of blood and worse, red wicking up its sides. Her fingers shook as she reached for his arm —outstretched like Sid's—and pressed two fingers to his wrist. No pulse. She tried again. Tried his neck. Still nothing.

She was up then, snatching the phone off the counter, shoving it into one back pocket, the gun into the other. She backed away, carefully at first, to not slip again in the mess on the floor, Cricket coming with her, quiet now the man was dead. And then she was slamming down the hall for the bathroom. She dry-heaved over the sink and caught sight of herself in the mirror—blood spattered across her forehead, in a wide arc above her cheekbones, her face clean where her mask had been.

The water was a warm trickle but she didn't care. After one glance showed pink flowing down the drain, she kept her eyes closed until she was sure she'd gotten everything off. Then she waited another few seconds in case there was anything that needed to clear from the sink. The mirror showed her round face, framed with fringes of wet dark hair. She looked clean, but the expression in the mirror was one she'd never seen on herself. A blank mask of grief.

Her mask.

Masks. Everyone she'd seen coughing and convulsing, everyone she'd seen die—except China Box Lady, but that was different—hadn't been wearing a mask. The neighbor. Sid. The man at the printing press. The woman in the car. Only Josh had worn one, but he'd taken it down before the worst of the smoke—and it had only been a bandana, not an N95.

And her mask was on the floor, back in the kitchen. She had to get out of here, but once she left, she was never coming back in, and she couldn't leave unprepared. She ran to the bedroom, grabbed a *My Little Pony* backpack off the floor of Bailey Rae's room, jammed it with a stuffed animal from her bed, some clean pajamas, underwear, pants, shirts. Cricket stayed glued to her side as she threw open the man's closet, looking for the gun safe he must've been trying to tell her about. Nothing. She yanked open the door to the garage. A gas can! She grabbed it, then whirled to the workbench. On top were D batteries—her D batteries! He hadn't even *needed* them. She snatched them up, shoved them in Bailey's backpack. She scanned the shelves for anything that might be useful, but she couldn't think. She needed a mask, not all these tools. She pulled open drawers. So many tools. But in the bottom one, she found a package of masks—open, with a picture of a construction worker on the front. Better than nothing. She grabbed those too, put one on. In the corner, a huge black safe.

More ammo, the neighbor had said. 773. She punched in the code, and nothing happened. She tried it again. He must not have told her the whole thing, and she couldn't waste time figuring it out.

Back in the house, smoke was pouring through the front door she'd left open. She had to get home. But there had to be food in the kitchen. She went toward it. It was just a dead body in there. Nothing scary.

"Look folks," the radio blared. "These are no ordinary bugs. The casualties out of the Midwest are staggering, hospitals overrun, and the number of swarms keeps growing. The Northern part of California is aflame, and now Australia—" The man rambled on about the speed of the flames, how soon the fires might reach other states, the rate of drift from the smoke but she'd stopped really listening when he'd said bugs.

Swarms. Taylor Muckenfuss of Matreus had mentioned more than "Teff and the *infestation*"—there was something else he'd said off the record, what felt like days ago, but was not even 24 hours... *Australia*! That's where he'd said that specialist was coming from and she'd wanted to know why. She had her answer. Australia was burning too. It didn't make sense—what possible link could bugs and fires have?

She coughed behind her mask and Cricket whined. The smoke was getting worse. "I know *perrito*. I'm hurrying."

She forced herself into the kitchen. In the fridge there was milk, cheese, tortillas, wheat bread. In the cabinets she found packets of applesauce, cups of mandarins, peanut butter—kid food. She snatched a cloth bag from where it hung on a drawer knob and shoved all the food into it, keeping her eyes up, above the line of the counter, off the body sprawled on the floor.

But when she turned to go, she was stopped by the sight of her neighbor's gaping mouth. It wasn't the fire that had killed Bailey Rae's daddy. It wasn't the fire that had killed Sid, or Josh, or those first farmworkers. Papa had been ahead of the flames when he'd fallen. Papa had tried to tell her there was something dangerous about the Teff grass. He had wanted her to cover the story, not because of the fires but because of his friends who'd gotten sick before. Because of the *loco* grass. *Do something*. She'd been thinking about getting her local Ag-fire story, maybe exposing Matreus for encouraging hazardous workplace conditions. But if there were swarms of bugs in Illinois where Matreus was based, and fires were all across the West and Australia, and people far away from the original fires—like Sid, like her neighbor, like the casualties in Illinois, of all places—were dying, the fires weren't the real problem. It was the smoke... or the bugs. But she hadn't seen any bugs at Josh Bertoli's farm. That couldn't be it. But if someone from the seed company was spearheading a response, then there had to be some connection between the bugs and the fires and the Teff crop itself. Papa had told her people working the Teff fields had had breathing problems—

And no one seemed to know that. No one was talking about how people were dying from smoke inhalation in conditions that weren't usually deadly. She could do more than keep her family safe—that information could help keep lots of people safe. She'd been thinking too small before. But first she had to get her family away from the fires, away from the smoke.

She knelt next to her neighbor. "I'm sorry." Cricket whimpered while she rummaged through the man's pockets, her plan taking shape even before she'd pulled out his keys. She rushed through the living room, lugging the gas can, Bailey Rae's backpack, and food back toward the door. They'd take the neighbor's truck—it would be tight, but they'd all fit in the dual cab. His truck had to be running better than the van. And they'd have gas. She'd seen him filling up. They'd head East, away from the fires, and then North, toward Canada, maybe. The Midwest didn't sound safe, however much she'd like to get to Matreus' headquarters and talk to Taylor Muckenfuss, junior Agronomist. She'd have to find out what was in the smoke some other way.

She was almost outside, her stomach cratering at the news she would have to break to Bailey Rae, when she remembered the wireless radio. Her hand was on it when the first scream ripped through the walls.

On the doorstep, she stood frozen, disoriented. She couldn't see the houses across the street. And the horizon—that shot adrenaline through her veins and got her feet moving. It was a roiling orange—

not of dawn, but of fire. Flames shot up into the sky, the smoke boiling in a giant charcoal plume that meant more than grass was burning—buildings. The fire had reached the city. Footsteps pounded on the sidewalk, and people's screams reached her through the thick haze, but she couldn't see anyone. Headlights barely cut through the smoke, as car after car rushed by—an evacuation, an exodus. She blinked and the flames were closer, their glow more lurid. She didn't wait to blink again. She dropped the gas can where she was.

"The river!" She jerked open her own front door. "We have to get to the river!"

CHAPTER TWENTY

SAM LEARY. BERKELEY, CALIFORNIA.

Smoke filtered through the ceiling tiles and door frame as fire ate its way into the lab. Charcoal embers flaked and fluttered, flames arched around the openings, bits of burned ceiling exploded in uneven splotches, and several tiles thunked to the ground. Sam dodged debris, sidestepping left as another tile dropped. He couldn't believe the fires from the northern part of the state had gotten all the way to Berkeley.

Grabbing the fire extinguisher, he pointed the hose at the flame, and pushed down on the lever. A puff of powder came out the end and trickled to the floor. "What the...?" He dropped the cylinder to the floor and pumped the handle. Useless.

He rolled the steel out of the way and reached for the fire blanket, slapping it against the walls. The flames ignored his efforts and licked hungrily at the deeply eroded calcium sulfate. Henry barked nonstop at the door and shook his coat as bits of embers buried themselves in his fur. Sam threw the blanket over the overwhelmed pup to keep him from being burned, pulled him underneath a desk, and pulled another alongside it to create a mini-fort for his pal.

More of the ceiling collapsed, and the sprinklers' glass bulbs burst as a huge ball of heat consumed the room. The fire alarm split the air in warning. Sam ducked under the blanket and covered his ears as the deflectors shot water over the entire room in a heavy downpour, soaking everything. Within minutes, the blaze was extinguished.

Frank's voice boomed through the damaged blockade. "I told you Sam, you should've given me the laptop and kept your dog from attacking." He struck the boarded-up window, the soaked embers bursting into the lab. "I'll roast him alive for the holes he put in me."

Sam swore up a blue streak, but under his breath so Frank wouldn't hear him. Not the fires from up north, then. Something more confusing, but no less threatening. Frank was going to smoke him out, just for that laptop. Which, of course, meant he must never—ever, never-ever—get his hands on it. Sam had retrieved it from the gym locker under cover of dark, but his data was under threat as long as Frank had them in his sites. He crawled from under the desk, pulled the blanket off of Henry, and prodded him toward the door. The dog sniffed, crouched, and growled as Sam screamed at his nemesis. "Go away, Frank. If you come in, he'll bite you again."

A gloved hand thrust two fingers into a hole burned in the plywood window, prodding the area for weakness. Sam retrieved the fire extinguisher lying by the teacher's desk and rammed the butt of the steel cylinder into the wooden window. His aim was true, smashing the fingers flat.

Frank squealed before a woman's voice interrupted over the pain filled scream, "Burn it some more! He won't be able to stop the flames now."

Sam recoiled from the door, dropping the extinguisher in disbelief. "Paula?"

"Hand over the computer, Sam."

Sam peered through the hole. "What are you doing? Frank can't be trusted."

Paula pushed past Frank and leaned against the door jam. "Oh,

Sam. Honey, it's complicated. I've always liked you, but this is business."

"Right, so the fire in my lab is just an illusion? There's no possible way I could have burned to death?"

The end of an acetylene torch poked through the charred opening and flames licked at the edges of the plywood. Sam ran to the desk, grabbed the blanket, and whipped it at the torch. The flame only danced around the fabric as it curled around the side of the window. Thank goodness the maintenance department had installed half-inch plywood. The water-soaked wood refused to ignite.

Frank pulled the torch out. "It's too wet."

An exasperated screech belted through the opening in the window. "Use more combustibles! There must be something in these labs to start a blaze."

"I used all of it on the ceiling."

"So, break in. The wood should be brittle enough."

The plywood thumped twice. "It's not going to break unless we chop it down. Besides, that dog's still in there. You saw what the mongrel did to me."

Sam maneuvered closer to the damaged opening in time to see Paula grab the acetylene torch from Frank and push him out of her way. Her high heels clicked at a rapid pace down the hallway, the echoes a reminder that she was a woman, and scorned. Hell better watch it because Paula had a grade-A temper. Sam had only seen her in a rage once, and it was enough to make you want to hide.

He tested the brace. Still firm. He was drenched, and shivered as cold air blew on him from the central air above. Wringing the excess water from his cotton shirt, he hung it from the door knob and dug in his pack for a dry one, slipping it over his head, but not tucking it. His pants weren't too wet, but the waistband had absorbed some water. No point getting the clean shirt damp.

Henry shook his entire body, drops of water spattering out in all directions until his hair stood out three inches. He padded to the door, sniffed, and rose up on his hind feet. With teeth on display he growled and stuck his muzzle into the window's new viewport. Sam smiled as the thud of Frank's boots beat a hasty retreat.

Sam ran a cloth over the monitor wiping the few drops of water from the stand. The desk had directed most of the water flow away from the electronics. Dipping his head under the desk, and opening the small cupboard, he ran a hand over the computer. Not a single drop. Pulling up the forums, he blasted out an all call for Cockroach and went to investigate the storage closet.

The macaroni and cheese box ripped apart as he squeezed the cardboard container. Several layers of paper bowls and plates were stuck together in a clump. But that wasn't what he was worried about. The laptop? He tapped three bags of dog food, thumped on the fourth, and ripped open the wrapper. The inside of the bag was lined with plastic and the laptop was safe and dry. "Thank you, Jesus." Putting the delicate package to the side, he checked the other supplies. It was about what you'd expect: everything in paper, ruined, everything in tin and plastic, safe.

Sam rubbed the taut muscles in his neck. A throb was on the edge of becoming a full-fledged headache. "Selfish morons. Frank and Paula have about as much consideration for other people as buffalo would grass in a stampede." It was the kind of weirdo analog Cockroach would love. Why was it that all the cool people were digital and the analogy versions were primo assholes? Frank would never have appreciated that one-liner.

He grabbed the broom and brushed a pool of water toward the floor drain; small waves of debris clogged the opening. He slid the clump away with his toe, and the water dropped into the pipe. When the floor held only a thin sheen of slickness, he put his broom away and sat at his computer. He needed to think; not daydream-wander-think, but actual brain-cells-at-full-capacity-think. What the hell did Frank and Paula want with his data? His University employment contract, and the attendant NDA, was clear; his research was going to be used by the military. He'd always believed—or perhaps allowed himself to believe—that international agreements about the non-use of bioweapons meant that whatever he discovered would be put to some benign use. Memories rose—professors, teachers, parents, classmates—all telling him, in their own way, some kind, most not— that he'd missed the point. But the point was never pointy enough for him to grasp; it was invariably hidden under layers of their coded speech. But with Frank trying to smoke him out of his office, he couldn't ignore the data, it was definitely pointy enough for him to twig to the implications: he'd been working on a weapon, something dangerous and illegal.

The foam cushion splatted under his rear end. It had soaked up half a gallon of water. He leaned his head back. Things would dry out. No point crying over spilt water. Pulling the keyboard drawer out, he attacked the keys, hoping that his first message had alerted his friend that they were needed. "Cockroach. Ready for a mission?"

The cursor blinked, and he stared at the screen, willing his friend to show up. "Come on, I need you right now. Quit playing video games or whatever you do and answer me."

It was as if Cockroach could hear what he'd said because seconds later he logged in.

CR: Whassup?

Sam ran his palm over his face.

SAM: "I need some digital forensics done on Paula Dean. She works at the University of California, Berkeley. She has an office somewhere in the life sciences building and just assisted a colleague in an attempt to burn me out of my lab."

CR: "Why the aggression? Turn her down for a date?"

SAM: "Hilarious. They're after my research on the caterpillars. Your slip up the other day has them after my laptop."

CR: "Say no more, Watson. I'm on the case."

Cockroach went silent, and Sam leaned back in his chair. The cold sponge of water soaked the back of his shirt and down his trousers. He shivered and stood up, shaking his body in an attempt to loosen the cloth suctioned to his back.

Sam dug in the cabinets underneath the counter and produced four Bunsen burners. Fitting the rubber hoses to their ends, he connected them to gas nozzles on the counter. Preparing the flint lighter, he placed the head above the burner and started squeezing the arms to create sparks. Turning the handle so the valve was open to let the gas flow, he brought to life a lazy glowing orange flame. Adjusting the valve so the air hole was half open, the flame turned from orange to a shorter, focused blue. He repeated the task for the other three burners.

As the air started to warm, he placed his arm over the flame to dry out his sleeve. Was it energy-efficient? No. Did he care? Also no. The heat reached his skin, and he shrank back. Small hairs curled and blackened on the back of his hand and wrist. "Well, Henry, looks like we can't speed up the drying process, sorry."

Cockroach reemerged, a ding acknowledging his presence.

CR: Mission is a go. The main directory for Paula shows she is an administrator's assistant making sixty thousand a year. Her office hours are...

Sam interrupted the string of typing.

SAM: I need you to break into the servers at the school, not tell me what the people search website tells you. Her personal folders should give us an unrestricted view of who she is.

CR: Alright, Watson, keep your shirt on. We'll see what we can see. I'll need you to accept a remote access request after giving me your I.P. address.

Sam swished the mouse back and forth over the mouse pad until a small window appeared. He clicked 'yes,' and the cursor moved of its own volition. Cockroach was now in control. A command line opened, and a string of text blurred by as he worked to break into the servers on campus. 'Access denied.' Another string shot by. 'Access denied.' By the time Cockroach had quit, Sam's desktop was littered with windows filled with DOS commands, and failed attempts to crack the administrator's passwords.

CR: Sorry, man. My software isn't powerful enough to crack their firewalls. For once, an I.T. guy was paranoid enough to enter a password other than *Password*.

Sam slumped in his chair and swiveled until he was facing the burned hole in the boarded-up window. He tapped his knee in succession and swung back around, fingers flying over the keys.

SAM: You were able to remote into my computer. Could you do the same to her?

CR: Not without her permission... but... we could try to trick her into allowing us to see what she's doing. Take the horse to the gate, so to speak.

Sometimes Cockroach could be so cryptic with his codes even Sam couldn't figure it out, more so when it came to technology. He could be talking about the Trojan horse, but he could literally mean some other horse Sam had never heard of. If he'd learned anything it was that Cockroach was full of surprises and the best thing was to watch and wait.

CR: Give me some time and I'll get back to you.

SAM: Make it soon. They might try to break in here again.

Cockroach vanished from the chats.

Sam checked his phone: no messages. He clapped the lid closed and wrinkled his nose. Something foul filtered through his nostrils as he sniffed the air. Following the scent to the storage closet, he located the source. "Whoa, whatever that is, it needs to go out." Hauling out the bag of trashed food items, he slid the mass over the floor and propped it by the door. Henry trotted over and started sniffing. Sam used his leg to block the dog's nose. "You don't want this, trust me." Peering through the hole in the window, a shadow passed along the far wall and footsteps echoed off the tile. "I'm not going out there if I'm being watched. I can deal with stench better than pain."

He futzed with his supplies, stacking what he could salvage in the back of the closet and moving the spoiled goods to the door. Still no word from Cockroach. Sam would normally have fed his caterpillars next, but he was out of oak leaves. "Note to self, must do a supply run asap."

He checked the forum again, still no Cockroach. The hours ticked by with nothing to do and nowhere to go. He checked the chat rooms, his phone, the chat rooms again. Nothing, plus nothing, with a big side helping of nothing. He flicked his figet spinner around, harder and faster, willing Diana to call him with an update, or Cockroach to message with a work around, or even Frank to make his next move, but there was only the rasp of his sweet dog's sleepy breath and the sound of his own brain ticking over, making him just a little bit insane.

Sam wasn't designed for silence. He flicked open his phone and found Diana's contact.

"Thank you for being my friend." He backspaced over the message faster than he'd typed it. She already knew they were friends, he didn't need to say that again. What was it he wanted to say to her. *Don't leave me here, Diana. Something bad's happening. I don't know what, exactly, but it's giving me the jitters.* That was just dumb. Not grounded in fact and very far from scientific. What could she do with a message like that? Nothing! It wasn't actionable. No, best just wait until she called.

He scrolled down to Cockroach's entry. What a weirdo that guy was. The smile spread across Sam's face, all the way from his mouth, up past his eyes and into his hairline. Cockroach was his kind of weirdo, though; that guy was smarter than smart, took no prisoners, and got the job done.

Sam kneaded Henry's shoulders and steeled himself against the silence and the dark. He had a couple of really good friends. Not the fake kind he'd seen evaporate in High School when he was promoted out of his year group, time after time, but solid people he could rely on.

All would be well.

Probably.

CHAPTER TWENTY-ONE

**RON FROBISHER. THE FAIRWINDS.
SOUTHAMPTON DOCKS, ENGLAND.**

Crashing waves rode the harbor wall, sending plumes of spray over the steel walkway where Ron cussed and hollered at the loading crew. Bobbing on the horizon were the deep-bellied tankers and long-haul transporters; the kind of seafaring vessels that had professional crews and long-armed cranes and steel lashings to keep everything in place. Not so the good ship *Fairwinds*. The dockers' philosophy seemed to be something akin to, "Anything goes. If it fits, it fits." These were no TETRIS masters, more like irate toddlers throwing a hissy fit; "throwing" being the operative word. The crates went from hand to hand to the hold of the ship like a line of friggin' beachballs.

"Put it down. No, down." Ron's crates had been delivered to the dockside while he was in the pub. He wasn't late, they were early, but that wasn't the problem. The loading crew were stacking boxes higgledy-piggledy; steel containers stacked on top of wooden boxes abutting the honking great lion's cage Ann Pilkington had promised him. Ron needed his goods to be away from the main cargo and stashed in that steel cage, where he'd have direct access to them.

"Stop!" His crates were clearly marked with *Bio Better Inc's* logo: Caduceus, mounted with the Rod of Asclepius. But unlike most medical insignia, the parent company had encircled the serpents, physician's staff, and wings with a band of text. *'Terretur minimo pennae stridore columba unguibus, accipiter, saucia facta tuis.'* Great. Latin nonsense that no one but Ann Pilkington cared about. Upside: he could easily identify which of the boxes were his and extract them from the bowels of the ship.

He snatched a crate away from a dockworker. "My load goes in last. Over there. On their own. In the cage, capiche?" Why he was using Italian when talking to a Ruskie was just one of those head-scratchers. A lot like speaking *louder* to a foreigner made them magically understand English. "Where's the captain? Kaptiàn?"

"Captain no here." The dockworker was cross-hatched and weather beaten, his teeth chipped and stained from years of knocking back liters of vodka to compensate for having such a crappy job. Ron knew the type. The UK had been flooded with displaced Russians after the end of the Cold War. They did the jobs Britons were too stuck up, or too proud, to do for themselves. "Captain say we go pack, we go pack."

"Yes, we go pack. But not my things." Ron put the crate down and shoved his way back along the walkway, hands slipping along the rain-drenched railing. He boarded the vessel and made a beeline out of the rain and up to the control room. "Where's the captain?"

"Don't have a clue, sir."

"Who are you? Second mate?" It was a good guess, given that they were on the bridge.

"Third mate, sir. Oberon Kettering." He tipped his fingers to his cap in a half-assed salute. If he'd been a Naval OS he'd lost whatever good habits the Navy'd drilled into him. "Been with the *Fairwinds* for twenty years. Honored to be taking her out for one last spin. Gonna miss the old girl."

Yeah, yeah, not now. You can reminisce later. "I'm Peter Columbus. I'm the biologist accompanying the live cargo."

Kettering shook his head. "News to me, sir."

"Those crates with the medical insignia on the side? No one thought to check the manifest to see if there were special instructions?"

Kettering tsk-tsked and shook his head. "Not my department, sir. You need the harbor master. He's in charge of the dockside ops."

Ron swore under his breath. "What an absolute cluster. I need them taken out of the hold and placed in the space dedicated to *Bio Better's* cargo. All of them. Now. That's not dockside business, that's down to you."

"Keep your blummin' hair on." Kettering grabbed the radio, untwisting the cable which had snagged on an antennae. "Bridge to hold. Bridge to hold, come in please."

"Hold to bridge. What's up, Obi?"

Kettering held the speaker to his chest. "That's what they call me. Obi-wan-Kettering."

Ron grabbed the handheld radio from the third mate. "This is Peter Columbus." Dumbest cover name ever, but he had to roll with his instructions. "I'm here to escort *Pilkington Industries* cargo to Lagos."

The speaker crackled and sputtered. Like everything else on the *Fairwinds* it was the shoddy, third-rate, bottom-of-the-barrel version of a ship's radio making it impossible to understand the speaker.

"Say again. Over."

"Sorry, Mr. Columbus, there's nothing here from *Pilkington Industries*, sir. Over."

Wrong company name. Stupid, schoolboy error. "Right. That was last month." He knew better than to over-explain. "Today we're moving inventory for *Bio Better, Inc.*"

"Ah, yes." The man on the other end of the radio was upbeat. "Mr. Columbus, sir, your cargo is almost loaded."

Ron let his finger off the speaker button and swore. In Russian. "жизнь трахает меня." *Zhizn' trakhayet menya.* Literal translation, "Life is f**cking with me." It sounded better in Russian. "Get four of your best men—"

Obi-wan-Kettering, or whatever his name was, laughed. "Yeah, right."

"I want your best people on this and I want them now. They're going to move my samples to the steel crate."

"But, Mr. Columbus, sir..."

"Don't 'but' me. I want it done."

"It means offloading a boatload of other stuff."

Ron mashed the speaker up against his mouth. "I don't care if you have to hand pick splinters from a haystack. You're going to get my stuff out of there and into the cage."

"Cage, sir?" More white noise and interference overlaid whatever the guy was saying.

"Show me the manifest." Ron hung up the radio speaker.

"That's with the First Mate, Mr. Columbus."

"What kind of Mickey Mouse outfit it this? You can't *not* have a copy of the manifest on the bridge."

"The kind of Mickey Mouse outfit that transports goods for *Bio Better*, no questions asked." Ron swung around and came face to face with the secretary from the pub. The one who'd thwacked the drunk with her handbag. She'd changed out of her pub clothes and was dressed in the standard issue *Helly Henderson* waterproof overalls and the *Xtratuf* boots that were so popular with commercial fishermen. And... women. He had three seconds of abject confusion before the pieces fell into place. He'd been a friggin' idiot. Blinded by the zeroes tumbling into his bank account, he hadn't asked Ann Pilkington the most basic questions. Item one, is Captain Alva a man or a woman?

"Captain Alva, I presume." He held out a hand. She didn't take it.

"Mr. Frobisher. What are you doing on my vessel?"

Ron managed not to look at the third mate, who already knew him as 'Peter Columbus.' He'd never been caught out using an alias before, but he had an answer ready. "That's not the name I use professionally. I'm Peter Columbus." He forced a blush, something he'd perfected over the years. "Alimony issues, you understand."

"Classy." She eased past him. "A man who doesn't meet his obligations. Exactly who I want on board."

"It's complicated." He didn't need Alva to be his enemy, but if she bought the story about having two names and thought he was a cad, it was a small price to pay for having flubbed his own introduction. He was going to be locked in the lion's cage with a bunch of beetles —or glowworms, or whatever it was Ann Pilkington was sending to Nigeria—for the duration of the trip. The captain could judge him and it wouldn't make a blind bit of difference.

"You're working for *Bio Better?*"

"Correct."

"Obi, get down to the hold and tell Ellberry to get his ass in gear. Mr." She turned to Ron. "Columbus, was it?"

"Columbus. Right." The boat pitched and swayed, rolling on the tide that sucked and slapped at its moorings. Ron widened his stance. Wouldn't do to be thrown to the ground on his first day. He'd get his sea legs soon enough. "Peter Columbus."

"Mr. Columbus works for friends of ours, Mr. Kettering, and as a courtesy to *them* we're going to do as he asks."

"Yes, ma'am." Obi snapped a salute that was a good deal sharper than the one he'd thrown at Ron when they met. "Right away, ma'am."

"Listing?" Obi hovered in the doorway. "On the manifest; what are they listed as?"

"They're not on the manifest, but the crates have a distinctive stamp."

The job was turning out to be even more intriguing than Ron had first thought and that was saying something. The Right Honorable Ann had said Captain Alva 'didn't ask questions,' but not having cargo listed on the manifest contravened so many shipping laws in so many countries that he could only assume she was being paid as handsomely as he was.

Alva scratched instructions on her iPad and hit send. "Escort Mr. Columbus to the hold, Obi, and let him show you which crates are his."

Ron wasn't so ego driven that being dismissed by women bothered him, but to have it happen three times in one week was a little on the dispiriting side. He was used to being the charmer, the fixer, the one they turned to in their hour of need. Captain Alva wasn't going to ask him for dime one, let alone assistance. He shrugged it off. He had the mildest case of White Knight Syndrome that anyone had ever had and he wasn't going to let her opinion of him throw him off course. At least, not much. If the passage had been longer or the pay less outrageous he might have cared what she thought, but as always the money Pilkington Industries was paying him to do this job covered all manner of ills.

He followed Obi out of the bridge and onto the deck. The rain hadn't eased up but the dock workers weren't letting that slow them down. As Ron rounded the corner to the lower deck stairs, a shout went up.

"*Smotri chto ty delayesh'*" Watch what you're doing. "*Ty idiot?*" No translation needed. Same in every language. "*Ty chto sobralsya nas vsekh ugrobit'?*" You're going to get us all killed.

"*Vislushayte ego, on prav.*" Listen up. Ron pounded back down the side of the ship, projecting his voice toward the dockworkers. "*On prav. S gruzom nuzhno obrashchat'sya ostorozhno.*" He's right. You need to handle the cargo carefully.

"*Ty govorish' po-russki?*" You speak Russian? The dock worker who'd greeted him when he first arrived was all smiles. "*Yeshye kak govoryu.*"

"Yes, way." Ron's accent marked him as having spent time in St. Petersburg, but that was to the good. Russians told him that he sounded "educated" and "literary" and "not like that buffoon, Gorbachev."

"Your Russian is real good." The docker was from Moscow; he had that distinctive, heavy twang that marked them out. "I'm Veedal Smirnov." He pumped Ron's hand. "Like the wodka."

"Smirnov, tell them I need the boxes collected and moved to the designated area. They're toxic. *Toksichno. Yadovityy. Smertel'no.* Lethal. You understand?" Ann had told him a single drop could, 'Wipe out a colony.' Yet another detail he hadn't investigated.

A crate flew through the driving rain and into Veedal's back then dropped to the steel walkway, landing on a corner. One side of the crate split sending packing material spilling out of the crack.

Ron backed up a couple of steps before realizing that the crate didn't have the *Bio Better* stamp on the side. This was some other poor schlub's problem.

Veedal shook his fist as his colleague. "Oaf. Idiot. Son of a motherless dog. You make I sign for the dole office." Both men laughed. There were some advantages to working in the United Kingdom. If you were injured on the job, you could 'sign onto the dole' for benefits. There was every chance that, all laughing aside, Smirnov would sign on and collect money for doing nothing other than lying on his backside and sucking down gut rot.

"Before you go, Smirnov." Ron made sure every syllable was annunciated clearly. Russian wasn't spoken like English; you weren't immediately identified by class and region when you opened your mouth, but there were sounds that would land as authoritative. *"Peredayte muzhikam, chto im zaplatyat..."* 'Tell the men there's a reward in it for them. If they move my stuff, slowly and carefully, into the lion's den and stack it no more than three crates high and three crates deep, I'll cross their palms with paper.' He pulled a one-hundred pound note from his stash and pressed it into Veedal's calloused hand. "There's more where that came from."

Veedal lit up like New Year's, Easter, and Victory Day had all landed at the same time. He relayed instructions up and down the line, taking charge as if he'd been made for the job. "Yes, this; no, that; do what the man says and he'll make it worth your while. I saw it, with my own two eyes. He's not like her up there. Not some miser with the money. This one will pay you. No, I tell you, he will. Do it. Do it now."

And just like that, the *Bio Better* crates were moved—gently, tenderly; like newborns being passed from a wet nurse to a mother just days after they'd made their way into the world—like precious cargo, rather than some old garbage they didn't give a toss about.

Ron jogged down the stairs and joined Obi-wan-Kettering at the door to the lion's cage. "Leave a space at the front. Ten feet by ten feet." He turned to the third mate. "I'm going to need a mattress."

"Mattress?"

"You got it."

"Down here?"

"Right there, where I can see anyone trying to get into my stuff."

"Whatever you say, boss." Obi lingered, like a bell boy who'd ripped your bags from your hands in the lobby, insisting you couldn't carry a few measly shirts and a couple of pairs of trousers to your own room, only to hover while you fished around for your tip.

Ron peeled off a fifty pound note.

"Saw what you gave Veedal."

"Balance on delivery."

Obi took himself up the stairs, leaving Ron to supervise the final uploading of *Bio Better's* crates. He leaned up against the side of the cage. What had Ann set in motion? Here was a boat that was barely fit for service, captained by someone who was apparently going to take the moral high ground with regards to his alleged non-payment of alimony, but who was willing to transport something sight-unseen and deliver it to a port that was not going to inspect the incoming goods. That was primo-level gangland shenanigans. Not that he thought there were gangs actively in the mix, but contraband *anything* meant you were going to consort with the lowest of the low and the roughest of the rough. Captain Alva didn't fit the profile.

The *Bio Better* crates were loaded and stacked under Veedal's command. The man was on fire to please Ron, rearranging crates that weren't lined up perfectly; making sure the logos all faced the same direction. He stood back, hands on his hips, then smacked Ron on the back. "We do good, ya? *My vse zakonchili.*" We're all done. "There are four mens do good work. Two more is useless piece of crap. We pay four, yes?"

Ron tallied the crates. Three deep, three high, twelve long except for the front row, which was several crates short. He'd picked the stacking ratio at random. Without a packing or shipping manifest he had no way of knowing how many crates he was supposed to have. "One minute, Smirnov. I'll be right back."

He tapped a note to Ann's burner phone, picking each word with care, adding and deleting options until he had what he hoped was succinct, but clear. "How many?"

The three dots pulsed. Ron waited. She was doing the same,

adding and subtracting of words so they'd both be the right side of plausible deniability. "Unknown."

That wasn't right. She must have thought he was asking about the merch, not the crates. No way anyone would know how many glow-worms—beetles, slugs, whatever—were in each crate. For all he knew it was one per and the rest was whatever glowworms needed to survive inside a wooden box for five days. What was an innocuous word for 'crate?' He did a quick synonym search, but it was useless. Box. Package. Parcel. Everything sounded too much like 'crate' and far, far too incriminating. He didn't want anything that smacked of smuggling. It came to him while Veedal pared his nails with a peasant's knife. No implied threat there, then. "How many cartons?" He was traveling; he could have been referring to cigarettes. English people did that all the time, traveled to mainland Europe to buy off-duty booze and ciggies.

"108."

He only had 98 crates. "Ten missing, Smirnov."

"Nyet. No, all here, boss. I check."

"Ten missing."

Veedal rained insults down on his countrymen, urging them to find the missing crates, and was met with a colorful volley by way of return. "Cost is more. We take everything down, we put all up. Cost is more."

"One hundred pounds more for each man who brings me a missing crate." That was peanuts compared to what Ron was making. And worth it. Ann would not be amused if he started the journey short.

"Five hundred for me." Smirnov had lost his cheerful enthusiasm, instead sporting that most-Russian of all expressions: resignation. His mouth turned down, his eyes were hooded, and the rest of him had gone slack. Yep, Russian to the core.

"Fine. One hundred for each of the finders; five hundred for you, for *nablyudeniye*. Supervising."

The Russian grunted and stomped away to unstack and restack boxes. It was a grueling hour which turned up only seven of the ten missing crates.

Veedal wiped his face with his shirt. "We look everywhere. Is all."
He flicked the top of Ron's phone. "Message is wrong. All here."

There was nothing to do but pay the man and face the music.

"When you come Southampton, we drink, da?" Smirnov stuffed
the bills into an inner pocket in his trousers. "You ask for Smirnov,
like the wodka. I give you number. Here." He took Ron's phone and
tapped his contact details in.

"Da. We drink." Ron shook Veedal's outstretched hand and sent
him on his way.

In the cool calm of the rocking hull, Ron Frobisher debated the
pros and cons of telling Ann Pilkington that someone had lifted some
of her cargo before they'd even set sail. You'd expect that kind of
thing in an unregulated port, but Southampton? It galled him to type
the words. He wrote and deleted his message ten times before he was
interrupted by a text from Ann.

"All is well?"

He paused for a beat. On the one hand, she wasn't going to fire
him. There was no one else who knew how to navigate these waters.
He could tell her there were three *Bio Better* crates missing and keep
the job. On the other, she'd promised him a bonus and those could
wax or wane, depending on her mood. Better keep her sweet. "Fine.
Just dotting my I's," he typed. White lie. No one would ever be the
wiser. "All present and accounted for."

The three dots pulsed for several minutes. "Remember. One
drop."

Who could forget? One drop of this 'luciferase' would "wipe out a
colony." Colony of *what* was the question.

CHAPTER TWENTY-TWO

DR. DIANA STEWART. LINCOLN, NEBRASKA.

When Diana came around for the third time, Dan's kick slammed her back against the store wall. She curled into a ball, arms protecting her head, and coughed. She couldn't tell if the toxins were starting to get to her lungs or the kick had broken a rib.

"What did it get you, making that noble sacrifice?" Dan hit her again as she struggled to breathe. "Did you save the little children? Have you made up for your sad, wasted life yet? It'll take more than that. A whole lot more."

She didn't reply. Through the cage of her arms she could see a thread of smoke coming out of the shelves at the end of the aisle. The lighter had fallen into the pile of cans. It wouldn't light anything fast enough to be useful and that left her in a dangerous position.

He kicked her again, deadening her arm so that it fell away from her face. He crouched and leaned in to speak intimately right in her ear. "Are you—and I ask despite your massive, much-hyped intelligence—are you under the impression that giving yourself up will make a blind bit of difference? It won't. The kids will be going out that door and you'll get a ringside seat. I'm looking forward to seeing your face as they blister up and choke to death."

Another kick landed in her ribs and she grunted in pain, trying to curl in tighter to the wall. *Something's broken.* She had to get out of his line of fire, she had to! But everything had gone wrong, and she was helpless to stop him hurting the kids. Even if she could get past Dan, Aaron lurked near the end of the aisle, keeping one eye on the customers and the other on her.

"I'm supposed to bring you in alive, for some reason, but it would be a great shame if you had a terrible accident and died. And frankly, you're proving to be a bit dull so far. How like you. But as always, I know how we can remedy this." He turned to address Aaron. "We have no instructions about the kids. Let's send them for a little walk, shall we?"

She shut her eyes in despair. She'd failed, right at the last post. But as he grabbed her arm, an ear-splitting boom roared across the store. Dan slammed into the wall, crumpling on the floor next to her. A scorching wave of heat thundered over her and there was a cacophony of metal on metal as the cooking implements on the shelves nearby were sent tumbling to the floor. There were screams, dull and muffled and the fire alarm was similarly distant.

Diana rolled to her hands and knees and grabbed a bungee rope from the remains of the display. Cutting two lengths with her knife, she knotted loops over Dan's hands and feet and hog-tied him, tugging the rope with all her strength. She pulled his head up and shoved a glove in his mouth as he stirred. Awake now, but unable to move or speak, he struggled wildly but it was too late. She let his head thud back onto the floor and left him there, impotent and furious.

Aaron was unconscious and had burns on the side of his head and shoulder. She tied his hands and feet as she had Dan's, but he awoke before she could finish the job. "What the...? You!" He rolled over and swung his legs around in an effort to knock her over, but she jumped back. He was not immobilized and that was a problem, but she didn't dare go nearer.

She picked her way down to the front of the store. Fortunately, the blast had not done more than crack the windows' reinforced glass.

"We don't have much time." She cut Eli's bonds. He threw his arms around her. "Are you okay, Eli?" She felt him nod. "Go and untie Mrs. Beaufort and her friend, and we'll get everyone out of here."

"Those men?"

"Escape first, talk later." She cut Samantha's bonds.

Samantha got up. "I'm glad you're safe. What do we need?"

"Goggles, scarves, gloves, hoods or hats. You have the bag?"

"Yes." Samantha patted it.

"Good. There are enough masks for us and your mother and Jesse. If anything goes wrong, make sure you and Eli are covered and run back to the car. If I don't make it, go."

Samantha's face was pale. She handed the phone back to Diana. "But if that happens, ring Mom and we'll come and get you." She hurried away.

Diana cut the rest of the customers free. Mrs. Beaufort, Leon, the manager, the football player, the few others who were in the store were on their feet and finding protective gear within minutes. From the back of the store, there was a slam and a shout.

"We haven't got long. Can someone unlock the inner doors? If you can get out safely, do." Diana pulled on a coat. "There are fewer cicadas about. They won't stay in the city for long—they're looking for food— but every surface you touch will be toxic." She handed Leon a balaclava from the shelf. "Wear gloves and goggles, cover your face and don't let them touch your skin. The outer clothes you're wearing will be compromised and so will your shoes. When you're home safely, take them off wearing the gloves, put everything in a bag and throw it away."

Another crash, and two voices shouted.

"Hurry!" She didn't dare let Dan and Aaron find them. "Anyone who's ready, make your way out and take shelter in the nearest building."

"Let me clear the way, ma'am." The manager unlocked the doors and the football player straightened his gloves and moved into the entrance. He heaved the body of the man from between the outer doors and threw out the few cicadas gathered on the floor, then waved them to follow.

"Go, quickly. And be careful." Diana hugged Samantha and Eli briefly as they joined Mrs. Beaufort and a few of the others. When the entrance hall was full, Diana closed the inner doors behind them and they spilled out.

"Don't just stand there, untie me, you moron!" Behind them, Dan's voice was shrill with fury. "She can't get away."

Diana ushered the second group in, and pushed the doors closed. As they left, she caught sight of the bag, which Samantha had left in her hurry. She slung it over her shoulder and rummaged inside. She hadn't had time to find anything for herself but—

"There! Get her!" Dan was on the stairs, and Aaron was crashing through the shop toward her.

The last customers were in the space between the doors. She joined them. "Get out, quick! Go!"

A woman gestured at Diana's unprotected face. "But you're not—"

"*Go!*"

As Aaron reached for the inner doors, the woman opened the outer doors and the customers ran. Diana was left in the entrance, unzipping the backpack with trembling hands. In the split-second Aaron hesitated, she grabbed the large clear sheet from the bag and as he opened the inner doors, she ran out into the street, pulling it over her head.

Aaron swore and closed the inner door again one-handed, then clutched at his burned shoulder. Dan stumbled into view, burned and disheveled. He screamed at Aaron, who disappeared back into the store.

Diana's ankle was not up to a full run, but she hobbled as fast as she could, dropping to a walk as she began to cough. The other customers were out of sight; Eli and Samantha too. Diana limped between the corpses and crashed cars like a ghost in some ghastly Halloween scene.

Cicadas were gathering on the sheet; most slid off, but one of them crawled into the folds of the plastic where she was grasping it, and she did not dare release her hold in case the whole thing slipped off. Coughing harder, she leaned against a lamppost for support. Her breaths were fast and shallow, and her heart was beating as if it would jump out of her chest. Every inhalation made the pain stab through her ribs.

A shot zinged off the lamppost, and she stumbled. Aaron stood in the lobby with his hand out the door, wearing an incongruously cheerful pair of ski gloves.

She limped behind the car, trying to ignore the dead man sitting on the other side of the open door, a blistered mess with his tie loosened and his shirt torn open at the neck. The back window shattered, and she backed away. Her breath was coming quicker and quicker. She was getting light-headed, and her vision was losing its sharpness. Was her throat closing like Jonah's had? It was difficult to stay calm. Aaron's shots were getting closer. Her stabby ribs wouldn't allow her to duck and dive, but she couldn't let Aaron shoot her. It'd be bad enough being dead, but worse if the children came back to find her brains splattered all over the inside of the sheet.

A shot ricocheted from the roof of the car just in front of her, and she recoiled.

Her bad ankle gave under her for the third time; she fell, landing hard on the pavement with only the plastic sheeting between her and the corpse of an old woman. Her rib hurt as if she'd punctured a lung, and the old woman's agonized, swollen face oozed fluid onto the sheeting.

"She's down! Get her!"

The inner doors screeched open. Dan's metal heel-tips clicked across the street. She had to move.

But all she could do was lie there as the slow ooze of blister fluid made its way down the plastic, and fight to breathe.

"Ha. Pathetic. Utterly pathetic." Dan wore a full-face diving mask. He stopped by the car, watching her gasp and wheeze. "All I have to do is take your sheet, and you're as dead as your friend there. I hope the kids can find someone who'll look after them better than you did, because if not, they'll be wandering the streets on their own, in a city full of poisonous insects. That toxin is deadly. And if they don't die of asphyxiation, like you are—well, young children with no one to help them, in a city they don't know. Doesn't generally bode well."

There was a screech of tires, loud amongst the fading hum of the cicadas. A truck sped toward them, mounting the pavement to avoid a cluster of cars. It slammed a couple of café tables and a motorbike out of the way and sent a garbage can flying as it roared straight toward them.

Dan sprinted out of the way, drawing his gun. The truck missed him by inches and rammed the car, sending him tumbling across the curb.

The truck door opened and Samantha jumped out, still in full gear. "Diana! Quick!" She ran to Diana, who flicked the sheet back so that Samantha could pull her upright, glove to glove. They stumbled around the truck and Eli opened the door from the inside. As he scrambled out of the way, Diana fell into the truck. Samantha shoved Diana's legs inside and clambered in, shouting to Jane. As the kids strapped themselves in, the truck swerved around and screeched off up the road again, amidst shouts and flying bullets.

Lying limp on the floor of the truck as the pain from her rib ebbed, Diana couldn't immediately focus. Various thuds and bumps suggested that the way was not clear, but as the haze of pain and panic eased, tears trickled from the corner of her eyes. She didn't dare wipe them away in case she had toxin on her hands. She shook like a leaf, but at least she was out of direct danger for the moment. And her breathing was easier, though her rib was still stabbing her innards and making her sweat. She concentrated on slowing her breaths and her pulse, calming herself. *Breathe in.* If it wasn't the toxin affecting her... *Breathe out.* Ha. Could it be as simple as a panic attack? Maybe it could, after all.

As the ride got clearer and the car slowed, the panic faded. Everything had happened so fast! But now she was lying with the plastic sheet bundled inside out next to her and the rucksack pressing painfully in her back. She struggled into a sitting position, clutching at her ribs.

"Are you okay?" Eli was peeping over the top, hiding behind the headrest as if he were watching something scary on TV. Samantha had an arm around him.

Diana coughed again. It hurt. "As shopping trips go, it wasn't my favorite." She mustered a smile, and he sat back down, apparently reassured. "Thanks, Samantha. That was some good work out there. Jane, all well with you and Jesse?"

"Good to hear your voice, Di. That was terrifying." Jane paused to turn onto the freeway. "Jesse's here in the front with me. He's fine, and so are the rest of us, thanks to you and your quick thinking. Are you hurt? Do we need to stop?"

"Let's get some distance in between us and Lincoln first." As Diana shifted herself into a more comfortable position, a movement caught her eye: there was a cicada caught in the plastic sheeting. She shuddered.

Moving stealthily so that the children didn't notice, she opened the cooler and took out another sample box. The creature was crawling along the plastic, and as she reached toward it, it dangled from the edge, about to drop onto the carpet. She caught it in the box and put the lid on, prickles going up and down her spine at the thought of it being loose in the truck.

It was different from the rest, though. Odd. Still, not the time to examine it.

As she put the box into the cooler with the others, the quiescent cicadas woke up, inching to the edges of their boxes and pressing themselves closer to the new cicada. Diana took the new bug out of the cooler again, but still the newly-wakened bugs were agitated. She didn't want them to wake up too much and scare the kids, so she closed the cooler and left the new cicada on the top, enclosing the sample cage in a plastic box for good measure. *Strange.*

"It looks like we're catching up with the swarm. What do you want to do, Diana?" Jane leaned forward, peering through the windshield.

"Keep going. They can't keep up with us at this speed. We'll outpace them soon enough. Everyone, check your windows, though. We don't want to take any chances." Outside, the occasional cicada turned to a handful, then a cloud, and soon their vehicle was crawling along the freeway, cicadas all over the place.

"The window's getting smeary. The windscreen wash just doesn't cut it." Jane's voice wobbled. "And I think there's a car close behind us, but it's hard to see—"

There was a smash, and the truck jolted sideways. The kids cried out. A scream of tires, and another jolt followed.

"It's lining up again!" Jane accelerated forward, for a few feet. "I can't see where I'm going but their lights are behind us. They're reversing again—wait! Oh, thank goodness. They're off the road. They can't get back on." Their own truck jolted to a stop. "What do we do?" Jane twisted around in her seat to look at the other car. "I can't see well enough to go forward without wiping the windscreen. But, obviously, I can't go out to do that."

"It's them. Those two men." Samantha peered out of the side window. "Their windscreen is as gunked up as ours. But the one who said he was a policeman is waving a gun at the side window and arguing. I think he wants to shoot but doesn't dare break the glass."

Diana wracked her brains for ideas. "Okay. We have to assume that when the cicadas thin out a bit, Dan will put his mask on and come over. And we can't afford to let him shatter any of the windows, so I'll have to go out to him. Samantha, grab one of Jesse's blankets. Here's a roll of tape. And—ah...."

"Are you okay?" Jane twisted in her seat.

Diana doubled over, hissing with pain. "When we have a chance, I need you to bind my ribs. I can't afford a punctured lung. But it'll have to wait. Right now, I need to get into my PPE before the cicadas leave."

It wasn't easy, wriggling into the suit in the confined space, and she had to keep stopping to let the pain from her rib ease, but she managed it with Samantha's help.

"The cicadas are far fewer now," Jane called. "How's it going?"

Samantha helped pull the harness for the compressed air tank onto her back. Diana hissed again at the weight of it on her broken rib, and checked the gauge. It wasn't full, but it worked. "You know what to do?" She handed her a roll of wide tape. "I need to get out the back. You need to make a barrier that separates the trunk space from the rest of the truck so no cicadas can get in with you when I open the door."

Samantha nodded, and with Eli's help, she attached the spare blanket to the hooks on the inside of the truck ceiling, then taped it to the walls and ceiling where the back seat met the trunk. She dropped the roll of tape over the back of the bench seat and sealed the blanket to the seat. Diana made herself another layer of protection with the clear plastic sheeting. With the air bottle on it was painful to maneuver, but she did what she could. If it would just hold for the few moments she needed.

"He's putting his mask on!" Samantha's voice wavered, and she cleared her throat. "Now he's got his gun."

"Wish me luck." Diana pulled the full-face mask down, tucking her hood over the top. She got out of the back of the truck as quickly as she could and took the sample box out of its plastic container. She batted away a couple of cicadas that flew up from the bumper. Then a couple more from the ground. Then a handful more. They began to settle on her shoulders, on her hood, crawling on her mask and tumbling off her shoulders.

"What the hell?" Dan stood by his car. His gun, pointed at her, wavered as she limped nearer, gathering a mantle of cicadas as she went. They clustered thickly over the sample box that held the strange cicada, and with every step, more insects zeroed in on her from all around, covering the box and her arm, and her shoulders and hood.

The cicadas' shrieks vibrated, twitching the suit as if the toxin was seeping through and eating away at her skin. She didn't know if it would soak through, but the thought kicked her breathing up a notch. She took another step toward him, and another. Fear coursed up and down her spine, but Jesse lay helpless in the truck. She had to defend him.

Dan retreated to the trunk of the car, his feet crunching on the cicadas scattered across the tarmac. He had left his door wide open and inside the car, Aaron was rummaging frantically to get something to cover his face.

Diana's feet slid out from under her and she fell heavily to the ground. The sample box skittered across the tarmac, and out of reach.

Dan stumbled forward to stand over her, gun pointed at her face, and grinned like a shark. "Goodbye, Diana. You won't be missed. Certainly not by me." Then he pulled the trigger again.

CHAPTER TWENTY-THREE

**ANAYELI ALFARO. EAST SACRAMENTO,
CALIFORNIA.**

Everyone in Sacramento was on the river. The gravel parking area of
River Rat Rafting Company was completely full. More than full.
Anayeli had never seen it so packed, even during the summer heat
waves, when it hit 110 degrees and everyone who didn't have a pool
flocked to the water. Cars and trucks and SUVs were parked and
double-parked, filling every available space. Others were slanted at
awkward angles, or pulled up onto the curb, while still more spilled
out into the street, rear bumpers jutting out toward traffic because
no one had time or inclination or skill to parallel park properly in a
panic. But the full parking lot wasn't the worst of their problems.

"Ernesto! Do you see any rafts?" Her brother was squeezed into the
other front bucket seat with Mama, and as Anayeli blasted past what

would ordinarily have been the entrance to the lot, he craned his neck.

"I don't see any..."

It was the answer she already knew. Usually the open area between the rafting company's storage sheds held at least a dozen of the yellow inflatable rafts that were a summer-time fixture on the river, but there was no tell-tale splash of sun-shiny yellow in her peripheral vision.

She cursed as she sped down the road, looking for any space she could wedge the truck into. In the back seat, only Roxy was quiet. Bailey Rae sobbed, Luz murmured kindnesses, Carlota zipped and unzipped her backpack over and over, and Cricket whimpered. The radio in her jerk neighbor's truck—which also had a full gas tank and working AC—blared the horrible buzzing alarm of the emergency broadcast system followed by evacuation orders for most of the city every three minutes in rotation. The problem was the announcement didn't say where to evacuate *to*.

Anayeli couldn't think. She had no Plan B. The river *was* plan B. Or, by this point, probably Plan P. The fire was bearing down on them. Every time she checked the rear view mirror, the sky was only more ominously dark, the smoke a churning, living, moving thing, and sure, objects appear closer in a rear view mirror, but when she looked over her shoulder through the back window, in between Carlota, Luz, Bailey Rae, and the dogs' heads, there was no doubt that the smoke, and the orange glow lighting the horizon, was nearer, even though she was driving away from it.

She'd run from the fire before, and if the flames came as close as they had on Bertoli's farm, the six of them plus the dogs could never outrun it. They had to take advantage of the small head start they had, because if the fire was moving like it had back at the farm, it was devouring the blocks between them in seconds. They had to get on the water. Fast. It was the only thing she could think that would save them—surely the fire couldn't jump the river. Or if it did, at least they could survive it. She'd read about people and animals using lakes, swimming pools, any body of water to shelter in during the terrible fires that had ravaged the state in years past, dunking under water when the heat or smoke got too intense, popping up when they got too cold—a constant dance between asphyxiation and hypothermia.

"Bailey Rae! Can you swim?"

In the rear view mirror, the little girl's head nodded. But still. She was only, what? Nine? Ten? The chances of her being a strong enough swimmer to last hours in the river were not good. The water was deep and cold and though the current looked calm enough in most places, it was deceptive. There were rapids, and plenty of hidden snags beneath the surface. They needed a raft. Without one, not only would they have no way to keep their bags dry, but there would be no way to keep their group together. If she could just find a parking spot, she at least knew where the path was that would take them down to the river. And maybe once they got there, they'd find an abandoned raft. Or maybe some kind people who would share. It was a stupid idea, but it still gave her hope, and hope was what she needed.

She yanked the steering wheel and whipped into a U-turn, wedging the truck's nose between two cars that were spaced just far enough apart to accommodate their vehicle, the truck bed sticking out into the street. It was a terrible parking job, but she didn't care. They were never coming back for the truck, not if the fire did what she was afraid it would.

"Grab your bags! Hurry!" They piled out of the truck in a head-long rush, Cricket and Roxy scrambling out first, before Anayeli's feet touched the pavement. Then Ernesto slid out, the telltale wheeze of his asthma coming with every breath. She hoped his inhaler was in his bag, but was afraid to ask. Nothing they could do about it, if it wasn't. The girls all spilled out of the back seat on Anayeli's side, leaving Mama alone of the far side of the truck. As Anayeli reached into the back seat to grab her bag, a white lifted truck squealed around the turn from the main road, then skidded to a stop at the blocked entrance to the rafting company parking lot. Someone else with the same idea. New plan. "Ernesto! Bailey Rae! With me! Run!"

She took off, zig-zagging through the haphazardly parked cars. "Mama! Meet us down there!" Ernesto, Bailey Rae and the dogs pounded after her. Anayeli prayed Mama, Carlota, and Luz could manage all their bags, and that if there weren't any rafts, there were some life vests left. At the very least she needed Ernesto and Bailey Rae in vests.

She stopped in the clearing that was usually full of rafts. The nearest storage shed's outer wall was lined with hooks that were mostly bare, except for a few very faded orange life vests that dangled at random intervals, the kind of vests that had been old when she was a kid. She snatched at one that seemed a little smaller than the rest.

"Here, Bailey Rae. Put this on!" The girl stood still as Anayeli slipped the vest over her head, then grabbed for the straps. They were all too long, even once she'd managed to shorten them as far as they'd go. It was an adult life-vest, not a kid's one. At least Ernesto was big—the one he'd found almost fit him. "Better than nothing, sí?" She hoped that was true. The little girl nodded, tears spilling down her cheeks. Anayeli should have tried harder to get to know her neighbors. If she had, Bailey Rae wouldn't be stuck relying on people who were little more than strangers.

Ernesto yanked the last three life vests off their hooks and held one out. "For you, Yeli."

"No." She was a good swimmer, had even joined the swim team in high school, possibly because after overhearing too many so-called jokes about Mexicans in rivers she had something to prove. "Give them to Luz and Carlota and Mama." Their three dark heads were weaving through the cars, slowed down by the weight of their back-packs, probably. Everything in her wanted to yell at them to run faster, but she didn't. They knew there wasn't much time before the fire was upon them. They didn't need her adding to their anxiety. But then Ernesto, one arm draped with vests, the other free, ducked behind the storage shed. Cricket let out a low growl, ears trained on something out by the road.

It was a man, running from behind Mama, drawing closer and closer. Beyond him, near the street, a woman held a baby on her hip and a toddler by the arm as she half-jogged, half-dragged the kids away from the white, lifted pickup truck.

"Ay, Mama! *Rapidamente!*" The anxious buzz of adrenaline

thrummed through Anayeli's veins. There was only one reason a man would take off running and leave his wife behind with their two little kids. He wanted something they had.

"Yeli!" Ernesto poked his head from behind the shed, his voice urgent. *"Ven aquí!"*

Hiding was a good idea. She grabbed Bailey Rae's hand and pulled her around the shed. The little girl wasn't crying anymore, and though that couldn't be a good thing, Anayeli was relieved. There was no time for crying, no time for soothing grief. The man was already past Mama and Luz. There was only Carlota left to pass.

Behind the shed though, Ernesto was smiling. He had found the *milagro* she'd prayed for. A raft. Only a four-person raft, but it would fit Bailey Rae and the dogs and the bags. It would be enough for them all to hold onto. It would keep them safe. And the running man must have seen it too.

"It's going flat." Ernesto stepped on the side of the raft. Instead of the taut surface of a fully inflated raft, the whole side gave, collapsing under the weight of Ernesto's foot. Next to it lay a patch kit, scattered across the ground, and one of those battery operated air pumps Papa had kept in their camping supplies to blow up air mattresses.

"I'll take it." The voice was male, and full of confidence, the words a command, not a request.

She whirled, filling her lungs to make herself taller, the way her tío had taught her to do when working with horses. She pushed Bailey Rae behind her, and both dogs came to their side, Cricket in the hunched, stalking position herding dogs used on sheep, Roxy with her hackles raised. From the warmth at her back, and the wheeze in her ear, Ernesto had moved behind her too. She had to look powerful. Sound fierce. "No. We want it."

Mama, Carlota, and Luz came around the shed and the calculus changed, along with the man's entire demeanor.

He put out both his palms, fingers wide in supplication, changing tack. He was about Anayeli's age, maybe younger, with the kind of neck beard all the outdoorsy redneck type guys had and a T-shirt advertising the popular IPA from one of the local micro-breweries.

One of those local-and-proud, born-and-bred type guys. The kind who went hunting and off-roading and boasted about being half-feral. "Please—" he gestured toward his wife. She had a kid on each hip and was doing an odd shuffling scurry toward them, the kind of run you did when you were carrying too heavy of a load and had to hurry before you dropped it. "My kids—"

A wail rose from the parking lot as the mom leaned to put the toddler back down. She dragged the boy again, his feet barely touching the ground as she clutched at his arm and ran. On her hip, the baby's head bobbed in time with her steps. The man's voice had gone pleading, and Anayeli guessed he wasn't the kind who liked to beg. "Please. My kids can't swim. We can't make it without a raft. Or life vests."

The wailing grew louder, then doubled as the baby joined her brother's cries. The man half turned, like he was going to go help his wife, but then he stopped. "How about we take your littlest sister in the raft with my wife and kids? Head down the river to the evacuation center, meet you there—"

It was a ludicrous suggestion. Whatever adrenaline had been fueling her burned suddenly hotter with fury, and something less than a glance, more than an electric current passed from her and Mama and her sisters. Cricket growled. Anayeli reached behind her and found Bailey Rae's hand. She gave it a squeeze and kept holding on. No way she was sending the girl off with total strangers. "What evacuation center?"

"At UC Davis Medical center. We can go near to the whole way in the river. It'll be safe there. We'll wait for you—"

The little hand in hers was trembling, and that same hot wind that had blown from the fire on Bertoli's farm had picked up, bringing with it swirling gusts of ash-filled smoke and the ominous crackling that raised gooseflesh all along her arms. There was no time for negotiations. "Yeah, no. We're all sticking together. We're not sending anyone"—she gave Bailey Rae's hand another squeeze—"with people we met in a parking lot." She couldn't believe the audacity of the suggestion.

"What's going on, Jason?" The harried mother came up alongside her man. Even though she had that exhausted, put-upon look of frustration every mother of a toddler wore, the girl was pretty—in a slim, high-maintenance, manicured, and highlighted hair kind of way. A wine-o'clock-mom, prettier than a guy like Jason deserved.

"We're just talking. Seeing if we can figure out the raft situation." His tone made Anayeli bristle. The way he downplayed what was happening. As if the raft were some used item she'd listed for sale online, available for best offer.

"Up! Daddy! UP!" The toddler pulled at Jason's pant leg, his face screwed up in a way that meant a scream was coming. Jason ignored his son.

The wine-mom hitched the baby up on her hip and threw a glance over her shoulder. "Jason..." She did not sound on board with the river plan, or else she'd had it with Jason leaving her to wrangle the kids. It couldn't help that the trees, the car windows, everything was lit a lurid orange, and charcoal gray smoke boiled where blue sky and clouds should be.

"Savannah! I'm talking to these nice people!" The restrained anger was unmistakable, and even though Anayeli's feet stayed planted, she drew away from him. She got the feeling the couple had been arguing well before they'd arrived at the parking lot. Savannah looked near tears. The baby, staring at Savannah's face, started bawling, and the little boy went from pulling at Jason's pants to clutching his mama's leg. That was when Savannah dissolved into a coughing fit, and Anayeli realized for the first time: none of them had masks.

It was the babies that did it. That and the coughing and the hot gust of wind-that-wasn't-wind. The fire was doing the same thing it had done on Bertoli's Farm, sucking in oxygen, fueling itself, sending up plumes of smoke that made whoever wasn't masked cough—and worse. They were out of time for negotiating, but she would not have the lives of two babies on her head. It was too much. Not one more life, not on her watch.

"This is what we're doing." Everyone's attention snapped to her. "The kids are going in the raft. Your two. Bailey Rae. Anything else that needs to be kept dry. The rest of us can hold onto the sides if we need. We'll get you as close as we can to the evacuation center—"

Mama let out a torrent of objections, all in Spanish, just like Anayeli had known she would. Anayeli made a sharp hiss but Mama kept going. *"Cállate, Mama!"* She'd yelled it at her siblings millions of times, but she had never been so rude to tell her own mother to shut up, and the shock of it made it work. Once they were on the river they could argue about whether it was safe for Mama—for any of them—to go to the evacuation center.

"Deal." Jason stepped toward the raft, as if he were going to grab one of its handles. Cricket and Roxy both moved to block his path and behind him, his wife sagged, her face etched with exhaustion and her mouth pinched with resentment.

"You carry your son. We've got the raft." At her words, everyone burst into action. Ernesto, Carlota, and Mama peeled off and went to the raft, put the remaining life vests and Bailey Rae's, Anayeli's, and Ernesto's bags inside, then hefted it up and took off at a jog toward the towering oak trees and the path that meandered through to the river. Luz came to Bailey Rae's side, took her other hand and led her after the others. Cricket stayed glued to Anayeli while she snatched up the air pump, but Roxy ran back and forth between the two groups, as if she were counting her people, trying to keep them all together.

As Anayeli ran to catch up to the others, Jason, his son on his shoulders, left Savannah to bring up the rear with the baby. He jogged alongside Anayeli, matching her steps in a way she didn't like. He didn't trust her word that they'd share the raft. But whatever. She didn't have time—or inclination—to reassure him. They needed to get to the water, put more distance between themselves and the fire. She prayed whoever had been patching the raft had finished the job and that they could blow the raft back up at the shore.

In all the times Anayeli had been rafting down the river, she'd never moved so fast and the path had never been so long. Somewhere along the way, Luz started singing *Vamos to the Beach*—the upbeat, trumpet-filled song Anayeli used to play on her phone, any time the family had been on the way to the water. The sweetest sister, always trying to make things better, urged Bailey Rae to join her, but got Carlota and Ernesto to instead. But when they finally rounded the bend and the river stretched out before them, the song died in their throats.

Instead of the rippling water sparkling under the summer sun, its surface dotted with bright rafts full of laughing families, there was no river to see. The entire waterway was completely clogged with floats of all description—yellow rafts like their own, kayaks and canoes, loungers crowded with three or four abreast, a giant white unicorn crawling with people. It was a teeming, splashing, screaming mess, as the people clogging the shoreline pushed and jockeyed for position, everyone trying to get into the water as quickly as possible. But the current was too slow, or the water too crowded to carry the mob downstream quickly enough to make room for all the new people lining the shore, or the stragglers like them that were still coming from all the various paths that led down to the beach.

Jason was the only one who didn't stop at the sight. "Let's go!" He barreled past Anayeli and Ernesto and headed straight for the water, with all the confidence of a man on a mission. It worked, too. By the time they got there with the raft, a small space had cleared near Jason and they were able to set the raft down. As they waited for Savannah to come huffing from behind, Ernesto got to work with the pump, its thin, high whine drowned out by the noise of the crowd.

Anayeli took the remaining life vests from the raft and held them out to Carlota and Luz. "Put these on."

Carlota did as she was told, but Luz took the vest and gave Anayeli a little smile, then went toward Savannah. "This is for you. Want me to hold your *hija* while you put it on?"

Savannah gave Luz a searching look, but everyone loved Luz and it was exactly zero surprise when the woman handed over her daughter. The instant the baby let out a squall, all Luz had to do was take a few dance steps and start up her beach song again. That made the baby giggle, and Luz kept it up while Savannah fastened the life vest's straps, stopping to cough every few breaths. She didn't have a bloody nose though, so that was good.

Anayeli turned to Jason, held out the last life vest to him. "Here. You should have this." If the raft didn't end up holding air, Savannah and Jason would need all the help they could get, keeping their kids afloat.

"Yeli!" Ernesto straightened from the raft's air valve and put the air pump inside, then pushed on the raft's wall. It barely gave under the pressure. "It worked!"

Ernesto and Jason inched the raft closer and closer to the water as the crowd thinned. Anayeli tried not to, but every few seconds she checked the skyline, watching and listening for the telltale signs that the fire was close. Ash landed on their shoulders and heads, caught in their lashes, but there was no sign of actual flames.

Finally they nosed the front edge of the raft into the water. As it bobbed up and down on the current, Ernesto splashed into the river, steadying the craft while Bailey Rae clambered in. When Roxy scrambled after her, Jason scowled and pointed to the shore. "Get out!" When the dog didn't acknowledge his order, Jason grabbed her by the collar and made to haul her out, but Bailey Rae wrapped her arms around Roxy. "No!" It was the first thing Bailey Rae had said since she'd realized her dad wasn't coming out of the house to join them.

Anayeli was at just the right angle to catch the moment Jason smoothed his irritation away as he turned back to help his son aboard. Even though the back of the raft still touched the shore, it shook and bucked as the boy wobbled around inside, and she wondered about the wisdom of putting the kids in first, before Savannah was aboard to manage them. Luz must have had the same thought.

"Come on, Savannah." Luz, still holding the baby, took the woman's arm and led her to the water's edge. As the woman stopped to cough, Anayeli pulled her pack out of the raft, shouldering it while she dug for a mask to give the young mother. Mama and Carlota hung back, the pair of them muttering in Spanish, disapproving of everything she and Luz were doing to help the young family. Anayeli couldn't disagree—she wished it was just her family on the raft—but as Savannah settled into place and reached for the baby Luz held out to her, Anayeli knew she'd made the right decision.

Ernesto splashed forward into the river, dragging the raft farther out. She hoped he wasn't making his asthma worse with the exertion, but her heart swelled with pride at her baby brother, taking responsibility. They were among the last of the people gathered on the shore to make it into the water, which at least meant there was more space around them.

Anayeli handed the mask to Savannah, who gave her a wan smile just before she secured it over her face. The moment Savannah's arms tightened around the baby again, and the raft began to bob, fully in the water, Jason exploded into action. He burst forward, crashing into Anayeli and knocking her backward. He barged toward Ernesto, panicked as his wife and children floated away from him and probably afraid Ernesto couldn't manage the raft alone. But as Anayeli struggled to maintain her balance, Jason didn't stop. He didn't apologize for bumping into her. And he didn't grab the raft handle to help Ernesto guide the raft out into the deeper water. Instead, his arms were tense, and the moment he was within reach of Ernesto, his right fist flew out and landed a punch squarely on Ernesto's jaw. Everyone around them erupted into shouts as Ernesto dropped into the water.

Time stretched into slow motion. Roxy scrambled out of the raft and into the water, swimming straight for where Ernesto was splashing. Carlota and Mama ran through the water toward Ernesto, both of them screaming. Luz and Cricket came to Anayeli's side, and Bailey Rae shrieked, leaning over the side of the raft as if she wanted to jump in after Roxy, tipping it precariously. All around them, the other people in the water paddled furiously, trying to get away from the commotion, making it easier for Jason to pull the raft into deeper water.

The only people not screaming were Jason and Savannah. That was when Anayeli knew. That had been their plan the whole time. They'd used her and her family to get the raft to the river, but they'd never had any intention of honoring the "deal" Jason had agreed to. She went cold with fury and time slowed even more as her hand went into her backpack and closed on hard metal.

She stuck the pistol straight into the air. "Jason! Stop right now or I'll shoot!"

Jason didn't stop. At the sight of the gun, the splashing panic around them grew more frenzied, as everyone tried to put distance between themselves and whatever was unfolding. Bailey Rae went over the edge of the raft with a splash, desperate to get away from the strangers who were dragging her away.

"No! Jason! Don't! Please!" Savannah clutched at their children, shielding them with her own body as Jason ignored her and plowed ahead.

Anayeli was done making deals. Jason was not allowed to hurt her brother. He did not get to take all their supplies. Her family would not be left without the safety of the raft. She had important details she needed to get to the authorities, to people who would be able to make use of the information that there was some connection between the Teff fires and the toxic smoke, and she refused to let an ungrateful *pendejo* stop her.

She lowered her arm, sighted down the line of the barrel, aimed for Jason's heart, and pulled the trigger.

CHAPTER TWENTY-FOUR

SAM LEARY. BERKELEY, CALIFORNIA.

Sam's body itched as if ants were crawling under his skin. The burned tiles and mildew had created fumes that reeked. His adrenaline was way past its effective state. He was a nervous ball of raw energy. Henry woofed in his sleep and Sam jumped, sloshing the black coffee in his cup. Running his hand over the jagged edges of the damaged plywood, he inspected the hole for the tenth time in as many minutes. Someone could push their hand through and undo the door brace. It was only luck—and the butt of a fire extinguisher—which had prevented Frank from doing just that during his last attack.

Sam sipped the scalding beverage and spat the offending liquid back into the cup before setting it by his bed. He was circling the edges of exhaustion and he knew it. If he couldn't even remember: 'Coffee, kettle, boiling water, equals too hot,' who was he to set himself up as the scientist who could solve the cicada invasion? Actually, no. He was exactly the right guy. He'd been studying something directly adjacent to this and his research was valuable enough that he was being hunted. *HUNTED! For crying out loud!* He checked his watch. Twelve hours had elapsed since Diana had cut off communication, and he hadn't heard a peep from Cockroach for hours.

He shuffled to the computer and scratched his head. His fingers came away sticky with the oil and grime of the last few days. He wiped them on his pant leg.

Slumping against the keyboard with his elbow, random letters filled the chat window, which became a black-and-white blur through lidded eyes. Henry lapped from his coffee mug. "No way." Sam snatched the cup away and grimaced at the mysterious floating debris circling his wake-up juice. *Today's going to be a very long day.*

Cockroach made his appearance online over an hour later in usual Cockroach style.

CR: Email the unsuspecting Paula Dean the trojan horse I have created for you. Once it's delivered, monitor incoming messages for any activity from her computer. If you're caught, I'll disavow all knowledge of this activity. This message will self-destruct in five seconds.

Five, four, three, two...

Sam opened the email and scrolled through its contents. A PDF stood out from the text and he hovered the cursor over the icon.

A second message from Cockroach appeared underneath.

CR: Don't open the attachment! We only get one shot to track her, and we don't need your computer in the mix.

Sam pulled his hand off the mouse and scolded himself for almost ruining the sting.

CR: The keylogger will automatically install as soon as it's opened. It tracks whatever our target types or clicks on. It's a basic kid monitor that allows us to see everything done on one particular machine. If you opened the pdf too, the software installed would track your computer and hers.

SAM: So what am I sending? I need to put the correct wording in the subject box so she'll open it.

CR: I created a fake invitation to a ball with fancy lettering and everything.

Cockroach, you're amazing, but sometimes so clichéd. To each his own. If he hadn't needed to figure out who Paula really was, he would have ended the chat. But Cockroach had taken the time and energy to create the Trojan Horse. In any case, Paula pairing up with Frank was enough of a red flag that Sam had to investigate what was going on from her end. He read over the details of how to send the message and replied in the chat.

SAM: Are you sure she'll open the pdf, let alone the message?

So many of the faculty members at this university ignored important emails.

CR: Please. Staff rarely touch official email, but they open junk mail all the time.

Sam quirked an eyebrow. It was true. He wasted time on messages in the past that had nothing to do with work. Most of the time they were fun memes and video clips about animals. Maybe this scheme would work.

SAM: When do I start this 'mission?'

CR: The sooner the better. If the email is in her box before she gets into the office, there's a greater chance of seeing everything she types today.

Cockroach had a point.

Sam stripped out everything identifying Cockroach from the email and copied the pdf into another message addressed to Paula. "Let's see if she comes in today and brings a treat to distract you." Henry sat up and gave a doggy grin; his smile spread from ear to ear as his tongue hung out. Selecting the box for a digital read receipt he clicked send; the swoosh informed him the document was delivered.

Clicking echoed down the hall and Henry went to investigate. Lifting up on his hind legs, he sniffed at the hole in the plywood. "No, there isn't anyone out there. It's the echo effect off the hard surfaces. Someone's heading upstairs." Sam threw the ball as a distraction.

He'd just sat down to a peanut butter and honey sandwich, when his email brought up the requested receipt. Paula had opened the package. *Let's find out what she's up to.* Another email dinged in his inbox minutes later.

PAULA: Hilarious, Sam. If you think this will keep me from

pursuing the laptop, you're dead wrong. Although the offer to dance is sweet.

What else did Cockroach put in the invitation that he didn't tell Sam about? He opened up the email from Cockroach and found the link to view what was going on. A window opened and a string of text with time stamps populated in list form.

1:00 p.m. Outlook.

1:10 www.amazon.com

The string continued for forty lines, showing every key Paula pressed. Most of the list was about shopping. Man, if Dean Collins found out about her using sites like this on the school's computers...

Thirty minutes later, Cockroach sent a message.

CR: Has the prey taken the bait?

Sam clicked the accept box so Cockroach had a remote view of his desktop and took another bite of his sandwich. His mouse cursor floated around the screen, enlarging the keylogging window, and scrolled through a hundred lines of information.

CR: Oh, shopping. So exciting.

Sam licked the peanut butter from his fingers. Sticky keyboards were the worst.

CR: Go find Frank and make him think you're up to something. If he and Paula are working together to get your laptop, you can guarantee he'll pass on whatever he heard.

SAM: What if he talks to her in person?

CR: If they meet in person, make sure to be in hearing range of their conversation.

Sam slumped. Cockroach was many things: smart, computer savvy, funny, but 'worldly' wasn't one of them. There was no way Sam was leaving his laboratory to sneak around like one of the Hardy Boys, just *hoping* to overhear the right conversation between the right people at exactly the right time. The real world didn't work like that. That was what you got for hanging out in the digital world. The nerds might have inherited the Earth, but they had no more clue what to do with it than their parents had.

The phone rang and he picked up his cell. It wasn't buzzing. He followed the bell tone to the school phone. "Hello?"

"Sam, what's going on? I heard about the fire. You okay?"

It was Janine, from the DNA lab. Her voice was distinct enough he could pick it out of a crowd of a hundred people. "Fine thanks." It was a lie, but who could he trust? For all he knew, she was in on it.

"You didn't hear this from me. *Entiendes?*"

Sam squirmed in his seat, grabbed a pen and flipped over one of his drawings, ready to take notes. "Yeah, I understand."

"The U.S. Government has been in contact with the school. For over two years they have been searching for a new kind of weapon that can be used in stealth missions. When your caterpillar venom came across our desk, they were extremely interested. It took less than a week for the paperwork to be signed. Since the venom comes from an insect any death would look benign to those looking for a cause and no one would be the wiser as to who was involved."

Sam jumped to his feet, the handset cord yanking the base into the air. The phone hovered for a second before it clattered to the floor, busting the corner open. The line went dead. *Dammit.* That was the first real lead on his work and he'd botched it with a stupid stunt in his excitement. The dots connected at warp speed; he wasn't paranoid or wrong; they *were* out to get him and his research and they always had been.

As he picked the phone off the floor, the hair on the back of his neck stood on end and he turned in time to witness an eye disappear from behind the plywood. The shuffling on the other side of the boarded-up window confirmed he was being spied on. Grabbing his cell phone, he flipped the device open and pressed the earpiece to his face. Henry went to sniff the door jamb. If Frank was on the other side of the door, there was no time to call Janine back. He made a mental note to contact her later.

"Hello, Di? Can you hear me?" Sam waved the phone in the air, pretending to scan the room for cellular strength. Moving closer to the intruder, he raised his voice so Frank understood every word. "Hey, I wanted to pass on some terrific news. The DNA lab cracked the molecule. They have a way to create the anti-inflammatory I was telling you about. What? Yes, the caterpillar venom." It was crude, but then so was Frank. You might not be able to beat fire with fire, but he could try a blunt force info dump to the neural network of an idiot.

Sam used his peripheral vision. Frank inched past the window. Cockroach was right, they did eavesdrop. He would have to thank him later. Turning sideways so the hole in the window was at his back, Sam continued to pretend he was feeding Diana information.

"Well, now for the bad news. The military has been working in tandem with the school on a weaponized version of the venom, one that can be used for assassinations. The lab rats discovered it three months ago. If they add another protein instead of subtracting one and place it between a couple amino acids, the venom creates arrhythmia strong enough to induce a heart attack. It's been tested over the last few months on animal subjects and they are ready for field tests."

He paused again. It was fun, having fake conversations. Even more fun to think about Frank freaking out and grabbing the wrong end of the stick.

"I don't have the foggiest clue how they got the..." Sam slapped his forehead and kicked at the trash can. He missed by inches. It was the kind of thing Frank would have done so even missing the trash can was a work of genius. "The samples. I gave them to Janine. I should've done the work myself, but they can be so protective of the equipment over there. It's too late now; let's hope the field trials don't go as planned. If they have to start at ground zero I might be able to sabotage their research." Another short pause for maximum effect. "All right, drive safe."

Sam peered out of the broken window as Frank's side loomed in front of it, blocking the hole. Moments later the hallway was empty. *Got you where I want you.* Sam ran to his desk and jabbed the keys in excitement.

SAM: Sting operation is underway.

Cockroach was seconds behind in his reply.

CR: Roger that.

The key-logger text streamed fast and furious as Frank conversed with Paula on Windows Live.

FRANK: Came from Sam's lab. He said the school has succeeded in creating a weaponized chemical from the caterpillar venom. It's real.

PAULA: Terrific. What's our time frame?

FRANK: I think late this afternoon. He won't be expecting the attack so soon after the last one.

PAULA: We need the information intact.

FRANK: Keep your skirt on. I'll have the laptop tonight. Even if I have to rip the device out of his hands.

PAULA: Make sure you don't kill him.

FRANK: Don't tell me you're sweet on him.

PAULA: It's none of your business whether or not I like him, just keep him breathing and in one piece. What about the mutt? How are you going to deal with it?

Sam grinned like the proverbial cat while scratching Henry's head. "Good boy, Henry. Good, good boy." How gratifying to know that his big ball of love and fluff could scare the bejeezus out of Frank.

FRANK: Won't be a problem, not with what I have planned. Don't visit the first floor after six. It's not going to be a pretty sight. Come to think of it, it'd be better if you weren't here at all.

Frank disappeared from the keylogger text while, to Sam's utter amazement, Paula continued to shop. She'd discussed stealing state secrets and gone right back to designer handbags and stilettos.

Deviating from the regular stores, she navigated to a site labeled *Cheaper Than Dirt*. Sam opened a search window and pasted the information into the address bar. A list of weapons filled the page with the choices of hand guns to rifles. Oh, so not *exactly* handbags. Scrolling through the options, he followed the path Paula made. The trail dead ended with a snub-nosed, double-action three-fifty-seven revolver.

Sam fumbled with the keys, misspelling words as he freaked out.

SAM: Cockroach, she just bought a gun.

His body buzzed and he pushed his chair away. Nervous energy coursed through his veins and with trembling limbs he circled his lab. *If Paula is willing to kill for the information, what's next? She doesn't want Frank hurting me. Does she want the pleasure of doing it herself?*

After a hundred laps around the lab, the adrenaline slowed, and he resumed his watch of the keylogger. Finishing what he assumed was her wish list, she opened a web browser labeled TOR and pasted in several odd sites that didn't fit with the normal naming conventions for the internet.

SAM: Cockroach, what do these sites do? I've never seen them before.

The cursor floated around until it hovered over the up arrow and the text scrolled backward several lines. The small white pointer underlined the letters and numbers strung together in odd formats and stopped moving.

CR: She's going to the dark web: places you can buy and sell contraband. You can bet that if she's visiting these sites at the school, she's hiding behind the internet protocol addresses that are masked when they travel through the firewall. I wonder how she found a way through the tech servers to do this. Most schools don't allow access to sites like this.

SAM: Hey, focus. Where do they lead?

Cockroach vanished for several minutes.

CR: Okay, got my notebook here. It pains me to have this list because it cost me some of my anonymity with the Government when I first explored the dark web many years ago. Long story. Let's see... the first tab is a site called the *World Market*. It's for drugs of all types. Uh, the second one, is... for Bitcoin and PayPal. Hold on a minute. Looks like she is leaving a message for someone.

Paula's text came across slow and methodical.

PAULA: To interested parties: in possession of a DOD chemical specified for assassination. Bidding will commence in forty-eight hours on website money market, tag: Mega. At the end of bidding, and confirmed payment, a drop site will be designated. Buyer is responsible for item once delivered to agreed site. Bitcoin or Ethereum payment only. Use trusted market for transaction, tag: cooking. Sale is for data sheets on weapon and one live sample, all sales are final.

Sam's jaw hung open. She was trying to make money off of his research. Oh, man. If word got out that the venom was on the market, he'd be toast. He'd given terrorists the perfect weapon. But she didn't have the laptop, so that would be the next step, which would be sometime tonight.

Cockroach stepped on Sam's thought process.

CR: Your girlfriend is a terrible person. I wonder if her partner knows what she's up to?

Sam ignored the quip and shot back.

SAM: How reliable are those sites she mentioned? Can they be hijacked?

CR: The dark web isn't like the average website you find with Google and Bing. These sites aren't indexed, so you have to know the exact address they are located at, and chances of them having higher security than the Government is assured. It makes up only five percent of the world wide web, and these people hide better than I do. Face it, your only chance at keeping this thing from getting into the wrong hands is to keep the information away from everyone, or destroy the laptop and the sample before Paula and her conspirators can get their hands on it. Good luck.

Sam turned the monitor off. Well, that settled the question of Paula. Saboteur, spy, or criminal, she was about to sell something that could land him in jail or worse.

CHAPTER TWENTY-FIVE

DR. DIANA STEWART. OUTSIDE LINCOLN, NEBRASKA.

In all the time he'd been giving her a beat down, nothing had changed. Dan still had murder in his eyes.

Sprawled on the tarmac Diana's ribs spasmed in pain. She could barely breathe for a few seconds. She couldn't get to her feet and run, and the sample box with the new cicada—the queen or whatever it was—was out of her reach.

He set the muzzle of the gun against her mask and pulled the trigger. Nothing happened, not even a click. He pulled it again and again in increasing fury, and then ejected the magazine. Empty. He swung at her mask, trying to break the glass, but she jack-knifed and slammed both her feet into his knees. He crumpled sideways. The strap on his mask snapped, and it rolled away.

As he kicked the sample box, a shrill sawing note went up from the creature within. There was a whir of wings as every cicada in sight launched itself into the air. A great cloud of them converged on the box, on the car, on Diana and Dan, hundreds upon thousands of them.

Diana clambered to her feet, clutching her ribs. Behind her, Aaron cried out. She couldn't see him for the cicadas on the outside of the car.

Dan struggled to his knees, flailing frantically to get them away from his face. "Help me! Diana! Save me!" She backed off so he couldn't grab her again; but he was already coughing and wheezing. It wasn't a trick. He didn't deserve her help, but she couldn't just leave him.

She staggered to Dan's car. Maybe there was something there she could use. She opened the trunk to find a great roll of plastic sheeting, some wide tape and a series of saws and axes. And several boxes of lye. "What the hell?!"

"We wouldn't have. Not really." Dan choked on his own blood. "Victor said…" But his choking turned to great wheezing convulsions. His eyes bulged, bloodshot and blistering, and the skin of his face split, blood flowing over the cicadas and pooling on the ground. His wheezes slowed, became tight and squeaky, then stopped. Jerking, he fell backward. He clawed at his throat, and again; then his hand went limp and dropped to the tarmac. His body went lax and he lay still.

Diana's breathing was fast and heavy, despite the pain. The cicadas settled over him more thickly, crawling up onto the mess of blisters that had once been a face, and in and out of his swollen lips.

It happened so fast. But he was dead.

Behind her, Aaron rolled out of the car and crawled for the shoulder. He didn't even get clear before the convulsions set in. She wanted to retch, but in a mask that would be bad news. She turned away and concentrated on her breathing, slowing it down to a more normal speed. By the time she'd gotten control of herself, he wasn't moving.

The cicadas were calming from their initial frenzy, but they were everywhere.

A saw and an axe and a machete, all ready in the trunk, her brain repeated. She shuddered, and it hurt so much that she had to lean on the car, toxin or no toxin. This was not the administrative disciplinary matter. This was real, serious, deathly trouble, and she was in deep. There was some kind of secret about these cicadas that they thought was worth killing for. She had to work out who Dan was working for, and what they wanted: Her boss, Victor, would never be a part of murder.

Her mind was remarkably clear and focused for someone who'd just been through an insect attack of Biblical proportions. She'd seen men die under the weight of the bug toxin and lived to take their machetes. Perhaps it was the pain keeping her anchored. There was too much to do to indulge in hysteria, so she busied herself with clearing up the scene and making sure the children did not see the horrors lying on the tarmac in front of her.

The truck's windows were obscured by the cicada goo, but they would have heard the fracas. She went around to the other side, where they couldn't see the bodies, then wiped away a section of the goo and gave them a quick thumbs up. Jane looked ready to burst into tears; she seemed to be saying something but through the window and the hood of her suit, Diana couldn't hear it. She tapped her ear and then shook her head. Jane reached down to open the door and Diana pushed it so it would not open, shaking her head, then gestured up in the air. Jane nodded, Samantha's face white behind her. Hopefully that would reassure them enough to buy her a few minutes.

She bundled up the roll of plastic and the tools from the trunk of Dan's car. Every movement made her ribs scream, but they were too useful to leave so, gritting her teeth, she carried them to the truck. She set them down on a loose piece of plastic. She didn't want to let any cicadas in there with the children – and if the truth be known, she couldn't quite face talking to them just yet. Aaron had brought a backpack containing ammunition, food and water, and a couple of maps. She took those too, but her mind was running overtime.

It didn't make sense. There was no way Victor knew what Dan was doing. She had to talk to him, face to face. But, first things first, she had to take the samples to Sam, and hopefully by then she would've found some details about Jesse's relations.

The cicadas were settling, and the urgent piping had stopped.

Evidently the queen did not feel she was in imminent danger any longer. That had to be the explanation for the frenzy, nothing else made sense. The sky had cleared, and the remaining cicadas drifted away up to soar onwards on the breeze. She cleared away the cicadas from Dan's body—though not his face. She didn't want to see what it had become beneath the blistering and ooze. The cicadas crawled back, in fewer numbers but she brushed them aside again and checked through his pockets, and then Aaron's. She took both guns. The holsters would be covered in toxin, but the guns themselves could be cleaned.

She went back to the truck for the plastic container she'd kept the queen in and placed the sample box back inside, fitting the lid carefully. Once the lid was sealed, the other cicadas lost their focus and dispersed. It was that simple. And that terrifying.

The cloud of insects thinned and cleared. She rolled both me face down in case the children could see them.

She grabbed Aaron's jacket from the car and used it to scrub the yellow fluid from the truck's windshield. She waved at Jane, sitting inside, who put on the windshield washers and eventually she got the glass clean enough to see through. It hurt her like crazy, and she paused to lean on the truck while the spasm of pain eased.

"Diana? Are you all right?" Samantha's voice was muffled through the window.

Diana nodded. "Not injured. Bruised though." She closed her eyes and shook her head, trying not to replay Dan's bulging eyes as he asphyxiated in front of her. "I'm going to wait till there are fewer cicadas around so I can get back in the truck. No point in risking them getting past the plastic sheet. Might be a few minutes. And I need to make a phone call."

Jane straightened the blankets over her passenger. "Jesse's waking up, but we're taking it slowly in here. Take whatever time you need."

Diana went around the back of the truck and leaned on it. *Oh, to hide under a duvet and have a good cry right now!* The past couple days had been so overwhelming that she was emotionally numb. The same could not be said for her ribcage, though, and her head hurt, and her shoulder was on fire, but there was no point grumbling about them.

The cicadas had all settled or gone – at least enough to risk a quick call. Cautiously, she pulled up her facemask onto her head, and unzipped her suit to get at her phone. She did not take it out of its plastic bag but dialed through the plastic, and waited.

"Diana? Is that you? Is everything okay?"

"Victor, Dan's dead." She had no time to waste. "The cicadas got him, and Aaron too."

"Hang on. There, that's better." Victor flicked the phone over to video. "Diana, what happened?" She bit her lip as her mentor's face registered concern and horror all at once. "Are you okay? You look like you've been through the mill."

"Victor. Dan. He tried to kill me." She swallowed, trying to keep her voice level. Hopefully the kids and Jane couldn't hear too much of this, but she wandered away from the truck anyhow. "He was going to throw innocent people to the cicadas. He tried... he tried to drown me—" A sob came unbidden, and she averted her face for a moment.

"What the hell was the man thinking?" Anger surged across Victor's face. "I said quite specifically that he was to make sure you got here unharmed. I want you safe with us and helping us to work this out. You're unhurt though?" He frowned. "Your face?"

She brought a hand up to the broken skin on her forehead and cheekbone but was careful not to touch it. It was sore but not tingling any more. "I thought it was toxin, but he did slam me into the wall a few times, so who knows."

"He did *what?*" His outrage was real; she'd known him long enough to see that.

"It got physical. But apart from a broken rib, the rest of it is all superficial." *I hope.*

Victor slammed his fist into the desk. "That's unacceptable. It's *unacceptable.* I'm so glad you're safe, Di. I'm sorry. Get back to Chicago and we can have you checked out before we head for the lab. I want to get to grips with this as soon as I can. We need to work out where it came from, pronto."

A wave of dizziness swept over her, and she squeezed her eyes shut, forcing herself to relax. Why had she doubted him? Of course he wanted to help. Victor was many things, but he was not the sort to let people die. And the thought of going back was tempting, so tempting. Diana had used the company's executive suite in Head Office before, when her flat flooded. It was a luxury penthouse, and what she needed more than anything else was sleep and a bath and time away from all the horrors she had seen in the last day or so.

"Di, it sounds dangerous out there, and with more and more swarms emerging, things will only get worse when people really start panicking." Victor typed something. "Why don't you head to the nearest airport right now? Just tell me which one, and the jet will bring you straight here. You'll be back in time for a whiskey before bedtime."

"That sounds blissful." She could get there in hours, depending on the airports. But she couldn't drag Jesse back to Chicago and have him kicking around in a lab indefinitely, not if he had a relative nearby. "Look, there are a few things I need to do here first. I'll come straight back when I'm done. And what do we do about Dan and Aaron? The police will want to know their next of kin."

"They'll be in the files. I'll get someone on it straight after the call. Have you called the police or ambulances?"

She held back a laugh. "There are no ambulances, Victor. When the cicadas hit, everything was overwhelmed in minutes. The cicadas took out the city. Dan was firing at me quite openly in the streets, and the police didn't turn up. If it's like Watseka, they're probably all in the hospitals too because of the toxin." She flicked an exhausted cicada off Dan's car with her gloved hand and leaned back on the hood. "People are already way past panic. This is a crisis—"

Victor cut in. "Where are you? Still outside Lincoln, right? And Dan too?" He tapped on his keyboard again. "I'll send someone out. Just wait there."

A warning flag was fluttering in the corner of Diana's mind. She hadn't mentioned the name of the city, she was pretty sure. But she was too shaken to work it out. "I'm shattered, Victor." Her English background slipped out of her mouth when she was uber-stressed and/or exhausted, all of which was true in that moment. "I need sleep and a shower. Dan's not going anywhere. If you can have someone come and sort things out with the authorities, I need to go and rest."

Now that the adrenaline was wearing off, she just wanted to sleep. "In all honesty, I'm not even sure when I last ate. I'm going to take Jesse back to his people and check in with a friend. But once that's done, I'll be right back."

Victor smiled. "Sam? Or have you picked up a love interest since last we chatted?"

She snorted. "In all that spare time I have, right? Yeah, I need to go and see Sam. It's a bit of a trek, but you know how close we are. He won't do well with all the change and chaos, and he hasn't anyone else to check in on him really." Realizing she was telling too much, she stopped. Victor had been like a father to her once, but she didn't want to fall into the trap of assuming he still was.

Victor frowned and scribbled on the pad on his desk. "Well, do what you must and then let me know where to send the jet. But don't take too long, Diana. We need your help here."

The only remaining cicadas were the ones on the ground. She headed back toward the truck. "Gotta go. It's getting toward dusk, and we have a long drive in front of us. I'll be in touch."

"Soon as you can. Take care, Di."

"Soon as I can." She tucked her phone back into her inner pocket then dragged the supplies into the back and set them on the end of the plastic sheet. It hurt like crazy but once it was done, they could go. "Everyone okay in there?"

"Just about." Jane's voice was much stronger than before. "You?"

"It's been a funny old day." Diana closed her eyes for a moment so she wouldn't have to consider everything that had happened. "Once I've gotten these supplies in, let's get going."

"Where? I just got in and drove. I don't know where we should go."

"Let's head to Wyoming, to your family's place. I don't want you guys mixed up in this mess." She wriggled painfully out of the harness for the compressed air tank, turned off the gauge, and stacked it on its side.

"But those two? They won't be coming after you anymore." Samantha pulled aside the blanket barrier so she could peer through the plastic sheeting. "Aren't you safe now?"

"I don't know. I don't know who else is involved. Hopefully no one, but..." Diana took off her protective suit, gasping at the stabbing pain, and rolled it into a bundle inside out.

"What?" Samantha peered out of the side window. "It's not the cicadas, is it?"

"No." Diana stopped what she was doing, struck by a thought. "Sorry, one more phone call, and I'm with you." She got out again and closed the truck door behind her. "How did Victor know where I was?" She wasn't one for talking to herself, but this puzzle required talking out. "How did Dan find us? How do you track someone along a random freeway and still know where to find them? That would be so unlikely as to be almost certainly impossible. Unless there was something you were tracking."

She set her phone to do a backup to the cloud. Dammit, it had to be the phone. She spent a few minutes exporting all her contacts to her email. Then she rang Sam to let him know why she was out of touch.

When she'd finished, she reset it to factory settings then bent and set it under the back wheel of the truck. "Dammit, Victor, if Dan used that to track me, you owe me a new phone." Not that she could text him and say so now.

"Right." She took off her gloves and climbed into the back of the car with Eli and Samantha. "Are you okay to do the first shift, Jane?"

"I just want to get home."

"Sounds like an excellent plan. Let's go." Diana listened for the crunch of tires going over her phone as Jane reversed. It came into view from under the car. The phone was crushed, glass scattered. A little rain and a few more cars driving over it and it'd be way beyond fixing.

In the passenger seat in front of her, Jesse stirred. "Diana?"

She leaned forward so that he could see she was there. "Hey there."

"Where are we?"

How to answer that one? "We're on the road again, sweetheart. But when we get to the other end, we'll find a hotel and sleep in comfy beds and eat burgers and pizza, I promise you."

He blinked. "Can I have ice cream?"

"Or pudding, maybe."

"But ice cream isn't pudding."

She brushed his hair out of his face. "It is in England, where I grew up. That's what we call dessert. Pudding! How are you feeling?" His face looked better than that morning. Maybe the antihistamines were helping.

He yawned. "Don't leave me."

"I won't. I promise. I will always come back for you till we get you to your family. And when you're happily settled with them, I'll come and visit sometimes. Would you like that?"

But he was falling asleep again. Diana was tempted to do the same.

"Burgers and ice-cream?" Samantha murmured as Diana sat back in her seat. "I hope you've got enough for everyone."

Jane chuckled. "He'll keep you to that, you know. If it's three months from now, he'll still remember. Just you watch. By the way, I cut his morphine dose down by a half. He's nearly out, and it would be better to wean him off it gradually. The swelling seems to be going down though."

"I think so too, thank goodness." The truck rumbled along for a while as the sun faded from the sky and the landscape around them darkened. Though her body was a bag of aches and pains—some she'd barely tracked when she was rolling around on the sidewalk with a man's boot to her neck—Diana slept.

She awoke sporadically through the night, and she and Jane took turns to drive. The road was quiet in rural areas. They skirted the major cities, where chaos reigned. The night's run was reasonably uneventful. The cicadas would be settled on trees and bushes through the hours of darkness, and so they got some miles in.

In places, clusters of cars at the side of the road, and boarded up windows told their tale but in the pre-dawn, all was still. There were occasional vehicles here and there, and the odd burned-out wreck, glowing and clinking in the chill of the morning, but no signs of cicadas so early in the day.

They stopped at a truck stop to gas up and use the restrooms, thrilled to find a pump that worked. Diana took the opportunity to inspect her torso. Her shoulder competed with her ribs for the Pain of the Year Award. Her entire side was one big black bruise. She'd fallen so many times, and taken so many kicks, she could barely differentiate one contusion from another.. The biggest welt was pale against an ominous blue-black bruise. She'd have to buy ibuprofen on the way out. This was not the time to be incapacitated.

But there wasn't time to stop and process. She had left Jesse waiting anxiously outside the door, clutching Samantha's hand, and he hadn't been up and about for long so she didn't want to tire him out. Diana washed her hands and joined the others.

Miracle of miracles, the shelves were still well stocked, so they bought food for a couple of days. It was as if they'd driven through hell to get to a little patch of Normal, USA, and Diana couldn't remember being more grateful for "boring, normal truck stop food" in her life.

"Should we get more?" Samantha lingered by the Krispy Kreme stand. "Just in case, you know, the shops all sell out of food."

"We have some in the truck. We're just stocking up on fresh stuff." Diana grinned. "Sorry."

"You can't blame me for trying." Samantha wandered off to find Eli.

"She likes you." Jane added a couple water bottles to the shopping cart. "And she's at that age where she has no respect for anyone. I can't decide whether I'm annoyed that you've had more genuine conversation with her in the space of a day than I've had in months, or glad that she has a sensible adult she'll talk to." She straightened, rubbing the small of her back. "Do you want milk?"

"Do you like milk, Jesse?" He nodded. His grip on her hand was fierce, and he stayed right beside her, flinching at sudden sounds.

As they filled the cart, more and more people came into the store, despite the early hour, and by the time they got back to the truck, the parking lot was packed. People were running and jostling to get inside, and a fight broke out in the doorway.

"So much for 'normal,'" she muttered.

Jane hurried the children into the truck. "Thank goodness we got in early."

It was a relief to get them back onto the freeway. For the first time Diana was glad she'd taken Dan and Aaron's guns. She might need to learn how to fire the stupid things. Maybe Jane would know.

As the morning passed and the roads got busier, it became more difficult to make any headway. The traffic was heavy and slow.

They encountered two swarms as they approached Wyoming. One was little more than a distant shadow and a hum, but the second swarm was just waking up, hovering over the trees and bushes alongside the road, with increasing numbers flittering up into the air as they drove through. The morning drew on, and chaos became more widespread. Windows were broken or boarded up; cars were crashed into benches and trash cans and left; and every so often, a corpse was left bundled in the road with only a sheet or tarpaulin to cover it up.

So many bugs in such a short span of time; their spread boggled the imagination.

"Guessing emergency services aren't coping here either." Jane looked up from the map. "Not too far now, but if the police aren't keeping things in check…"

"I know."

On a road that branched off to the right, a house was burning. The fire engine was outside, but half the block seemed to have burned down, and the fire engine couldn't control that sort of blaze. A crowd had gathered around, and half of the people on the hose were civilians, with a couple of firefighters in their protective gear at the front.

As they drew into Evanston, everything was calm and quiet. Too quiet? The shop windows along the strip were smashed. Further along into the residential areas, the devastation was less acute, but still evident. Houses were boarded up and garden gates were bolted and barricaded. The few people on the street hurried on their way, checking around corners before turning.

"What has happened here?" Jane whispered.

One road they went past was blockaded off with a barrier of

wrecked cars. Armed people stood on the other side, their rifles in full view.

"That's where the big houses are. I wonder if they work for the rich people or whether they've just taken over the houses."

"Shush, Eli."

Jane navigated them through the streets to a cul-de-sac at the far side of town. When they drew in, Diana pulled over.

"Holy crap." No one told Eli off for his language.

Then Jane was out of the car and running toward the charred remains of her parents' house. Eli and Samantha were two steps behind her.

CHAPTER TWENTY-SIX

ANAYELI ALFARO. ON THE AMERICAN RIVER. SACRAMENTO, CALIFORNIA.

Anayeli swam hard. With her good hand she gripped the raft's handle, while she paddled with the other, trying to keep the raft closest to the north shore of the river, farthest from where the flames roared, closer and closer to the bank. It was stupid to allow herself to get so winded when the smoke was so thick. She shouldn't tire herself out when they had so much farther to go, but if she didn't put everything into swimming, her mind went places she couldn't afford to let it—Jason's wide-open mouth, filled with dark blood; Savannah's screams as he sank into the water, red blooming up and spreading across the river's rippling surface. Anayeli had done what she had to, to keep her family safe. But she'd taken someone else's papa from them.

Her shoes dragged in the current, pulling her lower in the water. Beside her, Cricket swam, his dark head barely above the water, his breath coming in sharp puffs, his claws occasionally scraping her arm

261

as he dog paddled. In the raft, Savannah sobbed out the same three sentences she'd been repeating on an endless loop ever since Jason's body had bobbed to the surface, partially buoyed by the orange life vest, one side spilling foam from the bullet hole torn through it. "Help him. Please! We have to go back!" She'd been saying it so long, the words had lost their meaning, the sound of Savannah's voice receding into the background of so many other voices screaming and yelling.

Anayeli kicked to force her feet to the surface, trying to avoid kicking Mama who was floating behind her, clinging onto the back of the raft with Luz and Bailey Rae. Like an *idiota,* Anayeli had forgotten paddles for the raft, and so there was no way for Savannah to steer it. Not that Savannah was in any kind of shape to be useful, or like they could trust her if she were. The bags were all in the raft, but no one else, not sweet Luz, not Bailey Rae, not even the dogs, could be persuaded to get out of the water and back into the raft with the sobbing woman and her shrieking children. Instead, they were all in the river. Mama and Luz flanked Bailey Rae at the rear of the raft, and it was up to Anayeli on the left side, and Carlota and Ernesto on the right to pilot the raft as best they could.

Anayeli wished for the millionth time she'd dumped Savannah out of the raft right after her husband had decided he was a true maverick, but instead Anayeli had dropped the gun in the water, grabbed hold of the raft and run, splashing bloodied river water everywhere, leaving her family to hurry after her. She'd had to get away.

"Make room!" The shout rose from the other side of the raft where a beer-bellied man clung to a pool lounger, along with a woman and a teenager, the three of them kicking to move faster through the current. Behind them, a two-person kayak floated right next to Luz, the grim-faced man in front dip-dipping his oar quickly from side-to-side, narrowly missing Luz each time he paddled on her side.

Anayeli couldn't blame anyone for wanting to get past, or keep whatever space they had, but the last thing she needed was for someone to get hurt or her family's raft to get shoved closer to the south bank. Frenzied people were still bolting out of the trees on that side of the river, fire devouring their hair, their clothes, everything.

Embers swirled on the hot air and landed in the shallows. No one wanted to be over there.

"You're too close!" There was a smacking sound—oar against skin.

"Hey!" Ernesto bellowed and erupted into a flurry of kicking and splashing, shaking the entire raft. Savannah stopped her sobbing long enough to clutch at her kids while the raft bucked in the water.

"Get away from us!" Carlota's voice rose above the din as the man jabbed at her—or maybe at the raft—with his oar. Carlota let loose a stream of Shakespearean-level creative curses in Spanish, just as the rubber wall of the raft barged into Anayeli. The handle slipped from her grip and when she gulped for air, instead she got a mouthful of water as she was pushed under. She was sputtering when her head popped to the surface, the raft already moving away from her on the current, leaving her behind as she struggled to catch her breath, while other rafts bore down on her.

Cricket and Roxy, who'd been swimming just behind Bailey Rae, angled toward her, but they were no match for the current and try as they might, the pair of them made no headway.

Anayeli took a breath and got more water, the mask she was wearing soaked through. She yanked it around her neck and put her head down, pulling at the water in the s-curve she'd perfected on the swim team, grateful the cold water had numbed her burned hand, the makeshift bandage long ago lost in the current. She allowed the river to speed her downstream and when she popped her head up again, she was closer to her family's raft, but another kayak had moved into her path.

"Yeli!" Luz held to the raft with one arm hooked over the side, her body half-turned backward, her free hand outstretched as if she might reach Anayeli.

"Keep going!" Anayeli lifted her head up so she could keep her eye on the raft as she tacked across the current, working twice as hard as she would if she just let it take her downstream. But she was afraid it would send her farther away from her family, and with the congestion on the river, she'd never be able to get back to them. Worse, without the raft to hold onto, she'd never be able to last the hours it would take to get downriver to where the evacuation center was—assuming Jason hadn't been lying about that, too.

The wind gusted, strong enough this time to send embers over the water, some of them landing around Anayeli, sizzling in the water. A few must have landed on rafts and floats, because yells went up, and splashing. Something—a raft?—bumped into her from behind. No one was paying enough attention to anyone except themselves—

"Yeli!" Luz pointed at something just ahead. At first it looked like a shiny black rock, jutting out of the water, white current foaming around it.

But then Bailey Rae started screaming. "Roxy! Roxy! Here girl! You can do it!"

In her own struggle to cut through the current, Anayeli had lost track of the dogs. Cricket was still swimming in the raft's wake, but in trying to reach Anayeli, Roxy must have been swept sideways toward the center of the river. Even though the dog was paddling hard toward the raft, she was slowly being dragged toward a gap in a dam made up of sodden logs.

It wasn't even a thought, not even a question of if or whether. *Not another life*. Anayeli changed directions, swimming fast with the current toward Roxy. She was dimly aware of Mama's shouted protests, but they faded at the memory of Sid, the photo of Roxy clutched in his dead grip.

She was so close when the dog was sucked through the gap and went under. She screamed, or maybe it was Bailey Rae's scream filling her ears, and though the water was shallow enough she could put her feet down and stop herself from going through where the dog had, she hesitated for only a moment—just long enough that if Roxy was going to pop back up to the surface, she should have already.

Anayeli let the river take her, spreading her arms wide and ducking below the water. The water was so murky she could see nothing, but if there was anything to catch in her path, she would feel it.

She barged into something firm and warm—Roxy!—and clamped her arms around it, her lungs near bursting as she kicked and kicked and kicked.

The only mercy was that the current rushed into a calm stretch. Anayeli struggled to keep both their heads above water, Roxy's claws tearing at her as the dog fought to stay afloat too. But she kept swimming and they gained on the raft.

"Grab on!" Luz's trailing hand brushed hers. "I got you!" But Anayeli couldn't risk dragging her sister down.

Mama crawled hand-over-hand along the side of the raft, moving up to the handle Anayeli had been holding, making room for Anayeli at the back. Finally she touched the raft itself and kicked hard enough to throw one arm over the side, even as she clung to Roxy's middle. They were both heaving, and Bailey Rae was crooning the dog's name over and over and over again, her small hand slipped under the dog's collar. Only then did Anayeli rest, letting her legs sway in the current, Cricket paddling anxiously in her wake. She tried not to let his panting bother her, or see the way Luz's lips were trembling again, or how Carlota's face had gone fierce in the way that meant she was close to the end of her rope, which was never that long to begin with. Most of all, she tried not to hear Ernesto's wheezing, to ignore the paddle mark that reddened his cheek. But she couldn't.

"We can't keep on like this." She forced the words out between each heavy breath, speaking in Spanish so they could make a plan without having to account for Savannah. The woman had finally shut up, but her expression was flat, her eyes unblinking and unfocused. She could be plotting their murder for all she knew. She'd watched her husband die at Anayeli's hand and now that the shock was wearing off—or setting in? Anayeli couldn't be sure—she'd turned to stone. On the outside, at least. She wouldn't even look at Anayeli. "We've got to go to the evacuation center. Get out of the water."

"No." Mama's voice cut through the noise. Even Savannah shrank away from it. "You know I can't go someplace like that."

It was the same thing Mama always said. She had never once gone to any official school function—not a single back-to-school night or parent-teacher conference. When she had to drive, she always kept just under the speed limit, terrified of getting pulled over. She wouldn't camp in a national park—any place with a park ranger. And she refused to cross state lines. She wouldn't fly or take any public transport—"They've got *el policía* on there." She went to her job. She went to the *mercado* and the *carnicería*, because they were safe. She went home. Even though she'd lived in California for most of Anayeli's life without any incident, Mama lived in fear. "I can't let *la migra* take me." The evacuation center would be run by government officials, that was as far as Mama could think.

"But Mama!" Anayeli tipped her head toward Roxy and Bailey Rae. "We can't do this forever."

Beside her, Bailey Rae's teeth were chattering behind her mask, what was visible of the little girl's face pale and bluish in the snow-melt cold water. Even with the wind breathing heat and smoke and ash over their heads, it wasn't enough to warm them. The dog's difficulties were only a precursor to what could easily happen to Bailey Rae. She wished Carlota or Luz or Ernesto would say something, would back her up, but they all stayed silent; younger siblings, letting the eldest do all the work for them.

"No. We get these *niños*"—Mama jutted her chin toward Savannah's kids—"and this *traidora* close enough to the center, let them onshore, and then we've done more than anyone else would. Without them, we'll be good. We'll have the raft and we'll all be together."

All together. It was Mama's mantra, the thing she cared about most, even though it had made her life so small.

"But, where are we going to go, Mama? You want to take the river all the way to the ocean?" Plan B had evaporated into nothing, and the ocean wasn't even close to a plan. Bailey Rae wasn't going to make it that long, if she stayed in the water. And neither were the dogs. But none of those arguments would convince Mama.

"You think I know? It was your idea to come here. You're the one with all the plans."

Her mama wasn't wrong. It had been her idea to come to the river. She had to fix it. "We can't stay on the raft forever—It's hours already and look at us! We're cold, and tired, and hurt." She left off hungry, because mentioning it would only make Carlota more crabby.

Instead Anayeli flashed her palm. The skin around the wound had gone white, water-logged. But the burn itself was just as angry as ever, and now her arms were scratched too, from Roxy's claws. Who knew what was in the river water. "I think it's infected. They'll have doctors there. It'll be safer. And maybe I can contact—" She cut herself off just in time. She could never tell Mama the secondary hope that had been festering ever since Jason had mentioned the evacuation center. Because the evacuation center would have not just doctors, but working communications, officials who could shunt information to the proper channels to actually make a difference.

If she could get the information she already had to the right people, maybe they could stop whatever was happening. If she could talk to Taylor at Matreus again, she could get him to tell her more, she was sure of it. She'd convince him to release whatever Matreus knew about Teff, then get him talking about the breathing problems Papa had told her about. With the right prompt at the right time, she could find out why people were bleeding from their noses, coughing up bloody foam, convulsing in their office hallway or on their kitchen floor, dying miles away from the torched fields. Finally—with a flourish that would have made Sid proud, she'd get Taylor to say the words she already knew to be true: *it was all because of the smoke.*

She kicked hard, even though she had hold of the raft, triumphant! She'd ask him what he'd meant by 'infestation,' and if there was any truth to reports about swarms of bugs. And if Taylor wouldn't talk to her, some official at the evacuation center could compel him to. If she could make that happen, that might start to make up for everything else she'd done—for Papa and Sid and China Box Lady, and Jason...

"Contacts." Mama spat the word. "Always with your story. You're saving dogs and thinking about your job when you should be protecting your family—"

"I am protecting my family!" The emotion rose in Anayeli so instantaneously, she didn't even have time to check herself. If they had been on land, and she hadn't been clutching onto a dog, she might've slapped her own mother. If she could've swam right up to her Mama and screamed the words in her face, she would've. But she had to keep hold of the raft, because that was what her family required of her in this moment. She had to keep hold of Roxy because she was Bailey Rae's only comfort. She had shot a man because that was what her family had needed. "I'm protecting *everyone*! That's what I'm doing!"

"You tell yourself that. But if you go there, to that evacuation center, all you're doing is tearing your family apart. If that's what you want, then fine. You see just how much they want to listen to you. You see what contacts"—again the word was full of venom—"answer your call." Mama faced forward then, went back to paddling with her free hand, but before the conversation was over, the responsibility all Anayeli's again, she spat one last thing. "You know who always answers your call? *Familia*."

Everyone went very small after that, and no one spoke for a long time. No one would make eye contact with her either. But if Mama was going to put the responsibility on her, she had to do something.

"Savannah!" When the woman didn't turn or blink or do anything to show she'd heard, Anayeli scissor-kicked and hefted herself up higher, reaching out to poke the woman's back. "Move up." Savannah didn't move. Anayeli poked again, harder. "Make room."

Without ever acknowledging Anayeli, the woman did as she was told, pushing the bags farther ahead of her. There was water at the bottom of the raft, the bags already wet.

"Bailey Rae—"

"I don't want to!" Somehow the little girl had read Anayeli's mind and gripped the raft harder.

The hot wind gusted again, giving her an idea. "I know, but I need your help." If having younger siblings had taught her anything, it was that there was no faster way to get a kid to refuse to do something than to tell them it was for their own good. But at least Bailey Rae was paying attention. She wasn't hypothermic yet. "I need you to make sure the sides of the raft stay wet. In case any sparks land on it." It was a risk, mentioning the sparks. It might scare the girl. So before the idea of danger had time to set in, Anayeli went on. "And I'm really worried about Roxy. She needs to rest, but she won't get in the raft without you." Even with Anayeli supporting her, Roxy's head was barely above the water, and though she was still attempting to swim, her effort was feeble. There was no way Anayeli could let her go and expect her to swim. Anayeli laid it on thick. "I don't think she can keep up if I let her swim. And someone might just let their raft go right over her."

"Okay. I think Cricket should come in too." Anayeli could have kissed the little girl.

"*Por supuesto*. He'll protect you." Savannah's back went tense, but Anayeli didn't care if the woman knew she was talking about her. If her husband had done what he'd agreed to, he'd be alive. If he'd kept his word like Anayeli and her family had, he would be the one at the front of the raft, helping steer it.

Bailey Rae was practically a gymnast, and managed to get into the raft with only a one-handed boost from Luz. As soon as she was in, Roxy pulled toward the space between Anayeli and Luz, as if she were asking to go into the raft too. But that was a problem.

"Everyone put your feet down! If we stop the raft—" The water was shallow enough, at least for the moment, that they could all touch bottom, but it was a risk, with the crush of other rafts and boats coming behind them. Anayeli couldn't see any other way to get the dog inside, not without the help of an adult in the raft to haul her in, and Savannah was still sitting in stony silence.

"C'mon Roxy!" Bailey Rae's voice was the high pitched one people always used with dogs. As the girl patted the side of the raft, encouraging the dog, Anayeli's heart lurched. The raft gave slightly, the side no longer taut like it had been after they'd first pumped it back up. Probably just her imagination. Just fear.

"Put your feet down!" She could hardly hold herself still, the current was so strong, but the raft slowed, water rushing against it, pushing at it.

"Hurry Anayeli!" Ernesto had gotten to the front of the raft, and was using his back to block it. The strain couldn't be good for his breathing. Behind them another raft was coming, the family inside paddling furiously, trying to steer away from them.

She wrapped her arms more tightly around Roxy's middle and lifted. The dog corkscrewed, flailing about awkwardly, but somehow she managed to unceremoniously dump her over the side of the raft. Roxy was up in an instant, licking licking licking Bailey Rae's face, making the girl laugh—a welcome sound after everything they'd all been through. Cricket was at Anayeli's side, and as she went to scoop him up, he somehow leapt, shooting out of the water, making getting him into the raft almost effortless. He was on his feet in a blink, shaking water droplets over all of them, making Savannah's little boy shriek at the cold spray.

It was the tiniest happy moment. The smallest success. Anayeli cheered—they all did—except Mama and Savannah. But Anayeli's attention slipped, and so must've everyone else's. The raft surged forward on the current and Luz lost her grip, falling backward into the water. The raft bumped into Ernesto, knocking him down. Anayeli leapt forward, hooking her arms over the raft's side, practically sitting down in the water, trying to slow them down long enough for Ernesto to get up. Luz staggered to her feet, waist deep in the water, and dove after them, managing to seize the back wall. Somehow Mama and Carlota kept their hold on the handles. It was only sheer luck that kept the dinghy from going right over the top of Ernesto, but he was a good swimmer, and kept just ahead of it until he could get his feet back under himself long enough to grab the front handle again.

Except then Savannah's little boy let out another shriek—a piercing one—and pointed ahead. It was suddenly, horribly clear why the people in the other raft had been paddling so hard, why so few other floats were anywhere near them anymore. She and Mama had been so busy arguing, and then they'd all been so focused on getting Bailey Rae and the dogs into the raft that they'd completely ignored what the strong current meant.

A large shelf-like slab of rock jutted out of the river, splitting it. On one side, the water was shallow, rippling as it rushed over the flat expanse and spilled out into a pool. On the other side, the river funneled through a narrow, rocky sluice, churning and frothing over a series of jutting rocks before plunging into a channel littered with branches and debris—one of the dangerous snags the river was known for. No one was going to that side of the river. Except them. They were headed straight for it, the current already dragging them toward it.

"Ernesto! Carlota! Pull! Hard!" If the two of them could swim hard enough toward the other bank, then maybe—but they only had one arm with which to pull. "Mama! Luz! Kick!" Anayeli put every ounce of strength into pounding at the water. But none of them could kick with enough force to even shift the raft.

Savannah clutched her baby to her and screamed at her little boy. "Colby! Grab onto me! Onto my life vest!" At the same time, Bailey Rae grabbed each dog's collar. Both were terrible decisions, but there was no time to tell either to do anything different, nothing better to shout at them, at all of them except, "Hold on!"

The raft bounced upward on the first rock, catching air even as Anayeli's shins barked against the rough expanse. With no handle it was all Anayeli could do to keep her grip on the slippery rubber of the raft as the air filled with screams—hers, her sisters', Bailey Rae's, she couldn't tell who was screaming or where the screams came from. Everywhere. They were probably all being battered against the rocks, but that was survivable. *Vive*. All they had to do was live through this. But quicker than thought, a nauseous dread hollowed out Anayeli's insides as the raft plunged downward at a steep angle, the nose diving under water. The entire front of the raft was submerged, water splashing over Savannah and the children, washing the bags out. For a sickening moment, as Savannah slipped forward, Anayeli was certain she and her kids were going over too. But the raft swept sideways. Luz jostled into Anayeli, then bumped against her hard. There was a cry—it had to be from Luz, but Anayeli had squeezed her eyes shut and was screaming and gripping with everything because they were shooting down, down, and she couldn't let another horrible image burn itself into her memory.

The raft landed with a heavy smack into the pool and that was when the wailing shriek began. It was the sound of a rending, piercing terror, full of desperation like nothing Anayeli had ever heard before, and it was coming from Mama. She took stock—they were all there, all alive. Everyone but Luz.

Anayeli's heart punched in her chest as she dove away from the raft, back toward the waterfall, toward the evil snag jutting from below, its branches clawing fingers. Luz was down there, down where the plunging waterfall made a whirlpool, down in the deep green water, dragged under and caught in the branches.

Vive. Vive. Oh por favor, vive!

Anayeli was a good swimmer. She was strong. And she swam harder than she'd ever swam in any race, in her whole life. She dove, and dove again, and every time the current was too strong. The whirlpool that had sucked Luz down somehow spit Anayeli out. She dove and reached out her hands like she had done for Roxy, feeling for anything that wasn't waterlogged rotten branches, and caught only water. She dove and only once did she feel the slip of skin. Just one time fingernails caught at her burned hand, scratched deep into the wound that was already there, the soft skin tearing. Luz. Her sweet sister who always reached for her. *La hermana dulce, siempre.* The sweet sister, always. Slipped away. Out of reach. Gone.

CHAPTER TWENTY-SEVEN

SAM LEARY. BERKELEY, CALIFORNIA.

It was raining inside the lab. Again. Water shot from the sprinklers in the ceiling. Was this the big surprise attack Frank was planning? Sam grabbed the trashcan and pulled out the plastic liner. Underneath was a roll of plastic bags. Thank goodness for janitors, they always liked to be prepared. He slid the first bag off the roll and covered the open laptop.

Henry bit at the droplets as they cascaded around him, and then ran in circles as he chased his tail. At least someone was enjoying himself. Sam rushed to the closet while tearing off another trash bag, covering as many supplies as he could before they were ruined. As he worked, water soaked through his shoes. What in the world? There was a quarter inch of standing water in the closet.

Sam stopped dead in his tracks, water sloshing over his ankles. That wasn't right. It should have been dissipating, draining, running all over the massive basement. Instead, it was accumulating in his office. The whole mess reeked of a Frank ploy. His nemesis hadn't been able to burn him out, so now he was trying to drown him. How?

Henry pranced in the water, splashing in one great puddle, oblivious to their predicament. A bag of dog treats floated by. Another distraction. Chasing after the bag he lunged and bit down capturing the prize. Then he splashed over to Sam and shook the bag back and forth before dropping the treats in front of him. With wagging tail, the grinning mutt stared at Sam. Why not, he'd had one hell of a week cooped up in the basement. Sam bent over to pick up the treats, which was when he saw the sealant under the door. He gave Henry a treat and stuffed the bag into his sweater.

No doubt about it, there was a foam seal squeezed between the floor tiles and the bottom of the door. Sam knelt and poked at the seal. It didn't budge. Frank must have wedged it in there.

There was a mighty thunk right above his head. Sam shot to his feet to find a brass nozzle hanging through the hole in the door. Where had Frank found a fire hose? He reached for the brass nozzle right as the water shot into his chest. He fell back, coughing and sputtering. The jet stream broke beakers and test tubes, as they washed off the counters and onto the floor. Sam crawled out of the war path and behind the desk.

It was insane. They were in the middle of one of the most prestigious universities in the country and he was being hosed down by a colleague. How was that possible? Where were the campus police? Surely the dean would have a cow if he knew about the harassment. Once again, the dots hovered in front of Sam's brain, taunting him. *Are they all in on it?* No. If anyone that high up in the administration was plotting to retrieve his results, there was no way they'd send a putz like Frank to do their dirty work.

Three inches of water accumulated in less than five minutes, the results of a clogged floor drain. He slogged to the slotted hole in the floor, kicking at the papers that were suctioned to the tile. The drawings of molecules and cicadas wouldn't budge. The sprinklers showed no sign of stopping and the fire hose's spray continued its rampage. It arced over the main desk and caught the laptop monitor straight on.

The bag over the laptop came off as the computer tumbled into the water.

Wading as fast as he could back to the desk, he fished around in the tiny indoor lake and yanked his hand back to find blood running from a slash across his palm. He plunged it into the water to wash away the blood, but that did nothing to stem the flow. Henry barked in his loudest voice and bounded to Sam. "Henry stay." The dog obeyed.

Sam shuffled his feet until he kicked the edge of rectangular plastic and stooped down to retrieve the laptop. Turning it over so the water drained out, sparks ignited bright blue through the fan vent and he juggled the clamshell to avoid being shocked. Sizzling followed with the acrid odor of ozone from fried circuits.

"You big, mindless baboon of a human being." He shouted over the gush of the hose, hoping Frank was dumb enough and self-seeking enough to be listening. "You destroyed the very thing you were after!"

Sixty seconds ticked by and the water stopped. The hose backed out and Frank appeared, settling his nose and one eye in the hole. "Show me."

Sam opened a drawer on the back counter and pulled out a flat head screwdriver and some tape. He wrapped his bleeding palm and popped the back of the clam shell off. Removing several screws, he turned the waterlogged device over so he could detach the keyboard. With the motherboard exposed, he previewed the damaged circuits in front of Frank.

"See the M.2 chip. Its blackened and the pins are toast. Did you really think computers and water were a good mix?"

"I still want that computer."

Sam turned his back on the door, careful to angle himself so he was out of Frank's line of sight. He put the laptop on the counter and jammed the tip of the screwdriver into the hard drive. The chip splintered, bits of silicon flying this way and that. He put the screwdriver back in the drawer. It was always a good idea to put your tools where they belonged. That way you knew exactly where they were the next time you needed them. Also, it gave him great pleasure to know Frank was waiting and squirming. "You can have the hard drive..." *which is now useless to you,* "but you have to give me time to gather my things so I can leave. Wait by the elevator. Once I'm out, you can retrieve your prize."

"You better leave the laptop on the counter, and keep that mutt of yours away from me, or I'll give you worse than you got on the baseball field. You have ten minutes." The foam seal squeaked as Frank removed it from under the door and the water lowered at a snail's pace.

Sam sloshed back to his desktop computer and tried the power button on his monitor. Nothing. He shook the mouse. When the computer didn't respond, he pried the cabinet door open against the standing water. He yanked the electrical cable out of the power supply with a couple of small zaps, and wrapped the cord around the door handle, out of reach of the water.

"Well Henry, we better find another computer so we can contact Cockroach."

Sam tilted the wagon until the metal flatbed was on all four tires and the base of the transport was submerged. The sprinklers had stopped but it was going to be a long time before he dried out.

He scooped the canned goods into the base along with the unopened jug of Sevin. Pulling the camp stove and fuel from the bottom shelf, he wedged them between the cans along with a camp plate that held utensils and a cup inside. Stashing the camp knife along with the magnesium fire starter in his soaked coat, he wheeled the goods to the exit and untied the brace.

Water flooded into the hallway, running into side channels and other labs as he propped the door open. Despite Frank's malevolent and arrogant nature, he waited by the stairs like he was told to do. As the elevator car reached the first level, the bell dinged and Sam pulled the dog and the wagon inside. He hit the button for the third floor and Frank shot him a stink eye as the doors closed.

The third floor was for the higher-ups, every fixture and furnishing blared "money." Plush carpet and real tile layered the floor and each office held the same solid steel door and a separate shatter proof window that spanned from floor to ceiling. Every door had its own name and number, stamped in gold. And every one of them was empty, which explained how Frank was getting away with his nonsense. People were listening to the news at last, and heading out. Sam passed several offices before pausing at one.

"I can't believe that toad actually has an office on the third floor." Sam tried the handle. The door's silent swing inwards gave him goose bumps and he pressed the button for the lights. A temporary plastic table was centered in the room illuminated by the garish tube lights hiding in the ceiling. A leather high-backed chair sat on the other side of the table. It must be something Frank had brought from home, it sure wasn't standard issue. Front and center the desk hosted a name plate with Frank Dorset's name in hammered copper and burnished wood. The corner held the smallest computer ever built with a phone the same size right next it.

He checked the corridor, found it empty, then locked the door, tapping the wall three times as confirmation that he'd turned the lock. Then he pocketed the key that Frank had so kindly left behind, and padded over to his enemy's miniature computer. Talk about symbolism. The room was stark and empty of all personality and the computer barely deserved the label "computer." The man and his office were a sham.

He tapped the wireless keyboard, and the computer came out of hibernation. The screen brought up a Windows desktop, the background was a house on a beach. Frank left his computer logged in. Hollow sham *and* clueless idiot; better and better.

Loading the science forums in an internet browser, he found his chat forum, and logged in.

SAM: Cockroach, I need your help. Someone tried to drown me and ended up destroying my laptop.

Sam rocked in the chair. That at least was a source of comfort. If he wasn't careful, he'd fall asleep.

CR: You okay?

SAM: I'm bleeding, most of my stored food and supplies have been destroyed by water, and I'm sitting in my enemy's office. I think that sums up my situation.

Sam twisted in the chair, and a clatter filled the office. He jumped from the comfort of the leather and slammed his back to the wall adjacent to the door. Lying behind the chair's casters was a backpack with a telescoping fishing pole strapped to its side. "It's nothing. Just Frank's stupid fishing gear." Sam returned to his seat and propped the bag against the side of the desk as another text flashed on the screen.

CR: Fight the good fight.

Sam hesitated, his fingers stalled above the keyboard. He was about to ask too much of Cockroach. He shook his head. There was nothing for it, Cockroach was the only one who could deliver what Sam needed. His fingers tapped away and hit the return button before he lost his nerve.

SAM: I must ask of you a small favor.

CR: Ask away, my good man.

SAM: You received the package I sent?

CR: Yes, the padded envelope arrived this afternoon. Quite clever, backing up your work.

SAM: I need you to bring it to me.

The chat went quiet and Sam shook the mouse to make sure the computer hadn't frozen. Cockroach must be making up his mind.

CR: You're insane.

SAM: Come on, Cockroach, this is serious. I can't leave the campus before Diana gets here and the thumb drives are the only data I have left on the caterpillar venom.

CR: Have you seen the news?

Cockroach even had the gall to add a smiley face.

A great many phrases went through Sam's head, none of them PG-13 but he swallowed down his irritation and tapped back a plea.

SAM: Please. I need you. You are my only hope.

The cursor blinked. Sam closed his eyes, holding out hope that Cockroach would change his mind. He lived in California, so the trip would be short if traffic behaved.

CR: What about the fires?

SAM: If you start driving now, you can be here before they arrive. The University has many buildings to hide in, and I'm sure that we can find more food. You'll be safe, I promise."

CR: You'd better be right, Sam, or I'll kick your butt when I get there.

SAM: Thanks, man. I owe you one.

CR: True that.

Sam logged off the chat and turned his attention to Frank's fishing gear. He set the pack on his lap and unbuttoned the top. Inside, scrambled in haphazard order were fishing lures, reels of fishing line, a first aid kit, a plastic box of hooks, fake worms, and some trail mix. Sam turned, caught sight of the seething face at the door, and leaped out of his skin.

Frank, broken laptop in hand, was pressed up against the door to his own office, face contorted against the glass panel. He reached for the handle but when the lever wouldn't turn; he dug in his pockets. Sam lifted the key up and dangled the ring from his fingertips. Frank snarled and rammed the door with his shoulder, putting enough force behind his hammering to shake the waste basket.

Henry barked and lunged, but Sam ordered him back to his side with a single word. The dog bristled, hackles up and teeth bared. He knew who the bad guy was.

"Leave my fishing gear alone." The man was off his nut. He was worried about his fishing tackle?

Still, it gave Sam the chance to mess with the man who'd tortured him for days. He pulled out a couple containers from the bag and organized them on the desk. Stacking them into a pyramid, he pushed them to the far corner inching them closer and closer to the edge.

Frank rammed the door again, but when the metal didn't budge, he smashed his fist against the window.

Sam pointed at the laptop. "Doesn't feel very good, to have someone take what's yours, does it?" It was childish and petty, but he didn't care. This was the language Frank understood and he had every intention of playing it out right until the end.

"I don't care what Paula says. When I come back with another key, you're going to wish you'd never been born. I'm going to tie you to one of the cadaver dissection tables in the biology lab. Then I'll drip hydrochloric acid onto your bare skin for several hours as your flesh is eaten in slow, agonizing moments of torture. And if you happen to last that long, there are the freezers they keep the cadavers in. You'll be turned into a human meatsickle in a claustro-phobia-inducing container."

Woah, dude. Angry much? Take a chill pill, as they used to say. No, please, take two.

Frank stormed down the corridor, spewing more threats and nonsense, leaving Sam to stew over the possible outcomes.

"What can we do, Henry? Cockroach is headed this way. So is Diana. We can't go back to the basement and this is no place to be trapped with that psycho on the warpath."

Sam turned the wagon around, went to the desk and counted the boxes he'd pulled out. *Does a man need all of those fake worms for one fishing trip?* A spool of fishing line glinted in the lip of the bag. He stuffed everything back into the pack and stashed it in the wagon. He cracked the door open, and rushed to the end of the hall.

The office was empty apart from a desk. A note was taped to its side. 'Move to Frank Dorset's room.' They had to be firing more people than he'd thought. He hauled the wagon inside, waited for Henry to slip between his legs, and closed the door with a squeak. The room was not as well maintained as Frank's and was being used as a temporary janitor's closet. Soap, toilet paper, mops, bleach, and other cleaning supplies littered the floor.

Sam locked the door, pushed the wagon out of the way, and grabbed the end of the desk. That thing had to weigh two hundred pounds. Putting all his weight into the effort, he tried to inch it toward the door. It was too heavy though, and despite his efforts—and Henry's well-intentioned nudges—he slipped and crashed to the ground. With blood slicked hands he tried again, with the same outcome. Running to the other side, he strained against the edge, but the desk wouldn't budge. Surely it wasn't screwed in place? He ducked his head under the furniture. Nothing, just six plastic feet connected to the walls of the desk.

He wracked his brain for ideas. Henry, who had been sniffing the wagon's handle growled at it and then, wagging, grabbed it in his mouth and backed away. The wagon obviously moved far more easily than he was expecting: the dog shied back as the wagon tipped and settled on its side.

"Henry, you're a genius. I need to tip the desk on its top. The flat surface will spread out the weight and the smoothness of the top will slide far better than the little feet that dig into the carpet."

Sam crouched under the desk and hoisted it up, using his back for leverage. The mass of wood tipped sideways. Rising up he pushed again and the desk thudded on its side. It didn't take much effort to get it to roll over onto its top. Sam edged the desk toward the door, made contact with the frame and stopped pushing.

Collapsing on the carpet, Sam lay prone, panting and gasping for air, as Henry licked his face. Whispering a few syllables to the dog, he rolled over. "Guard the door. I can't move a muscle."

CHAPTER TWENTY-EIGHT

RON FROBISHER. SOUTHAMPTON, ENGLAND.

For all his feigned nonchalance and American cheer, Ron Frobisher lived and, if push came to shove, would die by a code: "My word is my bond." A lesser crook might not care if they'd lost a bunch of beetles, but Ron needed to go and find them, for his own sake, if not for Ann's. He had a reputation, dammit, and he wasn't going to allow a bunch of leather-necked dock workers strip him of his impeccable record for delivering the goods.

"This work for you, sir?" Obi-wan-Kettering lugged a lumpy mattress down the stairs, oblivious to the fact that it was soaking up rain and collecting dirt.

"Guess it's going to have to."

Obi made a big show of getting the mattress positioned, "Juuuuu-uust right" inside the door of the cage before claiming his second fifty-pound note. "Much obliged."

"Five hundred to stay here while I go ashore for an hour." It was all good and well to lie to The Right Honorable Ann about the missing cargo, but there were people who could track those boxes down in a hurry. For the right price. He just needed an hour ashore and a two-minute conversation with Vinnie Cunningham (aka Vinnie Two Tone), and he'd be set.

"You what?"

"Five hundred quid do it for you?" Even if Obi-wan-Kettering made the top rate for a Third Mate, his salary wasn't going to be more than sixty dollars an hour; peanuts once you'd translated it into pounds.

"You've got to be joking, mate. If I'm not beside Captain Alva when she runs through the pre-launch plan, she'll have my guts for garters."

"How much?"

"Listen, mate. You're not hearing me. No can do."

"Thousand. A thousand pounds for an hour of your time."

Obi-wan-Kettering eyed the crates. He didn't need to say it. Madness. That much money to stay in the hold and watch a bunch of wooden crates? 'Utter, utter bollocks,' as the English would say. "One hour, then I'm out of here."

The rain was still coming down by the time Ron hit the pavement. He crossed the cobbled street, hopped up a stoop step, and sheltered by a boarded-up doorway. His pay-as-you-go burner phone had three numbers, no names. Vinnie had the London area code. He tapped in a text: "Cod and chips, twice." That was all you said when you wanted directions to the nearest dealer. Vinnie's network was legendary. He'd know where to find hot goods.

"." Came the reply. Excellent. Vinnie was available.

"Cessna." It was Ron's call sign, on account of the fact that his initials were R.A.F. The Brits thought they were pretty clever.

"?"

"Yeah, no." He didn't only want a fence in Southampton, he wanted the broker who was nearest to the docklands. How to say that in as few identifying words as possible. His thumbs whizzed over the tiny keyboard: "Scummer + water." 'Scummer' was the nickname the neighboring city of Portsmouth had given Southampton. 'Water' would be obvious to anyone with half a brain. And Vinnie had way more than half; Vinnie was a certifiable genius.

"23 St. C's Cl. Dan." Google confirmed the meet was at number twenty-three St. Catherine's Close. His contact was Dan. Or at least that was who he was to ask for. He opened Google Maps. Damn. The address was way up some hill in a residential neighborhood. It was close enough to the River Itchin that it wasn't a total misfire, but Vinnie had identified the wrong body of water.

"Tide," Ron typed. That'd narrow it down, but not enough to tip Vinnie off to his exact location. What else could he add? He scoped the street. The pub name. That'd do it. "The Duck & Downer." He hit send. It would've been so much easier if they could have spoken, but Vinnie spoke to no man and no man spoke to Vinnie. It was burner phones and cryptic text messages all the way.

The little dots in the text field weren't moving. "Come on, come on." He only had fifty-five minutes before the goods in the ship's hold went unprotected. The fact that someone had already boosted three crates meant there was talk on the street.

The other two numbers were every bit as useful as Vinnie's, but The Right Honorable Ann wasn't someone Ron wanted to talk to and her business partner, Boyd Miller, was a nutjob if you got on the wrong side of him. Question was, did Boyd know what Ann was up to? She'd lied about the cargo which meant she didn't want *someone* to know what she was trading.

The rain had eased, but there was no point walking when he didn't know which way Vinnie was going to send him. Time to kick the hornet's nest. "Boyd..." he typed. "Got a sec for your flying buddy?" Unlike Vinnie Two Tone, Boyd did take calls, but not from numbers he didn't recognize. Texting ahead of time was the only way to get him to answer.

"Sure."

Ron hit call.

"Ann hired *you?*" Boyd got straight to business, as always, but the question was perfect. He obviously didn't know what Ron was doing in Southampton.

"Under the radar. Something for *Better Bio.*"

Boyd had several annoying habits. One was to tap his teeth with his pen when he was thinking. Tap, tap, pause. Tap-tap-tap. "Feedit?"

"Yeah, related." Ron had no idea what 'feed it' meant, but Boyd didn't need to know that.

"How can I help?" There was no vitriol in Boyd's voice, no rancor, which meant he hadn't heard about the mission, let alone the missing cargo. Time to steer the conversation in a different direction. "Is Cape Town the only destination?" Little misdirection to see if Boyd knew where he was headed. Tap tap. Tap tap; that irritating pen on teeth sound was twice as loud through the phone. Boyd was cycling through all the reasons Ron would ask about his mission. Time for another redirect. "I'm wondering if there's another voyage after this one, is all. Clients can be shuffled to make room for you, but only if I know what's on the docket."

Tap, tap. Tap, tap, tap. If Ron could have reached through the phone and snatched that pen out of Boyd's hand, he would have done it in a heartbeat. The taps were faster than usual and went on for a full minute; not a long time unless you're standing in a piss-filled doorway in the Southampton drizzle. The silence stretched to a second minute. Boyd had to be tracing a lead before he answered.

"Need to know, only." Boyd's tone was so smug, he might as well have added a congratulatory 'Ha!' which was more interesting than it was annoying. He genuinely didn't know about Ann's glowworms but he'd already found out that there were stolen goods for sale *somewhere* close by.

A text flashed across the top of Ron's phone. A new address and contact name from Vinnie. "Lindsay & Sons. Devon Tract." That had taken longer than usual, which meant Vinnie was checking him out, too; looking into what was being fenced in Southampton, getting in on the action. The price of retrieving his stolen cargo had just doubled. Still cheaper than admitting to Ann that he'd been burgled.

Boyd hung in the silence on the other end of the phone waiting for Ron to spill the beans. The unasked question lay between them: why are you *really* calling? But you can't con a conner. Boyd could wait until the cows came home; Ron would never fill the silence for the sake of filling it. "Keep me in mind for the next job. You know you and Ann are my favorite customers. I can cancel and rearrange if needed."

"Yeah, right." Boyd hung up before Ron could shoot back.

He turned his collar up against the charming English weather and hiked the few blocks to the address Vinnie had sent. The sign over the door was chipped and weather beaten, the name almost obliterated by time. He could just make out, 'Lindsay & Sons, Off License,' though there was every chance the sign was stolen, just like everything else in the joint. There were fewer goods in the window than there were cobwebs. "Sheesh. Your people are letting you down, Vinnie." Nothing telegraphed *this is a front* like not having anything for sale. What would it have cost to operate a Newsagents or a chip shop?

The door to the off license was slightly ajar. The hinges creaked and moaned as Ron eased his way inside. It wasn't just the display window that gave the game away; there wasn't enough merch on the shelves for it to pass as a legitimate business. Whoever this Devon Tract was, he'd done a piss-poor job of making a show for the public. Then again, the liquor store was in a part of town that included chop shops, pawnbrokers, and loan sharks, so chances were good that anyone who came looking for "a Smith Corona typewriter" or a "jar of elbow grease" knew what they were getting themselves into.

Ron hovered by the open door, his spidey senses tingling and the hairs on the back of his neck standing to attention. "Anyone home?" He was half-in, half-out, wishing it was the States and he could have a concealed carry.

"Mr. Lindsay I presume?" Devon Tract, if that was his name, was a tall, wiry man with ears too big for his head and a flat top buzzcut. Some people never grew up, never changed, remained the rebel they thought they were going to be at sixteen. "You here for the..." He tapped the side of his nose. "...you know what."

Ron took a step closer to the counter using his size to crowd the light from the front door. He neither confirmed nor denied his name. If Devon was expecting Mr. Lindsay, that worked.

"If you'll give me a minute, sir?" Devon backed up toward the store room, but there was something about his gait—a sideways shuffle that wasn't quite a drag—that suggested he was stalling, weighing his options.

"Okay if I come with?" Ron didn't leave him a choice. He rushed the 'shopkeeper's' position and chivvied him into the back room.

The ceiling was low and the lightbulbs had been removed from the wall sockets, giving the room a creepy, rather than a cozy ambience. This wasn't a place you went for High Tea and scones. This was a side of England that never made it to the Anglophile shows that dominated the American imagination: seedy, squalid, entirely lacking in sophistication.

A single *Bio Better* crate was stacked behind a small desk, easy to spot with its distinctive stamp. "I was expecting more."

"Ah." Devon wiped his hands down his trousers. Either he hadn't been doing this for long or he was phenomenally ill suited to the work. "See, what happened—"

"Vinnie will not be pleased."

Devon cocked his head to one side, his mouth opening and closing as if he had something he wanted to say but knew he shouldn't. He might as well have taken a neon sign and hung it over his head, declaring: 'Vinnie authorized the sale of the crates to another buyer.'

"Who has them?"

Devon shrugged and sucked air between his teeth, two of Ron's least favored means of non-verbal communication. Could mean anything; the man was disgusted, resigned, underpaid. What? *Use your words, people. Use your words.* Ron didn't have time to teach the man a lesson in communicating when working for a crime boss. "Three bills for what you've got. Delivered back to the docks, yeah?" He pulled a wad of cash out of his jacket.

"Vinnie didn't say nothing about delivery, my friend."

"I'm not your friend and you're going to deliver this crate. End of."

The bell over the front door rang. "Hallo!" It was a London accent, layered with the sheen of rough-talking movie gangsters. "You got something for me, me old mucker?"

Devon rushed the door, eyes bugging out and sweat staining his underarms in record time. Truly, the man should have been stocking shelves at the local supermarket for all the finesse he brought to the task.

"Mr. Lindsay, here for pickup."

Ron held up his hand and shrugged. *So there are two Mr. Lindsays in play. Deal with it.*

Devon skidded to a stop, head swiveling like a bobblehead doll. If you were that frightened of Vinnie, you had no business being in the business.

"Stay back here." Ron gave Devon a light push. The man stumbled and fell, arms flailing, then did his best impersonation of a spider making for the relative safety of a dark corner.

Ron stepped from the back room to the appalling excuse for a fake store.

"I'm Mr. Lindsay. Vinnie's friend. I take it you're Mr. Tract? Devon Tract?"

"Yep." Ron's British accent wasn't the worst, but it wasn't the best either. Words were going to be kept to a minimum.

The customer plopped an envelope down on the counter. "Pick up."

"Follow me." Ron turned toward the back room.

Mr. Lindsay cupped his hands over his crotch, legs wide. "Not happening, matey."

Ron waited. There was another shoe and it was about to drop.

"Ms. Emmas is in the limo, see. Can't keep the ladies waiting."

Ron had never heard of an Emmas, but that didn't mean much. He wasn't paid to keep tabs on every low-rent hoodlum in Southampton. He slid the stuffed envelope into his jacket pocket and weighed his options. "Give me a sec." He strode into the back room, opened the desk drawer, and found the first tool that could double as a weapon. Office scissors had so many interesting applications.

Devon was still crouched in the corner, an arm thrown over his eyes. There was no way in hell Vinnie had recruited the guy; his people were tough as nails. This bloke was barely Jell-o-level on the criminal 'hardness' scale.

"Remain calm and this will all be over before you know it." Ron ran his hand over the shelf. Most of the boxes were unmarked. "Know what's in these?"

Devon didn't lift his head. Ron took two steps, grabbed him by the collar and hefted him to his feet. "I said, do you know what's in the boxes?"

"No. Sir. No. Nothing. I don't know nothing," Devon stammered, sweat pouring down his temples.

"Open these." Ron pushed a couple of large boxes toward him. "We're looking for high end merchandise. Something that will make our friend out front leave us alone."

Devon ripped off the tape and dug into the first box. "Nintendo Switch?"

"No." Ron eased the scissors into the top of the crate and pried the nails free of each corner. "Something they can't get on the open market. They're expecting a payday."

Devon went back to his task with renewed vigor, ripping the tape off box after box. Ron didn't want to break it to him, but he was bringing a whole heap of trouble down on his own head by being so cavalier about the task. Most of what he was unwrapping was going to need to be rewrapped and moved on to the right buyer. Vinnie didn't like his merch to be handled.

"Gucci bags?" Even in the dimly lit backroom Ron could see that the logo was a poorly made knock off. He shook his head.

The crate he'd opened had a layer of shoe boxes that didn't fit in neat rows. Ron lifted a pair of sneakers out of their box and eased his hand under the tongue of the left shoe. Bingo. A brick of cocaine, no bigger than his palm. Exactly what he'd been looking for. Four more shoe boxes yielded four more bricks. That was enough for Mr. Lindsay et al.

As he passed the desk he snagged the packing tape and threw it at Devon. "You're good. Seal them back up."

"We're done?" Devon's face was pallid and drawn, his lips etched in white.

"Almost." Ron tucked the scissors into his pocket, always glad to have a little helper, just in case.

"Mr. Lindsay." Ron stopped in the doorway to the shop. The

driver—because that's what the man was, nothing more than the limo driver—hovered behind an imposing specimen of a woman. She'd have been five-eleven without the heels, but with the spikes she topped six foot. Her head was shaved to a light, stylish crop and her lipstick blared, blood red. "Mr. Tract. I believe you have something for me." She waited while Ron stepped around the counter, both hands in her tailored suit pockets.

Ron didn't want to overplay his hand. The wrong word with the wrong accent and these interlopers would stick around and mess up his transaction. He held out the white brick for inspection.

The click of metal on metal was Ron's signal to duck. He dove behind the counter, jammed the scissors into the plastic wrap that bound the cocaine, and flung the powder at his assailant.

Trouble was, Emmas wasn't the one with the gun. Devon was.

CHAPTER TWENTY-NINE

DR. DIANA STEWART. EVANSTON, WYOMING.

Diana helped Jesse out of the truck as Jane ran toward the charred remains of her parents' house, the kids trailing behind her.

Jesse's blistering had eased enough that he could open his eyes about halfway. "What's going on? Where are we going?" He blinked and winced. "Ouch. That hurts."

"Do you need some more drops?" Diana took the vials out of the meds bag and measured a couple of drops out for him. That way Jane and the kids had a few moments to themselves. "Better?"

"They're so itchy." Jesse wiped the saline solution off his cheek.

"They should be better any day now." As far as anyone knew. She held out her hand. "Come on, let's find Jane."

As they walked down the drive to the burned-out house, the neighbor's door cracked open and someone in a beekeeping suit slipped out onto the balcony. "Was that Jane I just saw?"

"Yes. Do you know what happened, where her parents are?"

The neighbor pulled up the veil to reveal an older woman with a worn, worried face. She glanced up and down the street. "Look, you can't stay here. The bugs might come back any minute. And we don't want any more trouble."

"Barbara?" Jane hurried over.

The woman leaned over the railing. "Jane, dear. I'm so glad to see you're well. Your parents went into the commune on Jackson Street to get medical attention. I would have had them here but..." She whipped her head around at the sound of an approaching engine and pulled her veil back down. "I'm sorry I can't offer to put you up. It's against the rules now. Don't antagonize them and you should be okay." She darted back into the house just as a Jeep came around the corner.

"What does that mean?" Jane came to stand with Diana, Samantha, and Eli following.

The Jeep screeched to a stop behind Diana's truck and four men jumped out, all wearing camouflage and armed with semi-automatic weapons. "Hey! Is this your truck?"

"Yes." Diana walked back to meet them, keeping her body language relaxed. "Is there a problem?"

"Who are you and what are you doing here?" The leader was a muscular man with a moustache. He was shorter than she was, and his frown deepened as she got closer.

Great. One of those. She stepped off the curb onto the road as she approached so his eyes were on a level with hers. "I brought my friend to join her parents but..." She gestured at the burned-out husk of a house behind her. "Are you local? Do you know what happened?" It was less challenging than just asking who they were.

"We're in charge here." Moustache stood with the self-conscious pose of a bully given power; trouble looking for an excuse to happen.

"Are you police?"

"There have been some huge fires in Salt Lake City. The emergency protocols kicked in and most of the police are there dealing with the fires. A few of the older ones stayed and were killed or injured by the cicadas. After that, a gang of thugs moved in so a pile of us who used to go hunting together decided it was time to step up, just like we always talked about around the campfire. We're in charge

292

now." He walked around the truck, peering through the windows. "What are your plans?"

"We need to find Jane's parents."

"The people who lived here? They're in the commune." He kicked the tires of the truck. "Follow us."

Jane helped Jesse into the backseat with Samantha and Eli and slipped into the front seat next to Diana where they could confer. "I don't like the sound of this, or the look of these people."

"Me neither." Diana drew away from the curb, following the Jeep. "The neighbor – was it Barbara?– said your parents went to the commune. Surely they would contact you though, to tell you about the fire if not to say they were okay."

Jane watched the Jeep as it lurched around a corner too fast. "I didn't like the way Barbara reacted when they turned up."

"Nor the way those guys were looking at the truck." Diana turned left and they followed the Jeep until they came to the barbed wire barrier, complete with a complement of guards. The Jeep screeched to a stop. Moustache got out, talking on his cell phone and waved at them to follow. She slowed and pulled into the side. "Looks like we're here."

"I'll go." Jane unfastened her seatbelt. "I'll know if my folks are not okay."

"Wave if you need us. And be careful."

Samantha unbuckled herself. "I'm coming too!"

"I need you two to stay in the car till we know it's safe." Jane opened the door.

"I'm not a kid anymore, Momma. I want to see Grandma."

The mustached man strode over to them. "Your mother's been informed you're here. She'll be at the gate shortly."

"Stay in the car, Samantha." Jane slammed the door, her hand in the small of her back. If she was uncomfortable, because of the baby weight, she'd never let it show.

"Fine!"

Samantha continued to mutter mutinously but Diana tuned it out. Moustache was up front gesticulating, and the other men casually sauntered around. It did not escape her notice that they were slowly moving to encircle the truck. The body language between Moustache and Jane was setting her hackles up as he postured more and more aggressively, but after a few moments the gate opened and an older lady hurried out. It had to be Jane's mother; they looked so alike. Jane threw her arms around her, and they burst into tears. There was a quick exchange. Jane threw a hunted look back at the truck but did not wave.

Diana rolled the window down enough that bits of the conversation drifted across.

"...smoke inhalation... only place we could get him seen to...all our savings but what can we do? The hospital was—"

So, are you gonna bring your family in or what?" Moustache put his phone in his pocket. "You know the buy-in. How many of them are there?"

"There are four —"

"Three. Alex—" She couldn't finish the sentence, but the tears said it all. Her beloved husband was already dead.

"Oh darling." The older lady squeezed Jane's hand. "Mr. Stone, I have no more money. You know that. But she's my daughter and the baby's due any minute." Jane's mother's hand drifted to the curve of her daughter's belly.

"No money, no can do."

Diana was distracted by the sound of the back door of the truck opening. One of the men called, "Plenty in here, Boss."

Diana threw her door open and hurried around to the back. "What do you think you're doing?"

"You have food. We need it." He pulled out the first of the boxes of canned food.

"Stop! You have no right to—"

He shoved her away, hitting her shoulder, and she nearly buckled with the pain of it. "Your mom there, she owes us a lot of money. This can go some way to paying it back."

"Please—" The older woman called out. "Nobody needs to get hurt." Moustache noticed the exchange and marched toward them.

Diana clutched her shoulder. "Wait. Stop." Forcing herself upright, she confronted the man again as he unloaded the boxes. "If you need the food, take it. But I'm a scientist and the cooler is full of cicadas. If you open it, you could be injured."

"Yeah right. That's where the booze is, isn't it?" The man went straight for the cooler.

"Wait. Let me show you. Please? It's not like I can stop you from taking it" She put a mask on and opened the lid of the cooler. "Look. Those are foliage samples, and those are..." She fell silent. Tiny pale things were wriggling in amongst the leaves. "That's impossible. That takes six weeks, not three bloody days." A shiver ran up her back.

"Holy crap, there's a live one in there." The man stepped backward.

"Like I said, these are samples. I need to take them to the lab." She put the lid back on and stripped her mask off. "Take the food if you must, but I need those cicadas."

Moustache was bristling like a rabid dog as he rounded the end of the truck. "Steve, get the frickin' food out of here and take it to the Committee."

"Yes, boss." The other man grabbed the sack of food they had collected and backed away from Diana's truck, dragging the heavy bag behind him.

"As for you—" Moustache sneered at Diana, brandishing his pistol. "Get back before I make you."

Jane appeared and grabbed Diana's arm as the truck's engine roared into life. "Di. Come on. We have to go." Jane pushed her into the back and clambered in the passenger seat. The truck lurched forward and sped away. But if Jane was in the passenger seat, who was driving? Samantha turned the steering wheel sharply and Diana was thrown against the door, eliciting a flare of pain from her ribs.

"You okay?" Jesse clutched at her sleeve.

She patted his hand. "I'm fine, Jesse. Bit ouchy is all."

The truck lurched again as Jane fired off directions. "Left now. In here. Stop and turn the engine off."

"Stop?! Are you crazy?" Samantha brought the truck screeching to a stop between a house and a row of trees, which masked it from the road.

"We'll never outdistance them. I know it. They race their Jeep and it goes like greased lightning. But we might be able to lose them. And in any case if there's a chase, I'm going to be driving, not you."

"Everyone quiet. I'm going to see if they're following us." Samantha slipped out.

Jane moved into the driver seat. "We need to leave town. The hospital was overwhelmed with cicada patients, so Mom took Dad for medical help. The doctor's surgery is in the area the hunters blockaded off and Mom was desperate, so she agreed to pay to go into their compound. But they took her phone off her and now they won't let her leave till she pays their dues. They're charging them astronomical prices —they've gone through my mom's life savings already. Soon as Dad's better they'll be out of there, but right now, he can't be moved. We can't go in and she can't leave him. She told me to go to her brother, my Uncle Mark. He has money—he'll help us buy them back out. Those guys took everything they had, even her engagement ring. Mom said to get out of here while we still had a vehicle."

Samantha clambered back into the passenger seat. "They went past us and down the road. Do you think they went back to the commune?"

"Let's hope so." Jane turned the engine on again.

"What's that?" Eli pointed out the window. There was a glint of sunlight on metal, and at the shout, the sound of running feet.

"Go!" Samantha yelled. A spray of bullets rattled through the trees as Jane swerved into the road and tore off. Behind them, four figures scrambled back toward the hunters' Jeep.

Samantha twisted to get a clearer view through the back window. "They're following... quick, Mom. They're still behind us."

The lights turned red just as they passed, but the Jeep behind them did not stop. A SUV accelerated out of the other road and had to swerve to miss the Jeep. It skidded around with a screech of tires and mounted the curb, smashing into the building on the corner. The hood crumpled and it jolted to a stop, horn screaming.

"They're getting closer!"

"Jane, the freeway." Diana leaned between the front seats and pointed.

Jane dragged the wheel around and the truck cornered so sharply that it lifted on one side. For one heart-stopping moment it teetered as if about to roll; then the wheels slammed back down on the tarmac, and it roared down to join the freeway.

Diana was thrown against the door again and the pain of the impact against her ribs took her breath away. She clutched at her torso as Jane brought the truck into the fast lane, zipping in and out of the occasional cars.

Samantha leaned between the front seats. "They've stopped in the middle of the on ramp. Wait. They're turning around. They're driving off again. Whoa! They're driving the wrong way back to the road."

"It's okay, Jane. They didn't follow us onto the freeway." Diana kept her voice relaxed with an effort. "Good job. We lost them."

Jane eased off the accelerator, dropping back into the middle lane. "At least we're all safe." She slowed to a more sensible speed. "I have no idea what to do now though."

"We'll think of something." Diana tried, and failed, to drum up a single idea. She was so tired and her shoulder hurt almost as much as her ribs. "Let's stop somewhere for the night and discuss it in the morning."

"Not here though." Jane shuddered. "We need to get away from those men."

"We can't leave Grandma and Grandad there, Mom," Samantha objected in that strident, self-righteous way only teenagers could muster. "We should go back and rescue them."

"We will, darling, but Grandad is too sick to move. We can't do anything till he's back on his feet, and Grandma says the doctors are doing a really good job of looking after him. Right now, he needs to be there. But by the time he's better, we'll have found Uncle Mark and we'll have the money to get them out."

"He's gonna be all right though? Grandad, I mean?" Eli piped up from the back.

"Of course he is, darling."

Samantha plugged her phone into the car charger. "So where are we going?"

"Last we heard, Mark lived in Auburn, near Sacramento." Jane pulled out to avoid an overturned truck on the road.

"Let's head straight to Auburn then." Diana leaned her head back on the seat rest. "It's on the way to Berkeley. There should be a hotel of some kind. We can rest awhile, replace the food they took and go on."

The plan to break the journey as soon as they got far enough away from Moustache and his men went by the wayside within a few hours. The radio was on repeat with warnings of swarm sightings. There were fires in the Sacramento area and every gas station they passed had been stripped of supplies and was low on gas. The world was shifting way out of order and Jane was too restless to stop. After their second break, she suggested they go all the way to Auburn.

Samantha tried to call Uncle Mark for the tenth time, but once they reached the Sierra Nevada mountains, the cell service was almost non-existent. And as they went through the pass and began the downhill leg of the journey, the traffic got heavier and heavier.

"Do you smell burning?" Samantha cracked the window open, but the acrid smoke made them cough, so she closed it again. "I wonder what's... Oh."

Where the city should have been laid out before them there was only a pall of heavy smoke, like a dirty haze below them. Jane slowed. "They said there were fires. On the radio."

"I've been so worried about the cicadas I haven't really been paying attention to the fires." Diana let her head fall back on the headrest. Maybe she should have taken Jesse to Chicago after all. "Where are they? How bad?"

"Hang on. Oh, shoot. No cell signal, just when we need it." Samantha clicked her phone shut in irritation.

"Well, the road is too narrow to turn around here and it's packed with traffic." Jane frowned. "We can't pull off here."

"Keep driving for the moment and we'll put the radio back on." Diana wasn't particularly happy but if there was a way to get past the fires and down to Berkeley, Jane and her family could always stay with them for the time being. "If the fire sounds like it's too near to where we are, we'll think again, but I need to get the cicadas to Sam."

The sun had set by the time they reached the foothills of Sacramento, so they booked themselves into a motel. It had a noisy generator running out front and Diana saw the look on Jane's face at the cost of two rooms but there was a Family room with two doubles and a sofa, so they took that. "My company can pay the bill. It's no more expensive than the single I'd be taking anyhow. And frankly, they—and I—owe you for dragging you into the mess with Dan."

"You know you don't have to." Jane rubbed her throat.

Diana grinned. "I'm not. They are. Take it while we have it, eh?"

Jane took the kids to the little restaurant next door to choose their meals, and Di took the opportunity to have a shower. It felt wonderful to be clean, though it stung her face fiercely. She washed off the sweat of panic and exertion, and the filth of the puddle in the alleyway where Dan had nearly drowned her. It felt like days had passed. *How could it be only yesterday?*

Her shoulder was black and blue and yellow, and incredibly painful to the touch. The most tender spot was the dark purple print of the diving tank harness buckle which she didn't remember landing on, but which must have broken her fall. Her body was a map of pain, but most of the landmarks were little more than mysteries; a boot print here, a fist there, the story of what she'd been through at Dan and Aaron's hands was written on her flesh.

After a long and luxurious shower, she wrapped herself in one of the thin, scratchy towels and went back into the bedroom. Just as well her overnight bag was always in the truck. If she hadn't had a clean change of clothes she'd've had to wash the old lot in the shower.

She dressed, trying not to see the bruises on her body in the mirror and finally paused to towel her hair dry. Her face was one solid crusted scab along the right brow, from hairline to cheekbone, but given the scrappiness of the edges, maybe it wasn't the cicada toxin after all. It looked more like a nasty graze, thanks to Dan. And the cough could be explained away by the amount of puddle water she'd inhaled. She snorted. At least she'd been too frantic to worry about her lungs.

A knock on the door heralded Jesse and Jane. Jesse was holding two paper bags. "We got you a burger. Is that alright?"

"Perfect, Jesse, thank you." They'd driven through more than one hellscape, but emerged into a place where there were still burgers. She tried to push the thought away, but it wouldn't yield: how long was *that* going to last?

When Jesse had eaten, Diana put him to bed and once again he was out like a light. "He's sleeping a lot. Should I be worried?" Jane felt his forehead. "I don't think so. He hasn't got a fever. He's still healing and his face and hand are painful. That would wear him out even if he wasn't dealing with all the emotions of what's going on."

"About that. He hasn't cried."

Jane smoothed his hair back into place and returned to the sofa in the corner, lowering herself in the time honored fashion of pregnant women—arm back first, legs stretched, and a huge sigh as she sank into the cushions. "He's still stunned. It will come sooner or later, and it will take a while to pass. But he's out of his normal place and out of his routine so a lot of the things that might normally remind him of those he's lost just aren't there."

"How do you help a child through that?" Diana sat on the bed and looked down at the scarred little face below. "I don't have the first idea." No one had tried to help her through the loss of her brother; her parents had been too wrapped up in their own grief. And now she had to find a way to make Jesse feel better? "Even the idea is daunting. But hopefully by then he'll be back with whatever relatives his Aunt Sarah has, and in familiar surroundings. Being with his real family must make it easier, surely?"

Jane reached into her pocket and dabbed at her eyes briefly. "You can put it out of your mind for a while and then, bam!, something comes and it just takes you out."

Diana left the bed and busied herself with her gear. "I'm sorry." Jane had only mentioned her husband in passing. She knew none of the details.

"My husband. Alex. Such a good, good man. He..." A sob escaped her. "Our baby is due in eight weeks." Jane hid her face and wept.

Diana sat awkwardly next to her. Nothing she could say would make it better, but she recognized this sort of grief. When she'd had to pretend to be fine after Charlie's death, she had found it could be done for so long, and then she had to let it all out. Jane was trying to keep cool and collected for her children, but her heart was shattered as much as theirs.

Eventually Jane calmed, and her sobs became watery sniffs. Diana patted her on the shoulder and brought her a glass of water and a cool, wet facecloth from the ones provided by the motel.

Jane drank the water in three long gulps and held the cloth against her eyes to get rid of the redness before Samantha and Eli returned.

Diana took the glass and refilled it for her. "Your two aren't back yet. They've been a long time."

"I said they could eat in the dining area. There was no one else in there. The waitress promised to keep an eye on them for me." Jane puffed up the cushion and lay back on the sofa. "Ugh, my ankles are so swollen, too. It doesn't help. The kids need a bit of time on their own, and frankly I needed a time out too. I'm getting snappy with Samantha and it's not always her fault."

Diana took her computer out of her bag, plugging it in to recharge. "I need to go see Sam but he's a couple of hours from here. And we need to keep an eye on what's going on with the fires. We should keep everything ready to go while you find your Uncle."

"And we need to get my parents out of that place just as soon as we can. The bills get higher every day."

Diana rummaged in her bag for her phone, and then in her coat pocket. For a moment she was baffled; then remembered it was halfway to Lincoln, smashed up on the freeway. "Your uncle will help though, won't he?"

"Perhaps. He fell out with my mother many years ago and we haven't had much to do with him apart from Christmas cards. I have his number but if he's changed it, we'll have to hope he still lives at the old address." Jane rubbed the curve of her belly.

Diana set her bag away and went into the bathroom to get her hairbrush. "Don't worry. We'll get them out of there one way or another."

Jane struggled upright. "Let me try his phone number again." She hit his contact, putting it on loudspeaker. "I know that it's ridiculous when I've tried so many times before but..."

A man's voice snapped "How did you get this number?"

"Uncle Mark? Is that you? It's Jane Steele."

"I don't know any Jane Steele—"

"Jane Patterson, sorry. Helen's daughter. I've been trying to get in touch with you. It's important."

"Helen's daughter. Okay." Mark did not sound delighted.

Diana came out of the bathroom, untangling her hair into strands, as Jane wiped her palm on her slacks. "The thing is, Mom and Dad need help. Mom took Dad to get medical treatment and the people keep putting the price of everything up and won't let them leave till it's paid."

"I knew the scams had been getting worse of late, but you people are sick!" His voice was a growl. "If my sister was in trouble, she'd call me herself. I don't know who you are or how you got my details but don't try to call me again. I'm blocking this number."

"But—" Too late. The line cut out and Jane was left staring at her phone.

CHAPTER THIRTY

ANAYELI ALFARO. SACRAMENTO, CALIFORNIA.

Anayeli walked toward the light. She had no idea how long they'd been walking. Hours. All night. A lifetime. Or maybe it was only minutes. There were no stars, no moon, no warmly lit windows, nothing to brighten the deep, smoke-choked night—except the glaring white glow she used as a pole star, the light she prayed was from the evacuation center.

Behind her trudged Ernesto, Mama, Bailey Rae, Roxy, and Carlota. Cricket was at her heel, refusing to flag even the slightest. Somewhere even farther back, Savannah trailed, perhaps gone, possibly lost—but not the way Luz was. Savannah was still alive in the dark. But Anayeli would never be able to un-live the moment Ernesto had pulled her out of the whirlpool and made her stop diving for Luz, both of them choking with sobs. She would never be able to un-hear Savannah saying, "Karma's a bitch, ain't she?" That was the moment Anayeli had stopped caring what happened to the woman. Whatever Savannah might think of her, Anayeli wasn't a monster.

She hadn't wanted to shoot Jason. She would give anything not to have left sweet Luz, tangled in a snag in the middle of the American River.

Savannah was the only one who hadn't wept as they floated downriver, none of them bothering to pilot the raft anymore. The worst the river could do had already happened. By the time they'd gotten to a wide expanse of shoreline past the college campus, near downtown —Sutter's Landing Park—the sun was setting, a brilliant bloodorange disc on the horizon, the sky long since gone dim. By then a grim silence had settled over all of them, punctuated only by Ernesto's wheezing, which had gone from the rumbling purr of *el gatito* to a more sinister labored screech. When they'd pulled the raft ashore, Anayeli waited only long enough for Bailey Rae and the dogs to get out before she'd started walking, knowing only that she had to keep moving, that she had to get her family out of the smoke. No matter what Mama thought, there was only one place that was even a possibility: the evacuation center.

"I need some help, here." Savannah had stayed in the raft, her baby cradled, asleep, on one arm, her toddler's head leaned on her shoulder. No one had answered her. No one had moved toward her. The one person who would have carried Savannah's baby was in the river, at the bottom of a whirlpool, gone. On a different day, or maybe even the same day *before*, Anayeli would have thrown karma right back at Savannah and made her eat her words, but she couldn't risk anything that might crack her frozen shell and let whatever was roiling in her deepest darkest parts out. The numbness was the only thing holding her together.

But the closer she got to the light, the more labored Ernesto's breathing became, the harder it got to stop the thoughts of Luz's last gasp, of nothing but river water. And now Ernesto was on land, inhaling fire. Like Papa and Sid and Bailey Rae's daddy. Their masks hadn't worked. Her numbness melted, replaced with a desperate urge that made her joints buzz and the pulse in her injured hand throb. She had to do more. When the keening wail rose behind her—Mama, Carlota—she walked faster. She had to. The closer they got to the lights, the more ragged and raw they were becoming. They might all fly apart if something happened to Ernesto.

The solid ground disappeared beneath her, and she jolted hard. She'd walked off a curb. "Hold up!" She backed out of the street she hadn't seen in the dark. The lane on their side was deserted, but across the wide intersection, barely visible through the smoke, cars filled the lanes, the street clogged. A truck nosed out of line, the engine revving as it bumped and jounced over the concrete median, before speeding the wrong way down the boulevard, passing everyone as they headed toward the evacuation center. It was only a matter of time before more drivers did the same. Except no one did. Not a single driver honked. Either everyone in the waiting cars had fallen asleep, or...

"This is it—we need to hurry!" They had to get to the evacuation center. Before it got full. Before—she pushed away the thought of the woman in the newsroom parking lot, slumped dead across her steering wheel, of what might be in the cars across the street.

"Anayeli, wait." Each word came on a labored breath. Cricket whined and circled Ernesto. "Rest?" In the dark she could just make out the solid shape of him, his hands on his hips. It was the pose he used to do on hikes, before his asthma had been diagnosed. A way to open his chest, get more air into his lungs.

"Where's your inhaler?"

"With everything else." Everything else. Luz. Their backpacks, carefully filled with supplies. All of it at the bottom of the river.

Wait or run. Those were their two choices. Wait and breathe in more smoke. Wait and lose their spot at the evacuation center. Run and save Ernesto. *Vive.* That's what Papa would say. *Corré.*

"We have to go. *Ahorita.* Can you run?"

Ernesto's footsteps, Mama's and Carlota's and Bailey Rae's, were her answer. The dog's tags jingled. They ran for the beacon that was the eerie light from the evacuation center, the rectangle shape of the building indistinct, its edges blurred as it jutted up in the haze. She prayed her desperate calculus equaled the right sum.

They got as far as the first of the solar generator trailers, each running one of the tall lights that shone through the night, illuminating a city of tents set up in the hospital parking lot behind a temporary chain-link fence topped with barbed wire. Then they had to stop. Not because of Ernesto, but because in the wash of cool light, a clumped and clotted cord of people snaked out of the smoke. The woman at the back was slumped in the way that said she'd been standing there for a long time. She didn't even turn toward Anayeli. No one did.

Ernesto's wheezing and Cricket's whining blended together into a single noise that twisted her nerves. She tapped the slumped woman on the shoulder, jolting her out of some stupor in a way the pounding of a family of five running up on her hadn't. "Is this the back of the line?"

"Yeah. Ain't moved since I got here." Slumpy had no mask, and a trickle of blood trailed from her nose to her upper lip. She smeared it away with the back of her hand, her eyes landing on Ernesto as he struggled to breathe. "Sposably there's a triage nurse up there and a whole other line for sick people. But I dunno. I don't wanna lose my spot. It's like playing telephone, getting any kind of word."

They all went quiet again, except for Ernesto's labored breathing and Mama and Carlota's panting after the run. Muffled shouting came from somewhere up ahead, and Cricket sat on Anayeli's foot.

"Didya see the jack?"—Slumpy looked around Anayeli to where Bailey Rae had sat on the sidewalk, Roxy leaning against her, periodically sneaking little licks of the girl's face— "'Scuse me, little lady. The *jerk* who drove to the front?" The woman pointed through the smoke with her bloodied hand. "Bet that's him up there yelling."

"We saw a truck pull across the—"

"Shhhh. I wanna hear." How Slumpy could have an appetite for drama in the middle of the night, when the city, the whole northern part of the state, was on fire around them, Anayeli could not understand. She stepped backward into the dark night.

The shouting got louder. The feeling coming off the crowd was like a snake coiling, readying to strike. People would only wait quietly for so long, and one shouting *pendejo* might be enough to set off a mob.

Anayeli drew her family farther away from Slumpy. "What should we do? Stay here? Or go see if—" But she shouldn't have bothered. Now that they weren't walking anymore, Mama's arms were wrapped around her chest, her head down as she repeated the same words over and over, a mantra.

"Mija. Mi querido. Mi esposo." It was a phrase perfectly calibrated to remind Anayeli of her failures. *My sister. My father. My heart.* She would not fail again. She would not wait.

"We need to get Ernesto in to see a doctor. They can get us an inhaler at least." An inhaler wasn't going to stop Ernesto's asthma, not if he was still going to be stuck outside. The tents in the parking lot would offer little protection from the smoke. No. She needed to get Ernesto admitted into the medical facility, so he could be inside, breathing filtered air.

"Hey lady!" It was the woman ahead of them again. She pointed at Cricket. "You know they won't let you take dogs in there."

Mention of the dogs snapped Mama back into dragon mode. *"Nadie.* Not one soul. Not even the dogs! No evacuation center. *Nunca.* I told you." She linked her arm through Carlota's, and pulled at Ernesto's arm, but he didn't—couldn't—move.

"It's the whole reason we came. He'll be fine in there." What Anayeli meant was: He was born in the United States. He wasn't going to be taken away from them or deported or any of the things Mama was afraid of.

"You always put your family first when it suits, and ignore us when it doesn't."

The sting took longer than it should have to hit her. It was the worst accusation anyone had ever made about her—that she would ever willfully ignore—As if she had meant for Luz and Papa to— "No! I have never—"

But it was true. She had begged off from family gatherings on Saturdays more times than she could count because she had work. She had slept in and missed going to church with *la familia*. She had a full inbox of calls from Mama and Papa that she had let go to voicemail instead of picking up. But that didn't mean she didn't love her family. That she wished them gone. That she used them for her own purposes. It took everything she had left in her not to scream at

Mama. "Listen to him! He can't stay out in this smoke." She pointed, and Ernesto shrank as everyone's attention turned to him.

"Yeli, I'm okay." Each word was an effort, and sweat dripped from his hairline down his forehead. His face above his mask had gone paler than usual and he swayed as he stood. "Just give me a min—" He hated it when they argued, and when he got upset, his asthma would get worse.

"Look at him, Mama!" She grabbed his hand, held it up. "His fingernails are going blue." Even as she spoke, Ernesto doubled over with hacking coughs. "What did you even let me bring you here for, if you weren't going to let him go in?"

But it was Carlota, not Mama, who stepped forward as Ernesto continued coughing. "Hurry up. Before he gets worse. Bailey Rae! Roxy! *Vamos.*" Carlota marched down the sidewalk, toward the hospital and the shouting that was still growing louder, her chin lifting higher as the glares and muttered rumblings followed her, the people in line like rattlesnakes shaking their tails as they passed.

At the front entrance soldiers wearing camouflage, military caps, and guns slung across their chests stretched to block off the hospital parking lot while other National Guard personnel erected still more chain-link fence. The truck that had pulled out of the traffic and raced up the wrong side of the boulevard was in the middle of the street, its doors flung wide, the key-in-the-ignition alarm ding-ding-dinging. Off to one side of the guarded entrance, a pop up tent filled with white-gowned and gloved and masked medical professionals had been set up, and more people straggled away from it, queuing parallel-ish to yet another barbed-wire topped fence. The people in the new line were all coughing or bleeding or crying or writhing in some kind of agony. Some lay flat out on the concrete sidewalk, motionless, while loved ones hovered over them.

But it wasn't the line Carlota marched for. It was the tall man who stood in the glare of the truck's headlights, shouting.

"You have to help us! Look at her!" His arm was wrapped around a teenage girl. The kid's was covered with blood that seeped from some kind of horrific injury that Anayeli couldn't track. The girl groaned as the older man—her father judging from the similarity of their build and features—staggered, dragged the girl along the asphalt as they struggled forward. The girl faded in and out of consciousness.

A female soldier in a hijab blocked the men's path, backed up by three other armed guards. "Sir! You cannot— There is protocol. Sir, you must wait your turn!"

"She's dying! She needs help now!"

"Sir, I can see that she's very sick, but I can't—The triage nurses will—"

The girl let out a scream—the kind that reminded Anayeli of when Ernesto was little and used to have night terrors. "Don't let her go! No! Don't look! It's too awful!"

The words raised goosebumps on Anayeli's arms and her nose stung with the tears she couldn't let fall.

The military officer made a gesture toward one of the guards backing her up, sending the other soldier jogging for the medical tent. He came back with one of the nurses. She crouched to examine the girl and she screamed again, before the nurse had even touched her. The nurse said something to the military officer and the officer ordered her guards forward with a gurney.

The teenager was lifted onto the gurney and as the nurse put an orange plastic hospital band on both the father and daughter's wrists, Anayeli made her move. Pulling Ernesto after her, she barged toward the same officer, her whole family following behind.

The officer's face hardened, going flat and resolute before Anayeli even spoke. "No."

"He can't breathe—" She pushed Ernesto forward.

"Ma'am, if you would just step back into line, there is protocol—"

Ernesto coughed. The nurse, who had been headed back toward the medical tent slowed, turned back around. Some unspoken question passed between her and the officer, and the nurse shook her head. No.

Anayeli had to keep the nurse's attention. They took the sickest first. As much as Anayeli despised herself for thinking it, if she wanted to get Ernesto into that hospital, she had to make him even

309

worse. She pointed toward the nurse. "Yeah. Protocol that's so important you just let her break it for that white kid."

"OMG." It was the first OMG Anayeli had ever earned from Carlota. In another lifetime, she would have been secretly pleased. Racist call-outs were usually Carlota's territory, and Ernesto hated it when she went on one of her tirades.

"Yeli!" Ernesto wheezed, putting up a hand. "Stop. It's not worth—"

But she did the opposite. She pressed, hoping it would be enough. "Is my brother's life less valuable? Is that why you won't let him in?"

"Ma'am, there's a proper procedure and we cannot give special privileges to every—"

Mama rushed forward. She grabbed for Ernesto's arm, yelling a torrent of Spanish. "I told you, he's not going in there! None of us are going! We are staying together." She tried to pull Ernesto away, but he was coughing so hard that he swayed on his feet, his face flushed, even as his lips went blue-tinged.

"Look, my mother doesn't even want me to talk to you. This might be my last chance to get him help—" She almost couldn't make herself go on. But if she could upset Ernesto enough, the strong emotions would make his asthma attack worse. And if it worked to get him into the hospital—

It was the only thing she could think to do. "You know why she's so afraid? Because she's here illegally. She thinks—"

Mama's slap was loud and hard across Anayeli's mouth and it meant every eye was on them. Ernesto's expression as he straightened reflected the same horror Anayeli felt at what she had just done. Mama's biggest secret, exposed. But Anayeli couldn't take the words back, she'd gone too far. Mama hurled curses at her—*traidora* and worse. Much worse. Mama would never forgive her. But if it meant Ernesto lived—

"But my brother—he was born here. He shouldn't have to be afraid to get help!" Something in the officer's expression changed. It was now or never. Anayeli made her last bid. "Was that girl allowed ahead of us just because she was *blonde*?"

Ernesto's whole back arched as he tried to suck in a full breath.

Cricket, who had been pacing behind Anayeli let out a sharp bark, just before Ernesto fell to coughing again, this time so hard that he retched, and fell to the ground, blood splattering on the asphalt as he clawed down his mask. Mama cried out then—the same cry that had filled Anayeli's ears the instant Luz had disappeared into the river.

The nurse rushed forward, put her stethoscope to Ernesto's chest. "What city did you come from?"

As soon as Anayeli said, "Woodland" the same unspoken question as before passed between the officer and the nurse. "Please! You have to help us!"

"I can't let all of you in at once." The officer's mouth was set in a grim line. "And no dogs."

"It's just me and my brother going in." Before she'd even finished, Carlota reached for Cricket's collar, and Mama sank to the ground, sobbing.

Anayeli pressed Carlota into a hug her sister did not return, as a pair of soldiers wheeled a stretcher out for Ernesto. "Stay near the gate, even if Mama fights you. It'll be safer. I'll come find you as soon as I can."

She went to where Bailey Rae sat with Roxy. "You take care of the dogs, okay? They're both so special and I really need you to help Carlota with Cricket, too." The little girl nodded, but her lips quivered, and a tear spilled, making a track down one cheek. "I'll be back, okay? I won't leave you."

Last she knelt next to Mama. "*Lo siento*, Mama. I'm so sorry. But I had to get Ernesto safe—"

Mama spat on the ground and turned away. "My own daughter treats her filthy *perros* better than her own family."

Anayeli held Ernesto's hand in her good one as he was wheeled toward the evacuation center entrance, the yellow bands around their wrists matching, except for the red stripes on Ernesto's. She did not look back at what was left of her family, split in two. She would not let herself cry. She had to be strong for Ernesto, for her family. She would not imagine what might happen to three women locked outside the evacuation center when the city was being devastated and devoured by flames. The guards at the entrance would help. The dogs would keep them safe.

The soldiers at the entrance parted to let them through. As she stepped toward the generator-lit hospital, a terrible howl went up. Not Mama. Not Carlota. But Cricket, saying goodbye.

CHAPTER THIRTY-ONE

SAM LEARY. BERKELEY, CALIFORNIA.

Frank's face contorted in murderous rage, a furious bull charging a red flag. He'd brought someone back with him and to say they weren't having a good time was the world's most massive understatement. Frank's victim was wearing a gray hoodie and baggy jeans. Sam couldn't get a good look at his face, though there was already blood spattered down his front. Whoever they were, they were much smaller than Frank, lighter, a lab rat who hadn't seen the inside of a gymnasium since his dodge ball days. Sam knew the type.

Frank body slammed his victim against the pane of glass, pressing his head sideways, until his lips drooled blood and saliva down the window in rivulets. Frank towered behind his victim twisting his arm. "I told you I'd make you wish you were never born. Since you've made it impossible for me to reach you, I'll take it out on your buddy, Cockroach."

Sam's stomach dropped at a million miles a minute. Cockroach? He'd made it *just* at the wrong time.

Frank ground Cockroach into the window so hard his bones and ligaments threatened to snap. "If you want to keep her alive, you need to bring me the backup files."

"Cockroach?" Sam's sweat drenched palms left streaks of perspiration on the glass as he got a better view. "Her?"

Cockroach gasped and struggled. "Hi ho Sam, off to work you go."

Sam backed into the middle of the room, jaw hanging open. *Cockroach is a she?* The female being tortured was more girl than woman. Her shock of hair splayed out against the window as her body was compacted into half her original height. There was very little muscle to cover the bones of the Ichabod Crane like scarecrow.

"Well, Sam? Are you going to help her or not?" Frank twisted Cockroach's arm harder; she winced and cried out as her legs buckled but the pressure against her upper body kept her upright. A single tear ran down her nose.

Sam inched closer. It was a selfish, awful thing he was about to say, but he had to say it. "Where did you hide the thumb drives?"

She gasped again. "Treasure... island ...buried... "

Frank yanked Cockroach back and wrapped his arm around her neck in a choke hold. His massive bicep cut off her air as she struggled for breath and went still.

Sam banged his fists against the glass. "Let her go Frank, you're going to kill her."

"That's the idea. Since you two have conspired to keep what I want, she's my bargaining chip. It took considerable convincing for the twerp to tell me about the thumb drives in the first place, but after searching her and her car, they couldn't be found." Frank Dorset, stating the obvious since forever.

"If she dies now, you lose your leverage."

Frank let go of Cockroach's body and she crumpled to the floor.

"Huh, she even looks like a cockroach right now." He drew an invisible sad face on the window and skewered the non-existent nose with his index finger. It was right in line with Sam's face. "Here is what's going to happen. I'm going to drag your friend to my office and lock the door. You're going to find the thumb drives with the data on the caterpillars and bring them to me. Place them on the floor in front of the door and come back to this office. Shut the door tight so that brute of yours won't get out. Once I have what I want, I'll release your friend."

"I don't believe you."

"I don't care if you believe me or not. Your friend does." Frank kicked Cockroach in the stomach, rolling her over onto her back. He placed his boot on his victim's chest and pressed his weight into it.

Sam threw his hands up. "Okay. Stop. Stop!"

Frank grinned. "You have one hour to find them."

Through the skylight the evening's amber glow was already dissolving into night's velvet blue. "It's getting dark out. Give me two hours."

"Fine, but no tricks." He pointed at Sam and then at Cockroach and slid the two fingers across his neck in a slicing motion.

Sam shivered as Frank dragged the girl across the carpet. "All right Henry, let's find those drives before he exterminates Cockroach."

The dog paced back and forth, on guard, as Sam levered his body against the wall and inched the table away from the door. Sam squeezed himself into the corridor. Henry slipped under his legs and the two ran down the hall, light feet almost silent on the carpet.

The evening haze crept closer as they ran for the only car in the lot. She hadn't locked it, which didn't shock Sam. Rummaging through the vehicle, he scanned all the opened cubbies. He ran a hand through the nooks and crannies while Henry sniffed around the outside.

Sitting in the driver's seat of Cockroach's car, Sam concentrated as hard as he could. What was it Cockroach had said? 'Treasure Island.' She couldn't have meant the real treasure island, that would have been too obvious. Besides, she was a literary savant. No, the drives had to be somewhere in the car. The night turned a shade darker and the closest street lamp cast a blaring yellow cone down on the car. Its refraction off the front windshield gave off the illusion of another mirror as the interior of the car was displayed.

Henry crawled half way into Sam's lap, his front paws resting on Sam's thighs. Sam scratched the dog's head while he puzzled and stared into the reflection in the front windshield. A bird flew past the rear window. Sam bolted upright and whipped around. A vinyl sticker clung to the rear window right above the brake light. He palmed his forehead with a light smack and crawled into the back seat. Why didn't he think of that earlier? The clear sticker was a palm tree in a lump of sand, x marking the spot on a two-dimensional map.

He pried the cover off of the brake light and fished inside the housing. Taped into the back were two thumb drives. He returned the cover and swung the car door closed as he raced for the Life Sciences building, Henry close behind him. Taking two steps at a time, he reached the front and body slammed into the doors, coming to an abrupt halt. They were locked. He hid the drives in his pocket. *Think. Racing around isn't going to help either of you. What happens when Frank gets these?* Government officials? Military secrets? Frank was working for the military? Directly. Bypassing the University; and perhaps double-crossing Paula. Or was he in cahoots with her, planning to sell the toxin on the open market? That had to be it, right? Nothing else made sense of the relentless rounds of torture he'd put Sam through.

He fished around in his pocket for the key, unlocked the door and slipped inside. Giving the drives to Frank was a double-edged sword. On the one hand, he couldn't allow Cockroach to get hurt. On the other, he understood—as perhaps Frank didn't—what his results could mean and what damage they could do in the wrong hands.

Sneaking past Frank's office to the last room on the corridor he grabbed several bottles of soap from the janitor's supplies and the fishing string from Frank's pack. Locking Henry inside the office he drew a mental floor plan of the atrium and surrounding hallways. He had an idea, not a good one, but it was all he had, and Cockroach's life was on the line.

He stuffed the roll of tape into his pocket right as Frank appeared at the top of the stairs. He leaned over the railing and waved for Sam to come up, then disappeared abruptly.

Sam took the stairs three at a time. "All right, let's finish this."

He padded down the carpet, counting the doors, then lay the thumb drives outside the room where Cockroach was being held captive. He tapped on the window and pointed down. Frank came closer, acknowledged the drives, and retreated. Sam peeked in at Cockroach to make sure she was still alive then dashed away and hid himself behind a pillar at the end of the hall.

Frank opened the door, stooped to retrieve the drives, and pushed his prisoner into the hall. Her body collapsed in a heap. Sam balled his fist. That loser was going to pay for that. Frank kicked at the lump of flesh and returned to his office. "She's all yours, come and get her."

Sam ran to Cockroach and turned her over. Blood crusted over her cheek, nose, and mouth. Her eyes fluttered open and she managed to croak out, "Run."

Sam wrapped his good arm around his friend and together they hobbled to the last office. After all the things Frank had done—and because of what he assumed was *really* at stake—there was no way he was going to run. He helped the scarecrow slide through the opening. She slipped down the wall, landing next to several empty bottles of clear liquid soap strewn about with the bleach and toilet paper.

"Look after her Henry, I'll be back."

The dog sniffed at the newcomer then pawed Cockroach's hand and she laid a weak palm on the dog's head.

Sam grabbed the supplies he needed from Frank's backpack and shut the door. Tiptoeing to Frank's hiding place, he took the spool of fishing line and wrapped it several times around the door handle, staying out of view from the window. Wrapping the line around the railing, three feet away, he tied it off and cut the spool free. The first stage of the booby trap was set. Sam went about his business, quietly and efficiently, setting up what he hoped was the world's most inventive snare. Frank wasn't the only one who'd played *Minecraft* and *Watch Dogs* and came up with whackadoo solutions to everyday problems. Sam ducked under the line and posed in front of the glass as Frank scrolled through the files on one of the thumb drives.

The familiar rectangle with an address bar at its top sat dead center on the monitor, and Sam focused on the folders. One file opened. Then another.

"Traitor!" Frank slammed his fist down on the mouse and flung the keyboard across the room. "Liar."

Sam waved through the glass panel, jeering at the buffoon.

Frank knocked the computer and monitor to the ground and charged. The handle twisted, and the door opened a quarter of an inch. The fishing line stretched as if a marlin was on the hook.

"You gave me dummy drives. Say your prayers because the eighth circle of hell is where you're headed." He pulled harder on the handle, but the line fought him.

Sam waited a beat more and took off down the hall, hopping like a rabbit every ten steps. He wasn't supposed to show people his 'inner child.' They got all weird and judgey about him. But it was good to be a nerd and have ideas and beat the bully at his own game. He was allowed a hop, most especially with no one around to smack him down and tell him to "grow up and act your age." A twang resounded like a gunshot as it echoed off the walls and Sam sped up.

Another twang snapped out, and a massive thud vibrated the floor. Frank lay on the ground, past the corner post, his head sticking out into the corridor, the rest of his body hidden from view. Frank got to his feet and took sideways shuffling steps until he reached the main passage where tile lined the path and no trip lines reflected. He picked up speed as Sam ducked around the corner. The thudding increased until Frank shot by, sliding on a patch of hand soap spread in a thin layer over the entire hallway. He tumbled on his back. The momentum carried him past the turn and twelve feet down the balcony. As soon as Frank hit the marker tied to the balustrade, Sam hopped over the slick and made for the main stairs.

Straddling the railing and holding on with one hand, he slid down the polished wood spiral to the main floor. Feet firm on the ground, he raced to a line taped to the main doors, pulled it away from the metal, and wrapped it around his palm. Standing on the far side of the tyrannosaurus, he hid his hand behind his back.

Frank struggled to his knees, slipping and sliding on the soap as he tried to get up. Latching onto the railing, he glared down at Sam. "You think that these little traps are going to save you? Enjoy your minor victories."

Frank reached the stairs, skirting the soap slicked path. Pausing at the landing, he crouched and shifted from side to side. It didn't take a genius to work out what he was doing. He honestly thought he could work out what Sam had in store. The glint of fishing line, strung from one side of the railing to the other, was a ruse, nothing more. Frank smirked and took a step away from the line and into the elevator.

Sam shuddered as the numbers above the elevator doors counted down to his floor. Sweat beaded on his forehead as Frank sauntered out of the box and strutted to the middle of the atrium. "Thought you were so smart. So much for the 'boy genius.' More like village idiot. Any moron could see the stairs were wired."

Sam kept space between them, backing up as Frank advanced. As they neared the front doors, Sam tripped over his shoes, falling backward, yanking the fishing string hard.

The pterodactyl that hung above the tyrannosaurus wobbled and broke free of its moorings, crashing down behind Sam in an explosive shattering of bone. Peppered with fragments of pterodactyl, Sam curled into the fetal position with his arms wrapped tight around his head.

Frank's boot slammed into his ribs. He wheezed and curled up tighter. Another kick sent pain arcing across his sprained shoulder before his arm went numb. He wished he had the strength to knock the smug grin from Frank's ugly mug. He rolled his body toward the tyrannosaurus, scrambling back to a fishing line taped to the floor. It ran to a board hooked to the railing.

Frank inched forward, crouched in a linebacker's stance, peering through the legs of the dinosaur.

Come on... Sam backed away further until he was near the column supporting the balcony. "Hold it right there!"

Frank lifted his hands in mock surrender. "All right, Sam, I'll play along. What can you do to me? You're not strong enough to overpower me, and your dog isn't here to protect you."

"I can do this." Sam rolled behind the column and yanked down on the line, freeing the board. It swung down, smashing into the tyrannosaurus. The supports which held it up exploded, bone daggers flying in all directions as the skeleton shattered. The T-Rex slammed to the ground, trapping Frank under the enormous rib cage.

The shock wave was overwhelming. Everything went white, and Sam dropped to the ground.

"Hey, you okay?!" The voice was familiar, but his blurry vision made it hard to recognize the hand waving in front of his face. The speaker was small, skinny, with a blonde pixie cut. Cockroach. It was Cockroach.

"Ugh. Never try that at home." He sat up and grabbed his ears as the buildings alarm tried to split his head in two.

"Are you hurt? I see blood."

Sam ignored her and twisted around so the column was to his right. Chunks of shattered tiles had left scars in the plaster, while small pockets of smoldering material pocked the landscape. The dinosaur's collapse was more spectacular and deadly than Sam had expected. The lizard king's backbone lay on top of Frank's body as blood pooled around his head.

"We need to get rid of the body before the police arrive." Cockroach's face was flat, her tone uninflected. She was simply stating a fact.

Sam wobbled on his feet, using her as a support. Edging nearer, he kicked the sole of Frank's boot. "Hey, can you hear me?"

Frank didn't move. His skull was half- shattered, the bone crushed under the dinosaur's skull.

Sam bowed his head. "I think I left a full bottle of hand soap in the office, could you get it please?" As soon as Cockroach was out of sight he leaned over the skeleton and vomited.

She returned faster than he expected. "I'm assuming this is for the body. Where do you want to put him?" She dismantled the top of the container and waited.

Sam wiped his mouth on his sleeve and pointed.

Cockroach measured out the straightest path and poured an even layer of goop to the elevator, spreading it with her hand as she went. Wiping the excess on Frank's shirt, each of them took a side. Grabbing an arm, they heaved the deceased—it was the only way Sam could bear to think of his former colleague—forward a couple of feet. He stepped over the pool of blood as they tugged the body.

"I thought the dinosaur skeleton had enough strength to remain intact. That it would hold him like a cage."

Cockroach remained silent.

Resting for a minute, they took hold and pulled again. Though they heaved and puffed, with the injuries they had, it took ten minutes to shift Frank's carcass fifty feet. When they reached the elevator, Cockroach dropped Frank's arm and broke her silence. "What are we doing, Sam? We can't hide a dead man in the elevator."

Sam pressed the call button and the doors opened. "Wait here." He stepped in, leaving Cockroach with the corpse. He pressed the top button and traveled to the third floor. Slipping into the janitor supply office he removed the wire handle from a mop bucket and returned to the second floor by the stairs. With the elevator car suspended on the third floor, Sam bent the wire until it was shaped like an L and shoved it into the slot above the right side door. He fiddled it left and right until he found the post and pushed up. The latch sprung free and the outer doors spread apart as he pushed on them. "Quick, get one of the bone fragments and wedge the doors open."

Cockroach found two rib shards that were shaped like door stoppers and shoved them under the left and right door. With a couple of heaves, they tipped Frank's body into the empty shaft. Darkness swallowed the body and Sam released the doors, their closing thunk the final chapter in Frank's story.

CHAPTER THIRTY-TWO

DR. DIANA STEWART. BERKELEY, CALIFORNIA.

Jane's sobs had turned to hiccups, then back to sobs, then coughing, and back again to wailing. She was inconsolable. It was only an hour or so of tears, but to Di it was an eternity. She wasn't so British that she avoided all public expressions of big emotion, but neither was she so American that she knew what to do with a woman in abject despair.

"He won't help." She'd said it ten times already. Her uncle was being a hard ass. He didn't believe Jane was his niece. He wanted a call from his sister. Which wasn't possible, seeing as Jane's mom was, for all intents and purposes, in prison.

Diana handed Jane a box of Kleenex. "We'll find a way. We'll convince him."

"What if he won't believe me?" Jane blew her nose.

"You look just like your mom." Diana put an arm around her. "Tomorrow morning I'll drive you over there. Even if he hasn't seen you since you were younger, he'll see the resemblance to her and he'll have to believe you then. He can't leave his own sister in that sort of trouble, can he?" That was a bit of a gamble, but it seemed to work.

Jane's sobs slowed to a stop. "No. Of course not."

"Now, you look exhausted. I know I am. What do you say we tell the kids to come back now and call it a night?"

The kids came back, full of burgers and shakes and tall tales of firebombs exploding all across the state. Jane hushed them and the room fell into silence. Diana took the couch, though she was hankering after a real bed, but slept sooner and sounder than she'd expected to.

The following morning, they left bright and early, much to Samantha's disgust. The GPS took them to the top of one of the little hills. It would have been a pleasant area with lots of trees and a view over the town in normal times, but in the dirty haze of smoke, everything looked more ominous.

Diana followed the road along the top of the rise, and they finally turned into a medium sized house that the owner probably thought of as a mansion. Diana turned in, the gates closing behind them. She followed the gravel drive through grounds so perfect that they didn't look real, with not a stray pebble trespassing on the lawn.

A man—balding and in bathing shorts, a towel draped around his shoulders—hovered by the mailbox. As they drew in, he shooed them away. "This is private property. Leave now or I'll call the police."

Diana stopped the truck and Jane clambered out. "Uncle Mark? This isn't a scam. My Mom's phone was confiscated. She didn't call me either." She rubbed the small of her back. "I just want to talk."

He pursed his lips and considered her words. "I suppose you'd better come in."

Samantha and Eli followed their mother into the house. Diana moved the truck under the shade of a tree. They'd agreed that it'd be better for her to stay with Jesse, ostensibly to avoid aggravating Mark any more than they absolutely had to. But given the week she'd had, Diana wanted to be sure that if there was trouble, the truck was ready to go.

"Do you think he'll help?" Jesse asked. "He must be rich if he has a swimming pool."

"I certainly hope he will." Jane had told her the previous night that she had no other relatives and no savings of her own. "How are you feeling today?"

"I can see out a bit more and my eyes aren't so sore. My arm hurts though. The skin is all cracky. Will it make a scab?"

Diana smiled, keeping an eye on the door of the house. "Probably a great big gross one."

"Cool." Jesse pulled at the edge of the bandage on his hand, trying to look underneath.

"Leave it be, scamp. Wait till it's properly scabbed over. Then we can think about taking the bandages off."

Jesse explored his face instead. "Will I have a big scab on my face too?"

"Maybe."

"Like yours?"

She glanced in the mirror. It was a terrible mess. Another reason for her not to go into Mark's. "Not exactly like mine."

"We could be scab twins."

That surprised a laugh out of her. "Lovely. I am very honored to be your scab twin."

"I can pick yours and—"

"Ewww, no! No one is picking anyone's scab, okay?"

"Okay." Jesse's eyes were alight with mischief—or at least the right one was, which was less swollen. "But we could have a sign that only we know."

"That sounds good. Did you have anything in mind?"

He pressed his lips together in thought. "I know. What about this?" He drew his thumb along one cheekbone and then the other with a flourish.

Diana copied him. "Like this? That's pretty cool."

"Yeah. Scab twins forever!" He did it again, with the air of a pirate threatening to cut his victim's throat.

Diana covered a grin. "Well probably for a week or two with the real scabs but..." She assumed an air of mystery. "Once a scab twin, always a scab twin. Even when they're gone, we'll know, won't we?"

"Yeah!" He giggled. "We will."

The McMansion's door slammed open. Jane ushered Samantha and Eli out and stalked after them.

Uncle Mark stood in the doorway. "Oh come on, Jane. What did you expect me to do? Give up my own life savings because your mother took a chance and it went wrong? There's nothing I can do. Besides, she's a grown woman, and she makes her own decisions, just like she did when she moved away and left us to look after Dad by ourselves."

Jane stopped in her tracks. "That was thirty years ago, Mark, and this is your own flesh and blood. They had to seek medical help, they're in danger and you offer fifty dollars, out of a safe that must have thousands and thousands in it? They took all her life savings, Mark, and all Dad's too. Five thousand might give us a chance, but you won't help her because you just put a down payment on a Tesla? Really? People are dying left and right, and you're playing 'better than the neighbors?'" She turned to walk away, but stopped. "I've always taken Mom's stories with a pinch of salt, always thought that I was only hearing one side of the story and she must be exaggerating how self-centered you could be. But I see now that she was understating it. This has certainly been a waste of your time and mine. I won't be bothering you again. Ever." She marched over to the truck, and slammed the door so hard that the samples in the back rattled. "Let's get out of here."

The journey to the motel was silent but for Jane trying to stifle her hiccupping tears and the kids whispering in the back. Diana drew into the parking lot, turned the engine off, and waited.

"What an ass!" Samantha burst out. "He could have helped, easily. He said he could barely afford the maintenance on his swimming pool! Like he was poor or something. He's got more money than I've ever seen in my life, all sitting in that safe like some kind of gangster—"

"Samantha, don't, please." Jane heaved herself out of the truck. "I can't deal with that now."

"But what are we going to do?" Samantha waited for an answer, but didn't get one. "Fine. Whatever. I hope the fires burn his house down. I'm going to the restaurant. I'm too angry to be calm right now."

The others walked back to the room. Jane plunked herself down on the sofa.

Diana sat beside her. "Look, this isn't the end of it. We'll get your Mom and Dad out of there somehow, I swear it. But we have a few days to think of a plan while your Dad gets better. Why don't you rest up here for today while I take the samples to Sam?"

Jane threw her arms around her. "Thank you, Di. This isn't your problem and I shouldn't get you involved, but I really need the help."

Diana extricated herself gently. "I need to get on my way with these samples but I'll be back tonight and we'll try to work out Plan B then. The fires don't seem to be coming this way just yet. Can you look after Jesse for me for a few hours please?"

"Of course. It'd be a pleasure."

Eli jumped into the pause. "Mom, can we go and play outside? There's swings and a playground and nobody's on them. Look, they're just out back."

Jane went to look out of the window. "Those ones? Okay, but stay in sight. And if I yell, you drop what you're doing and come running that second, you hear me?"

"Yes, Mom." Eli and Jesse raced outside. People were dying, most of the state seemed to be aflame, and the cicadas were laying waste to everything they touched, but the kids still needed to be kids and play.

Diana checked her backpack; her computer was in there, and the cooler box was near the door, plugged in. "Okay, got everything. Remember my phone is dead on the interstate somewhere, so I'm out of touch until I get a new one." She paused to glance out of the window. Eli and Jesse had been chasing each other but now they were deep in conversation. From the look on Jesse's face he was up to something. She hoped he'd behave for Jane. "I'll give you the number for Sam's lab. The minute there's trouble, if there's any talk of the fires heading this way, you call me immediately, you hear? I'll be listening to the radio but still..."

"We'll be fine." Jane followed her out to the truck as she loaded up her bag. "The prevailing winds are always to the north this time of year at home. I'm sure they will be here too. Oh, by the way, did you want that briefcase?"

Diana froze. "You didn't?"

"Pick it up for you? Yep. It's in the truck, right under the back seat." Jane pulled out Dan's briefcase.

He hadn't locked it in his hurry, and inside was his laptop, wallet, and a whole sheaf of papers in a file marked FEEDIT. "Oh my. You might just have saved the missing bits of my life's work, Jane. And this could be invaluable to Sam as well! Thank you so much!"

Jane slumped against the side of the truck. "Call from Sam's line, if anything changes. We'll do the same."

"I'll be back as soon as I can." She hefted her backpack over her shoulder, took the briefcase and waited while Jane dragged herself back inside the motel. She should go say goodbye to Jesse but she didn't want to upset him. Besides, he knew she was going out again and had gone to play with Eli so he couldn't be that bothered. She was obscurely stung by that thought.

The roads heading toward the University were much less chaotic than the ones around Lincoln had been. One of the gas stations along the road was just opening up as she got to the entrance, so she filled the tank as well as the gas cans, mentally thanking Jane for thinking of those and shooting off a prayer of gratitude that there was gas to be had.

She took Highway 80, but the road was thick with traffic, and the day was dark with ash and acrid fumes. Alongside the road, the fire was much nearer. Diana was not sure she wanted to go on, but she couldn't leave Sam on his own in Berkeley. There was no one who'd help him there. And without the data on the cicadas, there was no way of finding a way to control them. California had wildfires all the time, so the fire services must be reasonably used to dealing with them. But even so, with far off walls of smoke and the occasional flame coming into sight, she accelerated. The inferno that had everyone so worried was getting uncomfortably close.

As she neared Berkeley, the smoke grew thicker and there was a marked uptick in N95 masks. The traffic coming away from the city was growing heavier, and there were signs of people panicking. As soon as they'd done the analyses on the cicadas, she'd bring Sam and Henry out of the city and head for somewhere safe from fires and cicadas, wherever that might be. Maybe it was time to call for Victor's jet, after all.

A police truck was cruising along behind her. Diana glanced at the speedometer; nearly five miles above the limit. She moved into the slow lane between a station wagon and a Chevy, braking hard to match speed with them. As she hit the pedal, there was a thud from the back seat.

"Ouch!"

She knew whose voice that was. "Jesse? Is that you?" She pulled off the freeway at the exit before the university and pulled onto the hard shoulder. "Jesse Sanders, if you make me come around the back of the truck to find you it won't go well." She twisted in her seat and spotted a red sneaker peeping out from behind the blanket in the back. "Come out this minute."

Jesse didn't move. There was a whoop outside and the police truck pulled in behind her.

"Tremendous. Now the police are here. Get in the seat and put your seatbelt on, quickly."

Jesse pushed the cover back to show he was belted in. "My momma said I had to wear the seatbelt always. I've got it on. Kinda."

A policeman got out from the truck and straightened his sunglasses. Diana gasped. He was familiar. More than familiar. He hadn't changed since their University days, nor moved away, it seemed. Her heart started to thud as it did when he stalked through her dreams. "Jesse, pretend to be asleep. Whatever happens, you're asleep, okay?"

"Okay, but..."

"Shhh!"

Jesse pulled the cover over himself and shut his eyes.

The figure swaggered over to the car with the same old arrogance he'd always had. It set Diana's every nerve jangling, and she was suddenly twenty and afraid again. He knocked slowly on the window —he always did know how to reduce her to a wreck—and she rolled it down a crack to talk to him.

"Well, well, well. Hi, Diana. Small world, huh?" He bent down, bringing his face up close to the glass, inches from her own. "Long time no see."

"Garrick. You're with—the police now?" *How the hell did that happen? He was the last man on Earth who should be allowed to join the police force.*

He looked her up and down, a sardonic grin on that handsome face of his. "I'd like to say you look well, but in all honesty you're a mess. It looks like someone's taken his fists to you."

She shivered. "Not you this time, Garrick. I need to be on my way. I don't have time for reminiscing."

"Pleasant as it may be, I wouldn't be pulling you over for the pleasure of seeing your face, Di. 'Specially when it looks like that. I've been told to look out for a truck just like this. Think of it as a kind of unofficial Amber alert. Way I heard it, some woman kidnapped a child, you see, and this truck fits the details exactly."

Diana's pulse rate went up. It didn't make sense. Sheriff Ben knew exactly where Jesse was. "An Amber Alert?" It had to be Garrick twisting the truth again, surely. But someone had given him the description of her truck, and she couldn't believe that that was a coincidence.

"Yeah, nasty business, little boy about six. A lot like the one unconscious in the back seat there." He tutted. "Looks like you've been a bad girl, a very bad girl indeed. And bad girls need to be punished." He winked at her with that peculiar mix of threat and fake jocularity that turned her insides to iced water.

"I'm hardly a girl these days, Garrick. Grow up." But it was a brittle shell of bravado.

He laughed in her face with the same lazy amusement she had learned to fear when she'd been married to him. "Well, aren't you the little firecracker these days?"

She watched in her mirrors as he went back to his truck. He opened the door, picked up his radio and spoke to someone. She swallowed. She was clutching the wheel so hard that her shoulder was afire with pain, though it hadn't registered until this second. "Jesse, are you still belted in?"

"Yes."

"Hold on. This is going to get bumpy." Revving the engine, she reversed straight at the police truck, gas pedal to the floor. Garrick dove out of the way just in time. The truck smashed the door shut.

"What's happening?" Jesse grabbed onto the door handle as he was thrown forward.

"Shh! I need to concentrate." She could hardly get the words out. Her heart was pounding so wildly she could barely breathe. She drew forward again and aimed. This time she rammed the police truck right off the road and into a ditch, then accelerated away, engine straining.

As soon as she was out of sight, she swerved into a side street, and then another and another. She had to get out of there. She had gotten away from him once, all those years ago, and he wouldn't let her do it a second time. Behind her, a scream of tires; he wasn't far off.

She sped through town like the devil was after her. It wasn't far from the truth. At the intersection, a taxi and a freight truck were coming the other way. There was a smallish gap between them, but she raced through it, flooring the gas pedal to get out of the way as the freight truck thundered toward her. The brakes screeched, but at that speed there was no way he could stop in time. Missing Diana's truck by a hair's width, the freight truck juddered, hitting the pavement as it skidded, then toppled over with a crash, blocking the whole junction.

"Whoa! Did you see that?" Jesse twisted in his seat.

Diana's palms were sweaty on the steering wheel, but she'd won a few moments' grace. She heard Garrick's engine revving on the other side of the wreck. He'd be around the block in moments.

She floored the accelerator and roared along the street as the truck driver clambered out through the smashed windshield of his cab, shouting abuse. She only had moments before Garrick caught up with her. She had to get to the little short cut she'd found when she attended Berkeley. It looked like a dead end, but unless anything had changed—and she devoutly hoped not—she could get through the goods gate at the far end.

There. Slamming on the brakes, she eased the truck into the narrow little alleyway with inches to spare. Turning the corner scraped paint off all the side, which made Jesse cringe, but once in, she snuck through the gates and onto a maintenance track on the campus which led to the parking lot by the Science Department.

She parked in the hidden corner between the substation and the fenced area where the janitors put broken office furniture, just like she always had, and turned to Jesse. "You okay there?"

"That was soooo cool!" His face was alight with glee. "You're the coolest twin I ever had!"

"Scab twins forever." As she winked at him the screech of the gates echoed across the area. Her smile drained away. "Come on." She unlocked his seat belt, grabbed the cooler out of the trunk and hurried him across the asphalt to a cluster of bushes as the sound of the engine drew nearer. There wasn't time to get inside before the vehicle was in sight. "I used to have a den. Shall we see if it's still there?" Without waiting for an answer, she slipped into the space hidden in the greenery. She set the cooler down and gestured him to sit on it. "Hush now, let's see who that is."

Garrick's truck raced along the maintenance road and into the lot. He did a slow circuit, and paused outside the Science Department, then drove away.

"You don't like him, that cop?" Jesse was no fool.

"He... bullied me when I was younger and he would bully me again, given half a chance. We don't have time for that. We need to get to my friend Sam so he can study the cicadas and find out what makes these ones dangerous. Come on."

"Diana?" Jesse stared at the empty shell of a cicada.

"It's empty. It's an old one. But we'll be careful anyhow," Diana answered with a calm she did not feel. The cicadas were on campus, too! How? They didn't come that far West! Diana bit her lip. The earth around her was pocked with holes, and now she looked, there were far more casings than just one. She scraped the top layer of soil aside with her boot, and found more of the shucked shells.

"Oh my." She took a plastic bag from the cooler and put her hand inside it. She grabbed dirt and cicadas through the plastic, turned it inside out, and zipped it up. "Come on, we need to get to Sam right now.

CHAPTER THIRTY-THREE

RON FROBISHER. SOUTHAMPTON, ENGLAND.

Cocaine up the nose? Five minutes to impact. Cocaine in the eyes/nose/mouth, who the hell knows? Ms. Emmas Lindsay and her driver weren't necessarily going to get high, but they were temporarily blinded by the powder. The coughing and cussing was violent enough that Ron had the cover he needed to army-crawl his way through the dust bunnies to the door while his victims scratched at their faces, hissing and spitting in the featherlight dusting of coke.

Devon hadn't pulled the trigger, but neither was he incapacitated, so staying down until he was clear of the ruckus was of the utmost importance.

"Get me some water, right this instant." Emmas Lindsay had an upper-crust accent that Ron couldn't quite place. She thumped her driver between the shoulders, pushing him toward the backroom. She sneezed and wiped her nose over the back of her hand. *Not so classy now, eh.* "Do your job, Jake."

Jake was in no state to do his job. Tears snaked through the caked-on powder, creating a series of deltas on each of his cheeks. He hacked, doubling over and bracing his hands on his knees, then wheezed as he stood inhaling more cocaine with each breath. All to the good.

Devon disappeared from the doorway. "I've got this," he yelled. "Water. Coming right up, boss."

Ron leapt to his feet and threw himself at the wheezing driver, wrapping his arms around the man's torso and forcing him to the ground. He grabbed a fistful of the guy's hair and thwacked his skull once, twice, three times on the tiled floor, good and hard and guaranteed to knock him out. "Sorry, Jake. Nothing personal."

A stiletto heel stabbed the back of Ron's leg, Emmas Lindsay screeching and yodeling, as if her banshee wail could make the stomp more powerful. It was going to leave a nasty bruise, but it barely broke through the denim. Ron twisted at the waist and grabbed her calf, pulling her down on top of her driver and slipping an arm around her throat.

Devon appeared, a bottle of water in each hand, the gun a distant memory. Score one for cocaine amnesia. The guy'd had the upper hand and squandered it.

Ron smiled. "One step closer, Devon, and the lady gets choked out."

Devon hovered over the trio, hands over his head, eyes swiveling from the driver to Emmas and back again.

"Gun!" Emmas growled. "Go back into the store room—you big, useless lug—and get the gun."

Ron tightened his hold on her with his right arm while pushing himself off the floor with his left, dragging her upright with him. She might have been tall, but she was no match for a man who made his living taking out the trash. Each squirm and wriggle only served to tighten his grip on her scrawny throat.

"No guns, Devon." Ron stepped toward the wide-eyed clerk. "Back up slowly. Good. Hands in the air, like a good boy, and we will conclude our business so I can be on my way."

Emmas did a decent impersonation of a sack of potatoes, using her weight to resist Ron, but she was a socialite, grass fed and organically fertilized; there was no way her one-hundred and thirty pounds of sinew and muscle was a match for him. He shook her a couple of times, just to demonstrate who was in charge, then took a step closer to Devon.

"I don't even work here." Devon's eyes bulged, barely keeping the quake out of his voice. "I'm standing in for a friend."

"Yeah, well, you do now." Ron pushed Jake's limp arm out of the way with his foot and stepped around the sprawl. "Play your cards right and we'll all get through this without any further aggro."

Emmas raised her knee and lashed her foot backward. Not a bad move if your assailant was anyone other than Ron Frobisher, but his reflexes were razor sharp and he dodged the move with a single step.

"Shoes off, lady." She didn't budge. "You take them off or I do. If I do it, it's not going to be pretty." She kicked off her pumps, dropping several inches as her stockinged feet hit the floor. Ron pulled her in tighter. "Good. Now, let's get this transaction over with."

Devon stumbled as he backed into the dark of the store room.

"Easy does it." Ron propelled himself and his charge through the door and swung around back of Devon so he wouldn't have an opportunity to snag the weapon he'd so carelessly left on the desk. "Get a rope..."

"I d- don't have any..." Devon stuttered.

"Improvise. Grab one of the awful Gucci bags and rip off the shoulder straps."

Devon left the bottled water on the desk and rummaged through several boxes, muttering swear words under his breath.

"Third shelf down, three boxes over." Ron steered Emmas behind the desk and shoved her into the rolling chair then turned to inspect her. "Who sent you?"

Emmas spat in the general direction of his shoes. She missed.

"Charming." Ron's lip curled. "I take it we're not a chatty Cathy, then."

"Hands where I can see them." Devon's stutter had evaporated once he relocated the weapon. Funny how that worked.. "No sudden moves." Devon slid toward him, feet barely touching the floor. The man had moves. Ron ditched everything he'd assumed about the clerk and replaced that character sketch with a professional profile not unlike his own. The only thing that didn't fit was keeping him in play when he should have been on the floor, out cold, like Jake.

"Don't make me hurt you." Devon stalked the pair, his eyes never leaving Ron's. "Vinnie doesn't like bloodshed. Not on company premises."

Ron eyed the clerk. If he was a professional, he was relatively low down on the food chain. No one with mad skills would be parked in a Southampton dive when they could be in London, making real money for the boss. Wasn't a chance in hell Devon had the authority to pull that trigger. "Vinnie wouldn't want you to drop me."

"We'll see." Devon fished his mobile phone out of his pocket and hit a key.

Ron stared down the bore of the gun while Devon called his boss. Emmas lurched out of her chair and scrambled for the door, grunts punctuating her feeble attempt at an escape. Ron was on top of her before she'd made it three steps, arm around her waist, then a hand at her throat. She folded herself in two, jamming her teeth into his wrist. The coke had to be hitting her system because she was at least twice as strong as she'd been just minutes before.

Devon was having no luck reaching Vinnie, which only compounded Ron's sense that he was a pawn, not a knight or a bishop. Ron wrapped the pleather straps around Emmas' wrists, securing her to the bottom of the steel shelving unit, then took a stab at securing her feet. Easier said than done. She'd turned into an eel. An eel with long legs, a harsh kick, and the vocabulary of a sailor. The upside to her squirming all over the shop was that Devon didn't know where to aim his gun.

"Whoa there. Simmer down." Ron dragged her back into the ill-lit room.

She thrashed in his arms. "Turd-breathing Weimaraner."

Ron laughed. What did that mean? Coke hit everyone differently and Emmas was, it seemed, freed up to invent insults.

"May your progeny rot in the smaknlian of splan." She was devolving into nonsense. Ron bypassed Devon and headed right for the box of Gucci bags, dug the scissors out of his back pocket, and cut the bags free of their shoulder straps, all the while grappling with a woman who was higher than a flag on the Fourth of July. She was positively flying.

Ron stood and brushed his hands down his trousers. His wrist was bleeding where she'd sunk her teeth into his flesh, but other than that he was merely sweaty and irritated. He'd gone to the Off License on Vinnie Two Tone's say so, which, in the normal course of business, did not involve getting the run around from a two-bit gangster wannabe. With two moves he'd disarmed Devon and ushered him into the corner. "Give me the phone."

Devon flushed but slid the phone across the floor. Everyone knew you had to text Vinnie before calling. The light bulb went off. Dammit, he'd been played. Devon wasn't working for Vinnie. Ron scrolled to *RECENTS*. His heart juddered in his chest. He kept his breathing even, though the pounding behind his eyeballs made that a real feat of physical prowess. The number Devon had dialed belonged to Boyd Miller. Ann's second in command had sent someone to lift his cargo, which landed like a friggin' battering ram to the chest. No, that had to be the coke. He'd been breathing like the idiot he was. He wasn't as high as Emmas, but the accelerated pulse and rush of adrenaline, accompanied by that unmistakable *certainty* that he was unstoppable, told him he was high. They all were. Him, Emmas, knocked-out-Jake in the front of the store, and wild-eyed Devon who'd allowed himself to be disarmed and handed his phone over without a single word of protest.

The next ten seconds of Ron Frobisher's life—as he ran through all the permutations of what might unfold next—stretched out like a ribbon of fire, blazing across the room and lighting Devon up like a Christmas tree. He swung back, grabbed the shelving unit and heaved on it with all his might. The boxes came off in slow motion, crashing to the concrete floor with a pleasant series of cracks and booms. The shelves themselves were sturdy, but not bolted to the floor. It wasn't until Emmas threw her hands over her head that Ron realized she was going to be crushed.

Devon scrambled to his feet, pushing the boxes off Emmas and jabbering about "the cost of haulage." Another one who couldn't handle his high.

Ron stepped through the chaos and swiped a fist in Devon's face, the butt of the gun meeting cartilage in a satisfying crunch. The clerk went down, smacking against the floor. Ron was on top of the guy, raining fists into his face until the stillness took over.

In the wreck of fallen boxes, Emmas Lindsay groaned. Ron heaved the shelving unit off her. The gash in her side oozed blood while a thin trickle ran out of her mouth and toward her ears. She was a goner, with minutes left on planet earth.

"Tell me who you're working for and I'll put you out of your misery."

Emmas' eyes flickered. She had to know she was as good as dead. If their roles had been reversed, Ron would have welcomed a bullet to the brain.

"Have it your own way." He turned and left her where she lay. Devon was out cold. Ron pocketed his phone and retrieved both guns before pulling the *Better Bio* crate from its place on the shelf and hauling it out front. Jake the driver was still out cold. Ron ran through his pockets, mostly for the car keys, but he helped himself to the man's wallet and phone while he was at it. No need to let them alert Boyd right away.

He stopped in the doorway. Loose ends. Never good for business. He lowered the crate onto the counter and hunted for the two bricks of coke he'd dropped in the original attack. A brick each would do it.

He knelt beside Jake and unwrapped one end of the chunk of white rock. He crooked his elbow and rested his nose in the crease, then sprinkled the coke over Jake's bloodied face. Too slow. Not a guaranteed kill. He pulled his shirt sleeve over his hand and eased Jake's bottom lip open. "Down the hatch." He shook the snow storm into the driver's mouth, pausing when the man sputtered, but then emptying the rest into his throat.

Devon got the same treatment, death by overdose. Not Ron's finest moment by a long shot, but he had a job to do. A job that had gotten several degrees more convoluted and dangerous with the introduction of Boyd as an enemy. It was his own fault for calling the man and tipping him off to the operation.

Outside the shoddy storefront, the gleaming Jaguar seemed out of place. Whoever Emmas Lindsay was, or had been, she was one rich player. Ron popped the trunk.

The thump from behind sent the crate soaring. Emmas— drenched in her own blood, caked in coke, barefoot, and braying— swung a bat at Ron. Swung and missed. He grabbed the makeshift bat, splinters digging into his fingers, and wrested it away from her.

Out of the corner of his eye he spotted a black blur. It buzzed over his head and flew right into Emmas' face. She batted the insect away. Bugs. Big bugs. Big, beetle-like bugs hovered, then landed, crawling over her exposed flesh. It had to be a trick of the high he was still riding, but he would have sworn on a stack of Bibles that Emmas' face was puffing up under all that carnage. He turned in time to see the exploded crate lying in the middle of the road, but didn't pause to learn more. The winged monstrosities were creeping out of the corners of the *Bio Better* crate and taking to the air.

Emmas yelled—louder than before, and more desperate—before dropping to the ground. The coke had fueled her last burst of energy, but the blood loss had to have been profound. Coke only feeds your rage if it has a circulatory system to take it to the brain.

Ron hit the button on the Jaguar's fob, opened the driver's side door, and threw himself into the leather interior, slamming the door behind him.

The contents of the crate had crawled into the world, flexing their paper-thin wings and lifting off by the dozen. Could have been the blood, could have been the coke, or it could have been something Ron had no clue about, but those critters sure liked Emmas Lindsay.

"What have you gotten me into, Ann Pilkington?" It irked him that she'd lied to him, but that came with the territory. He was paid not to ask hard questions. He'd been tasked with transporting live cargo from England to Africa and he wasn't about to sit around waiting to see what that meant; if, indeed, it meant anything at all. He was still higher than he'd ever been in his life. Bottom line: the less he knew, the better.

He started the engine, backed the car over Emmas—mercy killing, definitely—and sped back to *The Fairwinds*.

CHAPTER THIRTY-FOUR

SAM LEARY. BERKELEY, CALIFORNIA.

The front doors to the Life Sciences building slammed shut and Sam poked his head out of the last office. Two more people walked through the main atrium, avoiding the shrapnel from the previous evening. He leaned over the railing on the third floor to get a better view. Great, it was bad enough that the place had been crawling with important people a few hours ago, now they had pedestrians. "Go away. The cops and firemen have already taken care of the situation."

Diana stopped and tilted her head. "It's rude to yell at someone before you find out who you're talking to."

Sam bounded downstairs. The day had turned from the worst ever to almost okay. "Sorry Diana. I didn't know it was you." He stopped, looking from her to the kid whose face was all puffy and scabbed over too. "What did you do to your face?"

Henry raced across to Diana, wagging furiously and skidded to a stop in front of her. "Hey, Henry, good to see you too, boy!" She set the cooler on the floor, clutching at her ribs as she straightened, and scratched the dog's ears. "Sam this is Jesse. Jesse, say hello will you?"

"Hello." The kid squinted through his swollen eyelid. "Hey, is that a T-Rex? Can I go and look at it?"

The world's favorite dinosaur was a broken shadow of its former, glorious self, and was still surrounded by yellow police tape. But the soap-goo had been cleaned off the floor along with Frank's blood, so there was no harm in letting Diana's kid-friend touch the skeleton. "You can." Sam remembered his first dinosaur encounter. The kid was in for a treat.

"But stay close, will you?" Diana stroked Jesse's hair then gave him a little push in the right direction.

Trotting over to it, Jesse measured his fingers against the teeth and wandered around the massive head. Henry licked Diana's hand before chasing after Jesse. Giggling echoed from the other side of the collapsed skull as Diana quirked an eyebrow at Sam.

He didn't know where to start. "It... I... Cockroach..."

Diana put out a hand. "It's okay. You're alive, and in one piece. You don't have to explain if you don't want to. Is he safe to play here while we examine these?" She pointed at the cooler.

Sam shook his head, placed a finger over his lips, and walked to the elevator. Standing by the metal doors, he placed his shoe over a spot and slid his foot backward so the rubber arch pointed to a red coagulated splattering in the grooves of the metal grating.

Sam wobbled, not enough sleep and too much adrenaline. "I've had nightmares all night." He let go of her and lifted his shirt. Several shallow lacerations crisscrossed his body. The shallowest were along his chest and stomach where bone shards had ricocheted off the pillars. The ones on his arms were deeper and covered in Dermabond. He ran his fingers over the rough surfaces and dropped his shirt. "The police think the blood is mine and Cockroach's. We told them it was an experiment gone wrong. But I have to meet up with the Dean on Thursday to explain what happened."

"You can tell me when you're ready." Diana was always kind, but not pressing him in that moment wasn't what Sam was expecting.

Who saw blood spatter and didn't ask a million questions? Only the very best friend you could ask for, that's who.

Diana turned toward the skeletal remains as Jesse trotted around the impromptu obstacle course with Henry, whooping with delight. "He isn't going to like seeing the cicadas. He's seen too many, already. Bad memories, you know?" She didn't wait for an answer. "Is there somewhere near the lab where he can play but we can see him?"

Sam pulled a ball out of his pocket and handed it to Diana. "He can play with Henry in the hallway. It should keep them occupied. And there are windows into the lab so you can go and look whenever you need to."

Diana raised her voice. "Jesse, we're moving on." The boy left his circuit and came to join her. Henry bounced along beside him with his jaw lolling open in excitement.

Sam grabbed the cooler and they headed downstairs to the first floor basement, Jesse talking to Henry all the way. Taking a right at the end of the hallway they reached the clean room stationed at the edge of the east side of the building. Setting the container on the counter, he dug out a couple of clean suits.

Diana stopped and knelt down so she was at the boy's height. "Jesse, Sam and I need to go into the lab and look at the cicada samples. I don't want to risk you being in the room while that happens, and Henry can't go in at all. Would you mind looking after him for a short time?"

The laughter drained out of Jesse's face. "Can't I come with you?"

"I'm sorry, no. But we'll be just through these windows here so you can come and wave at me any time you like. And you can play ball with Henry and stop him getting bored while he's waiting for Sam."

Jesse scowled at her, then winced. "You're just saying that to keep me out here."

"I am saying it to keep you out here, yes, but that doesn't mean it's not true. And if the cicadas get out of their boxes I don't want you in there."

Sam was impressed. She was so calm and cool, even though the kid had started to whine.

"Look, if you want to see the inside of a cicada I'll show you later with one of the normal ones, but these are a bit dangerous for show and tell."

"Really? The inside?" His eyes sparkled. "Ewwwww! That would be cool!"

"Deal?" She held out her hand.

"Deal. Scab twins forever!!"

Henry, picking up on the relaxed atmosphere, nudged Jesse and when the boy looked down, dropped his ball on the floor at his feet. Jesse picked it up immediately.

"He'll catch as long as you'll throw, I warn you!"

Diana reached over to tousle the dog's head. "Enjoy your game, don't break anything, and stay within sight of the windows, please."

"Okay." Jesse giggled as Henry nudged him again and dashed away. The boy threw the ball down the hallway and the dog shot off after it, rounded up the ball and came back to drop it in Jesse's hands.

Diana returned to the polypropylene garment and slipped her legs in first. Sam had finished suiting up, his goggles fogging due to the face mask. She zipped up the bunny suit, pulled on her goggles and gave him a thumbs up.

As they entered the clean room, Sam doubled over in a sneeze.

"Bless you, are you alright?" Diana stepped out of the way of the closing door.

"Yeah, I always do that when I come in here."

"Maybe you're allergic to science."

Sam wrinkled his nose and was about to reply when he caught sight of the laugh lines around her eyes. She was teasing. Diana'd taught him people did that with those they liked or were comfortable around.

They hoisted the cooler onto the stainless steel table and opened the lid. Diana grabbed a pair of forceps and pulled out the freshest samples, while Sam grabbed the killing jars and placed them in a line on the counter. He dabbed a swab with Ethyl alcohol and dropped it into one of the jars. As a team they extracted a cicada, trapped it in the glass container, and Sam twisted on the lid as tight as he could.

When the rest of the samples were contained, he marked the

time with his watch and counted down the seconds. When the insects stopped moving, he took another set of swabs, wiped each one down with the cotton balls, and placed the secretions into vials. He labeled the containers with a dry erase marker and held them to the light. "This venom is very similar in viscosity to that of poison ivy."

"Which would explain why washing with soap and water might assist in calming the effect."

He pointed at the cicada Diana placed in front of the others. "Is that the queen?"

"Looks like it. The others follow her whether she's in sight or not. As you'd expect, it's driven by some sort of pheromone or scent-related thing. When I shut her in a sealed box, they lost interest and wandered off."

Sam returned to the venom he'd collected. "We'll save it for last."

Filling the vials with reagent, he put them into the vortex unit and turned the machine on. The center rotated, swirling the mixtures in the vials. He grabbed a silver box and handed the tools to Diana. She opened the hasp and spread a set of scalpels on a sterile cloth, along with dissecting pins and several teasing needles. Sam brought the dissecting tray from a side bench and placed the shallow container between them. A timer dinged, and he checked on the vortex machine. Pulling the cotton swabs from the toxin samples with a set of tweezers, he loaded the first vial into the microplate spectrophotometer.

Diana prepped the first cicada, pinning its lifeless body to the tray and grabbing a scalpel. "So, who was the unlucky guy at the bottom of the elevator?"

Sam hit a last button, and the machine started to drip solution into the trays, one row at a time from a set of pipettes. "That would be Frank. He was after some data I had been collecting on the Megalopyge opercularis. Since he was going to take my job, I guess he figured he would take everything else as well. But there were reasons." He dropped his voice. "Government-army reasons. Industrial-military complex reasons..."

Diana held the scalpel out to Sam, studying him as she did. "So dropping him down the elevator was what? A tactical necessity?"

"Well, no." Sam flinched. He knew Diana didn't mean to make him feel stupid, but he wasn't sure she grasped the importance of his reveal. Frank was working for the bad guys. Bad guys who probably weren't going to give up, now they had his scent. He grabbed a couple of magnifying glasses and hauled them over to the table. "It was an accident. I only wanted to trap him with the dinosaurs but the bones weren't strong enough. If we hadn't hid the body the cops would have put us in jail and we wouldn't be able to investigate these." He held up the last cicada with a set of forceps underneath the largest magnifier, then took the scalpel from Diana.

He sliced through the joints of one cicada to remove the legs and wings. Pinning the body through the head, he cut through the side of the insect, its exterior crunching as the blade passed through its carapace.

"So, assuming this venom isn't unique, and is something with roots, what are you hoping to find with E.L.I.S.A?" Diana leaned closer, watching what he was doing.

Back on solid ground, Sam rattled off the facts. "Many of the venoms we've studied contain one of the amino acids; L-amino acid oxidase, phosphomono- and di-esterases, phospholipase A2 and peptidases. Since the venom is from an insect; acetylcholine esterase, phospholipase B and glycerophosphatase might show up as well. If the Enzyme-Linked Immunosorbent Assay process finds any of those, we can narrow down the type of venom and structures just like I did with the puss caterpillars. If none of them appear in the scans, we are looking at an unknown biological weapon with little hope of creating an antitoxin or vaccine in enough time to save the masses."

Greenish yellow ooze spilled out of the carcass as he lifted back the exoskeleton. Sam coughed and backed up. "They're putrid." He continued to slice into the dead insect, pulling back layers of the shell. Muscle fibers ran from limb to main body with spaces around the strands for other biological functions.

That gave him an idea. He put his scalpel down, moved to the computer at the end of the table, and removed his gloves to type on the keyboard. A visual diagram of documented cicadas filled the monitor. He clicked a button and a virtual ruler marked out the insect's length and width with small dots. The exterior of the drawings' organs was outlined in thick black contour lines. He ran the tip of his little finger around the thorax. "Isn't this where that greenish junk oozed out?"

Diana used his discarded scalpel to point out the location. Digging into the flesh a little more, green drops cascaded out of the cavity. "I wonder what function the fluid has inside the cicada. Most of the organs are up here. Did one get punctured by accident?" She prodded the eyes and stopped. "Don't species differentiate themselves by eye color?"

"Yeah, why?"

Diana waved an arm for Sam to come over and pointed at the adults and larvae.

He stooped as close as he dared and compared each mature cicada to the last, picking up details of the skewered insects.

"They all have red eyes. And your point is?"

Diana put the blade down and tilted her hands inwards, resting her wrists on her hips. "So. These are from three different swarms in different locations around the United States. Which means, they all belong to the same species. Right?"

"Oh." He straightened and walked away from the table. "Strange. I was just telling some guys on the forums, it was impossible these could be over in Egypt because different genus live in different climates. I think we've discovered a new super species."

The spectrophotometer whirred away in the background. Sam snapped on a fresh pair of gloves and fiddled with the first cicada in the lineup. Taking the wings and pinning them beside the body where they would have been attached, he reassembled the insect, spreading out the parts enough so they could be labeled. He glanced at the monitor and scribbled down 'forewing' on a piece of paper. Sticking the tag and the wing with a pin to the wax, he prodded a limb into position and repeated the process.

Finished with the samples, Sam grabbed a stool and climbed on top of the unstable wooden seat, his peripheries picking up the entire lineup of cicadas. "There is no deviation of size, shape, or color. What are the chances they're all drones? You know, like bees."

Diana shrugged and moved to the opposite side of the table. "Let's dissect the queen, maybe she'll give us the answers."

The spectrophotometer stopped testing, and Sam went to investigate. "Ding ding, and we have a winner. Glycerophosphatase takes home the gold." Sam cleared his throat and started another test. Rejoining Diana, he removed one side of the queen's exoskeleton while Diana peered over his shoulder. Prodding the muscles, he put a pin down to keep the organs separated. He placed the scalpel on the clot, reached for a teaser, and used the metal tube to prod the back end of the cicada. "We know the insects' morphology is different from any that have been studied so far. Have you ever seen an ovipositor shaped like this?"

Sam grabbed another teaser and pushed several of the organs around while Diana leaned over to look through the magnifier, adjusting it several times.

"I can't see the part you're pointing at." He scooted over to give Diana more room. "Okay... there... Take a look at the distal valvulae, the diagram you pulled up on the computer is drastically different."

The view was distorted from his angle so Sam swung the larger magnifying glass around with his arm, placing it so they could use it at the same time.

He used the teaser to help Diana locate the area. "See the serrated blades? That's the first valvulae. They have those edges to saw into plants, so they can lay their eggs. That's no surprise."

Diana made eye contact over the top of the protective glasses.

Sam swallowed. *Uh, her posture is tense and she's lowered her head so she can see me without a barrier between us. What did she say the motion meant?* He reached up to scratch his head and she swatted the hand away.

"You can't touch your skin. Even with these suits on. You might expose yourself to the venom if you touched your face by accident."

Sam tucked his head down to avoid her gaze.

She softened her voice and inched closer. "Hey, I'm not mad, alright. I just don't want you to get hurt."

He continued to stare at the ground.

"But what's really interesting here is the second valvulae. It surrounds the first one but has the same blades. Like you said, the reproductive tracts of these cicadas are fundamentally different from anything on record."

The spectrophotometer's whir stopped indicating the second round of testing was complete. Sam replaced his gloves and punched several buttons, focusing on the digital readout. He inched closer to the screen, went to rub his eyes and stopped. He waved Diana over to the tests and pointed at one word.

She read the word out loud, emphasizing the last syllable. "Dimethylpyrrole?"

"So I'm not imagining things."

Sam returned to the cicada queen, and pried apart another part of the exoskeleton as Diana looked on.

"Why does that matter?"

Sam hooked his foot underneath the stool and slid the four-legged seat over. He sat, paused, and lifted two fingers to get her attention. "As of now, I know of two toxins with that specific element. One is the puss caterpillar. The other is a certain type of frog that natives of South America liked to dip their darts in. They use it to poison targets. If we continue, I suspect we will find all three venoms are similar in chemical composition." He pulled another limb from the queen cicada with some forceps.

"They don't have an antidote for the poison frog do they?"

Sam shook his head, returned to the computer and hit print. "If we can get this information to someone who works with poisons they might be able to extrapolate possible methods for counteracting this stuff." The printer shot out several pages. He grabbed them and placed them next to the cooler.

Diana glanced at the papers as Sam teased out the queen's digestive tract, following it down to the anus, explaining as he went along. "From what we have here, I would hazard a guess we have a mutated apparition lying before us. The gut is larger, and the intestine is much longer. It makes sense. The cicadas would have to evolve in order to handle the plant matter they are digesting. So the question is, what do you want to do Diana?"

"Keep digging. The more we know, the better chance we have at stopping these things."

"Can we? Stop them, I mean."

Diana looked Sam dead in the eye, which made his stomach squirm. *She's a friend. It's not a threat. I can return her gaze.* "I don't know, Sam. But if we don't, no one will. And if no one does, we're all going to die."

CHAPTER THIRTY-FIVE

DR. DIANA STEWART. BERKELEY, CALIFORNIA.

In the clean room, Diana was keeping an eye on Jesse who was playing in the corridor with the dog. "I'm going to call it a day, Sam. Jesse's not right yet and he'll get tired any minute. Are you happy to clear up here?"

"Yes, I can do that. What will you do next?" Sam took her slide and set it with his own.

Jesse waved to catch her eye, and then did their secret sign, drawing his thumb across one cheek and then the other. She did it back; his face lit up with such glee that she had to smile. "Now that Garrick knows I'm here, Jesse's in danger. I need to take him back to Jane. We're staying in the Motel 8 in Auburn, so I'll take him there now and come back first thing tomorrow. What about you?"

"It will give me more time to look through these and compare them with my results. I have some data that you ought to see." He followed her to the door. He hit the button and the door closed behind them with a hiss. "Cockroach has the other copy but I'm not sure where she is. She's supposed to meet me here today but if she saw you or the police driving around, she might have decided it was better to stay away."

"So, Cockroach—you finally met her? And she's a she?" Diana unzipped the suit. She twisted to free her arms of the sleeves, earning a dizzying stab from both her broken rib and bruised shoulder. She hissed at the pain, losing track of what he was saying for a moment.

"...Frank beat her up. That's why it all went wrong. He was going to kill her and me too." Sam struggled out of his own suit. "You know, I never thought I'd be able to kill anyone. But he's dead and I can't blame anyone else."

"From what you've told me, it was self-defense." She stepped out of her suit and lowered herself to her haunches to pick it up. "You can't ignore it and hope it goes away though. We need to tell the police what happened, but not Garrick. If he's in charge in Berkeley, he's quite capable of making trouble for you out of pure spite. I don't know who else to contact." She got up again with a grunt, bundled up the suit and put it in the container next to the door. Sam was biting the quicks of his fingers, something he only did in times of great stress. "We'll sort this out, Sam. We just need time to work out what to do."

A trickle of blood ran down Sam's finger. "You haven't got time now."

"I will as soon as Jesse is safe with Jane." She fished in her pocket and took out a packet of Kleenex, handing him one. "Maybe if we—" She broke off as Jesse dashed around the corner, Henry trotting behind him. "Hey, twin. Did you have a good game?"

Jesse giggled. "Hey twin! Yeah, I like Henry. He's a good dog."

Sam twisted the Kleenex around his finger. "Twin? You aren't twins."

"*Scab* twins!" Jesse glanced sideways at him, a big grin on his face, still reveling in the grossness of the concept.

Diana laughed. "It's perfectly logical, but only by six-year-old standards." She paused. Henry stopped dead in his tracks. He sniffed once, twice; and then his hackles went up. He set himself between them and the corridor ahead, standing stiff-legged and ready for trouble. A low growl rumbled through his chest.

"He's not normally like this—and it can't be Frank." Sam's voice wobbled; he was not as cool as he was making out. But then, he was all of eighteen years old. He might have had the genius to gain a Ph.D. at the age of twelve, but that had separated him from his peers at an early age and, emotionally, he was still a kid.

"I'll take a look. It's probably nothing." Diana kept her voice light.

Henry was on high alert, ears up and posture tense. Time to get them out of the way. "Sam, is there somewhere you two can hide?"

Sam gestured at the doors just ahead of them on the right. "My lab's wet but we can lock the door."

"Let's get you shut in there." The lab doors, opened with an alarming creak to reveal the basement lab, charred and with pools of water around the drain. "What a mess!" She picked Jesse up and followed Sam down into the flood, setting the kid on the table where he would be dry.

"It's taking ages to drain." Sam whistled for Henry and when the dog splashed across, he lifted Henry onto the table too. The dog curled in Jesse's lap, embracing the cuddle.

She patted Henry's head. "Jesse, wait here with Sam. I won't be long."

"I want to come with you—" He grabbed her arm.

"I know." She took his hand in her own. "But you can't always come everywhere with me. This is one of those times when I need you to stay here just for a few minutes. I'll be back in a moment or two."

Jesse let her untangle her hand from his. "You won't go far?"

"Not far at all. And I'll come straight back. I made a promise, remember? A Scab Twin oath of a most solemn and binding nature." Diana extricated her hand from his and put on a very serious expression, although half her attention was still on Henry. "I, Diana Stewart, do solemnly vow and declare on my honor as a Scab Twin—" She did the sign again and a twinkle came into his eye. "...That I will always come back and find my twin, whether I am two minutes away or two hundred thousand miles away. I will always come back for you, Jesse, always."

He nodded. "Now you've made an oath you have to." He still wasn't happy about it though.

Voices echoed down the corridor. Diana hesitated. She could join the boys in the basement, but then they wouldn't know who was here, who they were and when they left. And if it was Garrick, she wanted to be sure he had left before bringing the boys out. No, she had to investigate. "Sam, keep Henry with you, and keep him quiet if you can. Lock the door, and don't open it till I come back."

They waded across to the door. Diana waited till the lock clicked, and Sam gave her the thumbs up through the charred hole in the boarded-up window. The voices were nearer now, all men. She edged out into the corridor, which was still clear, and darted across to hide in the stairwell.

It was too echoey to make anything out. She went up a few stairs, ignoring the water squelching about in her boots. She could make out what they were saying, though she was careful to stay out of sight.

"This is a wild goose chase. What're we doing wandering around an empty building? I could murder a burger right now." A male voice.

"Don't ask me. I'm just doing what the boss says. He's got some sort of bee in his bonnet about some woman here, and a kid too." The voices came nearer, and she retreated. "If you ask me that scientist guy who was handing out dollar notes like they were candy wants her trussed up and heading to Chicago as soon as possible. We just have to catch her first."

"Hah. Well looking at the roll of notes he handed over, we're all in for a decent payday for tonight's work. And for that sort of cash, I don't much care what we're doing." They laughed.

Time to go. She stepped back and bumped into something behind her.

"So, there you are."

She froze. Even twenty years on, Garrick could petrify her just by being there.

"You should know by now that running away from me is pointless."

She shuddered, mustering the courage to turn and face him. "What are you doing here, Garrick?"

"Looking for the fugitive who damaged my police car and fled. What have you done with the kid? Social Services want him." He grabbed the top of her arm. She gasped as it jolted her shoulder and he was on it like a terrier on a rat. "You look uncomfortable."

"It's nothing."

He ripped open her shirt. "It doesn't look like nothing." Buttons fell to the floor, and he tutted at the purple bruising which spread from the neckline of her undershirt up to her collarbone. He let go of her arm and gripped her shoulder hard, pressing his thumb down into the bruising.

She yelped, which only made him press harder. She'd forgotten what a sadist he was. "Take your hands off me, Garrick. You're hurting me. There are laws about this sort of thing."

"There are laws about kidnapping too, and yet here we are." He pressed harder, grinning at the flicker of pain in her eyes. "What are you doing dragging a kid around the place? I'm surprised you haven't managed to kill him yet, like you did your brother. What was his name? Charlie? Or was it 'Beloved son of...'"

"You're just as damaged as ever," she panted. That hurt. He hadn't lost the knack of inflicting pain with a minimum of visible damage. She tried to pull his hand away from her shoulder, but he was stronger than her. The familiar feeling of helplessness began to wash over her, but she refused to succumb to it. "Sorry, Garrick, if you're expecting this to reduce me to a sniveling wreck, you're twenty years too late." The pain was making it difficult to catch her breath, but she was damned if she was going to let him win this time. "I see your bull for what it is now. Took me a while, I grant you, but once I admitted to myself that you didn't love me and you never were trying to look after me, it finally clicked." It was difficult to keep her tone even but she'd made a vow to Jesse, which meant she had to.

"Goodness, aren't you the feisty one these days? This is going to be fun." He ground his thumb into her shoulder until pain arced through her like electricity and black dots danced in front of her eyes. She refused to make a sound this time though, and he shoved her away so hard that she fell, landing on hands and knees in front of him. Leaning into the stairwell, he hollered up the stairs "She's here, guys. Get your asses down here!"

She knelt and tried to catch her breath. She had to find a way to get him away from Sam and Jesse, but the pain and fear was fogging her brain just like it always had, and her rib made it difficult to breathe.

Footsteps thundered on the stairs and the two cops hurried down. One dragged her to her feet, and the other took out a pair of handcuffs and clicked them onto one wrist. She twisted free from him, but Garrick was waiting and he jerked her bad arm up behind her, hard. Agony danced through her whole torso. Tears spilled down her face and this time she nearly blacked out. They hurried her along the basement corridor which led outside to the parking lot. She tried not to look at the lab door, but it was no good.

"Diana!" Sam shouted through the door. "What are you doing with her, you bullies?" Henry splashed into the water and was barking madly, jumping up and growling.

Garrick strode over to the door and tried the handle. When it didn't open, he smashed his shoulder against the wood a couple of times but though it rattled in its frame, it still didn't open. He peered through the hole into the flooded basement. "So this is where you stashed the kid. And is that a friend of yours? Guessing it is. Emmot, keep a watch on the door. No one gets out without my say-so."

"Yessir." The second cop went to stand outside the lab.

Garrick turned back to Diana. "I've been talking to your boss. Turns out he's angry with you. He hasn't seen you in days. So I'm going to take you in."

Her shoulder was on fire, and the pain was making her nauseous. "Dan's dead, Garrick. Whatever he was going to pay you, he isn't here to do it. You might as well let us go."

"Oh, don't you worry about that. I demanded payment ahead of time, and his sidekick gave me clear instructions about where to take you and what to do."

Trust Dan to leave it to Aaron. But if they had back up, she had to get away. Garrick was vicious, but Dan's men were out to kill her.

Her fear must have shown in her face. Garrick laughed and went to talk to the cop standing by the door.

She licked her lips, wracking her brains for ways to make him let her go. Defying her ex-husband was dangerous, but she had to get away. Her knees were weak just with the threat of him so near, but if she lost her nerve, she'd fall prey to that soul-destroying fear that he'd crafted so long ago. And if she did, she and Jesse and Sam were all lost. "I'm not going quietly, Garrick. Soon as I see another human, I'll scream and shout myself hoarse. They have mobile phones. They'll film anything for hits on their social media. Sooner or later, your bosses will start asking questions."

Garrick's eyebrows went up. In two strides he crossed the distance between them. He pinched her chin, forcing her head backward. "People asking questions isn't my problem right now. My problem is that we have witnesses. I'm not in the habit of leaving witnesses wandering around to make trouble." He let go of her chin. "Chad, you should really be careful with that weapon of yours. It'd be terrible if the kids got shot because you thought they were looters."

The cop loosened the tab of his holster. "What a terrible accident that would be. We'd be very sad if anything like that happened."

Diana shoved him away. "Don't you touch them, Garrick. Don't you dare."

Garrick grabbed her arm and kicked her feet out from under her. As she fell, her whole weight was suspended from his merciless grip, the impact dislocating her injured shoulder. Pain thundered in her ears and her vision went white for two breaths, maybe three. Then she was crumpled on the floor, tears running down her face. In the lab Jesse's shouts were high-pitched and panicky, and the dog barked like a wild thing.

Garrick crouched down as she struggled to get to her knees. "You know, Diana, with that convenient hole in the door, Chad could shoot them where they stand."

Her shoulder felt like it was on fire, and she couldn't move her arm properly. She could barely breathe with the pain of it. "Please, Garrick. Don't hurt them. Please."

"Don't hurt them? And why on earth wouldn't I?" There was only one answer. They both knew he had won, but as always, he wanted her to beg and this time the stakes were too high for her to risk defying him any longer.

She dropped her head and bit back a sob. "Please. Don't hurt them. I'll come with you. I won't make a fuss. Just promise me you won't hurt them."

He didn't answer immediately. He'd always liked to savor his triumph. "I won't hurt them."

"And neither will any of your men?"

"No, they won't lay a finger on them."

"Or shoot them?"

He slammed a hand on her shoulder hard, and she cried out. "Are you questioning my word?"

"No, Garrick. Please. I just want them to be safe." The sob escaped her before she could catch it.

"Fine. We don't go in there, we don't shoot them, we don't go anywhere near them. Does that cover it?" He was pleased with himself for some reason. That meant trouble, and Diana was losing her grip.

"Yes, Garrick." The old fear was lurking and she was running out of the ability to fight it. Fear and pain: that was how it had always been with him and she was sliding back into the abyss of the old mindset. If she just stayed quiet, if she just stayed still as a mouse, he might stop hurting her. She was nothing, just a girl-shaped space in the air. She just had to stop provoking him.

There was a movement behind her. The handcuffs clicked free, and then Garrick dragged her to her feet, this time by her good arm. "Chad is going to stay here." He nodded at the burly cop standing by the lab door. "If you step out of line, he'll shoot. If you make a fuss, he'll shoot. If you comply, he'll walk away and leave those two unharmed. Do you understand me?"

"Yes Garrick." She cradled her arm in front of her, but it didn't help the pain. "Can I say goodbye? Tell them to stay quiet and not make trouble?"

He slapped her face, hard. "Was that part of the deal?"

She staggered, caught her balance. "No. But it will make it easier for your guy."

It was a stupid excuse, but from the malice in his grin, he was in a good mood. "You have thirty seconds."

She wiped the tears from her face and hurried over to the door.

Sam was white as a sheet, his pupils big and panicky. "Diana, what do I do?"

"Listen to me and stay calm. I only have a few seconds." She wished she could think straight.

"Diana! Diana!" Jesse banged on the other side of the door, and Diana fought the urge to sob.

Sam lifted him up so he could see through the hole, and Diana reached through the hole to take his hand. "Jesse. I need you to stay here and help Sam. I have to do something and it might take a couple of days. I need you to help Sam find Jane, okay?"

"Motel 8. Auburn." Sam's eyes were dark in the pallor of his face. She nodded.

"You can't go! You can't. You promised!" Jesse sounded half-hysterical.

She withdrew her hand and leaned close to the hole. "I promised I will always come back for you, Jesse, and I always will. It just might take a little time, okay? Sam, if I go with them you two should be safe. Watch the forums for news. And make sure Jesse gets back to Jane, okay? She will help. The truck's in the usual place." She fished in her pocket and passed him her keys.

Garrick finished his conversation with Chad and turned to her. "Time's up. Let's go."

Diana wanted to scream and fight, do anything to stay with them, but the only way to keep them safe was to let Garrick win.

"I said, *let's go*! Now."

Turning back to Jesse, she made their secret sign. He just stared.

Garrick pushed her toward the doors. She stumbled along the corridor with him, her world crumbling about her. *I promised I'd stay with Jesse and I failed him. I promised I'd help Sam with the cicadas, and I failed him too. And if Dan is dead, where's Garrick taking me?*

It wouldn't be good. Not with Garrick involved. Her chest tightened so it was difficult to breathe. Her broken rib stabbed like a dagger in her side. She had only barely gotten away without serious injury last time, and he hadn't taken it well. This time... this time she was already hurt. How could she possibly escape?

He hustled her out the doors and across the parking lot to the police truck.

He yanked her shirt back over one shoulder and injected her with a syringe that looked very like the one Aaron had wielded. She didn't fight it. Whatever it was, it was the price for Jesse's life. Her vision lost its focus and became blurry.

Chad jogged across the parking lot and joined them.

Garrick grinned. "All done there?"

"All done, boss."

Diana frowned. It was difficult to think straight. "What's done? You promised they'd be safe."

"I never promised that."

Her breath was coming in pants now. "You... you promised—"

"I promised that we wouldn't hurt them." He grinned like a shark. "We haven't gone anywhere near them."

"But..."

"We don't have to. They're in a basement that's slowly filling with water."

Suddenly Diana understood. Her knees gave way under her and she staggered back against the side of the truck. "You turned the water back on." She slid down and toppled on her side. There was pain, but it didn't seem to matter so much as before.

"If you'd have been more specific your little friend wouldn't be drowning." Garrick winked at her. "Chad handcuffed the door shut, too. He'll be back later to retrieve his cuffs of course, but what a tragedy it will be to find the kid limp in the water, drowned like a rat."

She scrabbled at the asphalt. "You promised."

"I didn't promise that they would live." His voice was harsh.

Her body was heavy and unresponsive and all that happened was that she rolled onto her back. "Bastard." Then there was nothing she could do but gasp for breath. The sky was spinning, her vision faded, and everything dissolved in darkness.

READ THE NEXT BOOK IN THE SERIES

Swarm Book 2
Available Here
books.to/QJnWP

Printed in Great Britain
by Amazon

24883968R00208